DEC 2 0 2018

P9-CCO-697

WITHDRAWN
Salina Public Library

A WILD CARDS MOSAIC NOVEL

TEXAS HOLD'EM

The Wild Cards Universe

A WILD CARDS MOSAIC NOVEL

TEXAS HOLD'EM

Edited by
George R. R. Martin
Assisted by
Melinda M. Snodgrass

Written by

David Anthony Durham

Max Gladstone

Victor Milán

Diana Rowland

Walton Simons

Caroline Spector

William F. Wu

TOR

A TOM DOHERTY ASSOCIATES BOOK

New York

This is a work of fiction. All of the characters, organizations, and events portrayed in these stories are either products of the authors' imaginations or are used fictitiously.

TEXAS HOLD'EM

Copyright © 2018 by George R. R. Martin and the Wild Cards Trust

All rights reserved.

A Tor Book
Published by Tom Doherty Associates
175 Fifth Avenue
New York, NY 10010

www.tor-forge.com

Tor® is a registered trademark of Macmillan Publishing Group, LLC.

The Library of Congress Cataloging-in-Publication Data
is available upon request.

ISBN 978-0-7653-9059-2 (hardcover)
ISBN 978-0-7653-9061-5 (ebook)

Our books may be purchased in bulk for promotional, educational, or business use. Please contact your local bookseller or the Macmillan Corporate and Premium Sales Department at 1-800-221-7945, extension 5442, or by email at MacmillanSpecialMarkets@macmillan.com.

First Edition: November 2018

Printed in the United States of America

0 9 8 7 6 5 4 3 2 1

SALINA PUBLIC LIBRARY
SALINA, KANSAS 67401

Copyright Acknowledgments

"Bubbles and the Band Trip" copyright © 2018 by Caroline Spector

"The Secret Life of Rubberband" copyright © 2018 by Max Gladstone

"Jade Blossom's Brew" copyright © 2018 by William F. Wu

"Beats, Bugs, and Boys" copyright © 2018 by Diana Rowland

"Dust and the Darkness" copyright © 2018 by Victor Milán

"Is Nobody Going to San Antone?" copyright © 2018 by Walton Simons

"Drop City" copyright © 2018 by David Anthony Durham

Texas Hold'em

The most popular poker variant in casinos.

Two hole cards are dealt facedown to each player.
Then five community cards are dealt faceup in three rounds:
the flop, the turn, and the river. Each player seeks to make the best
five-card hand from the combination of the community cards
and his own hole cards.

A WILD CARDS MOSAIC NOVEL

TEXAS HOLD'EM

Bubbles and the Band Trip

by Caroline Spector

Prologue

"**WHAT DO YOU MEAN,** you need a chaperone for the band trip?" Michelle didn't like where this conversation was going.

Adesina kept packing her electric bass. It was a sweet StingRay 5 with double humbuckers. That it was done up with a purple sparkle finish was the icing on the cake according to Adesina. Michelle had been learning about the whole jazz band thing from her daughter for the past year and a half, but she always felt a step behind. And the humbucker thing was just baffling to her.

"Sean's mother was supposed to go, but then she came down with the flu and now we need another chaperone. Besides, Wally's going to be there," Adesina replied, as if her mother filling in as chaperone was the most natural thing in the world. "Oh, and so is Mr. Ruttiger, you know, the school counselor. Remember, you met him at the open house. He was on season two of *American Hero*. They called him Rubberband. He's all stretchy."

Michelle felt a coil of fear in her gut. "I can't," she sputtered. "I have . . . things . . . aren't there other mothers who can fill in?"

Adesina flicked the latches on her case closed. "Jeez, Mom," she said as she put her sheet music into a folder. "It's just five days in San Antonio with a bunch of band nerds. It's not saving the world."

Michelle watched in dismay, knowing this was a battle she'd already lost.

TUESDAY

Bubbles and the
Band Trip

Part 1

THE BRAKES GAVE A farty hiss as the bus pulled up in front of the Gunter Hotel. Michelle sighed with relief. Being cooped up with her daughter and the rest of the Xavier Desmond High School Jazz Band for eighteen hours straight was about as much fun as she could stand. The kids sometimes called themselves the Jokertown Mob, but mostly just the Mob to keep it short.

"Ms. Pond!" Peter called from the back of the bus. Peter was the band's trumpet player. He called himself Segway because his legs were fused together and he moved by rolling around on keratin wheels. "Can we get out now?" Michelle guessed she wasn't the only one ready for a break from the enforced confinement.

"In a second, Peter," she said. "Let me see where we're supposed to check in first, so we don't have to lug the instruments and suitcases all over the place."

The driver opened the bifold door and Michelle stepped out into the beautiful, cool San Antonio spring morning.

And discovered she was in a little slice of hell.

Coming at her was a group of about twenty people carrying an array of placards that read: *SPAWN OF SATAN! FREAKS! JOKERS ARE SUBHUMANS! JOKERS ARE WICKED ABOMINOTIONS: PROV. 15:9!*

Michelle strode toward them. They kept coming at her. At her and the bus full of her kids.

Bastards.

"That's far enough," she said in her very best I'm-from-the-Committee-do-not-fuck-with-me voice. They actually stopped.

Okay, so far so good. They're not complete morons.

"Where exactly do you think you're going?" Michelle asked. She aimed at the protesters generally. She couldn't tell if there was a leader or not, but right now she didn't care. They were going to stay the hell away from her kids. Especially when she saw that a couple of the protesters were carrying sidearms.

Texas, sheesh. Also, compensating much? She wasn't sure which bugged her more, the open-carry douches or the concealed-carry jerks. There was so much badness waiting to happen. At least if one of those guns went off and hit her, it wouldn't do a damn thing except give her more fat. And she could totally deal with that.

"You and those freaks are abominations unto the Lord," said one of the protesters, pointing at the bus. "He will smite them. They are wicked, for the Mark of Satan is on them." She wore oversize cat's-eye sunglasses and an electric-blue polyester pantsuit. Her hair looked like pink cotton candy. It rose at least seven inches into the air.

The bigger the hair the closer to God? Michelle thought. *Yeesh.* Michelle narrowed her green eyes and cocked her head to one side. *Wow, toots, big mistake. And not just the ensemble. You just bought yourself a world of hurt.*

"The only abomination is your spelling and grammar. 'ABOMINO-TION'? Seriously? Also, your manners are appalling. Yelling at children? Total dick move."

"You don't frighten us, Miss Pond," the woman continued. "For the Lord shall protect me. He will protect all of us."

A round of "That's right" and "Praise Jesus" rumbled through the protesters. "You tell her, Betty Virginia. You tell that filthy freak."

A bubble began forming in Michelle's hand. After Kazakhstan, her temper was shorter and her desire to bubble was sharper. It wasn't a good combination. "Yeah, you wanna test that theory," Michelle replied.

The protesters were an odd bunch. There was a pair of twins in their thirties who wore identical clothing and bore a striking resemblance to Tweedledee and Tweedledum minus the beanies. A woman with greasy hair wearing a muumuu carried a sign with a picture of a dead and horribly deformed joker on it. Off to one side, a pimply-faced teenage girl stood slumped-shouldered, looking as if she were about to cry. The men in the group wore jeans, T-shirts with *God Loves Humans* written across the chest, and gimme caps. The women seemed to take their sartorial lead from Betty Virginia. There were a lot of big, back-combed bouffants in a variety of shades. These gals loved the blackest of blacks and the reddest of reds. And they had embraced neon-colored pantsuits in the most sincere of ways. The protesters all had the same angry, hateful, self-righteous expressions on their faces.

God's Weenies, Michelle thought. She knew they were here to protest the Mob playing in the Charlie Parker High School Jazz Competition, as they were the only band playing that had any jokers. Okay, so they had *all* the jokers.

One of the men in the back had dropped his hand to his holstered piece. Michelle gave him a cold smile. "I'll be happy to show you *my* open carry. And you know bullets don't scare me."

Betty Virginia turned to see who Michelle was speaking to. He was a plain-looking fellow with cat-shit brown eyes and a comb-over. His sidearm was holstered, but he had the snap lock undone. His denim cowboy shirt was rolled up at the sleeves.

"Now, Earl Walker," Betty Virginia said with a honeyed tone as she gave her cotton-candy hair a pat. "You just keep that snub nose where it belongs. We don't advocate violence. You know that."

"Oh, that's hi-larious," Michelle said. "You just rile things up to make sure someone else gets their hands dirty. Stay away from my kids."

She released her bubbles then. The protesters shrieked. But these bubbles weren't designed to kill or maim, they just boxed the protesters in, keeping them from moving. A box of iridescent, translucent, and very strong bubbles.

Pretty, Michelle thought with a smile.

And as she was admiring her handiwork, she saw the other chaperones—Wally and Robin—the band, and the music director, Sharon, hustling past the protesters into the Gunter Hotel.

♣

The lobby was packed with teenagers carrying instrument cases and talking excitedly. The adults—chaperones, parents, and music teachers—looked like they were about to lose their minds.

"Gosh, where are the cowboys?" Wally asked, looking around the lobby. He was good-natured and sweet, but his large size, iron skin, and yellow eyes made him look intimidating. His skin would rust, but he'd done a good job at keeping it well-scrubbed on the trip down. It helped that his daughter liked to help him scrub it.

Wally had insisted that he come along as a chaperone on the trip. His daughter, Ghost, was the sax and clarinet player for the band. She was ten years old and had only recently started playing with them. Though she was an ace—and still in elementary school—the band members had embraced her. And not just for her smoking sax solos. Her indifference to them being jokers had won them over. And, after all, her father was a joker, as was her best friend, Michelle's daughter, Adesina.

"Wally!" Ghost said, tugging on his sleeve and pointing across the lobby. "There's the clarinet player from the Modesto Melody Makers. She's awesome!"

Michelle smiled at Ghost's enthusiasm. Ghost and Adesina had hung out at Michelle's apartment watching YouTube videos of all the other bands in the competition. By now, the girls knew the band members from the other bands by sight. Michelle surveyed the room, wondering how the girls could keep this many players straight.

A young girl, tiny compared to Michelle's six-foot height, came up to her. "I'm sorry to bother you," the girl said. She had long chestnut-colored hair, and was wearing a floaty floral print dress with black Converse sneakers. "But aren't you Michelle Pond?"

Michelle gave the girl a wan smile. She wasn't feeling up to a fan encounter, but she felt a strong obligation to not be a jerk when someone just wanted a moment of her time. She'd had her own fangirl moments in the past and knew how much it meant to have contact with someone you admired.

At least Michelle assumed she was being admired. Sometimes it was difficult to be sure. "Yep, that's me," she replied.

The girl beamed at her. "So, that's the Mob?" she said with a nod to the joker kids grouped by the door. The door to the hotel opened and the bleating of *"Jokers are abominations!"* and *"Spawns of Hell!"* floated in. Michelle thought about going outside and introducing them to less gentle bubbles.

The girl followed Michelle's gaze. "They're from the Purity Baptist Church. They're awful."

"Yep," Michelle replied tersely. "I've already had a super-special moment with them."

"I'm Kimmie," the girl said, reaching out her hand. Michelle took it and gave it a quick shake. "Would you mind if I met the band? I don't know any jokers. But from their YouTube videos, they sure can wail. I play flute in the Plano Originals." She blurted this all out while tucking a stray hair behind her ear nervously. "This is our third year in a row being invited. But we haven't won yet."

Michelle looked at Kimmie suspiciously. Most nats would be freaking out about seeing a pack of jokers, but the only thing she saw on the girl's face was clear and honest curiosity.

"Sure," Michelle said. She led Kimmie over to the Mob. "Guys, this young lady would like to meet you. She's in the Plano Originals band."

Adesina came forward immediately. "Hey there," she said. Her wings spread out, then snapped shut. She'd been having trouble controlling them of late. "OMG, your band is awesome! I loved that video you guys posted playing 'The "In" Crowd' in last year's competition. Your flute solo was hella kewl."

Kimmie looked down and her cheeks got red. "Thanks. I'm pretty proud of it. I like your wings. And your dreads. And your bass is awesome! I've never seen a bass tricked out like that. I mean, someone using one in a jazz band."

"Thanks," Adesina said, a smile blooming across her face. "I figured, I already look like this"—she gestured to her body—"so I might as well go big or go home. And who doesn't like purple sparkles, ya know?"

Kimmie laughed. She leaned forward conspiratorially. "I never would have had the guts to do something like that."

Michelle decided she liked Kimmie a lot. Her daughter may have been a joker, but Michelle had always thought she was beautiful. Adesina's skin was leathery and the color of obsidian; her eyes and dreads were coppery. She did have four vestigial insect legs, but they were small. Antennae sprouted from her forehead. Adesina and Michelle agreed the physical part of her latest transformation was filled with awesome sauce.

"Who's that?" Kimmie asked, gesturing toward Peter. Instead of pants, he wore a kilt. Michelle was pretty sure he wore it in the traditional way, and that brought up a lot of other questions she decided weren't really her business. But then she saw him grin at Kimmie and Kimmie smile back, and Michelle realized that Peter was also a cute boy and Kimmie was intrigued by him—joker or not.

Peter rolled over to Kimmie and bowed at the waist in front of her. That he could easily keep his balance always amazed Michelle. "O beautiful maiden," he said with a slight British accent that was totally put on. "How may I serve you?"

Michelle rolled her eyes. Peter was a gamer and especially into role-playing.

Kimmie laughed and held out her hand. He took it and made much of kissing it.

"Oh, for the love of Mike," Michelle said with a groan, "I cannot believe . . . hand kissing!"

"Mom's a monster when she's annoyed," Adesina said, laughing. She posed then, standing with her hands raised palms up, her feet firmly planted, and her face set in a stern expression. It was a perfect imitation of Michelle's usual "fight mode." Michelle glared at her.

Adesina smiled. "Yeah, that is *so* not working, Mom." She turned back to Kimmie. "Antonia is our drummer." She gestured at the girl with tentacles for hands. Antonia nodded at Kimmie. "And Marissa plays keyboards.

"This is Sean, our other sax player." Kimmie smiled and gave him a small wave. Colors began rippling across his skin until they ended in bright neon shades.

Adesina leaned in close. "He likes you and he's also totes embarrassed," she whispered.

"Am not," Sean cried.

"Are too," Adesina retorted.

"Oh, here's Asti—" She pointed at the boy holding a guitar case. "He plays guitar, obvs. And he's totes cute with that peach fuzz all over. Now don't be embarrassed, dude. And those bubbles coming off his head? They smell like peaches. So yummy." Her voice dropped and she leaned in to whisper in Kimmie's ear, "And OMG, you should see his abs."

The kids shook Kimmie's hand, chatting about the songs each band was going to play.

"Michelle, what are we going to do about those protesters?" Robin asked. "They're going to hassle the kids for the entire time we're here."

"They're obviously reptoid people." That was Jan, Robin's landlady. Jan was a conspiracy nut. Pure tinfoil hat stuff. Michelle wasn't entirely sure why Jan had come along on the trip. But she was getting on Michelle's very last nerve.

"They're not lizard people, Jan," Michelle said with exasperation. She'd had about enough of the whole lizard people, gray aliens, Denver Airport, and MKUltra conspiracies to last a lifetime. Well, in all fairness, the MKUltra stuff was true.

"Jan," Michelle continued. She glanced over at the kids. They seemed to be enjoying meeting Kimmie and talking about music. It was a relief. She'd been afraid that everyone would treat her kids the way God's Weenies did. "You do know that all this conspiracy stuff is just, well, bullshit?"

"Ha!" Jan said with maniacal glee. Blue sparks glittered between her teeth and the veins in her temples pulsed. Despite Jan's all black attire and dark sunglasses, she couldn't hide that she was a joker. And it was clear she wasn't really trying to hide it much anyway.

"An alien virus created all the wild cards," Jan continued. "And MKUltra is a real thing. It just follows that there are other secret shenanigans going on. And they're reptoid, *not* lizard people."

"Sweet baby Jesus," Michelle groaned. "That doesn't follow at all."

"Well, you're a part of the Committee and we all know they're nothing more than lackeys for the New World Order. And they're butt monkeys for the Gnomes of Zurich. Also, you're a product of aliens messing with human DNA."

Arghhhhhh, Michelle thought. Just enough truth balled up with the crazy to make things sound real.

"Give it up, Michelle," Robin said. "You've lost that fight. Those suitcases should have been here already."

Michelle took a real look around the lobby of the Gunter.

The Gunter was sponsoring the competition and had also discounted the rooms, which made them affordable for the students. Most of the kids in the Mob came from families without a lot of disposable income, and instruments and music lessons weren't cheap. Michelle had paid out of her pocket for the band's transportation to San Antonio with the promise from the band's director, Sharon Oberhoffer, that no one was to know it was from her.

Sharon was a joker, too. When her card had turned, she'd been a professional trumpet player, but now her lips were freakishly small and puckered tight like a rosebud. It had prevented her from playing trumpet professionally anymore. Because she couldn't speak, she whistled or used ASL to communicate. But mostly she whistled. It was like trying to carry on a conversation with Harpo Marx.

"Snazzy place," Michelle said as she looked around the lobby. Sharon gave a low whistle in agreement.

Adorning the lobby ceiling were intricate, bright white crisscrossing moldings. Enormous chandeliers hung from medallions centered in the squares created by the crisscrosses. The walls were painted Texas sky blue. The second floor had a balcony overlooking the lobby.

"I'll check us in," Michelle said to Jan and Robin.

She walked to the front desk and gave the clerk her best professional model smile. "Hello, there are five rooms under the name Pond."

"Yes, Mrs. Pond," the clerk replied, returning Michelle's smile. "Your rooms are ready."

"It's Ms. Pond. Are the rooms together?"

"Oh yes, we planned for that." A few moments later the clerk slid the keycards across the desk. "You're on the sixth floor. Elevators are just over there." The clerk leaned forward and said, "But you should know, that floor is haunted."

♠　♥　♦　♣

The Secret Life
of Rubberband

by Max Gladstone

Part 1

THE BAGS WERE LATE, protesters howled outside, and Robin Ruttiger, guidance counselor of Xavier Desmond High, had lost a student.

"You have so many," observed his unhelpful friend Jan Chang, who nobody called Sparkplug where she could hear them, before she turned the page of her highlighted and ballpoint-pen-annotated *National Enquirer*. She wore black jeans and a black leather jacket and would have looked completely foreign to San Antonio, Texas, even without the pulsing blue veins that webbed her skin. "Surely you can miss just one."

Robin scanned the posh chaos of the Gunter lobby, which boiled with teachers, parents, and kids who wore the T-shirts of eight different high school jazz bands. He covered the mic of his phone, even though the hold music probably didn't care about the noise. "Antonia was over by the ferns a second ago. You're sure she didn't come out this door?"

Jan did glance up this time, over the rim of the thick black sunglasses she wore to protect other people's eyes from hers. Robin raised a hand to block the electric glare. "That would require my having any clue what she looks like."

"Why did you even come, if not to help?"

She rolled her eyes, then pressed her sunglasses back into place. "I'm here because my niece is competing against your students in a band meet or match or whatever they call these things; said niece, charmingly devout, is convinced that residing in a historically haunted hotel puts her soul at risk; my breeder kid sister indicated that if I showed up to protect her against the ghost, she'd stop bugging me about having forgotten the birthdays of her various spawn for the last six years; and you owe me half a month's rent and don't get to throw shade." She turned the page. "If one of your kids has been kidnapped by our reptoid overlords, that's your problem."

"I'm more worried about those asshole protesters, who do exist, than about the reptoids, who don't."

"Spoken like a reptoid stooge. And I don't think they're protesting assholes."

"When there are real aliens in the world, I don't know why you feel the need to *invent*—" He stopped himself. "Antonia's a dark-haired girl, about five four, black gloves."

Jan raised the tabloid between them.

"Fine." He turned from her, covered the mic again—the hold line had started playing what he really hoped was not a Muzak cover of James Brown's "I'll Go Crazy." "Wally, have *you* seen Antonia?"

The enormous pile of iron whose birth certificate read Wally Gunderson, and whose ace name was Rustbelt, though most people shortened it to Rusty, shrugged. Joints creaked and red flakes drifted down to the lacquered wood floor Rusty was trying not to scuff with his enormous boots—or were those feet? Rusty didn't need to wear clothes, but Robin was glad he made the effort, even if his sharp metal edges pressed disconcertingly against his lime-green polo shirt and dad jeans. "Oh, she's here for sure, yeah. We brought them all in from the van, right through the door, and then Bubbles told off those jerks outside. The kids are fine. Have you got through to that delivery company there about our bags yet?"

Robin didn't know what he expected an enormous metal man to sound like, but the strong North Range accent always caught him by surprise. "I'm listening to the hardest working hold music in show business." Outside, the protesters' roars gained a rhythm: *Hell no, jokers gotta go.* Christ Jesus. "I just—I really need to know where everyone is. Okay?" How could he have lost a kid already?

"Well, that's Yerodin right there." Rusty pointed through the crowd, past mounds of instrument cases, to his adopted daughter, Yerodin, who he hadn't let out of his sight all day. Yerodin, who the other kids called Ghost, hovered over the arm of a couch, hugging one leg as she talked with Adesina Pond, who looked like an animate obsidian statue with cobalt wings.

"That's two out of seven, at least." The speaker on Robin's Nokia hadn't worked right since he dropped the phone in a vat of acid six years back, but even with the pops and fuzz he could hear the bad synths had marched on to "Try Me." "Hold this." Wally took the phone with the care of a man trying not to break a butterfly wing, and raised it to the geared pit where his ear should have been.

Robin craned his neck over the crowd. He was six feet two, and would have had a decent angle on the lobby even without playing his card—especially since most of the crowd were teenagers. But he was here to chaperone the students of Xavier Desmond High, and he'd just shouldered through a horde of angry nat protesters after an armed standoff. No use pretending to be normal.

So he stretched.

Body mass pressed up into his neck. Skin expanded. The bones he was very good at pretending to possess stopped mattering. His chest caved in, his arms grew frail, his watch clattered to the floor, and it all felt so relaxing. He smiled, and made himself stop when his neck was only twelve feet long.

From up here he could see most of his students, though the Xavier Desmond High School Jazz Band—the Jokertown Mob—was certainly living up to the "Mob" part of its name. Lanky Peter Jacobson, aka Segway, zipped through the crowd on his wheels. Morpho Girl, there, was still talking with Ghost—a ten-year-old girl raised, if you call it that, by people who hoped she'd one day be a weapon. Ghost, intangible, glanced over her shoulder at the crowd beyond the hotel doors. Marissa, aka *something*—she changed her handle every few weeks—had struck up a conversation with a Chinese girl wearing a bright silver cross and a Detroit Detonators T-shirt. He spotted Asti and Sean showing something he really hoped was not a fake ID to the lobby bartender, and—

"How's it going, Mister R?" Jacobson hopped over a luggage cart, spun midair, and landed with a squeal. A bellhop glared.

"Fine," Robin called down. "Segway, have you seen Antonia?"

Jacobson beamed at being called by his card name. Robin often wondered what it was about drawing the card that triggered an obsession with pseudonyms. Not that Robin Ruttiger himself, aka (no matter how he tried to forget it these days) Rubberband, had a leg to stand on in that regard. "She looked tired. Maybe she, like, went upstairs for a nap?"

"Thank you." He snapped back down to size. Segway swept past, bent down, and tossed Robin his watch. He stretched his wrist thin to slide it on. "Wally, can you watch the door? And stay on the phone?"

"You bet." Rusty stuck up his thumb, ground his jaw, and listened to James-less Brown.

Robin flattened himself, everything except his feet. (He didn't need shoes, but he liked wearing them.) He caught his watch in his hand this time—no sense testing the "full shock-absorbing power" any more than necessary—as he snaked through the crowd. "Excuse me. Pardon. Pardon me. Passing through." The mothers and kids and hotel employees didn't notice, or did and didn't care, or did and recoiled in horror, for which he didn't blame them. Flattened out, he looked like people did in cartoons after they'd been bulldozed by an enterprising coyote. He wriggled to the stairs, stretched his arms up fourteen feet—ten years of practice and it still felt weird reminding himself he didn't have shoulder joints anymore—caught the overhead railing, pulled his skin like a, well, like a rubber band, and snapped up through the air to land on the second floor in a tangle of overextended limbs.

The mezzanine, at least, was quiet. He sorted himself out, adjusted his watch, and straightened his collar.

Antonia Abruzzi stood alone by the window, staring down in silhouette at the protesters' flags and signs. Her long dark hair perched on her head, wound in intricate braids. She looked fifteen and fifty at once. She wore gloves, even if her hands didn't fill them right. She had removed her left glove, and the long thin tentacles she had instead of a hand fanned over the window like brush bristles mashed flat.

He approached. The chant rhythm outside had changed; he couldn't guess the words, now. Below, Sean led the kids in a chant of their own:

Jokertown, Jokertown, Jokertown Mob!
Stick that bullshit in your gob!

"Hey," Robin said. "I know it's a mess down there, but Ms. Ober-hoffer and Ms. Pond and Mr. Gunderson and I really need to know where everyone is."

"You know where I am," Antonia said.

"I do now, yeah."

She didn't turn.

"Would you like to talk?"

"No."

"Antonia, I know walking through that crowd was hard. They're small-minded, angry people. But we won't let anyone hurt you." It was hard to keep the anger from his voice. "Until Ms. Pond has us all checked in, we really need to know everyone's in the same place, and safe. Could you please come join the others?"

Jokertown, Jokertown, Jokertown Mob!
There aren't many words that rhyme with "ob"!

Antonia turned away from the street. Her face was another country. He thought she might be about to speak.

A slow wave passed through the protesters outside and below; placards and crude signs parted to reveal a black delivery van. Rusty shouted from the lobby: "Hey, Robin! I just got through! They say their fella's arriving now." His volume would have been perfect on a construction site, but was out of place in a four-star hotel.

Robin spread his hands, apologetic. "Those are the bags. I really have to go. Could you please come downstairs with me, and join the others?"

"Fine." The edge in her voice meant he'd screwed up. He told himself he was okay with that, for now.

Robin had worked with teenagers long enough to wait for her to descend the stairs first. When she was back with the herd, he vaulted the railing, fell to the lobby, and slithered through the crowd to Rusty's side. "Let's go."

♠

Thank God the delivery guy was a nat, or looked like one. Robin didn't think the protest would get violent—more violent, anyway, since words had a violence all their own—but it helped that they wouldn't think the delivery guy was bulletproof. Scared and angry people turned to violence when they thought they lacked other options—and to violence more vicious the less hope they thought they had. Fifty years of American public education had barely scratched the comic book myths: people still thought bullets bounced off aces and jokers. There was always a chance those myths would make it easier for some asshole to pull a trigger.

He wished Bubbles had thought up a better way to defuse the situation than reminding the protesters she was invulnerable, but, hey, spilt milk.

Robin signed three times on the delivery guy's iPad—once they found a stylus, since neither his nor Rusty's skin conducted normally, though for different reasons—and wheeled a cart piled with a suitcase Jenga tower down a ramp to the street. Someone tossed a tomato that splattered on the hot sidewalk and sizzled.

"What the—"

"Keep walking, Rusty."

The cart's left wheel wiggled. A hotel doorman rushed to open the side doors, and they pushed through air-conditioned steam into the lobby. Another tomato flew, and landed by Robin's feet. People shouted nonsense Robin tried not to hear. The tower of bags teetered overhead.

Together, Robin and Rusty shoved the cart through the door. Jacobson applauded. Bubbles, still arguing with the front desk, glanced over her shoulder and grinned. Marissa, who'd left her new friend with the cross to nap in a chair, tried to high-five Yerodin, but passed through. Wheeling the cart over toward the packed instruments, Robin felt, briefly, like he had everything under control.

Then he heard a high-pitched giggle, glimpsed a grinning, bleeding spectral face, and felt the luggage cart lurch to one side.

Robin and Rusty both grabbed the cart, but one particularly heavy suitcase on top of the stack had already tipped loose and arced through the air, tumbling toward the Jokertown Mob's piled instruments.

Time did its slow-motion crisis thing.

Robin cursed. He and Rusty lunged for the suitcase at once. Robin's arms stretched out, caught the case, pulled it clear of the instruments—leaving Rusty in midair, diving to intercept a case that did not exist. Which would have been fine, if his arc wasn't set to bring several hundred pounds of iron down on top of the band's brass.

Robin dropped the suitcase and reached for Rusty, thinking, *Too late, too late—*

He heard a whoop and saw a familiar flash of gold, and Rusty landed hard on the floor, three feet to the left of the instruments. His iron elbows dug deep gouges in the wood.

The milling musicians of the Gunter lobby had hushed in horror as they watched the suitcase fall. They held their breath as Wally dove through the air. The applause after the averted disaster, Jacobson hopping on his wheels, Yerodin cheering, even Ms. Oberhoffer whistling approval, deafened.

Years had passed since Robin had last seen the golden lasso that snared Rusty's shoulders, but he recognized it at once, as he recognized the voice raised in a triumphant *"Yee-haw!"* and recognized the jangle of spurs. Because Jerry Jeff Longwood—or, God love him, Kozmic Kowboy—did nothing by half measures. Not even the hearty backslap that almost knocked Robin double.

"Howdy Robin! Buddy! Sorry 'bout the lasso, there, partner, but you looked like you were in a sore spot."

Jerry Jeff knelt to help Wally free of the lasso, which had snagged on his shoulder gears. The Kozmic Kowboy wore his full regalia: chaps and vest and hat and boots and crossed belts, his big iron on his hip. (Robin hoped it wasn't loaded.) His mustaches drooped beautifully, and if there were streaks of gray in that dark hair these days, the cowboy hat covered them. Riches and fame and family life seemed to have added nothing to Jerry Jeff but a few smile lines around the corners of the eyes.

"Thanks," Rusty said, which Robin should have said first. But, in Robin's defense, he hadn't yet remembered how words worked.

"How" was a good start. "Jerry Jeff, what are you *doing* here?"

"You didn't think you could come to Texas without your old friend Jerry Jeff dropping in, did you? This here competition's been all over the news, and folk knew your school was coming, and I thought, maybe he'll be in town. And good thing for you I did! Come on, put 'er there." Before Robin could pull away, he found his hand enveloped in a calloused handshake that, in a pinch, could double as a hydraulic press.

Jerry Jeff wasn't a big man, but they made men tough in whatever comic book cowboy land he came from.

"Robin," Rusty said, "you know this fella?"

"Yes." Robin did his best to smile. "We were on *American Hero* together." *American Hero,* the reality TV series spotlighting "tomorrow's heroes *today!*," was the opportunity of a lifetime for its contestants. Some applied for money, some for fame, some because they wanted to make a difference, and some because they didn't see much difference between the three. When the second season casting call went out, Robin Ruttiger had been two years into his new life as an ace, using his gifts to rescue cats from the treetops of Akron, Ohio, and Jerry Jeff Longwood was already the darlingest, dandiest star-spangled rider, roper, and cowboy crooner on the rodeo circuit.

And years later, here they were.

After saving the instruments, Jerry Jeff accepted Ms. Oberhoffer's half whistled, half signed thanks—he might not have been able to sign fast enough to follow <I'm your biggest fan> and the frantic list of his concerts she'd watched on YouTube, but he must have gotten the general notion, since he tipped his hat to her and bowed and said, "That's right kind of you." She blushed, and fanned herself.

Jerry Jeff tipped his hat to Ms. Pond, too—they seemed to have met somewhere, which he had to admit made sense, given Bubbles' fame—and asked if he could borrow Robin to catch up for an hour or two. Robin tried to look utterly occupied, can't leave the kids, first night in a new city, but Sharon was too busy swooning to object, and Bubbles wouldn't hear of parting old friends reunited. "The kids have their rooms, and I think after this morning we've all earned a rest. Take a few hours off. Wally and I can handle the orientation."

"Ah," Robin said. "Great." He wished he sounded more convinced. "I'll be back in time for the mixer."

<We'll keep an eye on things while you're gone,> Sharon whistled.

Bubbles and the
Band Trip

Part 2

A MIDDLE-AGED WOMAN STOPPED Michelle as she reached the elevator. The woman's hair was a dull gray and she wore a faded green cotton shirtwaist dress and espadrilles.

"Miss Pond," the woman said. She had a twangy Texas accent. *Miz Pawnd.* "I'm Priscilla Beecher, the band's liaison for the competition. I'll be taking care of y'all. My job is to let y'all know where the children are supposed to be and when. After you get y'all's rooms, we'll need to head to the Tobin Center for orientation."

It was a relief to have someone around who knew the ropes. And Miss Beecher seemed nice and didn't once look askance at the Mob. "We were just going to drop our things off in the rooms," Michelle said. "We'll be right down."

"I'll wait here," Miss Beecher said.

◆

The rooms weren't what Michelle had expected. There was an odd square-shaped protrusion from the west side of the wall in Michelle's room and she could hear the elevator going up and down. She checked the other rooms and they were somewhat better and much less noisy, but even a "bad" room at the Gunter was pretty nice.

If it's haunted, it's not doing a very good job of feeling haunted, she thought as she reentered her room. The pillows were fluffy, the bed comfortable when she flopped down on it to check how it felt. There weren't any creepy cobwebs, peeling wallpaper, or unexplained chills. Nope, her room at the Gunter didn't seemed to be haunted at all. Unless being haunted by nice marble floors in the bathroom was a scary thing.

The rooms were clumped together as asked. Asti and Peter were sharing one room. Adesina, Marissa, and Antonia were in another. Adesina and Michelle had argued before they left about whether or not she would be staying in Michelle's room or in the room with the other girls.

"Mom!" Adesina had said. Her antennae twitched furiously. "I'll look stupid if I stay with you! I'm grown-up now! You can't do this to me!"

Michelle flopped onto her favorite chair, a mid-century modern piece upholstered in a gray-and-yellow atomic print. "You're still my little girl," she said. She wasn't loving the newly adolescent Adesina much just then. "Why do you need to stay in their room anyway?"

Adesina's antennae went wild. It was disconcerting. "Because it makes me look like you don't trust me. Okay, Ghost is staying in Ms. Oberhoffer's room, but she's just a kid. I'm an adult. I don't need to be babysat."

It was some impressive teenage logic. As in not so much.

"Fine," Michelle said, not wanting to have the whole teenage scene right now. "But you better be on your best behavior. And you're not an adult yet. You're not an adult until you can keep your room picked up, do your own laundry, and support me in my old age."

One of the things Michelle was learning about having a teenager was to pick your battles. And this one had been too much of a pain in the ass to fight.

"You guys have ten minutes to get settled, then we're meeting downstairs," Michelle said. She thought she was starting to get the yes-I-am-in-control-of-you-kids voice down. "Don't be late."

But her words were met by closing doors. Wally gave her a look of sympathy, then he went into the room he was sharing with Robin. Sharon gave a whistle, signed, <See you in ten,> and shoved her own door open. Ghost floated inside and Sharon let the door swing shut.

Michelle turned. Her door had closed automatically and locked. And her keycard was inside the room.

Great, she thought. *Just great.*

♥

"I want to thank all the bands participating in the Gunter-Sheraton Charlie Parker High School Jazz Band and Ensemble Competition. Whew! That was a mouthful!" The director of the competition, Dr. Amelia Smith, beamed at them.

Laughter rippled through the small theater. It was a bare-wall, flat-floor theater. Between the bands, the chaperones, the parents, the music teachers, and the judges, they filled up about half of the space. Priscilla had explained that they were in the Carlos Alvarez Theater just for orientation and master classes. The actual performances would take place in the main auditorium.

"Most of you have put videos up on YouTube, so I'm guessing y'all are familiar with each other's bands. But I'm going to introduce everyone just the same." She looked down at her notes then said, "From Texas—and third-year attendees—the Plano Originals. Please stand up so we can see you!"

A group of five teenagers stood. They all wore matching outfits except Kimmie. Michelle saw her pop up and sit down quickly. The rest of the band could have been in a Ralph Lauren catalog. They were clean-cut and fairly reeked of money and privilege. There was enthusiastic applause from the entire audience, including the Mob. The Originals waved like conquering heroes, then sat down.

"Folsom Funkalicious Four, from Folsom, Louisiana." A quartet seated in front of the Mob stood. A gangly girl who had a cloud of umber curls flourished her drumsticks, then did an insanely fast riff on the back of the seat in front of her, then turned around to look at the Mob. Michelle flashed her a smile and the girl got a look on her face like she was about to faint. She whipped back around and sank down in her seat.

"All right, settle down," said Dr. Smith. "The Modesto Melody Makers from California are here in the front." Michelle was tickled to see that the Melody Makers were all girls except for a single dark-haired boy.

"Oh. My. God! It's Mindy-Lou Gutiérrez!" Michelle heard Sean say. "What's she doing here? I heard she was going to drop out of school and start playing professionally."

"Nah," Asti replied. "I heard her family wasn't going to let her. They're super-strict."

"Well, doesn't really matter. She's going to have record companies lining up no matter what."

Mindy-Lou was pretty, very pretty. Michelle assessed her with the eye of a professional model. With her brown hair and brown eyes and six-foot frame she would be a lethal combination on her looks alone. According to Adesina and Yerodin, Mindy-Lou was also all kewl and hep to the jive. Though Adesina was quick to explain that they totes lifted hep from Cab Calloway. And jive was, well, a jazz thing. Michelle looked at them blankly.

"Lubbock High School Jazz Band. Detroit Detonators."

When the Detonators were introduced, a pretty girl wearing a black Detonators tee with a dramatic silver cross around her neck blew a few bars of "Satin Doll" on her trumpet. Appreciative laughter ran around the room.

Each band stood as their name was called and the audience gave them all warm applause. "The Seattle Wailers—I see what y'all did there—and finally, the Xavier Desmond High School Jazz Band."

The Mob stood up. There was a smattering of applause, and then someone in the back of the house yelled, "Go back to New York, you freaks." Michelle saw that the Plano Originals applauded at the cat-call, but she did note that Kimmie hunched farther down in her seat, jammed her hands under her armpits, and looked as if she'd rather be anywhere else.

"That's enough of that," Dr. Smith said, tartly. She frowned, yanked the bottom of her jacket down, and then glowered at the audience. "The Xavier Desmond High School Jazz Band got here the same as the rest of you did. Blind auditions.

"And while we're at it, there are some people who are protesting the Xavier Desmond High School's participation. You are to ignore and not to accost them in any way. We are an inclusive organization with our sole measure of merit being music."

The Funkalicious Four started clapping, led by their drummer. The Modesto Melody Makers followed suit, and after them, the Lubbock High School Jazz Band. The chaperones for those bands were applauding as well. But there was only a mixed reaction from the rest of the bands. Some sat stone-faced. Others clapped but without enthusiasm. The Plano Originals glared at the Mob.

Adesina said loudly as the applause was waning, "We're just the Mob. It takes less time to say."

"Moving on," Dr. Smith continued. "You all know our judges: Buddy Robins." A lanky man with a shaved head and light brown skin stood. He wore a blue Henley top and black pants. His eyes were kind and he gave a wave to the kids. Adesina and the other bass players gave excited yelps. The bands applauded him warmly.

"Pipe down," Dr. Smith said. "Regina Carter, Mary Halvorson, and Wynton Marsalis." The bands erupted with excited applause. There was whooping and excited clapping. Michelle knew from Adesina that the judges were heroes to the kids and even Michelle had heard of Wynton Marsalis. "There are a few announcements, then we'll meet up at the mixer at seven and everyone can get acquainted.

"As you all know, we have a special visitor at the mixer this evening—film star Haley Mok, Jade Blossom from season one of *American Hero*." The Folsom drummer gave an excited squeak.

"Sheesh, LoriAnne, fangirl much?" asked the boy sitting next to her.

"C'mon, Howard," LoriAnne replied. She hiccuped and then gave another excited squeak. "This is, uhm, kewl. Is that how you say it?"

"Yes, but you're not a gamer so you just sound weird," he replied.

LoriAnne slunk down in her seat.

Dr. Smith continued, "She's here to promote her new movie, *Lord Jim*, and one of you was lucky enough to win an evening with her." She pursed her lips. "Cesar Chao, the judges chose your essay. You're the winner! Stand up so everyone can give you a hand!"

A short, raven-haired boy stood. His shoulders were hunched and there was a chagrined expression on his face. The rest of his band catcalled and clapped. But the chagrined expression didn't stay. He looked around at his bandmates and glared. Their applause died and he sat down.

"I can't believe Jade Blossom is here," Michelle hissed. "She's awful."

"Shhhhh, Mom, please." Adesina gave Michelle her very best you're-embarrassing-the-hell-out-of-me look.

"That's all the announcements I have, ladies and gentlemen," Dr. Smith said. "You're free to go. And I'll see you at the mixer at seven o'clock."

♠ ♥ ♦ ♣

The Secret Life
of Rubberband

Part 2

ROBIN FOUND HIMSELF AT a sprawling Tex-Mex place on the San Antonio River Walk, eating corn chips and drinking a margarita Jerry Jeff had ordered for him without asking if he wanted one. Robin told himself he would not have rather faced down the mob again. He would not have rather been stuck in Dr. Hastings's lab again, being experimented upon. He told himself that as he scooped another tortilla chip in salsa, keeping one hand underneath as he brought the chip to his mouth, to save his khakis from red sauce.

Jerry Jeff ate with a mannered disregard for manners, one elbow on the table, hat cocked back, jacket rhinestones glinting. "After the second album did so well, we figgered Grandpappy's ranch started to feel a bit small, so we found a nice big place, you know, rolling grass range, this house like you would not believe. And Jim Anne took to it real well, and the kids, they just can't get enough of the place." His face got a dreamy look, and—were those tears in the corners of his eyes? "But now you've got me going on and on about my business, and you haven't said word one 'bout yours! My money was always on you, you know, in the pool—there were big things coming your way, Mister Rubberband. Come on, you haven't even touched your drink!"

Robin clinked margaritas with him, and raised the glass to his lips, but tasted only the salt. Jerry Jeff was on his second already. "I'm working," he said, "so I can't drink too much. You know how it is."

"Aw, like them kids have never seen a body enjoy himself before?"

"Not a teacher, I hope. At least, not on duty."

"Shit"—which was a two-syllable word the way Jerry Jeff said it— "they can take care of themselves." He finished his glass and raised it, empty, to the waiter. *"¡Uno más, por favor!"* Back to Robin: "Come on, catch your old friend Jerry Jeff up on the gossip."

Robin looked down into his margarita.

He'd kept the conversation away from himself on the walk over, and through Jerry Jeff's first two drinks. It helped that Jerry Jeff welled with stories: he'd talk about anything and everything with a white-water rapidity of gab. And Robin liked to listen, even though he already knew most of Jerry Jeff's stories, or their outlines at least, from those square celebrity journalism ads that popped up at the bottom of articles he read on the Internet—not to mention the Google Alert he'd set up on his fellow contestants one night while depressed, and had never worked up the nerve to cancel.

Whatever Robin had to say about the second season of *American Hero*—and he could say so much that most of the time he preferred to avoid saying anything at all—the show had been a great launchpad. Some people, like Jerry Jeff, knew show business well enough to use their brief spotlight to leapfrog into a stronger spotlight. For Robin, who spent so much of his life trying to avoid notice, the cameras and the sets and the significance bubbled inside him, and he glowed, drunk on fame, until the hangover. And when the drop hit, he made the good hard choice, and stepped away. He didn't want album deals, and he didn't want a manor house. He wanted to help people. He wanted his own path.

He'd found it. And along the way he'd found a tiny basement apartment with mysterious stains on the walls, the rent on which he was half a month behind. And he'd found a public school teacher's salary, a love life in need of love life support, students who rarely listened, and a bank account balance so low cartoon moths flew off his cracked laptop screen when he logged in.

"I'm doing great," he said. Meaning: Help. "My students are wonderful. Tough. Determined." Thinking of crowds and chaos and Antonia's scorn and sullen silence. "New York is like nowhere else." Big and smelly and tangled and broken, with rising rents and trains that caught fire or stopped on bridges for no reason, surging, torrid. "It's a good life," he kept telling himself. "I have everything I wanted."

Jerry Jeff looked up through the bushes of his eyebrows. Did he doubt the act? But the silence passed so quickly it might have never been. "Well," Jerry Jeff said, "here's to that!" He raised his glass, only to find it still empty. He turned to shout at the server, just as she materialized with his third margarita. They toasted, and this time Robin took a sip. "You don't know how glad I am to hear that. I mean, boy, you had it all right there if you wanted it, right in the palm of your hand. And this is a good thing you're doing, that's for damn sure, but whenever they get the teachers on the TV, you know, they're talking about pay and the tests and the unions and how damn bad it all gets, I just think about you, you know."

"Oh, I'm fine." He wasn't. "Hey, so, your kids—how are they? It's hard to imagine you as a dad."

"Aw, I do fine. Kids ain't too different from cattle, you know, just give 'em plenty of hay and space to run."

It sounded simple when somebody else said it.

"Hey," Jerry Jeff said, "you ever run into Woodrow at all these days? Or Stacy?"

And just like that seven years evaporated and they were back in the house after a long day of absurd random challenges, drinking the bad beers with which Our Beloved Corporate Sponsors had stocked the fridge, sharing gossip.

The enchiladas came, and they tucked in. "Speaking of which, Robin, you will never believe who I ran into last time I was out in Los Angeles—" Pronounced, of course, with a hard *g*.

"Denise?"

"Naw— the Laureate! Poet kid, you know, him what wrote those words that sometimes came true? He's tryin' to make it in Hollywood, screenwriting—you remember when we had that team forest matchup and him and Crazy Quilt got caught in flagrante delectable?"

Robin considered telling him that wasn't how you pronounced that word, then ordered a second margarita instead. "She went back to grad school, didn't she? Alice?"

"Grad school in kickin' ass, maybe! Always thought she shoulda made it further, even if the old Colonel did theoretic'lly win that swimming challenge by freezing her in a block of ice."

"She might have been able to challenge it if she hadn't set his clothes on fire when the med team got him out."

"Aw, he's a coldster, a little fire weren't gonna hurt him none."

"I thought that was exactly how you hurt coldsters."

"Well, to be fair, fire *was* his weakness, but Alice didn't know that. And you dumped him into the lake to put the fire out, so, no harm done, and anyway it couldn't have happened to a nicer pain in the hindquarters. Weren't nobody sad to see him stung."

"Yeah," Robin said. "No arguments there. Had me fooled, though, at first—Colonel Centigrade really seemed like a nice guy until Terrell and I went public with our relationship."

"Speaking of which," Jerry Jeff said, a bit too drunk to realize he shouldn't, "Terrell's doing good—still run into him every once in a while when I'm up Chicago way."

"Thanks," Robin said, and guzzled his margarita. "I keep tabs." The booze sparked in his head. "Most of us turned out okay, I guess, more or less. Except Tesseract."

"Shit. Did you ever figger her for . . . well, did you ever think she could do anything like . . ."

"Like Kazakhstan?" He shook his head.

"And to think she and I—"

"Really?"

"Well, I didn't know Jim Anne at that point, you know. But a gentleman never tells." And then the fourth margarita arrived, and the afternoon blurred blue.

"Awright," Jerry Jeff said when he came back from the restroom, hitching up his belt by its dinner-plate-size buckle. "Let's get you back before that Ms. Oberhoffer comes huntin'."

"We have to pay the check."

"I picked it up."

"Jerry Jeff, come on."

"Naw, you can get the next one. I got us a table at Bob's Steak and Chop House tomorrow, if you can wiggle out another couple hours for an old buddy."

Robin's heart dropped. "Ah. I'll see what I can do."

♣

Robin managed the walk back, declining like the sun, slightly tipsy and cursing on the inside. He should have told Jerry Jeff he couldn't get away, the kids came first, always needed more chaperones in a strange city. He should have come clean about his finances. He couldn't afford a steak dinner for one normal person and a cowboy—make that two cowboys, since Jerry Jeff's card upped his metabolism to let him eat and drink twice as much as a nat. Maybe he could manufacture some crisis tomorrow, plead off dinner.

But Jerry Jeff would know, and he'd ask the reason, and then Robin would have to come clean. He didn't mind not having money. He didn't mind leaving public life. But every time he tried to explain himself, it came out all screwy. How could Jerry Jeff just assume he'd pick up the tab at the steak place? How could Robin have just accepted, as if of course it wouldn't be a problem?

Dr. Nelson kept reminding him: Don't obsess over your mistakes. You made them, or you didn't. Play the ball as it lies.

He needed, roughly, four hundred dollars.

Where to find it?

Another teacher? Fat chance. Especially since he didn't know when he'd be able to pay back the loan. The travel had maxed his credit card for the month—the school district would reimburse him, eventually, but that didn't help now.

Maybe Rusty or Ms. Pond could help—they were both higher-profile than anyone Robin was in close contact with these days. But Robin had just met them this trip, since their kids were both solid performers and neither of them old enough to think about college yet. He didn't want to spoil whatever good impression he hoped he'd made by asking for a loan.

Calling one of his other buddies from the *American Hero* days would just make things worse. Which left . . .

Well, it was worth a shot.

The protesters had thinned out over lunch, and those that remained had settled in for the long haul, resting their gross signs against their lawn chairs and drinking cheap beer from blue dew-slick coolers. The beer, Robin noticed, came from Our Beloved Corporate Sponsors, sell-ing to both sides of the aisle.

A skinny wild-haired man wearing very short shorts and drinking an Our Beloved Corporate Sponsor tallboy shouted, *"Jokers go home!"* in a squashed hoarse voice. Robin shoved the revolving doors, entered the arctic chill of the now blissfully empty Gunter lobby, dug the Nokia from his pocket, and smashed buttons until he found the number he, to be honest, didn't exactly want to call.

He closed his eyes, and pondered the depths of desperation one had to plumb before asking one's landlord for a loan.

Then he pushed the green phone button twice. (The acid bath, again.) It didn't work, so he pushed it a third time.

The phone rang.

Jan, hi, something strange has come up and I was hoping . . . No, that was a warning flag conversation.

It rang again.

Jan, hi, I need four hundred dollars. Hm. A bit direct.

Ring number three.

Jan, I know this is a long shot, but . . .

The phone clicked. "Hey, Rob**, t**** * ****** ***** *******," the speaker hissed. He shook the phone. Something rattled inside.

"Jan? Jan, sorry, do you happen to, could you say that again?"

"******——$$$—&#%."

"Sorry, my phone's being worse than usual—"

"I said," came the voice he expected, clear as crystal, and right behind him, "speak up. I can't hear you."

"Jan?"

Jan grinned, and little lightning bolts danced between her teeth. "Howdy!" Her faint Brooklyn accent and affected drawl mixed like oil and napalm, and whatever effect she meant her souvenir cowboy hat to have, it wasn't. "I need your help."

"I," Robin said, too late as usual. Then: "Wait. What?"

"You're good with kids, right? That's your job?"

"Can you loan me four hundred dollars?"

The words rushed out all at once, and once they were said, he wished he could have unsaid them. Not because Jan looked hurt. Because she was grinning.

He scrambled to cover. "I know I'm behind on the rent, I know it's a lot of money, but it would be a huge help, something big has come up, and I'll repay you next month—you can just add it to my bill."

"Oh," Jan said, "I think we can come to an arrangement. Follow me."

♠

He hadn't expected to recognize Jan's niece, but the girl wearing the Detonators shirt and the bright silver cross, perched at the bar drinking a Sprite and looking deeply uncomfortable, was the same one who'd napped in the lobby earlier.

Jan jumped onto a barstool and leaned back against the lacquered wood. "Robin, meet Vicky. Vicky, meet Robin Ruttiger. He's an ace. A hero. A TV star. He'll help you out."

"I'm," he said, remembered the terms of the deal, and squashed his impulse to argue on general principle. "I'm helping your aunt look for the ghost."

"Devil," Vicky said.

"Devil," Jan said. "Devil, ghost, whatever."

Robin frowned. "Weren't you trying to convince me that there were different kinds of black helicopters just yesterday?"

"You can tell them apart by albedo. But that's not the point! Those things are—" Jan cut herself off. "Tell him, Vicky."

"It's okay, Aunt Jan. I know you don't think devils are real. But they are. One knocked over the luggage cart Mr. Ruttiger was wheeling into the hotel." Her dark eyes were large and frank. "You saw it, didn't you? You heard it."

"I saw a big red smile. And I heard a laugh. I don't know what it was."

"A devil."

"My point is," Jan said, "the hotel claims it's haunted. Devils don't haunt things. Ghosts do."

Vicky shook her head. "Either way, I can't stay here. Not with that . . . thing running around. It could hurt kids. Tempt us to evil."

"There are other explanations," Robin said, uncertain whether this would improve matters.

"Aliens," Jan supplied, ticking them off on her fingers, "secret government conspiracies, men in black, reptoids, higher-dimensional beings, renegade Majestic program subjects—"

"A practical joker," Robin cut in. "Or an ace, for that matter. Someone who drew a telekinetic card, or who can make people hallucinate. Lots of things might be happening, none particularly supernatural." What exactly *supernatural* meant when a miracle could be "just" another card, he didn't know, and no preacher had ever explained to his satisfaction, but he doubted that observation would be useful at the moment.

Jan swung in to fill the silence. "The point is, there are lots of things it could be other than a ghost or a devil. I felt it when it showed up—like a buzzing in the back of my head. So it's electromagnetic somehow. Are demons electromagnetic?"

Vicky stared at her aunt. Robin couldn't read her expression. She said, "I don't know."

"So here's what we're going to do." Jan laid out the plan: "You go up to your hotel room and get some rest. Robin here, he's a big-time hero, real experience, he's been on television and everything. He and your aunt Jan, we're going to hunt down this demon, bring it to you, and show you it's . . ." She frowned. Robin imagined she had been about to say *it's not real,* which wasn't exactly the point. "Show you it's nothing to worry about. How's that sound?"

If supernatural forces were real, one of them probably would have answered Robin's prayer and shut Jan up. "Do you feel unsafe?" he asked.

Vicky shook her head.

"If you do, go to Jan, or me, or to your teachers. We're all here to help."

"Can you find the devil?"

Jan's eyes drilled into him, and he remembered the handshake. Four hundred dollars for a ghost hunt, on delivery of said ghost. Half in advance.

"We'll find it," he said. *After the mixer,* he thought. *I promised Sharon I'd be back for the mixer.* "Don't worry. Everything's going to be okay."

If he kept saying that, maybe he'd believe himself.

♠   ♥   ♦   ♣

Bubbles and the
Band Trip

Part 3

"WHAT CAN I GET you, Mrs. Bubbles?" the bartender said with a Texas twang. *Whut kin ah git yew, Miziz Bubbles?* He was a particular breed of pretty boy—blond with perfectly symmetrical, pleasing features corked by a glib easy smile. He had a lean, yet well-muscled, body. The mixer wasn't exactly going well, and Michelle was on her second drink. And a non-alcoholic one to boot.

"We've got soda, water, ice tea, and more soda. Just so you know, I'm a huge fan of yours," he said, practically fluttering his long eyelashes. "Name's Billy Rainbow, and it's a pure honor to meet you."

That southern charm might work on some girls, but Michelle wasn't one of them. A bad girl might work on her, but a pretty boy, not so much.

"I'll have Coke." Michelle scanned the room.

"Here you go," Billy Rainbow said, setting it on the bar. "You're right pretty, Mrs. Bubbles. I expect you're just about the prettiest lady I've ever seen."

Michelle gave him her very best are-you-freaking-kidding-me? look. He didn't seem in the least deterred.

"You *do* know I'm famously gay, right?" she asked. "Never been confused about that my entire life. Also, it's Ms. Bubbles. Not Mrs." *Mrs. Bubbles? Really. Really?! Do I look like a Mrs. Bubbles?*

Billy's smile grew even wider and he opened his hands, turning his palms up. Small, sparkly rainbows appeared in them. He was looking at her intently. "Why, I expect you'd help a poor boy like me out, wouldn't you? I'm pretty broke."

Michelle stared at the pretty rainbows for a few seconds. Then she looked up at him with a scowl on her face.

"Does this *ever* work for you?" she asked, dropping two golf ball–sized bubbles into his hands. "Because if you think some *My Pretty Pony* deuce power and junior hypnosis is going to make me your bitch, you are sorely mistaken. And really, in this crowd it might not be the smartest thing showing off like that."

Billy Rainbow looked flummoxed and dropped the bubbles to the floor. Michelle let them pop. "But, but . . ."

"There's only one way in which I'm suggestible and, believe me, you are not the kind of person who can do that. Don't try that crap on anyone else."

He jammed his hands into his pants pockets then shrugged his shoulders. "It's just a parlor trick," he said dejectedly. "Those rainbows are so pretty, and I kinda like showing them off."

"I wouldn't," Michelle said. "Because that's not the brightest thing in the world." *I'm guessing no one has ever accused him of being bright,* Michelle thought.

"And don't go flirting with the girls or trying to get money from people. I'm keeping an eye on you."

Michelle took her Coke then walked to the nearest window. It overlooked Houston Street and she had a view straight up and down the street. Across from the Gunter, the Majestic Theatre's marquee was lit up with that evening's entertainment: *Phantom of the Opera*. It was an old movie palace that hadn't been torn down. She hoped she'd get a chance to see the inside of it before they went back to New York.

"What're you looking at?" Rusty asked. She turned to face him.

"Oh, just that cool theater across the way."

Wally smiled, his hinges pulling up. He was dressed in overalls and a short-sleeved plaid shirt. The overalls were new and looked pretty spiffy.

The Gunter Terrace Room jutted out from the second floor of the hotel. It wrapped around two sides of the building, forming a portico over the sidewalk. The walls were made of glass and curved up to the ceiling. A busy, burgundy-and-navy-blue Victorian-patterned carpet covered the floor. The room was crowded with band members, chaperones, judges, and some of the kids' parents. The mixer was supposed to be in full swing, but, at the moment, each band was clumped together, looking nervously around the room. The adults just looked frazzled.

"Well, this isn't awkward at all," Michelle said.

Sharon whistled in agreement. Then she signed, <It might as well be a school dance.>

"Why don't you go talk to that Kimmie girl?" Michelle asked Adesina. "She's nice."

Adesina shrugged and jammed her hands into the pockets of her faded black jeans. Her vestigial legs gave a little twitch. "I don't know, Mom," she said, casting a wary glance at Kimmie. "She's in the Plano Originals, and now we know they're hella a-holes. They really seem to have a hate on for jokers."

"But Kimmie liked *you*. And she was nice to all of the other kids in the band." Michelle caught Kimmie's eye and smiled at her. Kimmie smiled back, but it was tremulous. A tall boy with short blond hair and an athlete's body leaned down and whispered something in Kimmie's ear. Kimmie frowned and then glared up at him. She turned on her heel and marched across the room toward the Mob.

"Hey Kimmie." Segway zipped around Michelle and intercepted her. Kimmie's face lit up and she gave him a sweet smile.

"Hey there, Peter," she replied. She tucked her hair behind her ears. "I'm glad we get another chance to talk. I'm sorry about how rude the Originals were at orientation. They're all a lot like Jax, that blond guy in the pink polo shirt. He's such an idiot. Anyway, he thinks having the Mob in the competition is a publicity stunt."

What the six degrees of hell? Michelle thought. "The Mob got in here same as everyone else!" she said. Her hands were clenched into fists at her sides. They itched to bubble. *Remember Kazakhstan? Stop thinking that way. Blowing someone up isn't a good problem-solving choice in a room full of high schoolers. Defeating an elder god from a different dimension, yes. Killing a privileged punk from Plano, not so much.*

Kimmie held up her hands. "Ms. Pond," she said quickly, "I don't agree. The Plano Originals are, well, they're morons. They're almost as bad as my moth—"

"Kimberly Coldwater!"

This time Michelle didn't know the imperious voice, but it appeared as if Kimmie did. Her shoulders came up as she tried to make herself smaller. Her bright smile faded.

"Why on the Good Lord's green earth are you speaking to these . . . these . . . creatures?" A woman dressed like a pastel tornado came barreling across the room. She wore heels almost as high as Jade Blossom would. Even so, she was only a few inches taller than Kimmie. But her presence made it feel as if she was more imposing than that.

She was impeccably attired. A perfectly tailored azalea-colored St. John suit matched her towering heels. Her long nails were lacquered a deep red. She had big hair. It was long with blond streaks and back-combed with a perfect flip at the ends. It was *big* hair. It was upscale Dallas hair. None of that low-class height, but plenty of volume. A red Hermès bag that matched her nails was slung across her arm.

Holy shit! A real Dallas matriarch! Michelle thought.

"What are you doing to my daughter?" the woman demanded.

"Pretty sure nothing," Michelle replied. The room had grown quiet again. "But you never know. We're diabolical like that."

Kimmie looked miserable. "Mom, please," she said. "This is Michelle Pond." Kimmie was trying to do the right thing. Michelle was impressed. Even if her mother was horrible, the daughter had been raised to be polite. "Ms. Pond, this is my mother, Bambi Coldwater."

"I know that name," Michelle said, reflexively sticking her hand out. "Hold on, aren't you the woman who brought the suit to prevent kids with wild cards from playing in competitions like this one?" She pulled her hand away.

Bambi positively preened. "Yes, I am. And I'm proud of it. The members of your band have an unfair advantage. Who knows what special abilities your freaks have? It isn't fair to the normal children who've worked hard to be here."

"The Fifth Circuit Court said it was," said Michelle.

Bambi waved her hand as if shooing away a fly. "We're taking that case to the Supreme Court. Thank Jesus we have conservative justices who will make things right." She smiled in a way that sent chills down Michelle's back. How could sweet Kimmie be related to this nightmare?

"Kimmie, come." Bambi turned on her stiletto heels and marched toward the Plano Originals without looking back. Kimmie turned toward the Mob and mouthed, "Sorry." Then she followed her mother.

"This is not off to a great start," Michelle said to Wally. "And speaking of trouble, look. Jade Blossom is here."

Rusty turned to look. Michelle suspected that his own memories of Haley Mok were no fonder than hers. "Gosh," he said, and then, "Maybe she's changed."

Michelle gave a sigh. "I wouldn't count on it."

♠   ♥   ♦   ♣

Jade Blossom's Brew

by William F. Wu

WHEN JADE BLOSSOM HEARD Dr. Amelia Smith announce her name, she tossed back her long, glistening black hair, put on her pouty catwalk smile, and sashayed into the Gunter Terrace Room.

Applause, cheers, and a few gasps welcomed her as she walked forward in her aqua, canary-yellow, and teal gown by Aquilano Rimondi. Her tiny silver Coach handbag, on a slender strap hanging from her shoulder, swung at the side of her slender frame. The four-slit skirt of Italian silk fluttered around her legs with her stride in silver Jimmy Choo sandals with five-inch heels. She had no interest in high school kids, but here she was.

"Hi, everybody," Jade Blossom called out, raising her right hand to give a pageant-style wave as the applause and cheers continued. At six feet tall plus the silver sandals, she was able to glance throughout the room. It was jammed with students, staff members, and chaperones, but she spotted a familiar face near a shiny, black grand piano near the center and worked her way toward it.

Ethan Bach, a slender, twenty-something guy in a black silk shirt, gave her a cheerful nod as he waited for her by the piano. He had come to represent Paramount Studios at the competition, which really meant reporting back on how she handled herself. With her personal assistant, Elaine, he constituted the other half of her minor entourage. Elaine was already in the crowd, ready to step up to Jade Blossom's elbow to obey her slightest whim.

Jade Blossom's duty at the event was to promote her upcoming film by making some introductory remarks and meeting a high school boy who would be her date for the evening. He would receive this honor by virtue of having written an award-winning essay that had been chosen by the staff members.

The kids parted before her like fish avoiding a shark until she arrived at the piano.

"Look at her," one girl shrieked with excitement. The giggles of high school girls and the cheers of boys followed.

"Are we here to have some fun?" Jade Blossom called out, holding her slender arms up in a big V shape. She forced a cheerful laugh. With her back to the piano, she turned and looked around at everyone.

"You have an interesting idea of fun." Michelle, the Amazing Bubbles, stood nearby in the crowd, distinctive given that she was as tall as Jade Blossom and had long, platinum hair. "Perhaps you're confused about the definition. Fun actually involves some level of enjoyment. And this, not so much." Bubbles' green eyes were locked on Jade Blossom's gaze as if in judgment.

Jade Blossom gave her a playfully fake grin and spoke with equally fake sweetness. "Michelle, how absolutely delightful to see you again."

Bubbles gave her a cool smile. "Really, that's what you're going with? Fake politeness? That is so sad. I mean, I feel so sad-like for you. In the world of sad, this is the saddest. You poor wee thing."

Jade Blossom let her grin turn to a scowl. She had first met Bubbles on the TV show *American Hero* a decade or so earlier. Jade Blossom had been on the Clubs team and Bubbles on the Diamonds. From almost the first moment, Jade Blossom had disliked her and felt her disapproval in return. Even so, Jade Blossom had worked with the ensemble well enough to reach the final six contestants. Since that time, she had become embittered about her career after a decade of work for Hollywood bottom-feeders. Now she had a reason to care about her public persona again—or at least pretend.

"Jade Blossom!" Dr. Smith called out. "Maybe you would like to tell everyone a little more about your career."

"Of course." Reluctantly breaking eye contact with Bubbles, Jade Blossom again forced a big smile for the crowd and raised her voice. "I've been a supermodel in international fashion all my adult life and I'm about to start filming my biggest movie role yet!" She expected applause.

Instead, the teens just stared at her.

Jade Blossom glanced at Bubbles and found a slight smile of amusement on her face.

"Bigger than your role in *Truck Stop Vampires 3?*" one boy demanded, laughing.

She turned her fake smile in his direction. "I'm not ashamed of any work I've done. I think that's an important lesson in life."

"She was practically naked in that one," a girl shouted.

"She was totally naked in *Naughty Beach Nymphs 5!*" the first boy answered. "That's my favorite!"

Laughter rippled through the crowd.

"Apparently you saw it," Jade Blossom called out. "Does your mommy know?"

The kids laughed again.

"I'm not here to slut-shame you," Bubbles said. "Your body, your choice." She kept the exaggerated sweetness in her tone. "But you are a *delight*. I'm certain the kids will be learning all sorts of new and different things from you today."

Jade Blossom turned away from her, addressing another part of the crowd. "Becoming a fashion model requires dedication. So does acting. And both require a thick skin."

"Is that why you show so much of it?" a girl behind her shouted, and widespread laughter followed.

Anger burned through Jade Blossom's blood but she pushed past it. "A lot of you will need the same traits in your lives after high school."

When she waited for a response, she received only a long silence, with an undertone of whispers and mutters.

"I got one!" A boy off to one side held up his phone. "A nude shot of her! I'll text it to my whole list!"

The staff members and parents looked around in alarm and ultimately turned their attention to Dr. Smith.

"Good grief," said Bubbles. "Please just . . . just don't."

Cheers and laughs followed, with many of the kids watching Jade Blossom for a response. The rest were checking their phones to see if the picture had reached them.

"I've been quite successful," Jade Blossom declared, hoping to distract them. "Find a vision for your life, a willingness to work at it—in your own ways. You could follow my example."

"Eeeyew, slut," a girl yelled behind her.

Jade Blossom whirled, searching for her in the crowd.

More and more of the kids were focused on their phones, laughing and joking with one another.

Bubbles came closer and spoke quietly. "You're like a tornado in search of a trailer park. You're self-destructive, you always have been. Please do everyone a favor and stop talking."

Jade Blossom looked past her, calling out to the crowd, "You want to compare your lives to mine? My new movie is a remake of *Lord Jim* starring Leonardo DiCaprio!"

For the first time, some of the kids looked interested. Others busied themselves at the punch bowl.

"Are there women in *Lord Jim*?" Dr. Smith muttered. "That doesn't sound right."

"There's one in it now," said Ethan. "Look, Jade Blossom, this isn't going so well."

Instead of acknowledging him, Jade Blossom held out her arms and shouted to the crowd, "We're here for jazz! Jazz is about rebellion! Have any of you ever rebelled?"

Most of the kids were glancing from their phones to Jade Blossom and back, talking and laughing louder than ever.

"Look at your damn pictures later!" Jade Blossom yelled. "I'm here in the flesh! I came to this tank town from L.A. to see if any of you losers might have a future."

"I don't think that's the right tone, Ms. Blossom," Dr. Smith said quietly.

"Blossom's not a surname!"

"I suggest we move to the next stage of the program," said Dr. Smith. "That would be meeting your date."

"I'm not finished," Jade Blossom said in a harsh whisper.

Bubbles stepped up in front of her. "Take Dr. Smith's suggestion. And for the love of all that's holy, try not to embarrass the poor kid. It's bad enough he has a 'date' with you. And who thought this was a good idea? Seriously, *such* a bad idea."

"Just because you can't wear this ensemble?" Jade Blossom sneered.

"Girl fight!" One of the boys in the crowd laughed. "Get her, why don't ya?"

Other kids laughed.

"You got screwed by everybody who required a front zipper on *American Hero,* didn't you?" Bubbles said quietly. "Drummer Boy, Candle, Spasm, Stuntman, Wild Fox, Hardhat, Berman . . . Did you nail Joe Twitch too? King Cobalt? *Toad Man?* Was there anyone who didn't sample your charms? The rumors were everywhere."

"And all the rumors are true! I had any man I wanted. But you're not my type." Jade Blossom had no problem with anyone else's sexual preference, but she loved throwing another dig at Bubbles.

"Color me crushed." Bubbles looked disgusted rather than insulted. "Honey, you are *so* not my type. I have some standards. Do what you want with your body—"

"I will!"

"—but don't pretend you were using any other skill set to get ahead."

Jade Blossom glared back at her. "My studio sent me here to—"

"Publicize a film." Ethan stepped up. "And we have already provided substantial publicity for this wonderful event." He lowered his voice. "Uh, Jade Blossom, I'd like a private word with you. Regarding your studio contract."

"Jade Blossom?" Elaine, her personal assistant, slipped between some kids and spoke up meekly. "Can I help in some way?" A failed model, Elaine had chosen to stay in the business by working for Jade Blossom. Still fashion conscious, she wore a navy-blue Prada suit and white blouse with a very short skirt and black pumps. Her eyes flicked back and forth between Jade Blossom and Bubbles.

"Jade Blossom!" Ethan said. "Come with me right now!" He took hold of her upper arm.

She gave a quick, practiced elbow jab into his solar plexus. "Shut up, little boy."

Wide-eyed and doubled over in pain, Ethan released her arm. Elaine gasped and pulled Ethan away. "Oh, my, I'm so clumsy," said Jade Blossom, without taking her eyes off Bubbles.

"Jade Blossom, gosh, so nice to see you again. Easy, all right?" Rustbelt came forward, speaking in his distinctive Iron Range accent as his shovel-scoop jaw moved up and down. He angled his body toward Bubbles. "We can go forward with the program, don't you think?"

Jade Blossom glared at his back. During *American Hero,* her teammate Stuntman had said Rustbelt called him a racial insult. She had not been present at the time, but she had always believed Stuntman. She and Rustbelt had a limited, awkwardly polite relationship during the show and she had not seen him again until now.

Rubberband walked in his loose stride from the table full of soft drinks to stand in front of Jade Blossom. He wore a green-and-white-checked sweater and had his hands in his pockets. "Nice to meet you, Jade Blossom. I'm Robin Ruttiger. I was on the second season of *American Hero.*" He offered his hand.

"I've heard of you." Jade Blossom ignored his hand.

"Cripes," Rustbelt said to Bubbles. "Come with?"

"For the sake of the event," said Bubbles.

"I enjoyed watching you the first season of *American Hero,*" Rubberband added to Jade Blossom.

"When the show was good," Jade Blossom said, though she kept her eyes on Bubbles' long, platinum hair as her nemesis turned and walked away through the crowd with Rustbelt. Jade Blossom knew Rubberband was trying to break the tension and she resented it. "You weren't good enough to make it the first year?"

"I'm sure you were better for the show than I was," Rubberband said with a little grin.

Jade Blossom watched Bubbles and Rustbelt exit the far end of the Gunter Terrace Room, passing long tables with cheese, salami, baby carrots, and a bowl of red punch that she suspected was spiked by now. By walking away, Bubbles was sending a message: Jade Blossom had been put in her place and they both knew it.

"Come back here, bitch!" Jade Blossom shouted, but she was just putting up a front. The kids laughed again.

"You do so much," Dr. Smith broke in, projecting her voice so the kids could hear. "I'm so impressed with your success. I'm a huge fan of yours. I can't wait to try that new skin cream you've endorsed."

Annoyed by the interruption, Jade Blossom looked down at the older woman's face. "Honey, you can't afford to wait!"

The crowd roared with laughter.

Dr. Smith's face tightened with anger. "We asked you here to be an inspiration—"

"Where's my date?" Jade Blossom demanded, putting her palm up in front of Dr. Smith's face as she looked over the crowd. "Let's get on with this charade."

"Yes, her date," Elaine called from the crowd. "Good idea!"

"Cesar Chao," said Dr. Smith, studying the crowd.

Jade Blossom could feel the air moving from vents in the ballroom. Before she took advantage of it, she glanced through the crowd, searching for some hint of Cesar Chao. A joker girl stood out, with a human body the color of obsidian and four vestigial insect arms in addition to two human arms, plus iridescent wings. She had copper-colored dreads and antennae growing from her forehead. Wincing, Jade Blossom kept looking. She spotted someone with wheels instead of legs. Another girl stood out, a slender, very pretty six-footer with dark hair and noticeably large hands. Another guy was covered in peach fuzz and had bubbles rising from the top of his head. Off to one side, a solemn girl in a green T-shirt with a faded logo and worn black jeans watched Jade Blossom without speaking or holding a cell phone.

This was not getting her anywhere. "Chao? Are you hiding, damn it?"

As the crowd buzzed with low-level chatter, she lightened her density to that of the finest French silk. Then she jumped into a current of air from the vents and, moving her arms and expertly using the three-quarter sleeves of her gown, she drifted upward. With just the right shifting of her body, practiced throughout the years since her card had turned, she could stay aloft quite a while at this density as long as she found air currents. Now she floated over the crowd on the slight artificial breeze, with the long, four-slit skirt of her gown fluttering about her long legs.

All the kids and the adult staff and chaperones in the room were watching her, many with mouths open. She knew she was giving the boys a thrill; any teen boys who made the effort could see she was braless and wearing only a thong for panties—and what teen boys wouldn't make the effort?

"Cesar Chao!" Jade Blossom called out again. "Where are you? Ya too chickenshit to show yourself?"

Finally a couple of boys, grinning like idiots, pointed to one guy in the middle of the crowd. Somebody shoved him forward and he stumbled into an open space.

She drifted over to him and carefully increased her density to land lightly, as the others in the crowd backed off. "So you're my date for the evening?"

He grinned, embarrassed, and looked down. "Uh, yeah."

Jade Blossom put her hands on her bony hips and assessed his appearance. He was about five feet nine inches tall, she gauged, making him eight inches shorter than her in the Jimmy Choo sandals. Free of typical teen skin problems, Cesar had black hair in an average haircut. He wore a blue golf shirt with khaki slacks and was a little soft—definitely no athlete. "I guess you'll do," she said.

Cesar shrugged and gave an awkward smile.

Hoots of laughter and shouts of encouragement rose up from adolescent male voices. The girls were giggling again.

"Cesar, let's go get acquainted somewhere," said Jade Blossom.

"Uh, sure." Cesar grinned as someone jostled him forward, pushing from behind.

"Come on, laughing boy." Jade Blossom raised her density to aluminum in case anyone caused trouble and clutched Cesar's arm. "Walk me out of here."

"Your hand's like a rock."

"Aluminum, damn it. In fact, because we're touching, you're about to increase to the same density." She glared at the kids, teachers, and staff in front of them until they parted to make way, again like fish aware of a shark.

"I am? What'll happen to me?"

She ignored him. Dr. Smith stepped up in front of her. Two uniformed security guards, both young, beefy men, came with her. "Jade Blossom," Dr. Smith said, "I'd like to have a word."

Jade Blossom stepped up close, in Dr. Smith's personal space, and looked down at her. "I'm going to spend time with my date, just as we all agreed."

"Your behavior has raised some issues . . ."

Jade Blossom planted her aluminum-hard hand on Dr. Smith's forehead and shoved, sending her stumbling backward.

The two security guards moved to block her way. One, with a brass nameplate reading *J. CARNAHAN,* reached out for her arm.

Jade Blossom knew she was stepping off a metaphorical cliff, but she had never hesitated to do so before. She leaned forward as though she was going to say something privately. Then, just an inch away, she head-butted him in the face, not too hard, and he stepped back, his hand to his nose.

"Oh, my, excuse me." Jade Blossom gave him her big, fake smile. "I'm just so clumsy, silly me."

Blood oozed between Carnahan's fingers. His face contorted with anger, he opened his mouth to speak.

She leaned close and whispered, "You want to show off your bloody nose in front of all these kids? Just shut up and let it go."

He glared at her, uncertain.

"All right, lady, let's go." The other security guard, whose nameplate said *H. BERBELIA,* reached for her arm.

Before Jade Blossom could respond, Cesar pushed the much larger Berbelia. He barely had an effect, but in return, Berbelia shoved Cesar back two steps. "Out, kid."

Jade Blossom stabbed her aluminum-hard thumb into Berbelia's solar plexus and spoke in a harsh whisper. "You're pushing around a high school boy? Are you going to shove me? The featured guest at this event?"

"Jade Blossom!" Dr. Smith called out. "I'm asking you to leave the premises for good. Cesar, come with me!"

Jade Blossom pushed past Dr. Smith and Cesar hurried to keep up with her.

"Jade Blossom!" Dr. Smith shouted. "This is unacceptable!"

With her signature catwalk pout, Jade Blossom led Cesar out. "Let's find a bar." She reduced her density to normal.

"I'm too young to drink."

"Then a restaurant where I can get a drink." She slowed enough for him to come up alongside her and then took his arm. "Dude, lead the way."

"Uh, yeah."

Protesters out on the sidewalk shouted as they waved their signs: *"Jokers no joke! Jokers no joke!"*

Members of the news media were asking them questions, snapping photos, and taking video. "There's Jade Blossom again!" One guy swung his video camera toward her. A man wearing a sidearm eyed Jade Blossom closely and shouted, "Aces ain't no joke, either!"

She had passed them on her way inside but had taken no notice. "Cesar, who the hell are they?"

"They're from Purity Baptist Church," said Cesar. "I gotta admit, jokers kinda give me the creeps."

"Keep walking, damn it." Jade Blossom didn't like jokers either. They reminded her of what she might have become. She had majored in microbiology at UCLA to learn about the wild card virus, and she understood how arbitrary its effects could be. "I heard something about them on my way in."

"Aces no joke!" the protesters shouted. *"Aces no joke!"*

Jade Blossom spotted Elaine, visibly anguished, waiting off to one side with Ethan. He had engaged a chauffeured limousine for her use during this appearance and now watched her warily. She decided they looked constipated.

"Elaine! Get in the limo and follow us!" Elaine, whose rust-colored hair was tossing in the breeze, waved acknowledgment.

Jade Blossom felt that breeze fluttering the long skirt around her legs. "I'm going to keep hold of your arm, but if you feel me slipping, grab on tight." She reduced her density to the lightest feathery seed bloom.

"What?" Cesar stared up at her.

Because Cesar was in direct contact with her, his density was also reducing. Jade Blossom swept up her free arm and, as she began to lift from the ground, she gave her legs a little kick. Cesar came up with her.

"Cool," Cesar muttered, looking down.

"Just don't lose contact with me or you'll fall," said Jade Blossom, as they gradually gained altitude.

"You can swoop down and catch me."

"I can't fly, you idiot! We're drifting on the breeze, updrafts, whatever air movement I can find."

"Oh."

"So if we let go, you'll switch back to your normal self and go splat on the pavement."

Traffic raced along the street beneath them and Jade Blossom knew the pressure wave in front of moving vehicles pushed air upward as well as sideways. She caught more of the air and took Cesar forward about twenty feet above the ground. Below them, pedestrians were staring. "Pick a place, kid," Jade Blossom said.

"I'm from Seattle!"

"Look anyway!"

◆

Eventually they spied an upscale tavern and Jade Blossom brought them down gently on the sidewalk, increasing her density, and his, back to normal. She let her knees bend slightly and found her footing even on her Jimmy Choo sandals.

Cesar stumbled backward, lost his hold on her, and landed on his butt. "Shit."

Ignoring him, Jade Blossom strode inside, her silken gown swaying around her long legs. The bar was airy, with a vaulted ceiling and exposed rafters of unvarnished wood. Brick walls, painted a sand color, stood at each end, and the wooden tables and chairs matched the walls. Three-foot potted plants gave the place some greenery. Easy-listening instrumental music played faintly from overhead speakers. In the center, an internal pavilion was surrounded by a three-foot wooden railing.

As Cesar hurried after her, she asked to be seated in the pavilion. It contained a table for six on a raised platform that probably doubled for musical performers. The aroma of sizzling burgers drifted from the kitchen.

Elaine came clattering inside from the limo with Ethan and up onto the platform. She turned two of the chairs to face outward in front of the steps that led to a break in the wall.

Without acknowledging her, Jade Blossom sat down in one chair, crossing her legs so that the colorful split satin gown fell away nearly up to her hips. She patted the other chair without looking and Cesar got the message to join her.

"Elaine, bring me a strawberry margarita and an iced tea for Cesar."

"Hey, this is a special occasion—" Cesar stopped when Jade Blossom turned her palm out and stuck it in front of his face.

"Got it." Elaine hurried off just as reporters and camera crews from the protest outside the hotel rushed into the bar. They set up just in front of Jade Blossom, as she had expected, below the dais.

Ethan stepped in front of Jade Blossom, this time at a safe distance. "I'm horrified by your behavior. The studio will hear about this. I think your role in the film may be at risk. You can't stop me from speaking up."

"You're blocking the cameras, asshole." She waved for him to move away.

Ethan strode away, pulling out his phone.

"Aren't you worried about what he said?" Cesar asked in awe.

"Worried? Not about that little pussy."

As photographers snapped stills and news crews took video, Jade Blossom turned to Cesar. "God, I hate that easy-listening shit. Well, then. How did I get stuck with you?"

He gave a nervous laugh. "Uh, I wrote this essay."

"On being a Chao? Is that why they picked you? Why didn't I get a Jones or Hernandez? Is that how they matched us up?"

"I wrote about 'What Jazz Means to Me.'"

"It means you get to be my date." She accepted her margarita from a server and sipped it, enjoying the salt, the sweet strawberry, and the cold tequila. "What did your essay say?"

"I said my favorite album is *Bitches Brew* by Miles Davis and explained why."

"*Bitches Brew*. Is that a joke?"

"Hey, it's real. It's considered a landmark."

"Jade Blossom!" One of the reporters, a young Latina, held up a hand. "What do you think of your new friend?"

Jade Blossom turned to Cesar, aware that all the reporters were listening. "You're from Seattle? Whoever heard of Seattle jazz? What instrument do you play?"

"The teacher told me you'd get a full report," said Cesar.

"I didn't waste my time on it."

"I play piano." He looked up as though hoping for approval.

Jade Blossom sipped her margarita, thinking, *He's just the kind of loser I expected.*

Another reporter, a young guy, shouted from behind a camera crew, "Jade Blossom, what do you think of Bambi Coldwater?"

"I'm as human as anybody, only more so," Jade Blossom shot back. "Ask the bitch what she thinks of that."

Cesar gave a goofy laugh.

She sighed. "You have a girlfriend, Cesar?"

Cesar hid behind his iced tea with a couple of big swallows. "Are you married?"

"Me? Ha!"

"I guess you can play the field a lot, huh? Have lots of relationships?"

"I don't do relationships. I do what I want."

"Okay, so, what do you want?"

"Looking for a turn-on, are you? A peek behind the curtain?" She leaned back, extending her long legs in front of her for the benefit of all the cameras. "I wanted Bruce Lee, for one. He was very fit and flexible even at the age of fifty, some years back. I'm taller, so when we stood together, his face was right at boob level." She giggled, remembering. "I wanted Golden Boy and he liked me right back. Same with Arnold Schwarzenegger—I heard he liked to grope, so when I had an early small part in one of his movies, I went to the density of a car tire and turned my butt toward him. Gave him a surprise!"

"You know a lot of celebrities, huh?" Cesar asked.

She sobered slightly. "I admired Bill Cosby, but when we met for drinks one night after *American Hero,* my margarita tasted funny, so I made excuses and got the hell out. The bastard sent word around Hollywood and stalled my career in low-budget shit for years." She savored the bitter memories and used them to stoke her inner fire.

"Old dudes," said Cesar. "Every single one of those guys is old enough to be your dad."

"They aren't the only ones, asshole. I had any guy I wanted."

Some of the reporters and camera crews were turning away. They had all seen this chatter in the tabloids and online long ago. Off to one side, Ethan talked into his phone, then let his shoulders sag as he lowered it. As Jade Blossom expected, she had little to worry about from him. She sipped her margarita and turned to Cesar. "What about that girlfriend? You don't have one, do you? She'd be way jealous right now."

Cesar slammed down his glass, sloshing iced tea onto the table. "I play piano, bitch, and I'm good at it! I'm human, so I'm better than you!"

At the sound of his raised voice, the reporters and camera crews turned back, calling out questions and recording again.

Jade Blossom was startled but she liked his response. "Somebody spike your iced tea? What's in that stuff?"

"I'm damn good on the ivories and I wrote a damn good essay! Girls don't like me, that's all."

Jade Blossom jumped on his weak spot. "Why don't girls like you?"

"I dunno." He drank more iced tea, the fire seemingly gone.

"Hey, Jade Blossom!" The Latina reporter was smirking. "You going to give him tips on getting girls? After all, he's got you for the day!" All the newspeople laughed.

Jade Blossom yanked Cesar's cold glass out of his hand. She poured a little of her margarita into it and slid it back to him. "You're not ugly. You need to work out, tubby."

"I hate my life."

"Think that makes you special?"

"My mom's really strict. But I like band. And I'm kinda shy." He drank some of his spiked iced tea. "I hate my life and I hate you."

Jade Blossom laughed. She understood hate. "Is it because of my ace?"

Cesar leaned forward and threw down a long swig of his drink. "Mom came down with our band, you know, to be a chaperone? Outside the hotel, she stopped to talk to the Purity Baptist Church people. I listened and you know what? They make some sense. Mom says so, too. You're not human. You're different now."

"If you can live in a world with dogs and cats, you can live with people like me."

He pounded his glass down on the table again. "Live with that Marissa Simpson? Are you kidding me?"

"Who's she? Some girl you've got the hots for?"

"She's a goddamn joker in Jokertown Mob!"

Jade Blossom had him hooked like a fish. "Does she play skin flute?"

Cesar stared at her, maybe not certain he had heard correctly. "She plays piano, only her hands are all weird."

"Weird how?"

"Her hands are all rectangular. She's hard and white, like piano keys. Her whole body looks like a robot made out of ivory, hard edges and angles and hinges on her joints."

"An exoskeleton," said Jade Blossom.

"And her face! Like a robot, all white and stiff, too."

Jade Blossom sighed. "If you hate wild cards, why did you write that essay to meet me?"

"That was before. Now I know better!" He chugged the rest of his spiked iced tea, then clanked the glass down, gave her a triumphant grin, and stomped out.

Jade Blossom judged it to be a good exit for a high school kid. The reporters and news crews followed him out. She had a moment alone, if you didn't count Elaine waiting for her off to one side like the toady she was and Ethan staring at the floor with his hands shoved into his pants pockets, willing himself to be anywhere but here.

Jade Blossom liked Cesar. Very few people tried to get the best of her—except that bitch Bubbles. Jade Blossom was not normally reflective, but Cesar's responses reminded her of when she had been a six-foot-tall, skinny fourteen-year-old girl named Haley Mok, who was ridiculed and ostracized by her peers. When her card turned, she learned to hurt people before they hurt her. She had maxed out her density and smashed through doors and walls at school, destroying desks, terrifying her peers and the adults alike. Then she knew she could speak her mind. Those memories still amused her.

She sipped her icy margarita, allowing Cesar plenty of time to go ahead of her. Her studio commitment required that she attend the mixer with him, but she had no idea if he was going back to the hotel. No matter what, she would have to go back and hang around for the evening.

"Elaine!" she called over her shoulder without looking.

"Yes?"

"Take the limo to the hotel." Jade Blossom set down her glass still half-full and sauntered outside into the dusk.

The breeze was still blowing lightly from the direction of the hotel, but she had plenty of practice working her way through the air. She reduced her density to the minimum, jumped lightly, and let the breeze toss her like a silken scarf. Once in the air, she angled herself to pick up a thermal from the restaurant's roof exhaust fan and rode it up high. Then, like a sailboat tacking against the wind, she altered her density in slight changes and turned herself to catch the pressure waves from passing vehicles and light gusts between buildings. Outside air was almost always moving, in more ways than most people ever noticed.

She felt emotionally drained. Cesar's complaints and accusations had taken a toll. The little snot was getting to her somehow and she hated that. Vulnerability was a sign of weakness and weakness was just about the only thing that terrified her.

As she drew near the Gunter, she saw that the protesters were still outside. Some of the news crews who had followed Cesar from the restaurant had returned. She slowly increased her density and landed on the sidewalk near them.

"Hey, look who's back!" One woman pointed with her arm extended like she was making an accusation.

Jade Blossom gave the crowd a quick glance, taking in a pair of twins maybe in their thirties wearing identical clothes and a woman in a muumuu carrying a sign that showed a picture of a deformed joker. Everyone in the group had hostile expressions as they looked back at her.

Always ready for a confrontation, Jade Blossom sashayed forward with her best catwalk stride. "This is a public sidewalk."

"You're even worse than that Bubbles," one of the other women spoke in an imperious tone as she came forward.

Jade Blossom's professional eye for fashion was offended by the woman's cat's-eye sunglasses and electric-blue polyester pantsuit. Her hair was in a kind of oversize pile that Jade Blossom had seen in old movies from the sixties.

"Betty Virginia." Jade Blossom had seen the protest organizer earlier, leading a chant. "You think you know something about the wild card?"

"The Lord's word guides us," Betty Virginia said calmly. "You aces just think you're better than everyone else."

"No, just better than you," Jade Blossom said in an exaggerated, childlike singsong. "Nobody needs an ace for that. Jokers are better than you."

"You're no longer human. Abominations before the Lord." Betty Virginia tilted up her face, challenging her. "If you can't put on a regular dress, at least you could wear proper unmentionables."

"And leave my son alone!" A petite, pretty, forty-something woman of East Asian descent, wearing a modest blue dress, came up next to Betty Virginia. "He doesn't want anything to do with you!"

"This is Lara Chao," said Betty Virginia. "You are certainly a menace to her family." She backed away slightly, letting Lara step up.

Jade Blossom looked down at her from more than a foot in height difference. "Cesar liked me just fine. Too bad, Mommy."

"Leave him alone!" Lara yelled, tossing shoulder-length black hair that was parted just off center. She took a deep breath and spoke with an intense calm. "I was proud when he wrote his essay. Now that I've met Betty Virginia and Bambi, I'm part of the Purity Baptist Church movement."

"Honey, you're part of a bowel movement."

"I don't see any need for that kind of language," said Betty Virginia.

"Listen, all right?" Lara insisted. "My Cesar is a prodigy. He played classical piano in local concerts by the time he was twelve. And he branched into jazz as a teenager. He has four full-ride music scholarships to choose from. And Betty Virginia told me how you wild carders take opportunities in life away from gifted human children like my son."

Jade Blossom heard her own mother's demanding standards in Lara's words. She felt sorry for Cesar. His tiger mother was smothering him. *No wonder the kid doesn't have a girlfriend.*

"I tried to put a stop to your so-called date, I'll have you know," said Lara. "I told somebody in charge here that I didn't want my son spending one minute with you. They put me on the phone with your studio and some jackass threatened to sue me for the cost of your precious promotion, so I dropped it. If Cesar stays away from you on his own, well, that's different."

"He's a teenaged boy." Jade Blossom took a sexy pose, with a hand on her hip and one leg angled out of a slit in her gown. "Of course he's hot for me. His mama can't do a damn thing about it."

"My son is naturally gifted!"

Jade Blossom understood: Lara wasn't any kind of true believer. She saw the protesters' position in pragmatic terms. Lara just wanted to get an edge for her son. Jade Blossom heard the echo of her mother's voice again.

The guy wearing a sidearm shouldered his way through the crowd with a confident grin, leering at Jade Blossom. He had a comb-over and wore a denim cowboy shirt rolled up at the sleeves. His gaze dropped to her shoes and came slowly up her legs and trim torso to rest on her face.

She began increasing her density in case she needed to defend herself. "Lara, if Cesar's truly gifted, he'll be fine."

"This ace has quite a mouth on her, doesn't she?" The guy stopped in front of Jade Blossom, his hands on his hips.

"I think she was just leaving, Earl," said Betty Virginia, giving Jade Blossom a hard look. She waved her hand in a shooing motion.

Jade Blossom had reached aluminum density. With her hard right hand, she gave Earl a pseudoaffectionate chuck under the chin that knocked his head back. "You're a cute little thing, Earl." With that, she sashayed away, knowing he appreciated the view no matter what his church taught.

"Inhuman bitch," Earl called after her.

Inside the ballroom, many kids were talking, some dancing to canned music, others mingling and joking around. Many were clustered around the table with soft drinks and the table with munchies. Jade Blossom spotted Cesar in the crowd, now wearing a black suit that was too small and tight, a white shirt, and a plain blue necktie that made him more nerdy than before.

He was running his hand over the polished black surface of the grand piano. Most of his peers were casually dressed in teen styles she found silly but genuine. She decided Lara must have bought Cesar his ill-fitting suit.

This time, the kids accepted her presence. Many of them watched her but no one interfered as she worked her way toward Cesar. She came up behind him as he looked at his slightly elongated reflection in the top of the piano.

"Waiting for your date?" Jade Blossom asked, projecting her voice over the buzz of the crowd.

Startled, Cesar whirled around. "Uh, hi."

"Why aren't you hitting on girls?"

"I suppose they're avoiding me because of you."

"Okay, I'm your date. But what's so fascinating about your own face?"

"I want a human girlfriend! Someday, I mean."

"Someday!" Jade Blossom laughed. "Someday never comes, Cesar."

She looked out over the crowd. Rustbelt was across the room, his big jaw moving up and down as he talked to Rubberband in his signature slouch. Near one wall, she spotted a girl who fit the description of the joker piano player Cesar had mentioned. Her body looked like it was formed of large and small piano keys, hard and white in modular rectangles connected by hinges large and small. She had an exoskeleton, Jade Blossom had said to Cesar. In her case, this meant a chiseled white face with dark eyes, softened only by lush chestnut hair that reached her ivory-white shoulders. A green dress of modest length hung on her body, revealing more hard angles under the fabric.

As Cesar eyed Jade Blossom, she nodded toward the keys of the grand piano. "Show me your stuff. You're my date, damn it. Try to make a good impression on me."

"Why would I care what a diseased mutant thinks?"

"You have any other girls begging to take my place?"

He frowned but settled himself on the bench and started playing, even with the canned music coming through speakers and the growing buzz of conversation.

She leaned down close. "Keep at it, dude, and I'll be right back." She ran her manicured nails along the back of his scalp for encouragement, but he flinched at the contact.

When Jade Blossom reached Marissa she didn't bother with niceties. "Don't you want to play?"

"I do play," said Marissa, as her mouth made rigid vertical movements. "Pleased to meet you, Jade Blossom."

"I know you are."

Jade Blossom nodded toward Cesar. "Is that guy any good?"

Marissa shrugged, her modular shoulders going up, slightly sideways, then moving in reverse. "I guess we're all pretty good."

"Show us what you got," said Jade Blossom.

"What? You mean, now?"

"Come on, joker girl. Have you got anything or not?"

"Where the hell do you get off talking that way?" Marissa demanded. "Are you always a super-bitch?"

"I'm a sweetheart." Jade Blossom batted her eyes.

Instead of responding, Marissa watched Cesar at the piano for a moment. Then she walked toward him, maneuvering awkwardly through the crowd.

Jade Blossom followed.

Cesar was toying with the keys, gazing out at the crowd in front of him.

"Can you play or not?" Jade Blossom demanded, as she came up behind him. She began raising her density, sure that Cesar might try to walk away.

"What?" When Cesar saw Marissa timidly sit down on one end of the bench, he rose to his feet. "Hey! I'm not playing with a joker!"

Jade Blossom's density had reached granite level. She placed her heavy hands gently on his shoulders and bent her knees slightly. Her weight slammed Cesar back down on the bench. "You're my date, remember? Pretend you're trying to get in my pants. Well, my thong."

Cesar glanced once more at Marissa, who pointedly looked down at her fingers on the keys in front of her. In a sitting position, her green dress clung even more to the sharp edges and angles of her body.

Cesar suddenly started a fast, complex piece.

Jade Blossom knew very little about classical music, but this had nothing to do with jazz. She believed it was a composition by Johann Sebastian Bach, but in any case, Cesar was showing off. Jade Blossom had challenged him and he was responding.

The kids nearby turned to watch and listen.

Marissa began playing. At first she watched Cesar's hands, but quickly found what she wanted. Her hard, white, rectangular fingers matched the white piano keys.

Jade Blossom listened and realized that Marissa was not just keeping up, but harmonizing.

Cesar made an abrupt change. Suddenly he was playing a mid-tempo atonal piece, leaving Marissa behind.

Jade Blossom finally got it—Cesar had no interest in impressing her. He was trying to embarrass Marissa. The little snot was angry about Marissa joining him, so he wanted her to look bad in front of all their fellow musicians. In return, Marissa was showing her stuff. Jade Blossom knew next to nothing about atonal music but she could see that their fast hand motions were precise.

Against the far wall, the slender, very pretty six-footer was talking to the guy covered in peach fuzz. Others in the crowd drifted toward the piano, interested in the impromptu performance. A moment later, the canned music stopped.

Marissa made the next move. She began a tune that Jade Blossom actually knew; her mother had listened to a lot of British-invasion-era rock music and this was "The House of the Rising Sun," bluesy and wailing.

Cesar hesitated, then followed her lead to the song.

Jade Blossom heard him improvising and saw that Marissa responded in kind.

The other kids were swaying, dancing, talking, and laughing. Many, though not all, were obviously tipsy, on drinks they must have smuggled into the event.

Jade Blossom swept her skirt out of her way and planted one Jimmy Choo on the piano bench. Then she stepped up onto the deeply polished top of the piano. She danced alone, moving to the jazzy version of the song she had pretty much gotten sick of hearing when she was growing up.

"Cool, bitch!" One of the boys held up a cell phone and starting taking video.

"Proud to be both," Jade Blossom shot back, and gave him a little hip move.

Cesar settled into the line of music that was traditionally instrumental, down low, working the bass with his left hand and an A-minor chord arpeggio with his right. Marissa was playing the melody that represented the lyrics as the song was usually sung, slowly making it her own.

Jade Blossom, still dancing and laughing as the kids crammed closer with their cell phones raised, realized that Cesar and Marissa seemed to have reached a musical accommodation.

Because Jade Blossom wanted to keep the moment between them going, she swayed and waved, moving around a little on the grand piano. She spotted the solemn girl she had noticed earlier. The girl stood close to the piano, watching Jade Blossom without a cell phone, still in her green T-shirt with a faded logo and worn black jeans.

Jade Blossom turned away from her, putting on her catwalk pout as she turned one way and then another. Cesar worked the piano keys cleanly as Marissa strained even higher for the melody. While Jade Blossom danced and posed for the cameras in the crowd, some of the kids, mostly boys, hooted and called out to her, sometimes with insults or taunts. Most were drowned out between the music and crowd noise.

From her high vantage point, she saw that more of the chaperones, staff, and parents were watching her from various spots along the walls. A strikingly pretty blonde with light eyes pushed past people with a hard expression on her face. A slender guy of East Asian descent was talking to a dude with short blond hair and a husky build, who was chewing gum as he gave off a kind of cocky air.

"Hey, Jade Blossom!" One of the boys, a tall, angular guy, waved his cell phone at her. "Did Cesar screw ya yet?"

The kids who heard him laughed, waiting for her response.

"A lady doesn't kiss and tell!" She swiveled her hips, making her dress sway.

"What's a slut say?" A girl in the crowd giggled.

"She doesn't blow and tell, either," Jade Blossom shot back, laughing.

Across the room, the adults turned to one another, maybe not sure if they had heard her right.

Cesar kept the arpeggio going and lowered the bass line even more, while Marissa blew on the melody, wailing high, sad, and lonely.

Some of the boys, fortified by whatever they'd been drinking and maybe smoking, started climbing up on the piano at Jade Blossom's feet.

The solemn girl in the faded T-shirt still stood nearby, not speaking.

Jade Blossom laughed at the boys and, remembering they were still kids, she approached them one at a time as she increased her density. She gently placed one Jimmy Choo sole against a shoulder and straightened her leg, pushing each guy back down again. Some laughed as they fell, staggering with an alcohol buzz. While some guys had friends who caught them, others hit the floor on their butts, still grinning.

The adults in the back of the room started coming forward through the crowd, led by Rustbelt. He made slow, careful movements, apparently to avoid colliding with anyone. One woman hurried out, probably looking for help. Cesar and Marissa kept playing, oblivious to the other kids.

Jade Blossom, still dancing, increased her density to aluminum as she waited to see what would happen next. She hoped Cesar and Marissa would keep playing. From what she could hear, she believed they communicated through their piano work.

"Geez, fellas." Rustbelt finally worked his way through the crowd and stopped near the piano.

Jade Blossom pretended she hadn't noticed him.

Rustbelt raised his voice, speaking in his distinctive accent. "Hey, Jade Blossom—"

At the sound of her name, she swung her hips, opening the slits in her dress and flashing a long leg up to her thigh.

"Jeepers." Rustbelt turned away for a moment, then looked up at her again. "That sure is some fancy dancing, you betcha. It's good, real good. But, uh, I'm wondering maybe this ain't such a good idea."

"I'm here to make a splash for the event, right?" Jade Blossom continued gyrating, swirling the split panels of her gown up high around her legs. "They wanted media coverage, they got it!"

Some of the tipsy boys were climbing up on the piano again.

"C'mon, fellas, knock it off, how about?" Rustbelt said to the boys.

A few backed away, but several ignored him.

Jade Blossom laughed and dropped into a crouch. She kissed one guy on the forehead and gave him a shove that threw him back. Raising her density again, she put a hand on another guy's chest and leaned forward, pushing him off the piano.

The two security guards, Carnahan and Berbelia, pushed their way through the crowd, grim and determined.

"Cripes," said Rustbelt, his expression pained. "Jade Blossom?"

On the piano at her feet, Cesar pounded away at the bass and maintained the arpeggio. Marissa took the melody into a high-pitched wail that took Jade Blossom by surprise.

"Get down here, bitch!" Carnahan gave her a hard grin.

"Whoa, now," said Rustbelt. "That ain't right."

Carnahan gave him a wary glance.

"Wanna dance, little boy?" Jade Blossom laughed and turned slightly, angling one hip toward Carnahan. She increased her density again, going past aluminum toward lead.

The two security guards reached up, Carnahan grabbing her ankle and Berbelia reaching for her arm.

Jade Blossom lifted the ankle with a hand wrapped around it and slammed her foot down. The polished surface of the piano cracked. Carnahan let go, wincing in pain, and walked backward.

"C'mon, knock it off, fellas," said Rustbelt, moving between Carnahan and the piano.

When Berbelia grabbed Jade Blossom's arm, she folded at the knees and slammed his hand against the wood, breaking the fine bones.

Berbelia gave a throaty growl of pain and released her, staggering back.

Rustbelt eased to one side, now blocking Berbelia from the piano.

"Jade Blossom?" Cesar shouted, though he kept playing.

Carnahan ducked around Rustbelt and launched himself at Jade Blossom's legs like he was making a football tackle.

Jade Blossom sprang up to avoid this grasp, though not very high given her great weight now. When she came down, her Jimmy Choos smashed through the top of the piano and through the wires.

Carnahan's tackle missed her and the music came to a stop. He bounced off the edge of the piano and fell to the floor, tangled in wires and big chunks of wood.

The crowd of kids burst out laughing.

Annoyed, Jade Blossom kicked out, breaking more wires and wood. Gradually she crashed her way down to the floor, knocking big splinters of wood aside with her hands and stamping a bigger opening even though she was trapped in the middle of the piano's wreckage. Then she pounded on the piano with her fists, splintering more wood so she could eventually break out.

"Awww, geez," said Rustbelt. "Didja have to go and wreck the piano? I'll bet them things are real expensive."

"Aw, Rusty, don't you know I always make a mess?" Jade Blossom grinned at him as she stood up straight, though she was still caught inside the remains of the big piano. She saw Cesar backing away, holding Marissa by her upper arm.

"Get away from my son!" Lara pushed through the kids, screaming. "What's wrong with you?"

"The piano was out of tune," said Jade Blossom, shaking her hair loose. Still using her great density, she smashed her way out of the piano, throwing chunks of wood ahead of her, forcing Lara back.

"Somebody arrest her!" Lara yelled.

"Okeydokey, I think we're done here," said Rustbelt. He turned to Carnahan and Berbelia. "Find Michelle, will you?"

The security guards turned and pushed their way through the crowd.

Ignoring Rustbelt and Lara, Jade Blossom kicked the remains of the piano out of the way and looked around. She found Cesar and Marissa standing together, staring wide-eyed at her and the ruined grand piano.

"You didn't have to do that," Cesar muttered, looking at the huge mess.

"Here!" Jade Blossom snatched up some loose keys and tossed them toward him as she reduced her density to normal. "Play all you want." She stepped between the two of them, blocking out Marissa with her body, and grabbed his arm. "Come on."

"What?"

Jade Blossom pulled him close and threw both of her arms around him. Before he could react, she put her lips against his and kissed him. He wriggled with surprise but she held on.

Around them, the kids cheered, hooted, and whistled. Boys shouted obscene suggestions. "Get away from him!" Lara yelled.

Still in the clinch, Jade Blossom spoke in a whisper: "Listen, turd brain, I'm making you the hottest hunk around. If you won't try to use your dick, I might as well rip it off your body myself. Just tell everybody you're leaving me, if your IQ is any higher than room temperature!" She increased her density, certain she would need it.

"Hey! I've got an IQ of a hundred and forty!"

Jade Blossom put her palms on his shoulders and shoved, using her greater weight to send him staggering backward to Marissa.

The crowd of kids, some of them more tipsy than ever, cheered.

"All right, then!" Jade Blossom shouted, with a melodramatic expression of horror. "Take your joker girl, you like her so much!"

Marissa's rigid mouth dropped open in surprise. Her shocked eyes stared out of her otherwise rigid, blocky white features.

The kids quieted, curious to see what would happen next.

Lara stared with them. When Rustbelt started toward Cesar, Lara gestured for him to stay back and he stopped.

Across the room, the security guards returned with the Amazing Bubbles, her platinum hair distinctive in the press of the crowd.

Jade Blossom knew she did not have much time before Bubbles stepped up to confront her. She watched Cesar's expression change from incomprehension to realization, but had no idea what he would do. Suppressing a laugh, Jade Blossom wailed, "Cesar! At least finish our date! Don't leeeave me!"

The crowd broke into laughter and hoots of derision at Jade Blossom but encouragement for Cesar.

"The bitch is hot for ya, Cesar!" One boy's voice carried over the general din.

Cesar glanced around at the other kids, astonished.

Marissa, looking mortified, took a few steps back.

The two security guards had advanced, but Bubbles was following them slowly, watching Jade Blossom without hurrying. She glanced over to Cesar and Marissa.

Jade Blossom glared at Cesar, thinking, *C'mon, idiot, work with me.* "Finish our date, Cesar!"

"What for?" Cesar asked, with a tentative smile.

"You're not leaving me for her, are you?" Jade Blossom wailed in an embarrassing display of overacting.

This time even Marissa's hard facial features seemed amused.

"You won't leave me for that joker, will you?" Jade Blossom pleaded.

"Now wait right there!" Lara edged around Rustbelt and stomped toward Cesar. "Cesar, you just get away from her!"

"Which her?" Cesar asked, with a hint of humor.

"Not me!" Jade Blossom whined, fighting down a laugh.

The other kids guffawed, enjoying the awkward moment.

Even Bubbles smiled with reluctant amusement.

Lara swiveled to Marissa. "Back off, you mutant!"

Cesar stepped in front of his mother.

Jade Blossom shifted her density to aluminum.

"Uh, Mom? Go upstairs, okay?" Cesar said.

"Are you talking back to me?" Lara shrieked. She eyed Marissa, looking over Cesar's shoulder. "Get away from him!"

"It's about the music," said Cesar.

"Don't you talk to me like that!"

Just as Lara reached for the front of Cesar's shirt, Jade Blossom leaned down, grabbed Lara's petite form below her butt, and hoisted her up on one shoulder. "No!" Jade Blossom shouted, just for the fun of it.

"You put me down!" Lara yelled.

Jade Blossom carried Lara, whose short arms and legs were kicking and punching, with her typical long strides, heading out of the ballroom.

"Don't worry, Mrs. Chao," Marissa called playfully. "I'm a lady and a lady doesn't blow and tell!"

"Psycho mutant bitch!" Lara yelled, still hanging over Jade Blossom's shoulder.

Jade Blossom strode out the front door of the hotel and saw the protesters turning toward her in surprise. Darkness had fallen, but she stopped in the light from the hotel. "Got a present for ya!" She leaned forward, set Lara on her feet, and made a catwalk turn that swirled her gown around her legs. Then she hurried back into the ballroom.

The room had changed in the moments since she had left. The crowd had parted in the middle, where Bubbles stood flanked by the two security guards. Rustbelt stood behind them with other parents and staff members.

"Whoa, now, fellas," said Rusty. He seemed trapped by the close quarters, reluctant to move forward for fear of hurting someone. "Maybe this ain't such a good idea."

Cesar and Marissa, stiff with alarm, remained close to the ruins of the piano. They made a distinctive pair in his too-tight suit and tie and her green dress hanging from her sharp edges and angles.

Jade Blossom looked from Cesar and Marissa to Bubbles. She knew perfectly well that Bubbles' ace was far more powerful than her own and decided to enjoy herself while she could.

In the silence, Rusty clapped one hand to his head, with a loud clang. "Aww, Judas Priest, what now?"

Jade Blossom spotted Ethan standing with Elaine against one wall. "Give the bill to my studio rep." She took a catwalk pose with one hand on her hip. "After all, I was forced to be here!"

"Why are you still here?" Bubbles asked, stepping up face-to-face with Jade Blossom. "Again with the making me sad-like. Except now you've really stepped over the line. You know I am going to have to kick your ass in front of all these people. And that's just embarrassing for both of us. And so much YouTube action is going to ensue. You're really set on full self-destruct mode, aren't you?"

"Maybe I'm just dense." Jade Blossom smiled at her little joke. "You expect me to care what you say? You're denser than I am. Come on, bubble-girl, join me. We'll make it a two-bitch fashion show."

"Seriously, you have a problem, Jade Blossom," Bubbles said. "You can't bear who you are. I pity you, I really do. No snark at all. Well, for now."

That stung. "I don't need your pity, or you, or anyone else!"

"If it weren't for the kids, I'd feel sorry for you."

"I wouldn't want you to strain yourself on my account." Jade Blossom started raising her density. Yet somewhere inside her, fourteen-year-old Haley Mok desperately ached for someone to like her. Jade Blossom forced away the feeling.

"Please don't fight," said Cesar.

"Take your girl out of here," said Jade Blossom. She raised her voice, adding a desperate tone. "You like her better than me, fine! Take her!" She put one hand over her eyes, as though she was on the verge of tears, and winked at Cesar.

Finally catching a clue, the kid with the slowest 140 IQ that Jade Blossom had ever seen took Marissa's arm and they walked away through the crowd of kids.

"Is this really the person you want to be?" Bubbles asked. "For your whole life?"

"I'm just myself!" Jade Blossom heard her voice waver and hated the moment of showing weakness. Like everyone, she knew her looks would go someday. Sometimes she wondered if she should end the hollowness inside her using a hard, brittle density in a high fall. Young Haley Mok would understand. She had thought about the same fate before her card turned.

"The curtain's coming down, drama queen," said Bubbles. "Take your bow and go home. No one will be sorry to see you go."

"Not without a finale." Jade Blossom, at extreme density, bent her knees and launched herself at Bubbles, her arms outstretched.

A dazzling rainbow-glazed silver blast flashed in front of Jade Blossom, as she had expected. The force knocked her backward. She stumbled on her Jimmy Choo stilettos and landed hard on her butt.

A bubble surrounded Jade Blossom and rolled her backward, legs over her head and then around again. She grew dizzy as the bubble continued rotating, bouncing her against its flexible wall repeatedly. As much as she disliked it, she knew Bubbles was not going to hurt her. Bubbles was just throwing her out of the Terrace Room, down the stairs, and out the main doors.

The bubble stopped rolling. Jade Blossom reduced her density, causing the bubble around her to do the same. She kicked out, popping the bubble with little effort, and got to her feet. Bubbles had gone easy on her.

Swaying and staggering a little from dizziness, she found herself out on the sidewalk. She was not far from the protesters, but they kept their distance. Even Lara, Earl, and Betty Virginia said nothing as they watched her. After taking her phone from her purse, she texted Elaine: *Outside main doors. Where the hell are U?*

The main doors opened again. Startled by the sound, Jade Blossom whirled to see if she was facing more trouble. Instead, she found the solemn brunette wearing the green T-shirt with a faded logo and black jeans.

The girl stopped a respectful distance away. "Jade Blossom, may I ask you something about being a model?"

The rented limousine glided to a stop at the curb. Elaine climbed out while Ethan waited in the rear seat.

"What's your name, kid?" Jade Blossom shook out the panels of her gown so they fell properly. The Aquilano Rimondi was destined for the trash heap after the beating it had taken tonight. She reduced her density to normal.

"Natalie. What advice can you give me about becoming a model someday?"

Jade Blossom let out a derisive breath. "Why aren't you asking that bitch Bubbles? She's a model and she's a hell of a lot nicer than I am."

"I don't want nice. I want the truth."

Jade Blossom liked that answer. She appraised the girl's appearance and saw that Natalie was attractive, though with an average build. "You have just barely enough height and the cheekbones. You need to lose fifteen, twenty pounds. I doubt you'll make it because most people don't. Prettier girls than you have failed and uglier ones have succeeded. Am I hurting your feelings?"

Natalie gave a defensive little shrug.

"Get used to it. You'll always be too short or too fat, too ethnic or too white. You'll be too outspoken or too timid. You'll always have some other girl ready to take your job and eventually you'll be too old. So maybe you should just go away and cry."

Natalie raised her chin defiantly. "No way."

"Good answer. How old are you?"

"Seventeen. I'm a senior."

Jade Blossom looked into her eyes but spoke over her shoulder. "Elaine! Give this loser my private cell number. As for you, lard-ass, if you haven't wised up after you graduate from high school, call me."

Natalie's mouth opened in surprise. "Really?"

"Get away from me before I change my mind! Elaine, take the limo to the airport. I'll meet you there." Jade Blossom turned her back to both of them and reduced her density. She walked away from the hotel and the protesters to a spot where she could feel a light breeze. As she reached tissue density, she jumped and found an updraft.

As she rose on the breeze into the shadows of evening, she looked down. The protesters had lost sight of her against the dark sky. Down the length of the hotel building, Cesar and Marissa strolled out of a secondary doorway, talking. Maybe they could have something together that teenage Haley Mok never had.

Forcing a laugh at herself, Jade Blossom drifted away on the wind. Haley Mok's girlish dream of being in a major Hollywood movie was going to come true. Jade Blossom would make it happen, no matter what it cost her.

♠ ♥ ♦ ♣

Bubbles and the
Band Trip

Part 4

"**UHM, SORRY ABOUT THE** fight," Michelle said awkwardly to the room. "Really, it doesn't happen all that often. Let's just get back to getting acquainted."

A lot of dubious expressions were aimed her way.

"No, really. I promise," she said. "No more ace fights tonight."

From the back of the room came a boy's voice. "As long as Jade Blossom doesn't come back, we're good."

"Works for me," Michelle replied. Then she saw Adesina pushing her way through the crowd.

"Hey, honey," Michelle said as some of the partygoers began to leave. They gave her excellent stink-eye as they passed by. The people who stayed behind started talking again, much to her relief. "How're things going?"

"Mom," Adesina said in a low voice. "You're really embarrassing me. You can't just go around bubbling people."

"Well, sweetie," Michelle replied. Having a teenager was turning out to be awful. Michelle was pretty sure *she'd* never been a teenager like this. "That's pretty much what I do. Perhaps you hadn't noticed."

"Do you have to do it *here?*" Segway and Ghost came up beside Adesina. They gave Michelle bright smiles. It made Michelle feel much better.

"Hey," Segway said as he touched Adesina's shoulder. For a moment, Michelle thought Adesina might pull away, but then she visibly relaxed. "Your mom was just trying to do the right thing."

Ghost wrapped her arms around Adesina and gave her a hug.

"C'mon," Ghost said with a giggle. Michelle was glad to see Ghost acting like a normal little girl.

"Your mom is awesome," Ghost said. "She's totes kewl. You're just being weird. What happened is already all over the place. Everyone here was recording it. Accept your fate."

"And what's that?"

"That your mom is filled with fabu and you're a big dork."

"I'm not a dork," Adesina said. She was trying not to smile. "I'm totes a nerd. Get your geek terms right. I have a Venn diagram that can prove it. Here, let me find it." She pulled out her phone. "And I won't even look at YouTube, Mom."

♥

"Those boys in the Plano Originals were so rude at orientation. If there's one thing I can't abide, it's rudeness," Priscilla Beecher said. She took a delicate sip of her sweet tea.

"Well," Michelle replied. "We're from New York. We're pretty used to rudeness."

Priscilla frowned. It wasn't a good look for her. It accentuated the lines around her mouth and the lines between her eyes. Then her frown vanished and she looked at Michelle with concern.

"Bless your heart," Priscilla said. There was the same kind of honeyed tone that Betty Virginia had used when chastising the gun-toting Earl. Did every southern woman learn that voice when they were growing up? ("And today, ladies, we learn how to talk like Melanie Hamilton Wilkes.")

"You and your band are just so brave to come here," Priscilla continued. "People can be so cruel."

Priscilla looked at Adesina, who was across the room talking to Peter and LoriAnne, the drummer from the Funkalicious Four. Asti was with them as well. Asti had informed Michelle that LoriAnne was too shy to come and meet her. Michelle thought that was goofy and told them they should bring her over anyway.

"It's remarkable how open some of the other children are to your band members. Why, I expected they would be shunned."

"Admittedly, the Plano Originals don't seem to like us much, except for Kimmie Coldwater," Michelle said, trying to make her voice more cheerful and upbeat.

"Kimmie is lovely, isn't she?" Priscilla replied.

"Yes, yes she is. And how long have you been helping with the competition?" Michelle asked.

"I started about the same time you were on *American Hero*," Priscilla replied. "Anyway, the last two years I was liaison for the Plano Originals," she continued. "And I was supposed to be their liaison this year, but Dr. Smith thought I was the best qualified to welcome your band and help them along."

Adesina came up just then. "Hey, Mom. Hello, Ms. Beecher."

"Oh, it's *Miss* Beecher, hon," Priscilla said. "I'm an old-fashioned lady, I suppose."

"Sorry, Miss Beecher," Adesina replied. Just then her eyes grew wide and she burst out, "Oh, there's Mindy-Lou Gutiérrez."

"She's so kewl," Adesina said with a sigh. "Her solo videos on You-Tube are awesome. She can play, like, every instrument and she even composes! And obvs she's, like, hep to the jive. Mom, that's old jazz talk. Yerodin and I are totes into that now."

Michelle looked at Adesina blankly. She could barely keep up with her own generation's slang much less whatever language Adesina's generation was using.

Michelle finished off her Coke. She knew it would be a bad idea to have another—too much caffeine made her jittery—but she went to the bar anyway. A different bartender was there.

"What can I get you?" the new bartender asked. She wore the same generic black-and-white uniform that Billy Rainbow had—though she looked a lot less like a model.

"A Coke, please," Michelle said. "What happened to the other bartender?"

"You mean Billy? He did what he does best: ditch the last half of the party so he doesn't have to do breakdown." The bartender wrapped a paper napkin around Michelle's glass and handed it to her. "He's not a bad guy, but he's always on the hustle. Even when there's not much at stake."

"Sounds like a not-so-great guy to me."

The bartender shrugged. "Oh, he's lousy at what he tries to do. He's mostly a doofus. Pretty, but a doofus."

"I can see that." Michelle might have said more, but that was when she heard Mindy-Lou Gutiérrez's voice rise in anger.

"*Stop picking on me!*" the girl from Modesto said hotly. "You're just jealous because I'm a better musician than you." Michelle knew that tone. It was someone on the edge of tears.

"Oh, please," was the reply. "Everyone knows you're a poser." It was the kind of nasty only a teenage girl was capable of, full of snottiness, contempt, and hostility.

"You're not nearly as hot as you think you are. There are *jokers* here who play better than you."

Michelle didn't know the other girl, but she kinda hated her right off the bat. She was about to intervene when Mindy-Lou spun on her heel and rushed out of the ballroom. The other girl smiled maliciously as she watched.

Adesina grabbed Michelle by the arm. "That's Jillian Bigelow, Mom," she whispered. "She's totes a bitch."

"Language!"

"Well, she is."

The ballroom was beginning to clear out. *Time to round up the kids*, Michelle thought. "You guys ready to call it a night?" she asked.

The Mob looked unhappy. "It's really early, Ms. Pond," Sean said. The colors of his skin rippled and gradually changed color.

"C'mon, Mom," Adesina said. Her wings gave a flap and almost knocked over a floral arrangement. "It's hella early."

"You guys have a super-busy day tomorrow," Michelle said. "It's time to head off to bed."

"Ms. Pond, it's only nine o'clock," Asti said. His peachy scent filled the air. "No one is going to bed at nine o'clock. Heck, curfew for the competition is ten."

Michelle had tried very hard to be Strict Mom and Serious Chaperone Woman, but it all seemed as if it was sliding away. The kids' request wasn't all that out of order. *Dammit.*

"Fine," she said. "But everyone back into their room by ten. Rusty's going to keep an eye out for all of you. If you're late coming in, I'm going to know. Also, stay away from those protesters."

"No problem, Ms. P," said Peter. He rocked back and forth on his wheel. "They went away when the camera crews left earlier tonight."

"And don't go down to the River Walk. Let's have one night before you start surprising the tourists. Just hang around the hotel. Okay?"

♣

Michelle discovered Jan, Robin's landlady, lurking behind one of the floral arrangements, looking fiercely at each partygoer as they left. Some of them didn't notice her, but the ones who did recoiled and hurried out the door.

"Jan, you're making the guests feel uncomfortable," Michelle said.

She got a glare in return. "I'm trying to figure out who're reptoids. Vicky could be at risk."

Michelle rolled her eyes. "Seriously, these are high schoolers with their chaperones and music teachers. Why on earth would reptile people be here?"

Jan stared at Michelle with amazement. "Reptoids! I thought I explained this to you. They're everywhere."

"And I suppose they want to be our scaly overlords?"

"They already are," Jan said darkly. "It's the conspiracy of reptoids and mind-control agencies." She pushed her face into Michelle's and looked deeply into her eyes.

"Unless you're about to kiss me," Michelle said, "you better back the hell off."

Jan shrugged, then did so. "I don't think you're one of them. But you can never be sure. For instance, the Bushes are reptoids. So is the royal family in the U.K. I think they were behind Brexit."

Michelle knew she shouldn't say anything. It would be a bad idea.

Almost as bad as coming on the band trip, but she couldn't stop herself. "And why would they do that?"

Jan gave her a you-can't-be-that-stupid look. "Because the queen wants British independence from Europe. Sheesh. Read a paper—or www.reptoids.com."

"Okaaay, how about we get you back to your room."

"No! I'm not finished patrolling." Sparks flashed between her teeth.

"How about we go together?"

"That's just what a reptoid would say to help throw me off the track."

"Jan, just let me come with you. It'll go faster with the two of us. I swear, not a lizard person here."

"Reptoid! You better not be," Jan said darkly. "I'd hate to have to kill you."

"Yeah, I'd look down upon that."

Thirty minutes later, Michelle escaped to her room. There was only so much glaring and staring at perfectly nice people she could take. Also, Jan was nuts and no matter what Michelle tried, Jan would double down on the cray-cray. It was with a sigh of relief that she sagged against the door of her room once she got inside.

♠

Michelle hit send and her e-mail made a swooshy noise. Just as she plugged in her tablet to charge, she had a text on her phone from Wally: *Bed check done. Everyone's where they should be. Cripes, this is a lot of work.*

One less thing to think about. She changed into her pajamas and robe, and tried to figure out what to do about God's Weenies, the Plano Originals, and Bambi Coldwater. Blowing them up wasn't an option, and that made her kinda sad.

Michelle grabbed the ice bucket, thinking a drink while she watched TV wouldn't be the worst thing in the world. *Keycard,* she reminded herself. She tucked it into the pocket of her robe and slipped out the door. The ice machine was at the end of the hall near the emergency exit. She caught a glimpse of the exit door closing. *Weird.*

As she reached the alcove with the ice machine, she could have sworn she heard a giggle coming from the stairwell. A girl's giggle. Then a lower-pitched voice.

Michelle's eyes narrowed. This could *not* be one of her kids. They wouldn't be that stupid.

She pushed the exit door open.

Sitting on the stairs were Segway and Kimmie. They were holding hands.

"Ms. Pond!" they said in unison. They dropped hands.

"It's the first night," Michelle said sternly. But not too sternly, just sternly enough. Not *I want to terrify you,* just *You've really disappointed me.* She held the door open. "Peter, go back to your room. Kimmie, what floor are you on?"

Kimmie stared down at her sneakers. "I'm on the fourth floor. Please don't tell my mother!"

"Ms. Pond, we weren't doing anything," Peter said. He looked scared. "We were just talking. Mostly about band stuff. And classes. Did you know Plano has special instructors who come in and give them lessons? Like they're doing here at the competition. But all the time."

Michelle narrowed her eyes. "And how did hand-holding come to be involved in this academic conversation?"

"Well, it's not like we were kissing or anything," Peter said. Kimmie's cheeks turned bright cherry red.

"You." Michelle pointed at Segway. "Get back to your room. And you, Miss Coldwater, go on now."

Segway and Kimmie exchanged longing looks, then Kimmie started down the stairs.

"I'm really sorry, Ms. P." Peter opened the emergency door and peeked down the hall, then rolled out.

"Go on," Michelle said. So far, it appeared as if she was the worst chaperone ever, what with Segway and Kimmie canoodling on the first night. Michelle went to the ice machine and filled her bucket.

She turned, and standing a few feet before her was a woman. Her gray hair was a knotted mess, and she had a hideous rictus expression on her face. Michelle was shocked, and gooseflesh raced down her arms.

The woman started toward her and a bubble began to form in Michelle's free hand. But before she could let it fly, the woman vanished.

Michelle closed her hand, letting the bubble pop, absorbing its energy. *Damn. I guess those ghost stories are real. Maybe I'll have all the vodka in the minibar.*

WEDNESDAY

Bubbles and the
Band Trip

Part 5

POP, POP, POP.

The report of the gun made her cringe. Soldiers screamed and collapsed. Michelle let bubbles go and they exploded. Then she blew up Aero.

Bam, bam, bam.

"Mom! Wake up!"

Michelle woke with a start. Sunlight was pouring around the edges of the drapes. *Why did no hotel make curtains big enough to black out a room?* she wondered. Adesina was pounding on her door. *Shit. This can't be good.*

"Just a second."

Michelle glanced at her phone as she stumbled out of bed. She opened the door, still disoriented from her dream. *Not a dream, though. Kazakhstan.*

"OMG, Mom," Adesina said, holding out her tablet. "You've totes *got* to see this."

Michelle took the tablet and let Adesina into the room. Adesina was having better luck with her wings this morning. They were snuggled against her back.

Michelle felt a little oogy from the drinks the night before. Those three vodkas from the minibar weren't a superior life choice. She wasn't much of a drinker and they'd hit her hard.

Adesina's tablet had a video queued up. Michelle saw herself frozen in motion, bubbles rising from her hands. She hit play. It was a .gif of her boxing the Purity Baptist Church with bubbles on a continuous loop.

Don't read the comments.

And yet she did.

I'malittleteapot1921: This is why people with the wild card virus should be locked up.

> Newton3: re: I'malittleteapot1921—You're an idiot. You should eat shit and die. When they were handing out stupid, you asked for an extra helping.

I'malittleteapot1921: re: Newton3—What's a matter bro? You a joker? You scum should be wiped off the face of the earth. . . .

Michelle handed the tablet back to Adesina. She picked up her phone and checked Twitter and sure enough, #stopBubbles and #withBubbles were trending.

Why do I look at this stuff? Really, it's like picking a scab.

"I have some more videos and .gifs if you want to see them," Adesina said helpfully. "The ones with Jade Blossom are awesome! Though not as good as the ones from her date with Cesar."

"Yeah, not so much," Michelle replied. It was already late, so she started taking off her pajamas. She could at least get a quick shower.

"God, Mom!" Adesina said, and turned away.

Michelle was perplexed. "Okay," she said. "When did you get so weird about me being naked?"

"Since I got all this," Adesina said, gesturing with her body. "It's just so gross. You're my *mother*."

It made Michelle feel bad. Nakedness was just what she was used to doing during changes at runway shows. Maybe body stuff was a teenager thing. She needed to find someone to talk to about that. *And that won't be weird at all.* She sighed.

"Okay," she said as she started to the bathroom. "I'll just hide in here until you're gone. Tell the kids to meet me and the other chaperones downstairs in fifteen minutes for breakfast."

She glanced at her phone again. "And I have a text from Miss Beecher saying we play last. Today at two P.M."

♠ ♥ ♦ ♣

Beats, Bugs, and Boys

by Diana Rowland

Part 1

LORIANNE'S STICKS FLEW OVER the drums, heavy beat pounding through the wild cheering of the stadium crowd. Led Zeppelin's John Bonham looked on in awe while, off in the wings, Drummer Boy sat on the floor, all six hands covering his face as he sobbed. From the front row, Buddy Rich gave LoriAnne a thumbs-up—which was a bit strange since she was pretty sure he'd died about thirty years ago. But she couldn't worry about that right now. Dave Grohl was about to finish up his solo, and then it'd be her turn.

"Take it, LoriAnne," Dave shouted. "*Eeeeeeeeeeeeeeeeeeeee . . .*"
Her rhythm faltered. "Huh?"
eeeeeeeeeeeeeeeeeeeeeeeeee
Dave Grohl and Buddy Rich burst into a million sparkles as the whine of a mosquito shattered the dream.

"Aw, man, that was cold," LoriAnne groaned. "You could've at least let me have my big solo." She cracked one eye open to give the nightstand clock a bleary peek: 5:24 A.M. "Go 'way, skeeter. Got six whole minutes."

No such luck. The skeeter had been content to stay by the window last night, but now it resisted her attempt to send it away. Instead, it crawled to her ear to sing a cheery skeeter wake-up song.

eeeeeeeeeeeeeeeeeeeeeeeeeeeeeeeeeeeeeeeeeeeeee!
"Okay okay *okay.* Jeez. I'm awake." She threw off the comforter, un-

able to keep from smiling as the skeeter danced happily around her head. It was tough to stay annoyed with the little thing. It had stayed tucked in her curls all the way from Louisiana and was probably just as excited as she was. Heck, LoriAnne was amazed she'd slept at all. Not only was this the biggest competition she'd ever been in, but it was the first time in her almost fifteen years she'd spent the night in a state that wasn't Louisiana.

Holeeeee crap. San Antonio. *Texas!* She'd been worried there wouldn't be any mosquitoes here, but San Antonio had *plenty.* She'd counted a dozen in the hotel lobby alone. It sure helped her nerves to have some of her little friends nearby.

And boy, did she have a lot of nerves. Not only was LoriAnne the youngest member of the Folsom Funkalicious Four, but she'd only been their drummer since December, after Reese Fowler's mom got a promotion at her job and moved the whole family to Australia. And *Reese* had been the drummer when the band got the invite to the competition. Sure, LoriAnne had busted her butt to learn everything, and the band director, Mr. Sloane, seemed real happy with how she played, but she couldn't help but be nervous.

Her roommate's bed was empty and neatly made. Man, Cassie was up and out *early.* Knowing her, she'd either found a quiet place to read or was off practicing piano. Not that Cassie needed more practice. She was ah-*maze*-ing.

LoriAnne flicked on the light then did a double take at the clock: 6:24, not 5:24! She scrambled out of bed, excitement shifting to horror. She *knew* she'd set the time for the alarm, but she must have forgotten to turn it on. And on an important morning like this! Mr. Sloane had a six thirty A.M. reservation for the five of them at the restaurant downstairs, and had warned them not to be late. "We don't want to lose our table," he'd said. "Plus, it's sure to be a madhouse in the morning, with eight bands all wanting to fuel up before heading over to the Tobin Center."

Now she was going to be late on the very first day of the biggest competition her band had ever been in. *Way to make an impression, LoriAnne.*

Good thing she'd laid out all of her stuff before she went to bed. But too bad she didn't dare skip a shower—not after spending eleven hours in the car yesterday on the road trip from Folsom, Louisiana. *And the award for Stinkiest Musician goes to . . . LoriAnne Broom!*

No time to wash her hair, which sucked, but her hair was so darn thick and curly that it took a good fifteen minutes to dry. A freezing shower and a manic scrub of her smelliest bits took less than a minute, followed by a frenzied toweling off, a quick slap of deodorant, and a dash for clothes. She wasted two precious minutes trying to tame her insane cloud of curls before she finally gave up and shoved a sparkly clip into it to get it out of her face, letting the rest be a dumb brown curl-palooza.

She pressed a hunk of curls to her nose and took a deep sniff. Ugh. Smoky, but at least it was from wood and not cigarettes. Halfway through the drive to San Antonio, they'd run into a hailstorm so nasty that the band ended up waiting it out at Buck's BBQ and Bait Shop. The food was great, but the whole place had smelled like mesquite smoke with a side of day-old minnows.

6:32 A.M. She was late, but maybe she could pull off being only *kinda* late? Makeup was a lost cause. She'd have to do it in the lobby bathroom after breakfast. Though she doubted she'd be eating much, with the way her stomach was busy twisting itself into knots.

LoriAnne slung her stick bag over one shoulder and her tie around her neck, grabbed her backpack, and spun to leave. Then stopped, door half-open. "Well, c'mon already."

With a happy whine, the skeeter settled at the nape of her neck.

At the elevator, she jabbed at the button then anxiously watched the numbers scroll lazily up toward "7." Eventually the elevator dinged, and the doors slid open.

The woman within the elevator gave LoriAnne a friendly smile. "Going up?"

LoriAnne stood frozen. Tall, blond, a bit chunky, and totally gorgeous. It was the Amazing Bubbles. *Here,* honest to God no lie, right in front of her! LoriAnne had watched Every Single episode of Every Single season of *American Hero,* and Bubbles was hands down one hundred percent her second favorite ace of all time—especially after she'd saved New Orleans. At the mixer last night, LoriAnne had been too worn out from the road trip and overwhelmed by everything else to work out something actually intelligent to say to her. And then, of course, everything went south when Jade showed up. Ugh. Cassie had darn near cried when the piano got destroyed.

"Going up?" the Amazing Bubbles repeated.

LoriAnne blinked, then flushed. "S-sorry. Down. Wrong button."

Bubbles smiled. "No worries. The Detonators are on eight, right? Oh, and good luck today!"

The doors closed. LoriAnne took a few seconds to quietly thunk her head against the wall then pressed the button for down.

"Smooth," she muttered. "Real smooth. You wasted a minute *and* totally froze up." LoriAnne desperately wanted to have an actual, real conversation with a wild card. Ace, deuce, joker—didn't matter one bit to her. There weren't *any* wild cards back home except for Miss Bethany, and she was old, more than a little crazy, and threw beer cans with her eleven-fingered hands at anyone who came near her house.

The down elevator arrived. LoriAnne dove in and pressed the button for the lobby, praying for a speedy trip.

No such luck. The elevator began a leisurely descent then shuddered to a stop on the next floor. A man in a business suit got on, briefcase in one hand and phone in the other. He glanced up to check that the lobby button was lit then returned his attention to his phone, ignoring LoriAnne completely.

"Hold the elevator, please!" a voice called from down the hall.

LoriAnne shot her hand out to keep the doors from closing, then had to clamp down on a gasp of delight at the sight of the new arrivals.

Jokers! Adesina and Yerodin—whom LoriAnne recognized from reading Every Single article she could find online about wild cards. She'd blown it with Bubbles, but here was a second chance.

Her delight dimmed as the businessman eyed the newcomers then shoved his phone into his pocket and eased to the back of the elevator. He acted like he'd rather be anywhere else, especially when *more* jokers came in. Two boys—one with *wheels* instead of feet, and one whose skin rippled with all sorts of cool colors. LoriAnne couldn't remember their names for the life of her, but she'd seen them at the mixer.

She'd also seen the picket line of protesters with their ugly-nasty signs and heard their anti-joker chants. Stupid discrimination wasn't new to her—not after growing up not-quite-white in a small, conservative town in Louisiana. Yet even though she'd followed the whole stink over the court ruling that allowed jokers to participate in the band competition, she'd still been shocked at how *horrible* the protesters were.

Yesterday, after the band made it through the lines and into the hotel, Mr. Sloane had sat them all down for a super-serious talk about how they were all to behave and not engage in any ugliness. He'd summed up with, "The lawsuits and rulings don't change anything for you four. You're going to participate and learn and play your best. Nothing else matters."

Easy for him to say. The rulings mattered to the jokers. How much harder would it be for them to learn and play their best with protesters screaming at them?

Meanwhile, all LoriAnne wanted to do was get to know them—in fact, had been dying to do so ever since she learned that the Jokertown Mob would be at the competition. Now here she was with *four* jokers right here beside her. This was her chance.

The elevator descended. LoriAnne's mind raced to come up with what to say. Something neutral and friendly that wouldn't sound weird. Easy. Right. Maybe she could ask what they played? Except they were all carrying instrument cases, so she'd come off like an idiot who had no idea what a clarinet or trumpet case looked like.

Argg. Why was this so hard?

The skeeter hummed against her neck in encouragement. A bit of her angst retreated.

The elevator stopped on the next floor, where two teen boys waited, each carrying a sax case. They started forward then hesitated, glancing at the occupants and then at each other.

"There's plenty of room," LoriAnne said with a cheery smile. "We won't bite!"

The boy on the left gave a tight smirk. "Not so sure about that." His gaze lingered on the jokers. "We'll wait for the next one."

Cold shock washed through LoriAnne. Adesina reached past her and pressed the button to close the doors.

"Oh. Sorry," LoriAnne mumbled, feeling as if she was apologizing for way more than the button.

Adesina's antennae twitched. "It's cool."

Great. She'd managed to exchange four whole words with a joker. And she only had a few more seconds before they reached the lobby. "Y'all headed to breakfast?" she blurted.

Adesina nodded. "Yup."

Awkward silence fell.

The instant the doors opened at the lobby, the businessman shouldered his way out and escaped. The joker with wheels muttered under his breath as he exited with the others.

LoriAnne cast a frustrated look after the jokers then sighed and followed them at a we're-not-together distance. A handful of the lobby mosquitoes drifted toward her, but she gently told them to stay back—all but one whom she allowed to settle behind her ear. A cloud of skeeters around her head would draw unwanted attention, but having the two tucked in her hair helped ease her general anxiety.

It didn't help that the jokers were walking—or rolling—at a normal, casual pace while LoriAnne itched to double-time it through the lobby and to the restaurant. But if she barged past, they might think she was trying to get away from them like Mr. Businessman.

Or maybe they'd just think you're in a hurry, LoriAnne chided herself. Yet she continued to amble a short distance behind them. It sucked to be yet another minute late, but that was better than coming across as a jerk.

Near the reception desk, an older yellow-haired lady watched Adesina and the others pass by then shuddered and leaned toward her husband. "The Purity Baptist Church folks are whackdoodles," she said, then lifted her chin toward the group of jokers. "But those creatures should *not* be allowed near children—" She broke off with a yelp and frantically waved away the cluster of mosquitoes that had oh-so-inexplicably targeted her, then struggled to sneeze out one that flew up her nose.

Adesina glanced back at the lady, and LoriAnne hurried to call the skeeters off. She didn't figure Adesina would guess that she was controlling the skeeters, but best not to take chances. And best to stop before the stupid lady killed them all.

Besides, LoriAnne knew that her dad wouldn't be real happy with her using the skeeters that way. After the Bobby Tripp incident a few years back, he'd grounded her for a month and delivered a long lecture that boiled down to: "Don't get dumb. Bobby's a useless piece of crap, and I can't say I blame you for siccing your skeeters on him after he got drunk and ran over your cat. But if you'd done killed him or hurt him worse than a few hundred bites, there'd be no end of trouble for the both of us. Y'gotta think hard 'bout what you're doing, and remember that there's a consequence for every little thing." That was also when he told her she needed to keep quiet about her little knack, at least until she was a lot older. "People can be real stupid," he said, and left it at that.

Then again, her dad didn't have a lot of patience with haters. There was every chance he'd be totally fine with her shooting a skeeter up the nose of that witch.

The four jokers veered off toward a sitting area to join two other Jokertown players—a dark-haired girl with tentacles in place of hands, and a bald boy with odd, pastel-hued skin. Now LoriAnne could hurry without any neurotic silliness holding her back.

Yet she couldn't help but give the group of jokers a wistful look as she speed-walked past. The one big problem with pretending to be a nat was that she had a zillion questions about wild cards and no one to answer them. There was only so much she could learn by watching American Hero and reading articles and interviews—and LoriAnne wasn't stupid enough to believe any of it was a hundred percent accurate. She wondered about the little things like, did she really need to eat spinach and broccoli to keep her skills sharp like her dad claimed? And the occasional bigger thing such as, was she an ace or a deuce? Or something in between? Yeah, she could call mosquitoes from a thousand feet away and then temporarily clone them hundreds of times over to make a swarm, but she couldn't see or hear through her bugs the way Jonathan Hive could, and her cloned skeeters needed to be within sight for her to control them. Plus, there'd only been a handful of challenges on American Hero where she figured a mosquito whisperer would've been useful, and surely that was the best test of all?

Of course it didn't *really* matter whether she was an ace or a deuce, especially since it was a secret. Right?

Sure. Didn't matter at all. Uh-huh.

Her Louisiana skeeter returned to sing by her ear, and she relaxed.

At the restaurant, LoriAnne spied Cassie's bright red hair where she sat reading a book at a round table in the corner. Beside her, Mr. Sloane sipped coffee and made notes on sheet music. Bass player Greg slouched across from him, swiping his fingers across his phone screen.

"I'm so sorry," LoriAnne gasped as she slid into an empty seat. "I set an alarm, but I guess I forgot to actually turn it on. I don't ever set one at home 'cause my dad's alarm always wakes me up, but today I didn't have—"

"Relax, LoriAnne," Mr. Sloane said with a kind smile. "We haven't even ordered yet. And we don't need to leave for the Tobin Center until seven thirty."

Greg glanced up through a lock of black hair. "Yeah, Howard was still pooping when I left the room." He grinned. "I think the barbecue from yesterday is fighting its way out."

LoriAnne made a face. "Ew?"

"You had another minute before I called you," Cassie said with a wink as she turned a page in her book. She was a senior and took all AP or honors classes, got kickass grades, did all sorts of volunteer work, and was pretty much the kind of girl that grown-ups wanted their own teens to hang out with. Plus, she was actually a really nice person.

LoriAnne didn't hang out with Cassie, but that was because LoriAnne was only a freshman, lived out in the boonies, and didn't have a whole lot in common with her except for the jazz band.

The "freshman living in the boonies" thing was a big part of why LoriAnne didn't have a rocking social life. That and the fact that she wasn't exactly a knockout. "Coltish" was how one of her teachers had once described her. "Tall and skinny and flat-chested" was how LoriAnne described herself, though she still held out hope for the appearance of boobs bigger than AA. She was one of the youngest kids in her class and wouldn't turn fifteen for another three weeks. Surely that meant she had a bit more growing to do in the right places? Not height, though, for the love of God. Five feet eight was more than enough.

Howard finally showed up, toting his alto sax case. The waitress came to take their orders, and as soon as she left, Greg elbowed Lori-Anne.

"Did you see this?" He shoved his phone at her. "Just popped up on Miss Bambi's Facebook."

"Ugh. What are you reading *her* stuff for?" But LoriAnne peered at the screen anyway. It showed a blurry night photo of a hooded man, his face shadowed. He held a beat-up Martin D-28 guitar, and a case lay open at his feet. A big red caption at the top proclaimed, *Joker Warning!!* At the bottom it read, "Parents and band directors beware! White-skinned freak a k a TheFeels spotted lurking in the vicinity. Keep our children safe!!!"

"Why shouldn't I read it?" Greg pulled the phone back and typed something in. "It's harmless, and there's loads of juicy comments. People are cray-cray funny."

She made a frustrated noise in the back of her throat. Bambi Cold-water was the lady who'd started the nastiness with the lawsuits. "Why can't she just leave people alone? So what if he's a joker? The guy makes kickass music."

Greg rolled his eyes and turned away, still smirking at comments. So much for not engaging in any ugliness.

TheFeels was the oh-so-mysterious musician who'd put out close to fifty amaaaaazing YouTube videos. Guitar mostly, but he could play *anything*. The comment trolls labeled him a joker since he never showed his face and because his hands looked white as paper. Plus, no nat could ever play *that* good. If TheFeels really was in the area . . . holy cats! It would totally *rock* if she could track him down this week. Hearing him play live would be the icing on the cake. In heaven. With ice cream on the side. Not to mention, maybe she could warn him to watch his back. After all, she wouldn't put it past dear Bambi to sic a few good ol' boys on him.

What sucked was that jokers like TheFeels and the ones in the lobby didn't have a choice about whether or not to live publicly as a wild card. It wasn't really fair that she could keep her skeeter knack a secret. On the other hand, those protesters out front were a prime example of Real Stupid, so maybe it was okay to keep it secret if you could?

The food arrived, and LoriAnne forced herself to eat, even though her stomach was a knot of tension. This wasn't her first competition—she'd been in two others since she started playing with the band—but this was the biggest by about a million percent.

After they finished eating, Mr. Sloane checked his watch. "All right, Folsom Funkalicious Four. Time to head out. Last chance to make sure you haven't forgotten anything." He eyed Greg. "Where's your tie?"

"In my bass case," Greg announced proudly.

A small sigh escaped Mr. Sloane. "And where's your bass case?"

Greg dropped his eyes to the floor by his chair then smacked his forehead. "On the bed!" He pushed up and dashed off.

Mr. Sloane let out a longer sigh. "I'll go get the car."

The Secret Life
of Rubberband

Part 3

SHARON OBERHOFFER SET THREE alarms every morning so she'd be sure to wake up before her fourth. With most teachers at Xavier Desmond High School, students obeyed a fifteen-minute rule— if the teacher was fifteen minutes late to class, class was canceled. If Sharon Oberhoffer was one minute late, they sent a search party.

So when Robin was five minutes late to the sixth-floor common room where the students gathered Wednesday morning before leaving for the Tobin Center, he expected a certain level of cold shoulder. He hadn't expected full piping conniptions and a barrage of sign.

"Sharon." He stepped back, raised hands, and stuttered out, <Slower, slower,> in ASL.

Her eyes narrowed, and she mimed slapping him upside the head, which was fair. <I understand English fine, Robin. I spoke it for twenty-five years before I drew my card.> Her dime-sized pursed lips tightened into a furious dot.

"I'm so sorry. What's the problem?"

<Can you count?>

He scanned the kids in the room, and bit his lip to keep from swearing. "Okay. Who here's rooming with Antonia?"

Marissa and Adesina raised their hands.

"When was the last time you saw her?"

"Breakfast." "Breakfast." "She said she was going down to the pool. Took her swimsuit."

"Okay. Great. Thank you. Sharon, do you mind if I . . . ?"

<The shuttle bus is waiting downstairs.>

"I can be fast."

He sprinted down the hall, considered the elevator, took the stairs instead. He vaulted over a railing and stretched. Arms attenuating, he swung to thread through the gap between the stairs until he reached the pool level and let go. His arms recoiled to their normal size with a gross wet *thwack*. After ten years of practice, that still stung.

The pool was, of course, empty except for a globular gentleman with a thick full-body coat of hair, swimming laps. Robin's "Excuse me" echoed back to him without impinging on the swimmer's consciousness. Robin tried again, with as little effect. Then he poked the fellow in the shoulder from ten feet away, which prompted a certain amount of flailing and splashing that eventually subsided into an angry glare. "Excuse me," he tried again. "I'm so sorry. One of my students is missing—a girl wearing gloves, she came down here to swim, I think. . . ."

"Oh, her," the fat man said in a tone of voice that made Robin consider violence, however briefly. "She left. Out that door."

Out that door led to the gym, which was locked, but wouldn't accept Robin's key for some reason. He made his arm long and thin, pinched it between door and jamb, and opened the door from the inside, to find a shocked janitor.

"So sorry," he said. "Guidance counselor. One of our students is missing. Gloves, sort of glowery expression?"

She'd entered wearing a towel, sat on the weight bench for ten minutes staring at nothing, then asked if the hotel restaurant was still serving breakfast, and left.

"Gracias," and Robin was off again.

The waiter at the hotel restaurant held an unpaid check and was very upset about it. She'd tried to charge the meal to her room, but their room didn't allow for charged meals, so she'd said she would head right up to the room and get her wallet, and never came back. "Here," Robin said, "bill it to mine," and hoped his would accept charges. Then he ran out, and back up to the sixth floor, past Sharon, who whistled, pointing to her watch. He knocked on 603, the room number she'd given the waiter. "Antonia. Are you in there?"

He heard footsteps.

"Everyone's waiting."

The footsteps stopped.

"We need to leave now, or we'll lose rehearsal time. But if there's something wrong—"

The door jerked open from within. The chain stopped it. "It's not my fault," Antonia said, "they didn't check the room again."

She'd waited until the others assembled before sneaking back in, but he wasn't here to win an argument with a fifteen-year-old. He tried: "Are you sick? I can tell Ms. Oberhoffer. They can do without a drummer for one practice."

She glanced away. Closed the door. He was about to knock again when it opened. "I'm fine," Antonia said, as if someone had asked her how she'd slept the night before her execution. "Let's go."

"Do you want to—"

She shouldered her backpack and stalked past him into the hall. "I said I'm fine."

◆

When kids at Xavier Desmond High School came to Robin for advice, he started with questions. He asked about their classes, their lives, their families, their problems. He rarely offered answers, but when pressed, his tended to revolve around a consistent theme. Find your path and follow it—find work that gives you strength, that helps the world and its people, figure out how to do that work happily, and in peace. Life's full of people and systems who want to tell you who you should be, what you should do. Don't listen. Or at least, don't listen naively.

The advice went double for kids whose cards had turned, leaving them with scales, tentacles, wheels for feet, or superpowers. Jokertown students had to be more careful than the rest. Just because you had a chameleon's skin didn't mean you had to live like one. Just because you had super-strength didn't mean you had to go out punching people for Freedom and Justice. Just because your body was as elastic as good rubber didn't mean you had to be some sort of stretchy crime fighter for example. Some people became guidance counselors.

The downside of this advice, of course, was that sometimes you ended up doing something you were bad at.

Robin sat outside the practice hall, failing to review his paperwork, and instead reviewing his students through the glass doors.

They played—music, basically. The rhythm didn't thrill, but he had to consider the circumstances—twenty or so hours cramped in a bus, until they reached the one place in the country with crappier weather than New York. If Robin were in their shoes, his spirits would be squashed enough without having to march through a nat protest. Hell, most of the kids were jokers—Robin at least knew, when he shouldered past people who hated him, that they wouldn't know they hated him unless he showed his card, and they couldn't hurt him unless they tried very hard. The world offered no such comfort to Jacobson, or to Marissa, or, for that matter . . .

Antonia played the drums as if she were taking a math test. And she didn't like math.

He had seen her play before. He visited extracurriculars every few weeks, on rotation—if you knew a kid only between the hours of eight and three you might see her exhausted slump between first and second period and miss her fire on the basketball court, miss his pride when he buzzed in for quiz bowl, miss the ferocity of their forensics. Antonia hadn't beat out ten other potential drummers for the Jokertown Mob by accident.

But she wouldn't have beaten them today. He'd hoped lunch, or the master class sessions, would have bucked up her spirits, but here they were, afternoon group rehearsal, and still, listless.

Something was wrong. You couldn't press kids—you could ask, you could tell them you were there if they needed you, you could keep them out of trouble, but the more pressure you gave, the more you became part of the problem. Politicians, papers, talk show hosts, they all talked about teaching like an industrial process, like kids were unstamped metal and good instruction could mold or melt them into this shape or that. All metaphors were wrong, but that was more wrong than most. Kids were seeds that transformed as they grew. And as they grew, how did you know if you were doing right? Maybe without your touch they would have grown stronger, truer—or withered. And even when you knew they were suffering, how could you help? Robin could count on one hand the number of adults of his acquaintance familiar enough with their own minds to know when they felt upset, let alone to know why. And teenagers?

The band shifted into a tricky passage. Antonia's brow furrowed as Jacobson tossed her the solo. Maybe people screwed themselves up worse as they got older, and if Antonia wanted him to know what was wrong, he would.

She hit the cymbals late. He couldn't hear the difference, but he saw it in her frown.

His pocket buzzed.

He read through the lines of dead pixels on the screen—acid bath, again—*GHST ALRT CM @ 1CE.*

Jan's number.

The kids had just finished their first break. Another hour and a half before they'd wrap up for the afternoon. Plenty of time to run to the Gunter, hunt a ghost, and get back before anyone noticed he was gone.

Speaking of not knowing the contents of his own head.

Beats, Bugs, and Boys

Part 2

HOLEEEEE CRAP. LORIANNE HAD told herself she wasn't going to gawk at the Tobin Center like a country bumpkin, but here she was doing exactly that. At least Howard and Greg were right there with her in the let's-look-like-idiots thing of gaping at everything, from the front entrance that looked like a castle in some ancient desert kingdom to the main performance hall with its incredible lighting and tiers and tiers of seats. Even Cassie looked impressed, and she'd been to awesome places like Carnegie Hall and San Francisco.

Greg and Howard set their instruments backstage in the area marked *Folsom Funk. 4* then everyone returned to the main hall for the master class, the first event on the schedule.

"Good morning," Dr. Smith said in a cheery voice. "We'll get started with the two-hour master class, then a half-hour break, then each band has twenty minutes to play the three songs they've prepared. Don't forget, one of them has to be ''Round Midnight' by Thelonious Monk." She went on to talk about the schedule of events and how the competition itself would work, though after the first few sentences Lori-Anne tried to tune her out for fear her voice would put her right to sleep. Besides, they all had the schedule and info in their registration packets.

Mr. Sloane had been super-cool and let the whole band have a say in picking the other two pieces they'd play. After a great deal of *intense* discussion, they'd settled on "Birdland"—which LoriAnne adored for its fun and upbeat drum line—and, finally, "Won't You Be My Neighbor?," a jazzy arrangement of the *Mister Rogers' Neighborhood* theme, because how could you not love anything to do with Mr. Rogers?

"And now, please welcome acclaimed bass player Buddy Robins!"

LoriAnne jerked her attention back to the stage and clapped along with everyone else as the curtain pulled back to reveal the famous Buddy Robins and the other members of his jazz quintet. Buddy waved at the crowd then immediately opened with a complex riff. A half-dozen beats later, his band joined in and together they treated the crowd to a solid ten minutes of killer jazz and blues.

When they finished, everyone gave them a standing ovation. Buddy applauded his backing musicians, then set his bass aside and picked up the microphone.

LoriAnne pulled her notebook from her backpack, pen poised to take notes.

"How many bands we got here?" Buddy asked. "Eight? I hear y'all are the best in the country." He chuckled as the hall erupted in shouts and cheers. "All right, who are my bass players? Stick those hands up."

Beside her, Greg shot his hand into the air.

"Real nice. How about piano-keyboard?" He smiled as new hands went up. "Sax?" He continued to list instruments, going through guitar, trumpet, clarinet, trombone, and even flute and violin before finally saying, "Lemme see the drummers!"

LoriAnne raised her hand then peered around at the other hands to try to identify the other drummers. Four, five, six . . . Where was the eighth drummer?

One last hand went up a few rows in front of LoriAnne. No, not a hand. A cluster of tentacles unfurled from the wrist of the dark-haired girl. A murmur rippled through the crowd along with a few sniggers.

"Freeeak!" screeched a boy in an exaggerated falsetto from the far side of the hall. Outraged, she craned her neck to pinpoint the source, but could only narrow it down to the general vicinity of either the Seattle band or the Plano Originals.

"Y'all play nice," Buddy said, tone mild but with enough edge to remind people that he was one of the judges. "You drummers are the backbone," he continued after the murmuring stopped. "Every band here got drums, keeping that tempo and juicin' up what needs juicin', sittin' back behind all y'all. Make sure you appreciate 'em."

Greg elbowed LoriAnne. "No pressure, right?" He chuckled.

LoriAnne managed a weak laugh in return. Yeah. No pressure.

After that, Buddy talked about his background and experiences and various lessons he'd learned along the way. LoriAnne took notes like mad, feeling ever so slightly out of her depth when he started talking about how using personal life experience can enrich the texture of playing. How was she supposed to enrich texture when she didn't *have* any life experience?

Eventually, he opened it up to questions. LoriAnne stretched her cramping hand then dove right back into note-taking, self-doubt rising as other competitors asked all sorts of knowledgeable questions.

The dark-haired joker girl stepped up to the microphone. "Antonia Abruzzi of the Jokertown Mob," she said, then went on to ask a detailed question that had something to do with optimizing the dialogue and contrast between drums and bass during polyrhythmic performance.

LoriAnne's head spun just listening to her. It was an awesome question, and one LoriAnne never would have even thought to ask. Holy moly, but was she in over her head. Mr. Sloane had made an awful mistake picking her for the band. Or maybe it was a "beggars can't be choosers" sort of thing? There'd been a few other people who auditioned for honors jazz when the drummer position had opened up, but maybe they'd all sucked super-hard, and Mr. Sloane had no choice but to pick her?

She dragged her tumbling thoughts back to the here and now and wrote down Buddy's every word.

Eventually, the questions wound down. Buddy and his band played another couple of songs, then Dr. Smith came back out. "How about another round of applause for the amazing Buddy Robins?" she said, nodding as the audience enthusiastically obliged. "The competitions will begin at ten thirty A.M. Band directors, please bring your bands backstage while the band before yours is playing. No earlier. Detroit, you're up first. Good luck, everyone."

LoriAnne checked her schedule for the millionth time. They were fourth to perform, which meant they'd probably be the last group to play before lunch.

Greg and Howard left to explore and socialize until things started up again. Cassie pulled out her book and resumed reading, while Mr. Sloane murmured to himself and once again made notes on his sheet music.

LoriAnne fidgeted for several minutes then decided she was too on edge to sit and do nothing. After leaving her backpack with Mr. Sloane, she made her way out of the performance hall. Apparently, she wasn't the only one who was stir-crazy. A couple dozen teens milled in the foyer area, chatting or checking their phones or just taking a moment to chill. Off to her right, a couple of girls peered at a phone screen, and a familiar melody wound beneath the hum of conversation. Lori-Anne smiled as she wandered past them. They were watching one of TheFeels's videos, one he'd put out only a week ago. Not that she had them memorized or anything.

She followed the corridor around until the crowd thinned to nothing.

Almost nothing. The wheeled joker whizzed by, passing Antonia as she strolled in LoriAnne's direction. LoriAnne gave her a friendly smile, but Antonia simply leveled a cool look at her and continued on without a word.

Sighing, LoriAnne turned to watch Antonia walk away. Okay, so the Jokertown drummer wasn't exactly outgoing. Maybe LoriAnne could try to strike up a conversation? *Don't be a stalker,* she reminded herself. Plenty of time left in the week to get to know a joker.

LoriAnne started to resume her wandering but paused as two vaguely familiar boys swaggered toward Antonia. Both looked sixteenish. One was slender with high cheekbones and perfectly styled hair, while the other had a bit more muscle on his frame and acne on his cheeks and forehead.

Pretty Boy smirked at Antonia. LoriAnne's eyes narrowed as recognition clicked in. These were the same two boys who hadn't wanted to get on the same elevator as jokers.

As Pretty Boy passed Antonia, he shot a hand out and jerked her stick bag off her shoulder. "You dropped something, freakshow." He held up the bag and backed away.

Antonia whirled with a glare, tentacles writhing. "Give. It. Back."

Grinning, he tossed the bag to Pimple Face. "Give that back to the joker, willya?"

LoriAnne started toward them. "Hey, cut it out, you jerks!"

Pimple Face ignored her and tossed the bag back to his buddy. Antonia tried to snatch it back, but Pretty Boy jerked it out of her reach.

Stupid, immature, mean jerks! She mentally reached for the pair of mosquitoes at her neck. It would take barely a second for her to clone them into hundreds and cover both boys with welts.

And Antonia will see it, she realized with a sick jolt. The two nats might brush it off as a weird quirk of nature, but the joker was used to wild card powers. Too much chance she'd figure it out, and then LoriAnne's life would change forever. All because these two were jerks.

But maybe one skeeter would be enough? LoriAnne sent the lobby skeeter toward Pimple Face and waited for the right moment.

Antonia swiped her tentacles toward Pretty Boy's face. He backpedaled then chucked the bag over her head toward Pimple Face. The instant it left his hand, LoriAnne sent the skeeter into Pimple Face's ear.

Pimple face yelped and slapped his hand over his ear. The bag went sailing past him then skidded another several feet across the floor. LoriAnne leaped after it and snatched it up. "Get lost, losers," she sneered at the boys.

Pimple Face balled up his fist, but Pretty Boy grabbed his arm. "This freak lover isn't worth getting kicked out of the competition," he said with a sneer. With a parting middle finger at LoriAnne, he hauled his buddy toward the foyer.

Relieved, LoriAnne turned to Antonia and held out the stick bag. "Are you okay? I'm so sorry they did that. I think it's just awful how mean people are to you jokers."

Antonia's chin jerked up as she took the bag. "*We jokers* aren't freaking crippled," she said, voice low but scathing. "I can stand up for myself just fine."

LoriAnne's face heated. "Sorry. I . . . I didn't mean to . . ." Her throat tightened. Gulping, she pivoted and hurried away in as fast a casual walk as she could manage, fiercely willing herself to not do anything stupid like *cry*. That would be the absolute nail in her social life coffin.

She darted into the first ladies' room she saw, locked herself in an empty stall, then sat and dropped her head into her hands. *Wow, I'm really on a roll,* LoriAnne thought miserably. She'd only been trying to help Antonia but instead managed to piss her off. This whole trip was turning into a train wreck, and they hadn't even performed yet! She didn't fit in—not as a drummer, and most certainly not with other wild cards. Antonia was her third strike. She was never ever ever going to talk to a joker, because she was done trying. The universe had spoken.

Her Louisiana skeeter hummed against her neck. She gave a wobbly smile. "Guess I can't hide in here for the rest of the week." Heaving a sigh, she left the stall, fixed her smudged makeup, then trudged back to the performance hall.

♥

As it turned out, the two jerks were in the Detroit band, which was the first to perform. To LoriAnne's savage glee, the trombone player seemed to have something wrong with his hearing and hit a number of sour notes. LoriAnne would never in a million years deliberately sabotage a competitor, but Pimple Face had more than earned a bug in his ear.

The Plano Originals were up next and—LoriAnne had to admit—played really darned well. As they worked through their set, her gut started tying itself into knots again. Those guys all knew what they were doing. Not a clueless freshman in the bunch, she was positive.

What if she ended up being the reason her band lost? She'd never be able to show her face at school again. Once they made it back to Louisiana, she'd find a way to tell Mr. Sloane that he needed to find a new drummer. A better drummer. Someone who knew what the heck they were doing. That is, if he didn't outright cut her from the group first.

The third band to play was the Modesto Melody Makers. Since Folsom was up next, Mr. Sloane ushered the Funkalicious Four to the back to get ready.

While Greg and Howard retrieved their instruments, LoriAnne checked her sticks then hunkered in an out-of-the-way spot while Modesto churned out "'Round Midnight." How could the judges stand to listen to the same song over and over?

"Hey, Folsom." Antonia stepped out of the shadows, tentacles twisting around each other. "I'm really sorry I jumped your ass." She winced. "You didn't deserve it one bit."

It took LoriAnne a few seconds to find her voice. "It's okay," she said, then offered a weak smile. "It's not as if you had any reason to be upset or anything."

Antonia gave a short laugh. "Right. Not a care in the world." She smiled. "Anyway, thanks for the help, Folsom. Good luck out there."

"LoriAnne. I mean, that's my name." She stuck her hand out then immediately worried if she'd made a horrible faux pas. Antonia had *tentacles*. Could she even shake hands? But pulling her hand back now would be even worse.

Cool, smooth tentacles wrapped around her fingers. Antonia shook her hand then released it. "Knock 'em dead, LoriAnne," she said, then slipped off into the shadows.

Holy crap! The universe had changed its mind! About talking to a joker, at least. She still didn't know a darn thing about being a wild card. And she also still had to face the performance without making a total ass of herself.

Modesto started their third song. Only a few minutes to go.

LoriAnne joined the others where they waited in the wings. Greg glanced up from his bass then frowned. "What's wrong?" he whispered. Loudly.

LoriAnne plastered on a smile. "Nothing. Just excited!"

He scowled. "Bullshit."

Howard leaned in to study her face. "Yep. Bullshit."

Mr. Sloane looked over at her then pulled the four of them away from the stage. "I should have dealt with this when we first arrived, but things were more chaotic than I expected." His kind eyes met hers. "LoriAnne. What are you?"

She went cold. Did he know about the skeeters? Was he asking her to confess that she was a wild card right here in front of the band? "I . . ."

"You're a musician," he finished for her while she quietly died of relief. "A very talented and driven and dedicated musician. One who is also quite human." He let out a rueful laugh. "It's normal to be overwhelmed and uncertain, and I should've helped you face it. You're such a solid member of the band, it's easy to forget that you don't have much experience."

"But all those other people who were asking such smart questions—"

"Are only half as good as you'll be when you're their age." His expression grew serious. "You wouldn't be in this band if you didn't belong in it. If you can't have faith in yourself, then have it in me."

Greg nodded emphatically. "Yeah, he'd boot your ass right out if you started slacking. Hey, Mr. Sloane, remember how you told Jordan Kelly to get the fu—"

Mr. Sloane cleared his throat. "Modesto just finished. We're up. Well, LoriAnne?"

The Louisiana skeeter sang by her ear like a teeny tiny cheerleader. LoriAnne abruptly realized that the tension that had been twisting her gut was gone. Every speck of it. She squared her shoulders. "Y'all better appreciate me, 'cause I'm your backbone!"

When they stopped laughing, the Folsom Funkalicious Four took the stage. LoriAnne settled behind her drum kit. They opened with "'Round Midnight." Mr. Sloane had spiced up the arrangement a bit, giving it a neo-funk flavor, but it was still sedate enough that Lori-Anne could sneak peeks at the judges. None of them were making faces, so that was a good sign. And Buddy wore a smile and nodded his head in time with the beat.

They transitioned into "Birdland." LoriAnne couldn't watch the judges anymore, but she didn't need to. She knew her group was kicking ass.

The band brought the song to an energetic close, waited for the applause to die away, then started the lovely "Won't You Be My Neighbor?"

It was over before she knew it. She hadn't messed up. None of them had.

The universe sure had changed its mind again. And that was okay by her.

Next challenge: make friends with a wild card and get some answers.

♠ ♥ ♦ ♣

The Secret Life
of Rubberband

Part 4

JAN CHARGED THROUGH THE doors of the hotel kitchen, one arm out, badge displayed. "Health inspector! Everyone stay calm."

Everyone lost all semblance of calm. One sous chef dropped a stick of butter into a stockpot, then cursed and grabbed for a spoon. Another looked up and froze, at least on a conscious level—some autonomous function continued to chop carrots until a third sous chef tackled her to keep her from chopping off her own hand. A shaven-headed kid punching dough cried out, "Chef!"

Chef was already blustering forward. "What the hell is this?" Her teeth weren't filed to points, but she gave the impression they were anyway.

Jan flipped her fake badge into the inside pocket of her leather jacket before the chef was close enough to read it. "Officers Chang and Samuelson, ma'am. We've received reports of spectral miasmas in the vicinity, class three health code violation. Have you seen anything out of the ordinary?"

"The only unusual things I've seen"—and the chef leaned in close—"are you. Can I see your badge again, please?"

"No time." Jan shouldered past her. "Our local ectoplasmic readings are off the scale. Everyone here is in terrible danger."

Robin followed her, and tried to look official. He didn't think health inspectors likely wore sweater vests. Or, maybe they did—just not the kind of health inspectors Jan was imagining, who probably didn't exist in this universe anyway. He caught up with Jan—wasn't hiding behind her, no, just catching up with her—as she neared the vat of dough the assistant baker was still punching. The chef ran after them. She was holding a knife. She'd been holding a knife when they came in. There was nothing necessarily violent about a chef holding a knife. She just had not put it down. *Yet. For very good reason.* He was sure.

"You can't just barge in here," the chef said, as Jan shoved the dough boy out of the way and plunged her hand into the vat.

The chef made a strangled sound, the kind that people, in Robin's experience, tended to make when there were too many curse words in their throat to come out one at a time. She raised the knife. (To be fair, she raised both hands. One of them just happened to *hold* the knife.)

Robin heard an unfortunately familiar laugh.

Then the dough vat exploded.

Dough chunks splattered the wall. Flour burst in Robin's face. A gray-blue figure sprang from the vat to the counter and crouched there—four limbs bent frog-like, a torso arched like a spitting cat's. A broad gash of a smile split its huge round eyeless head.

"Jesus!" Robin and Jan and the chef and the dough boy scrambled back.

The ghost cocked its head at them, as if reading fine print. It chuckled.

"Agent Robin," Jan said, "why don't you grab the ghost?"

"Agent Chang," he replied, "I thought that was your job."

"I'm the supervisor here."

Robin sighed, and gave it his best shot.

♣

Sprinting, he reached the rehearsal space five minutes after practice ended. Sharon Oberhoffer's voice piped and whistled with maniacal speed, and her signs came fast and furious. <Where the hell have you been? And why are you covered in flour?>

"It's a long story. I'm so sorry. I had to step out to take a call, and—"

<Another band is waiting for our space, for all we knew those mon-

sters outside had snatched you up, I couldn't even go looking for you—>

"You really wouldn't have wanted to," he said.

She paused. Her large eyes narrowed. Her fingers snapped out and snagged a glob of wet dough from his ear. <What is this?>

"Part of the long story?"

The kids stared at him. They didn't need sign to tell Sharon was furious. Her pipes and whistles left no room for debate on the subject. Most of the kids looked away. Antonia rolled her eyes. Robin agreed with her.

♠   ♥   ♦   ♣

Bubbles and the
Band Trip

Part 6

MICHELLE WAS SURPRISED AT the size of the H-E-B Auditorium at the Tobin Center. She'd expected something modest like the small auditorium they'd been in for orientation, not this sweeping expanse of gleaming, honey-colored wood walls and luscious ceiling-length drapes. The plush carmine seats were comfortable and well-sized. There were multiple levels and the entire place felt grand.

She'd wondered how the final competition performance could fill an auditorium this size, but Priscilla had explained that tickets had been donated to schools and colleges all over San Antonio, and that, as the competition was nationally known, jazz lovers from Austin, San Antonio, and Dallas would show up.

<We're starting off with "'Round Midnight,"> Sharon signed. <Then we go into "Jetboy Jump." When we're done, get off the stage as quickly as possible.>

Sharon gave a low whistle. The band whistled back.

"Xavier Desmond High School Jazz Band, please take the stage."

"Play great," Michelle whispered to Adesina. Adesina gave her a nervous smile, then followed Sharon.

Michelle, Robin, and Wally waited in the wings. The band settled into their chairs and put their music on the stands provided. Adesina and Asti plugged into their respective amps. Antonia set up her snare and played a couple of experimental riffs, then adjusted the provided drum kit to her liking. Marissa and Ghost played a few bars of "It Don't Mean a Thing (If It Ain't Got That Swing)," which made the kids in the audience laugh.

"If you're ready," said Dr. Smith.

Sharon raised her right hand, and the band immediately gave her their attention. Then she gave an upbeat and the band came in playing a medium-tempo version of Thelonious Monk's "'Round Midnight."

The bass laid down a soft beat with the drums. Asti started playing his guitar on the second bar. Peter, Sean, and Marissa each came in on subsequent bars. Peter stood and began playing the song's haunting melody. Playing it straight at first. Then gradually looping around it, changing it, playfully manipulating it.

He handed the solo off to Ghost. Michelle had expected her to play the sax, but she was on the clarinet instead. Ghost didn't toy with the melody as Peter had; instead, she played it straight, but so sad and mournfully it made Michelle want to cry.

Asti came in as Ghost finished her last note. Where her solo had been a virtuoso performance of wringing feeling from every simple note, his was complicated, building on some kind of internal variation of the melody he was channeling.

Then Asti stopped. A few bars later Marissa had her turn. Her fingers flew over the keyboard. Like Asti's, her solo was complicated, but where his had been strangely discordant to Michelle, Marissa's made sense to her uneducated ear.

As Marissa's solo ended, the band locked back into a tight groove. They played the original melody a few more times. Then they slowed and each instrument dropped out one at a time until only Adesina's bass remained. She played for another bar, then stopped.

There was appreciative applause from the audience. Everyone in the Mob broke out in big smiles. Michelle let out a sigh of relief.

But there was no time to wait between songs. Sharon counted them in and they zipped into a hot and fast rendition of "Jetboy Jump." As with "'Round Midnight" each musician took his or her turn at a solo— even Adesina. Between solos, the band would stop and they would all sing *Jetboy Jump* in unison, then whip back into the music.

This time after each solo, the audience applauded. At the end, they got whoops and yeahs! in addition to enthusiastic clapping.

As the Mob grabbed their music and started to leave the stage, black smoke suddenly began pouring into the auditorium, coming from beneath the stage. *Profoundly* stinky black smoke.

Are all the rotten eggs in here? Along with a generous topping of cat pee? Sweet baby Jesus! Michelle thought.

"Okay, guys," Michelle said, holding her hand over her nose and breathing through her mouth. Now it felt like she had rotten eggs and cat pee in her mouth. "We need to get out of here. Who knows what's going on. It might be a fire."

Sharon began whistling and signing. <Don't bother with your music and instruments. Let's just go. Wally, you and Ghost get out first.>

Despite this admonition, the kids picked up their instruments and scurried offstage.

Just then, there was an ominous creaking overhead. Michelle looked up. The bank of lights just behind the setup for the bands was swaying. *Yeah, that's so not good.*

"Look out!" Then Robin was sliding past her, stretching himself under the lights like a giant flesh pillow as they came crashing down.

The lights bounced off him and slammed into Michelle. They gave her a little whap and her belly pudged out with some fat. It felt wonderful.

What didn't feel wonderful was the stinking smoke, which seemed to be getting worse. It burned the hell out of her throat. She started coughing, then got up to see if Robin was okay. He'd pulled himself together into the semblance of a human shape and was pushing himself up from the floor. He didn't look quite right. Michelle grabbed his arm to steady him.

"Let's get out of here," she said.

Robin nodded. His face was contorted and squishy. "What an incredible smell you've discovered," he replied as he began coughing, too.

"Funny guy," she said. "Are you just trying to earn your geek badge of honor?"

They ran down the stage stairs and up the aisle toward the lobby doors. "Nope," he said, half coughing, half laughing. "Already got that one."

Outside, God's Weenies were in full swing. Their ranks had swelled to fifty and in unison they were chanting: "Jokers are scum! Keep us pure! Jesus hates jokers! Jokers are scum! Keep us pure! Jesus hates jokers! Jokers are scum! Keep us pure! Jesus hates jokers!"

New signs were on display: JOKERS WILL RESIDE IN HELL. JOKER LOVERS WILL RESIDE IN HELL. HELL IS FOR JOKER SCUM.

Oh, c'mon, God's Weenies, you can do better than that, Michelle thought. *How about JOKERS ARE ICKY AND WE DON'T LIKE THEM. Or maybe I'M AFRAID I MIGHT TURN INTO A JOKER, SO I'M BEING A BIG WUSS. Hmmmmmm, too wordy.*

It occurred to her that God's Weenies might have had something to do with the stink bomb. But she couldn't figure out how they could get into the building and set it off without someone seeing them.

Coming up the drive in front of the auditorium was a police officer on a bike. He looked sweaty and tired.

"Who's in charge here?" he asked wearily. He took his helmet off and mopped his forehead with a bandanna he'd pulled from his back pocket. Dark hair was sweat-plastered against his head. Across his forehead was a dark red mark where his helmet had rested. He had a broad nose, tawny skin, and walnut-colored eyes. And he wore the police bike patrol outfit: short-sleeved shirt and shorts that showed off his well-muscled legs.

Michelle looked around. All the other chaperones were with their bands and she couldn't see Dr. Smith anywhere.

"I guess I am," she replied. Her Committee voice kicked in. It seemed to be doing that a lot since they had arrived in San Antonio. "At least for now. And you are?"

"Officer Reyes. I got a call there was a disturbance here. Is it them?" He jerked his thumb toward God's Weenies.

"Well, they *are* being a pain," Michelle replied. "But the reason we called the police was because a stink bomb went off in the auditorium."

The officer gave her a long-suffering stare. "A stink bomb?" he said. "Really? You called the police for a prank?"

Now that he was saying it like that, it did seem a little bit of an overreaction. "Well, a bank of lights also fell on the stage right after the stink bomb went off."

"So, one of the lighting techs screwed up."

"It could have hit the children. I mean, the Mob had just finished playing. And they're jokers! And those ass clowns hate them." She pointed at God's Weenies and took a deep breath.

"Okay, tell you what. You and I will go back into the auditorium and we'll look around. You can't get hurt, right? You're the Amazing Bubbles, right?"

"Yes," she began. "But . . ."

"Ma'am, let's just get this over with." He sighed. "I don't know what I did to get the cycle shift and the kiddie calls, but here we are. You get a bunch of teenagers together, there's always going to be one idiot in the crowd."

Michelle pointed at God's Weenies. "Well, what about *them*?"

Officer Reyes got off his bike. He dropped the kickstand. Then he walked over to God's Weenies. "Okay," he said loudly.

The Purity Baptist Church continued to chant, "Jesus hates jokers!"

"For crying out loud, y'all settle down!"

God's Weenies just chanted louder.

"Protesters, move away from the auditorium stairs," he said again. "Or I'll make sure the press doesn't come close to here if you don't knock it off!"

The chanting stopped abruptly.

"Now move away from the steps, please," Officer Reyes said. God's Weenies shuffled down a few steps. "Now you know that's not what I meant. Go on down to the bottom, then down the driveway a piece."

"We might as well go home," said one of the protesters. Michelle recognized him from the other day: Earl Walker.

"That's right, Officer," said Betty Virginia. She wore an acid-green pantsuit today and her hair had a large magenta-colored, jeweled bow stuck in the middle of it. "We're just here doing the Lord's work. And also trying to make sure those jokers don't infect our city any more than it has been."

"It's wrong for our police to come and make us stop!" said the twins in unison. Today they wore T-shirts that had the word "Joker" with the universal sign for "No" superimposed over it.

"Well, there's nothing here to protest," Officer Reyes continued. He sighed. "I imagine things are over for the day."

With an impressive amount of whining, God's Weenies began walking down the driveway toward Auditorium Circle.

"Mrs. Pond," Officer Reyes said, "this is the way we prefer to deal with things of this nature here. I think we'll try and keep this as low-key as we possibly can."

"I realize that I may have overreacted," Michelle said acerbically. She did not like being on the defensive. "But they were threatening the children, some of them are armed, and all I did was restrain them harmlessly for a few minutes."

He shook his head. "Ma'am," he began. And now he sounded so long-suffering that it irritated the hell out of her. "Ma'am, this is Texas, where almost anyone can be armed. But restraining people against their will, now that's a crime."

"It's only a crime if there isn't a threat," Michelle said. She was bullshitting, but hoped he wouldn't want to get into it. "I'd argue they *were* acting in a threatening manner."

The cop shrugged. "I agree that you could see it that way," he said. "But let's face it, you scared the piss out of them and you *are* one hell of an ace. It's hardly a balanced situation. It being asymmetrical and all."

This really irked Michelle. "They weren't threatening me! They were threatening those teenagers. They had guns!"

"Ma'am," he said, "I shouldn't even be here. Childish pranks are childish pranks. But I'd like to get into some air-conditioning. It's beautiful weather, right up until you've been riding a cycle all morning."

♠

The stench from the stink bomb was horrible, but not quite as bad as it had been. The AC had been cranked up to the meat locker setting. And after a few hours of looking for any other threat, she had to admit that Officer Reyes had been right about it being a prank.

"Are you going to talk to the kids?" Michelle asked.

"Naw," the officer said. "I think whoever did this is probably scared as hell. Let's just let it ride. Teenagers can be idiots."

"I still think that light bank falling is suspicious."

"Ma'am," the officer said, "sometimes a stink bomb is just a stink bomb. And sometimes people forget to cinch the pulley tight enough.

Good thing the bomb went off when it did or someone might have been hurt by those falling lights."

Michelle crossed her arms. She'd been around enough hinky shit that this was pinging her something's-going-on sense. But she had no proof. Maybe she *was* being paranoid.

"I think we're done here," Officer Reyes said as they walked out of the auditorium. He put on his helmet and snapped the chin strap down. "I'm going to go file an incident report. Here's my card. Call and leave a message if you need to. But I think you really don't have a problem here." With that, he rode down the handicap ramp and out of sight.

Just then, Priscilla Beecher arrived. "Miss Pond," she said. She was a little out of breath, as if she'd been walking fast. "I've spoken with Dr. Smith. This incident is just a hiccup. Tomorrow morning she'll announce the bands who are moving forward in the competition."

Beats, Bugs, and Boys

Part 3

"WERE ANY OF THE jokers hurt?" LoriAnne asked with undisguised worry.

"They're all fine," Mr. Sloane reassured her, but his face stayed tense as he hustled them out of the Tobin Center and toward his vehicle.

LoriAnne desperately wanted more details, but she held back the rest of her questions. She'd never *ever* seen Mr. Sloane this angry. The jokers weren't even his students, and he'd been ready to tear apart whoever had set off the smoke bomb and dropped the lights.

A shiver raced down her back. Someone could have been killed! What kind of monster attacked *kids?*

Everyone piled into the SUV then remained silent as Mr. Sloane drove out of the parking lot. A small cluster of protesters huddled on the sidewalk, but they didn't do anything but watch Mr. Sloane drive past. LoriAnne had the feeling that if they'd set one toe on the street, he'd have gladly run them over.

After a couple of minutes he blew out a long breath, as if letting the anger go. "Y'all did a great job of keeping your heads back there," he said, glancing at them in the rearview mirror. "I was very proud of how you stayed calm and followed instructions."

"'Cause we're aaaaawesome," Greg said, preening.

Cassie frowned. "Mr. Sloane, you missed the turn for the hotel."

His eyes crinkled. "We're taking a little side trip."

To everyone's delight, the destination turned out to be an ice-cream parlor on the River Walk. "My treat," Mr. Sloane told them, and even got a triple-scoop cone for himself. Once everyone had ice cream, the Folsom Funkalicious Four sat by the river and watched the tour boats and people go by. By unspoken agreement, no one mentioned the competition or what happened or when they might find out which two bands would get the axe this round.

LoriAnne kept the skeeters away from her bandmates and let the roller-coaster tension of the day leach from her body. After the band finished their treats, they wandered the shaded paths along the River Walk, unhurried and with no particular goal in mind. When they grew bored of the river, they headed over to the Alamo, since they could hardly visit San Antonio without seeing it. The Alamo was a lot smaller than LoriAnne expected, but she took lots of pictures and read the various information plaques.

It was nearly six P.M. by the time they made it back to the hotel. Mr. Sloane gathered them by the elevators and praised them once again for how well they'd performed. "Dinner is at eight in the ballroom, and curfew is at ten for all competitors," he reminded them. "Everything else is free time. Y'all are good kids with good heads on your shoulders. Just remember, if you ever start to wonder if you're doing something stupid, there's a good chance you are."

Howard bumped Greg with his sax case. "That's easy for Greg. He's always doing something stupid."

"That's right!" Greg said.

A pained expression swept over Mr. Sloane's face. "Try to keep it to a minimum this week. For everyone's sake."

◆

Housekeeping had cleaned the room, made up the beds, and opened the curtains wide. While Cassie carefully put her things away, LoriAnne dumped her stuff on the bed and went to the window. They'd arrived after dark yesterday, so this was her first chance to see San Antonio from the room.

"Well, we have a great view of a parking lot," LoriAnne said with a laugh. Her gaze dropped lower. "And we're right over the pool." Oh man, a swim would be awesome right now. Not only did she still feel a bit grimy from barely showering this morning, but thanks to the smoke bomb, her mesquite-scented hair now also smelled like a rancid Fourth of July.

But best of all, there were jokers down there. Even from the seventh floor, LoriAnne had no trouble picking out shapes that weren't *quite* standard human. Sure, she'd succeeded in having a sort-of conversation with Antonia, but she still didn't have any *answers*.

"I think I'll go for a swim," she said, then, to be polite, added, "Wanna come?"

"Maybe next time," Cassie said, sorting through the books in her pack. "I'm going to do a little more sightseeing before it gets dark."

LoriAnne hid her relief. Under any other circumstance she'd be totally okay with doing pool time with Cassie, but how was she supposed to pick joker brains with her bandmate listening in?

Decision made, she dug through her suitcase and silently thanked her dad for insisting she pack a swimsuit. He'd managed his worry about having his baby going so far away by making meticulous lists in order to be absolutely sure nothing was forgotten. It was why she had fourteen pairs of underwear. For a weeklong trip.

"Extra undies don't take up much room," he'd told her when she protested packing so many. "There's nothing so sad as having a pile of dirty undies when you want clean ones."

Her dad was full of golden advice-nuggets like that.

She hurried to the bathroom to change, tugged on shorts and a T-shirt over the suit, then stuffed a towel, her phone, and her keycard into her backpack.

"You're taking your sticks?" Cassie cocked her head toward where they protruded from the side pocket.

"Just the practice ones," LoriAnne replied, and tried not to sound defensive. Truth was, she brought her sticks darn near everywhere and practiced beats whenever possible.

Cassie gave her a teasing smile. "And I thought *I* was a nerd."

LoriAnne grinned. "Dude, we're in band. We're *all* nerds."

♥

She took the elevator down, amusing herself with images of band-nerd jokers. As she approached the door to the pool area, a boy who couldn't have been much older than LoriAnne stepped through and held it open for her.

"Hey, a bit of advice," he said, and jerked his head toward the pool. "The jokers are out there, so you probably don't want to go in the water."

LoriAnne knew exactly what he was implying, but went ahead and offered him a perplexed look. "Why is that?"

He snorted, face scrunching in disgust. "You might catch what they have."

She widened her eyes. "Oh, no! They have impetigo?"

"What? No. They're *jokers*! You might catch the wild card virus."

"Ohhhhhhhhh," she said, then shook her head. "Whoever told you that was stupid. I mean *really* stupid." She beamed at him then continued outside.

Four jokers clustered near the deep end to her right. Adesina, Ghost, the boy with the color-rippled skin, and the bald pastel boy. No sign of Antonia, to LoriAnne's disappointment. At the opposite corner of the pool, a group of half a dozen nat teens sat by the shallow end—as far away from the jokers as possible. One brown-haired nat girl in a skimpy bikini kept sending longing glances at the water. LoriAnne could only assume she believed the crap about catching the virus.

Okay, you're at the pool. Now what? Be brave and go talk to the jokers? Shun them like all the cool kids were doing?

Well, shunning was obviously out of the question. LoriAnne started a casual saunter toward the jokers, but her bravery quickly fizzled out against their wary glares.

They're just kids, she scolded herself, but gave up and plopped her bag on an unoccupied chair halfway between the two groups. These were kids whose attitude screamed, *Don't mess with us.* Hard to blame them considering what had happened to them today.

The skeeter hummed a comforting melody in her hair as she tugged off her shirt and shorts. She loved having the skeeter near, but she sent it away before she forgot and went into the water with it.

"You're the drummer for the Louisiana band, right?"

LoriAnne whirled to see one of the nat boys standing a few feet away. Brown hair swept in waves past his jawline, and a nice smile hovered beneath dark and soulful eyes. "I saw you raise your hand in class today," he said. "I'm Basilio, the drummer for the Modesto Melody Makers."

"I'm LoriAnne," she said. "It's nice to meet you."

"You guys sounded great today." He gave a warm chuckle. "I saw a clip of one of your shows before we got here. I remember thinking your drummer had a lot of fire."

"That must have been Reese Fowler," she said. "He moved to Australia."

Basilio's mouth twitched. "No, it was fairly recent. Amazing drummer with really pretty hair."

"Huh. Then I guess it was me." She shrugged. "Did you check out the other bands beforehand, too?"

"Yeah, our director insists it's like football, where you watch the other team's old games to learn all their secrets." He rolled his eyes.

"And a one and a two and a *hut?*"

"Exactly!" His smile widened. "That's a quick wit you have there."

"Um, thanks," she said. "We watched videos of a few of the other bands, but Mr. Sloane told us to just trust ourselves and do our best."

Basilio shifted closer. "How long've you been drumming?"

"Since I was eleven," she said. "You?"

"I started when I was eight," he said. "You're really good for only playing a few years."

"It's about as long as the Mob's drummer has been playing, and she's pretty solid."

Basilio made a little scoffing noise in the back of his throat. "Sure, but she's a *joker,* so it's hardly a fair comparison. You're just as good without cheating."

LoriAnne stiffened with sudden sharp anger.

"No, wait, I didn't mean it like that—" He gulped as she speared him with her best ice-cold glare.

"Oh, really? You sound like one of those turdface protesters!"

Basilio's face twisted. "LoriAnne, please, lemme explain!"

As if. Keeping her glare at full throttle, she jerked her chin up and spun to march away.

And collided with a bare male chest. LoriAnne let out a yelp as she lost her balance and tilted precariously toward the pool. The boy made a grab for her. She clutched wildly at him, toppled, and—

Splash!

Mr. Bare-chest came down on top of her, pushing her under until the pool bottom scraped her hip. Water filled her nose and mouth, but before she could panic, strong hands seized her flailing arms and hauled her upright.

"Are you all right?" Mr. Bare-chest asked as she sputtered.

"Yeah," she said, coughing. "I'm good." At least the pool was only waist deep here. She cleared the water from her eyes then realized it was the pastel-skinned joker she'd seen in the lobby before breakfast. Except close up it wasn't odd at all, but a lovely light peach. His skin was peach fuzzy as well, and repelled the water the same way. Was it as soft? She let her hands drop to his forearms, as if she needed the help to remain standing. Yep. Soft. And six—no, *eight*-pack abs. Holy kamoley. Plus, now that he was close, she saw that the top of his head . . . *fizzed,* while an amazing peach scent wafted from him, subtle and enticing. It almost made up for the fact that everyone around the pool was laughing at her.

"I'm soooo sorry," she finally managed. "I wasn't looking where I was going. That boy was such an—ugh!"

"No worries," he said. His gaze tracked Basilio's return to the other nats.

She suppressed a sigh of disappointment as he released her. "I'm LoriAnne. From the Folsom Funkalicious Four."

"I'm Asti." He gave her a wonderfully kind smile then gestured toward his head. "Probably don't need to tell you I'm with the Jokertown Mob."

"I kind of figured that much out," she said with a light laugh. "I'm sorry, I didn't get to see much of your set. What do you play?"

"Guitar. You?"

"Drums."

"That's pretty cool. You a fan of Drummer Boy?"

"Ugh. No." Then she hurried to add, "But not because he's a joker! I don't like him because he's a jerk."

Asti laughed. "Yeah, I hear you. Antonia thinks Drummer Boy is a complete tool, and I can't help but agree with her. I don't know if you've ever watched *American Hero,* but—"

"Only every single episode," she said, but held off adding "twice."

"Yeah? Have you had a chance to meet the Amazing Bubbles? She's super-nice."

"Um, not yet." LoriAnne wasn't about to tell him that she'd completely frozen up when faced with Bubbles in the elevator. "I haven't met Rustbelt or Rubberband either."

"Maybe I can introduce you." Amusement flashed in his eyes. His gorgeous amber eyes. "I mean, since you obviously aren't afraid you'll catch the virus by breathing the same air—or being in the same water." He shot a look at the nat bikini girl.

"I'm not afraid of the virus," LoriAnne said quickly. "And it would totally rock if I could meet one of the aces. But what I'd like to know, um, ask you . . ." She groped for the right words.

"You want to know about this?" He swept a hand out to indicate the peach-skin and effervescent scalp.

She blew out a breath. "Yeah. Sorry. I'm being nosy. You don't have to tell me anything."

Asti chuckled. "I don't mind. I'd rather people ask than have them jump to conclusions."

Gorgeous and *nice*! "How old were you when your card turned?"

"Eleven and a half," he said. "I had eczema ever since I was a baby. Nothing too awful. I mean, I wasn't covered in it or anything, but there was always a patch on my legs and shoulders. One day the doc prescribed a new cream for it, and about a week later, the eczema spread to my entire body. I was one giant scab."

"Oh my God," LoriAnne breathed. "That must've been horrible."

"It was," he said. "Mom freaked and called an ambulance. I remember listening to her argue with the ER doctor. Then the itching went insane. I started clawing at the scabs, and where they peeled off, I had all this underneath. I was lucky. It all turned out okay for me."

This was okay? Yet LoriAnne also realized it could've been a whole lot worse. "You don't mind being a joker?"

"I'd be lying if I said it never bugged me," he said. "But I was a bit of a freak already with the weird skin."

"Still, because you have the virus, you're . . ."

"Labeled?"

"Yeah. That's not right."

"I agree, but—" His gaze went past LoriAnne, and his smile brightened. "Hey, how's it going? I'm Asti."

LoriAnne swung around to see Basilio wading toward them from the direction of the nat herd. Her eyes narrowed in a glare. What the heck was he up to? Why did he have to pick *now* to interrupt? And why did Asti have to be so darn friendly?

"Basilio," he replied, offering a hand to Asti. "Does the fizz make real air?"

Asti shook his hand. "A little," he said, then added with a laugh, "But not enough to keep anyone alive underwater."

LoriAnne ground her teeth in annoyance as she watched Basilio's display. It was obvious he was putting on this I-love-jokers act in a pathetic attempt to cover for being a turd.

"LoriAnne, I'd like to start over," Basilio said. "A few of us are going to walk down to the Alamo then get ice cream. A pre-dinner dessert sort of thing. Wanna come?"

"Sorry, I've already been to the Alamo today *and* had ice cream," she said with a tight smile. "Besides, I have to dry my hair before dinner. It takes a *really* long time."

His face fell, but then he shrugged. "That's cool. Maybe I'll see you around later. You too, Asti. It was nice meeting you."

"Likewise," Asti said. He watched Basilio leave the pool then returned his attention to LoriAnne. "What happened between you two?"

LoriAnne winced. She really didn't want to tell him about Basilio's joker comment and possibly upset him. "We got off on the wrong foot, that's all." One side of her mouth quirked up. "And I actually wasn't fibbing about drying my hair. It's too heavy if I leave it wet, and I end up with a crick in my neck."

"That's so tragic," he said, eyes sparkling.

Cell phones all around the pool began to ring, beep, and vibrate. "It's the results!" Adesina cried. "We made the cut!" With a whoop of delight, she seized Ghost up and tossed her into the pool. Or rather, at the pool, since Ghost went ghost right before hitting the water and hovered above it.

At the other end of the pool, several teens jumped to their feet with exultant shouts. "Plano! Plano!"

LoriAnne gulped. "What about Folsom?"

"Folsom made it," said one of the nat boys who wasn't cheering. His eyes skimmed over his phone. "Seattle and Detroit didn't."

Bikini girl burst into tears then grabbed her towel and ran back into the hotel. The boy with the phone shrugged. "Oh well. At least now I don't have to practice every night while I'm here."

LoriAnne spared a few seconds for sympathy then let the joyous relief pound through her. "Congratulations," she told Asti.

"You, too," he said, smiling broadly. "But I'd better let you go so you can dry your hair. I guess I'll see you at the competition tomorrow!" With that he turned, dove underwater, and swam toward the other jokers, leaving a trail of tiny bubbles in his wake.

Well, crap. So much for more time with Asti. Tripped up by the dumb I-have-to-dry-my-hair line. Jeez!

You have all week, she reminded herself. Plenty of time to find out everything she might ever want to know about living with the virus.

But later in the week wasn't *now*. And LoriAnne had to admit she was interested in Asti for reasons that went way beyond his potential as a source of information. Asti was *hot*.

However, even jokers had to eat, which meant he'd most likely be at the dinner tonight. Maybe it was a good thing she'd fibbed about drying her hair. Now she had ample time to get cleaned up for dinner.

♠ ♥ ♦ ♣

The Secret Life
of Rubberband

Part 5

IT WAS ALMOST—*ALMOST*—a relief when the afternoon performance turned interesting. Assholes set off a stink bomb, not even a threat, really, but it did concentrate the mind, and give Robin something to do. The falling lights, those pissed him off. Poor rigging or sabotage? Someone could have been hurt. But they kept the kids together, and their spirits up, and after Michelle's speech—she had a way with words—they walked the kids home.

He'd almost forgotten about his kitchen adventure by the time they returned to see fire engines parked in front of the hotel.

"Whoa, Mr. R—what happened?"

"Think someone set off a stink bomb here, too?"

"I can't say," he said, almost truthfully. "I heard there was an accident in the kitchen."

"Was it the ghost?"

Robin spent a critical few seconds searching for words, enough time for Jacobson to come to his rescue with, "We all know the place's haunted."

"I don't think it's a ghost," he said, though he wasn't certain what it was. Anyway, the ambulance had already left, empty, thank God—Jan found the dough boy's inhaler in time, and the burns from the spilled stock hadn't been anything a bit of overeager first aid couldn't treat, and the chef's ankle was probably only sprained anyway. Robin might have cursed the combat medic challenge during his *American Hero* days, but his skills—plus Jan's leather jacket, which contained enough ointments, creams, antibiotics, and salves to sterilize just about everything in East Texas that wasn't already wasteland—came in handy now and again.

He hadn't anticipated ghosts to be so slippery.

To be fair, he hadn't anticipated ghosts to be anything at all. In his experience, ghosts were something that most certainly weren't. (Excepting, of course, the occasional intangible wild card, like Yerodin, who just happened to *call* herself Ghost. But that was different.)

Whatever that blue-gray thing with the enormous mouth was, it most certainly existed. If Robin still possessed a circulatory system, he would have had the bruises to prove it. The "ghost" was solid—when it wanted to be. It was light—unless it wanted to be heavy. When he reached for it, it had grabbed his hand and swung hard enough to slam him into the wall, if he had bones like a normal person. Instead, it only tore his sleeve and bent one of his arms one hundred eighty degrees below the wrist, which had the positive effect of making the chef stop swearing, and the negative effect of making the chef vomit.

He'd wrapped his arms around the ghost, but it wriggled free; he'd wrapped his entire torso around the ghost, but it wafted through his skin, leaving only a clammy chill. Then it jumped on the stove, upended the stockpot, and life got interesting in the racist joke sense.

Entering the hotel lobby, he expected the desk clerks to point and scream and go for the whole *Invasion of the Body Snatchers* routine, but either his exploits or his description hadn't reached the desk staff yet.

Sharon, though, was signing at one of their hosts about the presence, or absence, of dinner. <What do you mean, there's no food?>

The attendant stammered something about a kitchen accident. The hotel was calling around, they were going to set up a Mexican buffet, but it was all so last minute and such a large order, so many kids, he couldn't say how long. . . .

"Sharon," Robin said, "it's okay. I'll go out with Wally and get the kids pizza."

She glared at him. <The hotel sponsorship *covers* restaurant meals.>

Shit. "I can—" He stopped himself, unsure what he could do. Pay for pizza? With the last of his cash, sure, if they found a cheap enough place. He could keep the receipt, get reimbursed. But they hadn't caught the ghost yet, and his chances of begging Jan for the second half of his ghost bounty without actually delivering said ghost were about the same as her chances of convincing him of the immediate reptoid threat beneath their very soles.

<I'm waiting for suggestions.>

"Shit," said Jerry Jeff Longwood in two syllables, sidling up spurs jangling beside Robin. "I don't mean to interrupt—"

Sharon wasn't good at keeping her emotions to herself. She colored beet red, then paled, then flushed an entirely different sort of violet. A slow whistle escaped her lips. If she could speak, this would have been the time to say "Mister Longwood," in the kind of low breathy swoon you only ever heard in movies after someone had applied vaseline to the lens. If someone swapped Sharon's and Robin's cards, she would have been a puddle.

"Anything I can help y'all with? I was just fixin' to drop by and wait until ol' Rob here could wiggle free for supper."

Perhaps there was an upside to this wrecked-kitchen fiasco after all. "Jerry Jeff, something went wrong with the hotel kitchen, and I need to find pizza for our kids. I won't be able to make it to dinner. I'm so sorry."

Jerry Jeff looked from Robin, to Sharon, to the kids—*Look hungry, kids,* Robin tried to tell them with his eyes, but they weren't looking at him. "Well," he said, and his shoulders slumped, and Robin's relief grew.

But before Jerry Jeff could say another word, vaseline-lens Sharon trilled protest, and signed, cutting, sharp, <Nonsense! Robin, you are going out to dinner with Jerry Jeff Longwood.> Her hands rounded when she signed his name. <And that is final.>

"We need to solve the dinner problem."

"I can help y'all take care of that! I know a great barbecue place, three, four blocks from here. Cheap, too! We'll drive . . . aw, no, we'll just walk over there, bring the barbecue back, all them kids get to eat, and then Robin and I dip out for supper. How's that sound?"

"Can you excuse me, Jerry Jeff?" He took Sharon by the arm and escorted her a few steps to the side. She craned her neck to look over her shoulder at Jerry Jeff. "Sharon, the kids should be our number one priority, here. I know I let things slip this afternoon, I'm so sorry, but I want to make amends—"

<You were five minutes late.> No mention of the flour, or the dough on his ear. <Thank you for the apology. The kids do come first. But Jerry Jeff Longwood—> Again, those awed, rounded gestures. <Jerry Jeff Longwood has just offered to help buy our students dinner. How many chances will they have to eat with someone like that?>

Entirely too many for Robin's taste, it seemed. No matter his thoughts on the subject.

♣

The steak smelled divine, looked better. Fragrant juices oozed, and the grill-seared fat crackled as Jerry Jeff cut in.

"Are you sure you don't want nothin' steak-like?"

"I'm sure," Robin lied, and sipped the cheapest glass of wine on the menu. "It's been a long, long day." True. "And I don't think a steak would do me any good." Manifestly, disgustingly, obscenely false, so false his stomach wanted to climb his spinal column to throttle his brain. But he gnawed his $20 chicken Caesar salad, and did his best not to eye Jerry Jeff's rib eye ($55), and to contain his appetite for mashed potatoes ($18), grilled asparagus ($16), and sautéed wild mushrooms ($don't ask).

"It's just that I'm feelin' right uncharitable, you treatin' me like this and then eatin' so much less. If it's about money—"

"No, no, no," *yes yes*. "Not about money at all, we're doing fine. Just like I said. No appetite. Been a bit worn out recently."

"Ain't that the truth." Jerry Jeff raised his glass of wine ($16) and touched the lip of Robin's ($7). The crystal rang. "To rest and recovery, once this whole bit is done for you. Glad those young'uns took to the barbecue, though. I figure it's not like anything they ever tasted before."

"You can get a lot of things in New York," Robin said. "But they did seem to like it." Jerry Jeff had ordered the barbecue—the cooks and clerk recognized him, cheered, snapped selfies—and he paid, too, waving off Robin's protests that the school would reimburse him, that he'd feel much more comfortable if Jerry Jeff wouldn't—

But Jerry Jeff did. He dropped a hundred on the counter, keep the change. The kids inhaled the barbecue; Ghost went back for thirds. Even Antonia seemed to like it, though her expression as she ate was one of grudging acceptance, rather than anything Robin would describe as "pleasure."

(There *had* to be something wrong. At school, she was intense, driven, quiet, but never this bad. Could she have trouble at home? Her mom was a paralegal, her dad the junior partner in a flower shop, they came to every teacher's meeting and were the kind of in love that made some people uncomfortable to be around—if family was the root of her problem, it must have been sudden. More likely something had come between her and the other kids. But there were four chaperones, not counting Jan, and none of *them* had seen anything. . . .)

Jerry Jeff, he realized, was talking, and had been for a while. "I'm so sorry. I was a million miles away."

"Shucks, it ain't nothing you need trouble yourself with. I was just, in my old rambling sort of way, working round to asking you for, you know, what your day was like, tellin' me a little about your life like it is now. I don't mind all this jee-jawing over what we've done that's past, the teevee shows and tricks, and I'll spin a yarn as easy as the next cowpoke, but I want to hear about the secret life of Robin Ruttiger."

His eyes were small black sharp points, and Robin told himself later that he hadn't shifted in his chair, hadn't played with his fork or touched his temples or looked up and to the right. "There's not much to tell, Jerry Jeff. Really there's not." *A dirty apartment, a bad salary, a job I love except when I'm sucking at it, like I feel I am now.* "I'm sure your life is a lot more exciting: career, kids, fame, fortune, and glory. You were all about that back on the show. You wanted to be Wild Bill of the new millennium, and now you are. What's Taylor Swift like in person? Any new movies in the pipe?"

Jerry Jeff leaned back in his chair. His hat brim dipped across his eyes. Mustaches twitched. They only looked prehensile—Jerry Jeff's card didn't turn that way. He stabbed a piece of steak, passed it between his thin lips, and chewed.

Great idea, Robin. Deflect every attempt your friend's making to express interest, throw his questions back in his face, and when all else fails dive into the kind of crap *Entertainment Weekly* interview questions the pop culture reporters spear him with whenever a new album drops.

"Actually," Robin said, knowing as he spoke that this was a bad idea, but not having a good idea to hand, "there is this one thing going on right now that might interest you."

Jerry Jeff's eyes emerged from the shelter of his hat.

Robin had started making this mistake—he might as well finish it. "I'm hunting a ghost."

♠ ♥ ♦ ♣

Bubbles and the
Band Trip

Part 7

WHEN MICHELLE, WALLY, SHARON, and the Mob returned to the Gunter full of barbecue, there was a buzz in the air. Over by the elevators stood the Modesto Melody Makers in a circle, most of them crying. Some of the kids from the other bands were scattered around the lobby, whispering to one another.

LoriAnne immediately rushed over to Michelle and the Mob and said breathlessly, "Mindy-Lou Gutiérrez is missing!"

The Mob started peppering her with questions all at once.

"Oh, this is something bad, you betcha!" Wally exclaimed. Sharon whistled in agreement. The kids all looked stricken.

Dr. Smith came over to join them. She took Michelle by the arm and dragged her away from the group. "Mindy-Lou Gutiérrez has gone missing!" she said. "It's horrible. We've never lost a student before!"

"I heard. When was the last time anyone saw her?"

Dr. Smith ran her hand through her hair nervously then tugged at the bottom of her gray suit jacket. "This afternoon, at her set. Some of the other girls said they saw her talking to a boy afterwards. An older boy, not one of the band members. Jillian said he was one of the bartenders from the mixer."

Michelle groaned inwardly. She had a sneaking suspicion she knew where this was going. "Who saw her last?"

"Bacho. He's the bass player for the Lubbock band. Is there any way you can help find her? Maybe contact the Committee? With all their powers . . ."

Michelle put her hands on her hips. She was thinner than normal today, having decided that walking around with bubbling weight might seem like she was spoiling for a fight. Which, in all fairness, she was. But defusing the Purity Baptist Church situation by looking less threatening seemed like a good idea. It also allowed her to wear her Levi's and a nice sea-green cashmere T-shirt that matched her eyes. She had her long, platinum-colored hair in a fishtail braid.

"This really isn't a Committee kind of thing," Michelle replied. "The United Nations doesn't usually deal with missing persons. Let me talk to Bacho. I'll see what I can do."

Dr. Smith went to fetch Bacho and led him back to Michelle. The boy had long dark hair and a sand-colored complexion. He seemed very poised for his age.

"Hey, there." Michelle held out her hand. He took it and gave it a quick shake. His hand was dry and warm. "I'm Michelle."

"I'm Bacho. And I know who you are. We all do."

"I heard you were the last person to see Mindy-Lou."

"Yeah. We were about to go on for our set, and the Modesto kids were coming off. She was talking with that bartender."

"The pretty boy?"

"Yeah, guess so. He was chatting her up and she seemed to like it. I remembered him from the mixer. He seemed a little dumb. How complicated is a three-drink order when two of them are Cokes?"

Billy Rainbow, Michelle thought. "Thanks, Bacho, that was a big help."

"It's cool," he replied. "Mindy-Lou is a great musician. And, well, I hope nothing serious has happened to her."

"Me too." After he had gone, Michelle turned back to Dr. Smith. "Sounds like she ran off with that bartender. She's probably infatuated with him, but he's definitely too old for her. Kids can be so dumb sometimes. I swear, they're walking hormones."

"Should we call the police?" Dr. Smith asked. "Her bandmates are worried sick, and her parents have been calling. . . ."

"She hasn't been gone long enough for the police to get involved,"

Michelle said. "Her parents could hire someone, though. A skip tracer or private detective should be able to find them quickly."

Dr. Smith looked relieved. "I'll tell them."

♠

When Michelle got off the elevator, she could hear the Mob playing. But they weren't playing jazz. They were doing a cover of "Gimme Shelter." Marissa and Adesina were on vocals. The music was also loud. Like call-the-cops loud.

The music was coming from the girls' room. She knocked on the door. Nothing. She knocked again, louder this time. "Don't make me bubble my way through this door!" she said as she pounded on the door.

The music stopped abruptly. There was frantic whispering, and then Marissa opened the door. The band was spread out. Some were sitting on the beds, some stood leaning against the wall. Adesina and Asti sat on their amps.

"Ms. Pond," Marissa said. "We, er . . ."

"Hi, Mom," Adesina said with only a hint of guilt. "What's up? I mean, what's going on with the whole stink bomb thing?"

Michelle narrowed her eyes. She put her hands on her hips. "You do know you could get into all sorts of trouble for playing that loud in here. Right?"

Asti, Sean, and Antonia got hangdog expressions on their faces. The rest of the band seemed equally chagrined.

"We just thought, since we were in here," Adesina began. "And nothing was going on . . ."

Michelle glared at her daughter. This new incarnation of Adesina was embracing stupid teenage shit at an alarming rate.

"Where's Rusty and Robin?" Michelle asked. Not only were the kids being morons, but now her other chaperones were AWOL.

"Wally told us not to leave our rooms. He took Ghost to get ice cream. And Mr. Ruttiger said he was going downstairs to meet up with Mr. Longwood. He also told us not to leave our rooms. And Miss Beecher told us to stay here, and she went to look for you."

Michelle cocked her head to one side. "And why are you all in one room?"

"Well, technically, we haven't left our rooms, we've just consolidated," Peter said. Then he looked mortified.

"I think you should all get to your own rooms and stay there. No consolidation!"

♠   ♥   ♦   ♣

The Secret Life
of Rubberband

Part 6

"I'M NOT PAYING MORE for the extra help," Jan said when Robin arrived at the Gunter with Jerry Jeff in tow. Or, more to the point, when Jerry Jeff arrived with Robin in tow. Having opened his mouth in the first place, Robin spent the rest of dinner and dessert—ricotta cheesecake with graham cracker crumble crust ($13)—trying to convince Jerry Jeff that no, he really did not want to join in Jan's madcap, destructive, and definitely illegal hunt for the ghost (or, depending on your theological position, demon) of the Gunter Hotel. Jerry Jeff couldn't afford to get his name mixed up in a lawsuit. Jerry Jeff was a public figure, and Robin would so much rather not end up in a paparazzi photo captioned *Ex-Star Goes Ghost Hunting*.

Jerry Jeff's response was to grin more. And the grin just got wider after Robin paid the check (all of Jan's first half in advance, plus fifty he had to borrow from Jerry Jeff, with promises of repayment when they reached the hotel), and led the way. By the time they found Jan, Jerry Jeff could have given the ghost (or demon) a run for its grin money, in breadth at least if not in malice.

"I ain't in this for compensation." He took Jan's hand and, without pause or warning, bent low and kissed the knuckles of her glove. She glared at him over her glasses. "Robin described the general outline of your predicament—y'all can find the varmint, and grab it, but you need to hold it once you have. You need a rope hand."

The blue lights of Jan's eyes vanished and returned as she blinked. "I never thought about it that way."

Jerry Jeff patted the rope at his belt. "Old Delilah's never yet let anything slip her loop, not so long as I hold her end."

Jan turned from Jerry Jeff to Robin, to Jerry Jeff, to Robin again. Robin hadn't seen Jan this flummoxed since someone suggested to her that the Franz Ferdinand assassination had been the work of an isolated anarchist cell, rather than a conspiracy between the Freemasons and the Bavarian illuminati.

"Whatever," she said once she solved the halting problem. "Follow me."

She led them through the lobby. The smell of chlorine grew fiercer as they neared the pool. "The ghost hasn't manifested for the last four hours—but I felt a buzz twenty minutes back, when I texted you. When the buzz started, it was faint, and everywhere, but it's been concentrating over time, shifting around, trying to avoid me: I'd chase the concentration to one part of the hotel, but it would disperse and reform somewhere else. So I just read the news"—she raised her folded *National Enquirer*—"and let it gather, which it's been doing, in the pool. If we're lucky, we might be able to catch it in the act of—"

Robin heard a spectral snicker, followed by a boy's scream.

He ran. The others followed seconds later.

Robin slammed through the door into the pool, and saw Asti dangling by the ghost's grip on his ankle over the deep end. The ghost rode the crest of a wave circling the pool, in contravention of all laws of physics anyone had ever explained to Robin, while swimmers scrambled for the sides.

The ghost saw Robin and Jan, and cackled so hard it bent double.

Then it threw Asti at them.

Asti screamed, tumbling heels over head through the air. If no one caught him, he'd break against the wall.

Robin thrust his hands out as far as they'd go, clutching light fixtures, and spread his chest wide and flat. His shirt and pants tore. His skin strained.

Asti hit Robin hard, and Robin's chest folded around him like a blanket. Robin gasped and gagged for air. The stomach he no longer had did a backflip. But Asti was safe. Robin let the light fixtures go and snapped back into a tangled heap on the floor around the kid, waiting for his body to sort itself out, too weak to move.

The few swimmers remaining had emptied the pool. The ghost gamboled atop its standing wave, and thrust out one spindly three-fingered hand. A whip of water cut across the pool deck, scattering lawn chairs and purses. It howled with joy, and lashed the deck once more.

Jan stepped over the stretched tangle of Robin's arms, removed her glove, and stuck her electrified hand in the pool.

A sharp pop cut through cries and laughter. Swimming pool light-bulbs burst. The ghost juddered like a lightning-struck cartoon char-acter, sharp teeth gnashing around its long red tongue. Its scream shivered the jelly beneath Robin's skin, a sound so high-pitched and furious it was barely sound at all.

Jan slumped.

The ghost, shaking, leapt free of the wave, and bounced off a wall. It landed on a running student, sprawling her flat, then jumped from her onto a tall boy's shoulders, pulling his hair. He screamed, slipped, and the ghost sprang free as he fell—

Only for a golden loop to settle around its shoulders and pull tight.

Jerry Jeff whooped. The ghost hit the ground hard, arms bound to its sides. It twisted and spit. Clawed feet found purchase on tile, and it forced itself upright. Jerry Jeff tugged the lasso, but the ghost crouched low and began to run. Jerry Jeff slipped on wet tiles, and the ghost, bound, pulled him into and across the pool, sputtering, hollering, but still holding fast to the lasso.

Robin, by this point, had recovered. Clothes hung from him like ribbons, but he wore elastic underwear in case of just such an emer-gency. Asti lay groaning on the tile, but fine. Robin staggered over to Jan. "Are you—"

"I'm okay! Go after that thing!"

The ghost burst into the gym, dragging a sprawled, soaked Jerry Jeff behind it. Robin followed, just in time to duck a thrown dumbbell as he ran through the door. The ghost kicked more weights his way; he dodged one, but the next bounced off his chest, and he fell over.

As Robin found his feet, screams and motion drew his eye to the corner of the gym: a red-haired boy, upright, adjusting his shirt, glancing around in confusion as if he had no clue how he'd arrived in this weight room, surely not in the company of a red-faced blond nat, who was, for her part, trying very hard to look as if she were not hitching up her bra. *At least they're not mine,* Robin thought. He made a mental note to check in with some of the other chaperones about appropriate behavior on school trips, after he hunted down this ghost.

The ghost darted between the bars of a squat rack, dragging the rope through a narrow gap in the metal. Jerry Jeff, dragged like a water-skier, swept his feet around to brace himself against the rack. The lasso went taut and the ghost snapped short, snarling. The squat rack scraped against the floor. Jerry Jeff tugged back, and the ghost flailed.

Robin ran toward it. "Give it more slack, Jerry Jeff!"

"I do and it'll just scramble away!"

"Trust me!"

"Gol-durn varmint!" Robin wasn't sure whether Jerry Jeff was talking to him or to the ghost, but he let out more rope—and before the ghost could take advantage, Robin stretched his arms to loop the slack around the ghost's ankles. The ghost landed on its side, hard, and fought to its feet again, but Robin pushed it over and rolled it back toward the squat rack, wrapping layer after layer of rope around the spectral form until only its wicked broad mouth was free.

Then, because Robin was worried about the fangs, he stuffed some rope in the mouth, too. The ghost kicked and hissed; they squeezed it through the squat rack, while Jerry Jeff held tight to his end of the lasso to keep the ghost bound.

They had taken care of everything when Jan burst through the door and rolled to her feet, forefinger pointed before her like a gun, blue light sparking about her nail. "Take cover!"

◆

Dripping, spark-scorched, smoking, they limped upstairs to Jan's niece's room. The ghost writhed between them, wrapped in Jerry Jeff's lasso and Robin's arms. Jan knocked; no answer. Jan knocked more; whispers from beyond the door.

When Jan started kicking, the door opened to reveal a teenager in curlers and unicorn pajamas. Before the girl could say anything, Jan brushed past. "Vicky! We've caught your ghost."

Robin and Jerry Jeff hesitated on the threshold, glancing uncertainly at each other. The kid in the curlers hustled after Jan: "She's sleeping. You can't wake her up!"

"Watch me," Jan said.

"No! I mean, you don't—you really can't wake her up."

"Nonsense. I'm her aunt. Robin, bring the ghost in here."

Robin glanced at the girl in curlers, who rolled her eyes and said, "Sure. But you can't wake her. She fell asleep doing homework about an hour ago. I dragged her onto the bed, and she didn't even stir."

"You didn't think this was weird?" Robin said.

The kid shrugged. "Happened to her this afternoon. She gets these episodes sometimes—narcoleptic." She looked proud of knowing the word.

Vicky lay, fully dressed, arms folded, on the bed, paler and more rigid than anyone Robin had ever seen sleeping. Jan touched her shoulder.

Vicky didn't stir.

"Hey, kid, wake up. We got your ghost."

No response.

Jan shook her shoulder. The ghost in Robin's arms twitched and snarled beneath Jerry Jeff's rope.

Jan shook harder. "Kid? Hey, Vick. Come on. Wake up."

The ghost spasmed and jabbered.

Vicky's lips twitched. Her fingers clutched the cross around her neck. But she didn't open her eyes.

"Vick, come on, you're scaring me."

And as she shoved her, Robin remembered Vicky, earlier that day, in the lobby, talking with Yerodin—then napping on a sofa while the ghost knocked over Robin's luggage cart.

"Vick, look, we caught it! It's not a ghost, or a demon, just some sort of plasma thing. A local ace screwing around. And we got him."

Robin turned to the kid in the curlers, and realized he didn't know her name.

"Angelica."

"Angelica," he said. "Sorry. Did—did you say that Vicky took a nap this afternoon?"

"Yeah. Around three. I came in and the lights were off."

Robin licked his lips. He thought about the card—thought about how he'd felt after his own turned, how scared he'd been, how alone. He thought about Vicky's fierce control in the hotel bar, about the thin line of her lips when Jan said ghosts did not exist. He thought about how scared you could be of yourself, especially at fifteen. "Jan, I . . ." Jan turned on him, glaring. "I think we should let the ghost go."

"Are you nuts? After how much trouble it was to catch the thing? I want to show Vicky she doesn't have anything to be afraid of."

"Jan," he said. "Look at her mouth."

Vicky's lips twitched, and the ghost yowled.

And the one happened at the same time as the other.

"Jerry Jeff," Robin said, "let her go."

Jerry Jeff looked from him, to her, to her. He released the rope.

The ghost vanished.

Vicky's eyes fluttered open. "Aunt Jan? What happened? What are you doing here?"

She looked afraid. Desperate to hide her secret.

She must have turned young, and woken from her illness full of power she did not understand. Power that scared her, that she loved, that she could not let herself love. Power she made into a demon.

He watched Jan's face. Jan, who'd turned as an adult. Jan, who worked so fiercely to expose truth, however weird that truth might be; Jan, who chased down ghosts and rooted out falsehood and had so little belief in comforting lies that she made up horrifying lies in their place.

Jan, who turned back to her niece, and said, "We found the ghost, Vick." The girl went still. "But she got away from us. And . . ." She searched herself a long time to find the next words. "I think she's not that bad a ghost after all. She's powerful. Mischievous. But not bad."

Vicky's mouth twisted. Her body wrung, and she curled the comforter about herself. She sat up, and brought her knees to her chest, and stared into the covers between her bare feet. "What if she hurts someone?"

"I'll be around," Jan said. "And I'll help."

♥

Jan slipped Robin the second half of the money before he left: a hand-shake with rumpled bills inside, to solemnize a conspiracy. He paid Jerry Jeff the fifty he'd been loaned at dinner, and walked him to his car.

The night lay heavy on the San Antonio parking lot pavement, and Jerry Jeff's boot heels clicked. Robin made no sound. Jerry Jeff hooked his thumbs through his belt, and looked back and up at the moon. "Boy, though, did you even *see* that? Just like old times, weren't it? You with the arms and me with the rope, and that friend of yours ain't half bad herself, could have used her on the set back in the old days I tell you what." He whistled through his teeth. "That's some proper hero-ing we did there."

Robin looked skyward for advice, but the moon had none to offer. "I don't know," he said. "I guess. I'm glad Jan handled it well. And the kid seemed to understand."

Jerry Jeff's eyes flicked sideways toward Robin, beneath the brim of his hat. They walked in silence past rows of cars. "You're good at this," Jerry Jeff said. "This is a good life for you."

"What do you mean?"

"You've always wanted to take care of people. I'm glad to see you doing it."

He stopped in front of a cherry-red pickup truck.

"Welp," Jerry Jeff said, "this is me."

A blanket covered the pickup's bench seat, and a pillow scrunched against one wall. Tufts of rumpled clothes sprouted from a backpack on the floor. A fly buzzed around a pile of takeout containers in the passenger seat.

Robin turned. Jerry Jeff looked down at the embellished tips of his boots.

"Jerry Jeff, are you sleeping in your car?"

"Aw," Jerry Jeff said. "Yes."

Robin set his hand on Jerry Jeff's shoulder. He didn't think he could say anything to help, so he said nothing at all.

"There's trouble at home," Jerry Jeff said. "All my fault, of course. I done wrong, Robin. In the music, in the lights, in the teevee, somewhere along the line, I just done wrong. I couldn't stay anymore, I couldn't hurt her like that. So I packed the car, and took the royalty check that showed up that afternoon, and I left. Didn't know where I was going. I drove north and then I drove south again. I ran through the money. I drove east, and I read your name in a paper in a diner, and I thought, shit, if anyone knows what to do, it's old Rubberband." His eyes glittered. "Happiest days of my life were on that dumb show. And here I seen you happy, with your kids and your life. You made something real. I just tried to be a shadow of a cowpoke."

Robin closed his mouth, and pulled Jerry Jeff into an embrace. Jerry Jeff breathed slow; his mustaches rubbed Robin's cheek. He felt light as dried wood.

Robin said, "I'm happy. And I'm broke, and I'm single, and I'm miserable, and I miss it all, too. I have debts and I'm failing my students one damn day at a time. I'm doing the right thing and I'm doing the wrong thing. I don't even know what I'm doing anymore."

Jerry Jeff's laugh was big and wet. "You're sure as hell doing something, though."

"Yeah," Robin said, "and when you showed up, I thought, there's my buddy Jerry Jeff, who had everything figured out way back when, who has this whole career set out for him, while I can't win for losing."

Jerry Jeff held the hug longer, and Robin let him. When he broke, Robin said, "I'll be here all week, if the competition goes well. But—come visit me in New York. You can stay until everything gets sorted out. Here." He slid the spare key off his key ring, and scribbled his address on the back of a receipt. "Go to my place. If the neighbors hassle you, tell them I said you could stay. The walrus next door comes on strong, but he's a nice guy when you get to know him. And . . ." He took Jan's money from his other pocket.

"Shit, Robin, I can't—"

"You can. It's a gift. You'll figure this thing out, whatever it is. It might take time. But, hey. Wrecks like us have to take care of each other."

Jerry Jeff looked from the money, to Robin. He took the bills. "A loan."

"A gift," Robin said.

"I'll be waiting for you in New York. I can get a job, I don't want to wear out your welcome."

"You're a guest," he said. "Stay as long as you need."

Jerry Jeff hugged him again. "Thanks, pardner."

"You can sleep in my room here, if you like. Rustbelt's already got the other bed, but we can split."

"Nah. Bessie's comfier than she looks. But don't you worry. I'll be around."

♣

Robin walked back to the hotel, hands in pockets, eyes on the stars (which still existed, somewhere, behind the choking clouds and light pollution). He tried not to think of Jerry Jeff; he couldn't help thinking of him.

As he reached the end of the lane of cars, he glimpsed a flash of color out of the corner of his eye. He knew better than to turn toward whoever was stalking him. One of the protesters, maybe, seeing a lone target? No sense waiting until it was too late, for him or for Jerry Jeff. Robin knelt, coiled his legs, and sprang.

The world inverted. He arced twenty feet up and back down again, and landed in a puddle behind the cars. His skin sorted itself out, and he resumed something like human form, hands up, filling his arms and shoulders, bulking like a cobra about to strike. He looked, for a second, like a hero.

Antonia Abruzzi stared up at him with wide dark eyes. Tracks of tears ran down her cheeks.

He deflated, and said, "Hi."

"Hi."

"Mind if I sit?"

She shook her head.

He sank to the asphalt beside her, and watched their reflection in the Ford fender opposite. "You heard?"

She nodded.

"I'm sorry. It's been a long day. For all of us. That's not an excuse, though. I'm just . . . I'm sorry. That's all."

Antonia inhaled, exhaled.

Robin waited.

"I'm not a joker," she said.

Robin waited more.

"The other kids. Stupid Peter. They're all about being jokers. That chant, in the lobby. Like they can take what those—assholes—" She glanced at him, but he didn't react. "Like they can take what those assholes outside call us, and throw it back. And maybe that's what I'm supposed to do. Maybe I should be that strong. But I'm not."

Fingertip by fingertip, she removed her gloves.

The tentacles began at her wrists, and with the gloves gone she had to shake them out from the fingerlike shapes into which they'd curled. They were thin and long, covered in shimmering scales the same gold brown as Antonia's arms. She raised them in the night. Streetlamps struck rainbows from their surface. She fanned them, braided them, unwound them again. They were beautiful.

"I don't like the name joker. People use it to mean broken. I'm not. We're not. Not Ms. Oberhoffer. Not Sean or Asti or Adesina, not even stupid Peter."

"No," Robin said. "You're not."

For a long while, in the parking lot, they did not speak, and other phantoms, unspeaking, clustered nearer. Robin watched the ghosts. "We all tell stories about ourselves, that say we've got everything figured out. We don't. But we're not broken, and no one can break us if we don't let them."

"And we won't let them."

He nodded.

In the end, she said, "I'm ready to go inside."

He stood, and stretched out his hand to her. She wound her scales around him, and he pulled her up.

Beats, Bugs, and Boys

Part 4

IT TOOK LORIANNE OVER an hour to shower and do her hair, but for once she was pleased with the end result. Whether it was the San Antonio water or the fistfuls of product she'd used, her curls had gone from insane to luxurious. She preened in front of the mirror for a couple of minutes then saw the 7:58 on the clock and raced to get dressed.

Luckily, clothing was easy—jeans, a T-shirt with skull-faced butterflies, and a light jacket since the hotel air-conditioning worked really well. Phone and keycard in the front pocket, drumsticks in her back pocket, and then she was off.

As she exited the elevator on the ground floor, she spied the back of a familiar peach-fizzy head. "Asti!"

He turned, a half-eaten ice-cream cone in his hand. "LoriAnne! I see you successfully dried your hair."

"Go me!" she said with a light laugh that she hoped didn't sound too dorky. "And you're melting." She waggled her fingers at the ice cream.

"Oops. Thanks." He hurried to lick the escaping trickle. "After hearing Basilio talk about ice cream, I had to go get some for myself." He lifted the mangled remains of the cone. "I'd offer you some, but, well . . ."

"That's all right," she said, though the idea of sharing ice cream with Asti was more than a little tempting. *Down, girl!* "Are you heading to the dinner?"

"Sure am. Right this way." He offered her his arm, which she took with delight. *"Allons-y!"*

"Allons-y," she echoed as she matched his long strides. Probably the only time her high school French would ever prove useful.

As they neared the ballroom, two boys and two girls stepped out, laughing and jostling one another. LoriAnne recognized them from the pool and started to give a smile of greeting, but to her shock, when they caught sight of Asti, their laughter shifted to sneers and whispers. To add to the insult, they made a point of edging close to the wall as they passed, then sniggered as they walked off.

Throat tight, LoriAnne glanced over at Asti. She fully expected to see outrage, but instead, he merely looked resigned—which was way worse. "You're used to that sort of thing, aren't you."

Asti popped the rest of the cone into his mouth and crunched it down before speaking. "Yeah." He twitched his shoulders in a shrug. "That was mild."

"I'm so sorry." To her horror, tears stung her eyes.

His fizz perked up. "Thanks, LoriAnne. You're really sweet. I'm glad you accidentally tried to drown me."

That made her laugh, which took care of the verge-of-tears thing. Probably his intention.

Within the ballroom, a buffet table ran along one wall, and tables and chairs filled the rest of the space.

"LoriAnne!" Greg waved at her from several tables away. With him was the rest of her group, including Mr. Sloane. Crap. Late *again*.

She gave Asti a wince of apology. "I'd better go join my band. Will you be around for a while?"

"Should be," he said, scanning the gathering.

"Sweet. See you soon!"

He gave her a distracted smile before making his way across the room. LoriAnne filled a plate at the buffet then wound her way over to the Funkalicious Four table.

"How was the pool?" Greg asked after she sat. "I didn't know you were going."

"Pretty nice. I didn't stay very long." She stuffed a forkful of enchilada into her mouth to avoid further questioning, then took a moment to enjoy the flavor. It was amazing—better than any Tex-Mex she'd ever had before. Of course, that was a low bar considering what she was used to in the boonies of Louisiana. She tucked into her dinner and let the conversation flow around her, pleased to feel quite a few of her skeeter friends in the room.

"Isn't that the Plano Originals?" Greg asked around a mini-taco.

LoriAnne followed his gaze several tables over to where half a dozen teens sat—including the ones who'd acted like jerks outside the ballroom.

"Yes, that's Plano," Cassie said.

"What are they doing?" Greg wondered aloud as two of them bumped chests then staggered around, laughing. "And why do they keep looking over at us?"

They were miming falling into a pool, LoriAnne realized. A flush crept up her cheeks. "'Cause they're jerks," she said with a savage stab of her fork into a tamale. No way was she going to tell her bandmates about her "big splash." Instead she informed every skeeter within a thousand yards exactly where to get themselves a nice juicy meal. "When I was walking with one of the Jokertown Mob players earlier, a bunch of them acted like they didn't want to get near him and made nasty faces like he smelled." She took a bite then realized everyone was looking at her. Cassie was outright staring.

"You were hanging out with a *joker?*" Greg breathed at the same time Cassie said, "Which one?"

LoriAnne put her fork down, relieved to see that Mr. Sloane, at least, was smiling. "The guitarist. Asti. I met him down at the pool. We talked and, well, he's really nice. I ran into him again when I got off the elevator."

Greg muttered something LoriAnne couldn't catch, but he looked more envious than upset. Howard wiped his mouth with a napkin. "That's the guy with the peach-fuzz skin, right, LoriAnne?"

"Yeah. And his head fizzes." Then she smiled. "Plus, he smells ah-maze-ing."

"He can really shred a guitar," Howard said. "He was killing it before the smoke bomb went off."

"The Plano shitbrains are still looking at us," Greg said with a scowl.

"And now they're doing that stupid laughing-behind-their-hands thing."

"Ignore them," Mr. Sloane said. "If you rise to the bait, you lower yourself to their level."

Greg's forehead puckered. "If you rise up then lower down, don't you end up in the same place?" He ducked as Cassie, Howard, and Lori-Anne flung tortilla chips at him.

Mr. Sloane laughed under his breath and placed his napkin on the table. "On that philosophical note, I believe it's time for me to retire. Enjoy your evening, don't forget the curfew, and be sure to get plenty of sleep tonight. We get to do it all again tomorrow, but even better."

He left to a chorus of "Good night!"

"I'm going to head upstairs, too," Cassie said, then added to Lori-Anne, "I might be asleep by the time you come in, so please be quiet."

"Gee, no impromptu drum solo?"

Cassie laughed and pointed to the sticks beside LoriAnne's plate. "Never know with you."

After Cassie left, Greg and Howard fell to talking about sports. Lori-Anne grabbed her sticks and escaped the table, scanning for Asti. She spotted him on the other side of the room, peering at his phone. Not far from him, Basilio sat slumped and alone except for a scrawny busboy clearing plates from the next table over.

Basilio was the last person she felt like talking to at the moment, but fortunately he had his back to her and didn't notice as she worked her way past him.

However, she was close enough to clearly hear the busboy grumble, "Don't get paid enough to clean up after joker slime."

She whirled, ready to rip the kid a new one, but Basilio shot to his feet.

"Joker slime? Do you have the guts to say that to a joker's face?" He made a sweeping gesture toward a startled Asti. "No? That's what I thought." Basilio took a step closer. "I bet you've never even *talked* to a joker before, but your bigoted little brain tells you it's okay to spout insulting bullshit."

The busboy's face went white as everyone nearby stared at him. With a gulp, he scuttled away like a roach seeking cover. Basilio turned to stalk off then stopped in his tracks at the sight of LoriAnne.

He flushed. "Um. Hey, LoriAnne."

"Wow. Basilio. That was incredible." No way was that staged. "I don't get it," she said, shaking her head. "What was all that by the pool?"

His blush went crimson. "I was just trying to flatter you," he said miserably. "It was so stupid. I swear I'm not really like that."

"Yeah." She smiled. "I see that now."

Asti ran up, grinning. "Bas, that was the coolest thing *ever*."

Basilio managed a sickly smile. "Um, thanks, but I probably came down too hard on the guy. I can be a real ass."

"Pretty sure that applies to everyone," Asti replied. "It was still wicked impressive."

A man in a suit approached, wearing a hotel name tag that read *Mr. Summit*.

"I'm sorry to interrupt," he said smoothly to Basilio, "but I noticed you had an altercation with Melvin." He flicked a glance toward the busboy just as the awkward teen knocked over a glass of water. Summit's face tightened as Melvin struggled to mop it up with his apron.

"It's all right," Basilio said. "I overreacted. I don't want him to get into any trouble because of me."

Mr. Summit pressed his lips together as if holding back from speaking his mind. LoriAnne had a feeling this wasn't Melvin's first screwup.

An incredibly tall and slender man stepped up to them. "Is everything all right?"

LoriAnne glanced up then stared. It was Rubberband. From *American Hero*. Beside her.

"It's no big deal," Basilio insisted, clearly growing uncomfortable with the attention. "We're good. I promise."

Mr. Summit looked at Rubberband then back to Basilio. He forced a tight smile. "Thank you for being so understanding," he said, then marched off. LoriAnne half expected him to smack the back of Melvin's head, but he settled for a death-glare.

"Thanks, Mr. Ruttiger," Asti said to Rubberband. "None of us wanted a scene."

"I understand completely, Asti. I'm glad it all worked out." He gave polite nods to Basilio and LoriAnne then walked off in an odd, flowing gait.

LoriAnne suppressed a groan as she plopped to sit at Basilio's table. An *American Hero* contestant had been right next to her, and she'd stood there like a lump of cheese. "Is Rubberband one of your teachers?" she asked Asti.

"Guidance counselor." He smacked his forehead, sending up a fountain of bubbles. "I forgot to introduce you! I'm so sorry. Let me go get him." He started to move off, but LoriAnne seized his arm.

"Jeez, not now! I'll look like a weird, pathetic fangirl."

Basilio sat and mock-furrowed his brow. "You're saying you *aren't* a weird, pathetic fangirl?"

"Guilty as charged." LoriAnne laughed and tugged Asti into a seat. "But that doesn't mean I want to advertise it."

"Speaking of pathetic," Asti said in a low voice. "Our friend Melvin is on his phone in the corner. Anyone else figure he's calling Mommy?"

"Nonsense," LoriAnne said with a straight face. "I'm sure he's simply checking in with his hot girlfriend."

Basilio snickered. "You mean his right hand?"

All three erupted in laughter.

"Okay, enough picking on poor Melvin," LoriAnne said, wiping her eyes. "Poor dude *wishes* he could be a wild card instead of a loser in the genetic lottery."

Asti winced. "You're probably right, LoriAnne. 'I'm not ugly, I'm a joker.'"

"Oh, crap!" She cringed. "Asti, I didn't mean it like that. I'm so sorry."

"I know. It's cool. Really." He smiled, but there was a whisper of sadness in it that made her chest tighten.

Basilio narrowed his eyes. "Please don't tell me you *ever* think of yourself as ugly—joker or not."

To LoriAnne's relief, a true smile bloomed across Asti's face. "Not lately, but everyone has their own insecurities."

She leaned forward. "Speaking of wild cards, have either of you heard of TheFeels?"

"Sure have!" Asti said. "I found his YouTube channel last month. Absolutely kickass."

"I've memorized all of his recordings," she gushed. "He's incredible."

Basilio looked at them blankly. "Who is TheFeels?"

"Nobody knows." Asti spread his hands. "'TheFeels' is just his online handle. He's this mysterious joker-ace musician who only comes out at night and never stays in any one place for long. No one's ever seen his face, but I've heard rumors that he's in town."

LoriAnne nodded emphatically. "I'm absolutely determined to hear him play while I'm in San Antonio."

"Wait." Basilio frowned. "Is that the guy Bambi Coldwater posted about? Wears a hood and has really white hands?"

"That's the one," LoriAnne said, with an *Ugh!* face for the Bambi mention.

"Okay. Yeah. Sure. TheFeels." Basilio rubbed his jaw, eyes flicking from Asti to LoriAnne. "Y'know, I heard someone talking about him in the elevator earlier today. Said they'd seen him busking down at the Alamo the last couple of nights."

LoriAnne lunged across the table and seized Basilio's arm. "They did? When? Where?"

"Ow! Yikes. Um, all they said was the Alamo. And I dunno when, but it would have to be after dark, right?"

LoriAnne released Basilio and eased back, pulse quickening as she checked her watch. "It's nine fifteen. Curfew isn't until ten. The Alamo is only four blocks away. A ten-minute walk at most. Plenty of time to get there, look around for him, and get back."

"And what if he's there?" Asti asked, eyebrow cocked.

"Then I'll have twenty minutes to listen!" And with luck, she could also warn him about Bambi Coldwater's nastiness.

"I'll go with you," Basilio said quickly, then gave a diffident shrug. "I mean, because it's a strange city and all. Probably best to not walk alone at night."

"Count me in," Asti said.

Basilio grimaced. "That's probably not a good idea," he said, waving a hand at Asti's fizzy head. "I mean, there's no mistaking you're a joker. And with those protesters around . . ."

Asti pulled the hood of his jacket up and stuffed his hands in his pockets. "It's dark. No one will see my fuzz or fizz." He grinned. "Relax. This'll be fun."

"Yeah," Basilio said with a weak smile. "Fun."

Excitement rose within LoriAnne, fierce and sharp. "Perfect. Let's roll."

♠

They slipped out of the ballroom then sauntered out to the street and headed east. Yet they'd barely reached the first intersection when Asti stiffened.

"Crap. That's one of our chaperones." At the far end of the next block, streetlights glinted off the distinctive metallic form of Rustbelt. "Damn. He's really nice, but he won't want to take any chances on us getting back in time."

"Then we'll avoid the problem," Basilio said, and steered them left at the corner. "Did he see us?"

"Can't imagine he did," Asti said. "I only knew it was him because of the metal."

They hustled up the street with a weird jostling for position. Basilio kept trying to walk next to LoriAnne, which was fine with her as long as she had Asti on the other side. But Asti kept shifting to put Basilio between them.

Is Asti mad at me for something? she wondered. *Or maybe I've been coming on too strong, and he's trying to get some distance from me. What if he doesn't really like nats? What if he thinks of me as just a kid?*

To distract herself from silly fretting, she pulled a drumstick from her pocket and began to twirl it between her fingers. At the next corner, they hung a right onto a one-lane street called Peacock Alley. Barred windows and NO PARKING signs dotted the walls along with unmarked metal doors that LoriAnne figured led to storage or maintenance rooms or the backs of shops. It wasn't *scary,* but she wouldn't have minded one bit if there were more streetlights and fewer shadows.

The who-stood-next-to-whom issue became moot as it ceased to be practical to walk three abreast. Asti fell back as a group of adults in dressy clothes walked by with barely a glance in the trio's direction.

A few seconds later, a college-aged guy skateboarded past from behind, all the while jabbering into his cell phone about the appetizers at the new bar and grill on Houston Street. As he rounded the far corner, a metal door opened on the right, and three guys stepped out, followed by a purple-haired girl wearing a beat-up leather jacket about ten sizes too big.

One of the guys paused to light a cigarette, then all four headed down the alley in LoriAnne's direction. They were older than high school age, but not by much. Eighteen or nineteen, she figured. The smoking guy and the girl led the way while the other two shuffled after them. One was tall and skinny with a wispy goatee. The other had a pirate tattoo on his forearm and a zombie-pirate face on his black T-shirt—with a rip through the eye patch, just big enough for a few scraggly chest hairs to poke out.

A shiver of worry ran down LoriAnne's spine. She was walking down a friggin' alley in a strange city . . . at *night*. Mr. Sloane's warning swam through her head, but LoriAnne didn't need to wonder if this was stupid. She knew.

Forget the Alamo. Forget TheFeels, she thought, gulping back a swell of panic. If she managed to make it out of this alley alive, she'd drag the others straight back to the hotel.

The smoker gave them a chin lift and a "'Sup?" then all four continued on by without showing the slightest desire to murder her or her friends.

LoriAnne released the breath she'd been holding. *Jeez, overreact much?* She checked her watch. Only nine twenty-five, and they were already more than halfway to the Alamo. She twirled and flipped her stick. They could still do this. No point chickening out now.

At the far end of the block, heavy bass pounded from a passing car, vibrating the ground beneath their feet, and loud enough that LoriAnne barely heard Asti's startled cry.

She spun to see him staggering back, fizzy head exposed. Behind him, Pirate Guy gripped Asti's hood in one hand.

"It *is* them!" Pirate Guy exclaimed, to LoriAnne's bafflement.

"I knew I smelled a freak," the girl said with an ugly laugh.

"Let him go!" LoriAnne demanded as she silently called for her skeeter friends. To her dismay, the closest ones were at least a hundred yards away, by a stand of palm trees around the corner. Why hadn't she thought to call her Louisiana skeeter back to her before she left the pool? Mosquitoes weren't fast fliers. Heck, butterflies could lap them. They were buzzing in her direction even now, but it would be a few minutes before any of them reached her.

Pirate Guy yanked hard on Asti's hood, sending him sprawling to the asphalt.

"Hey, peach smoothie!" Dumb Goatee jeered. "Is your girlfriend a freak, too?"

Basilio let out a howl of rage then charged Dumb Goatee and slammed him up against the wall. He managed one good punch to Goatee's ribs before Smoker grabbed him and hauled him back. Goatee punched Basilio hard in the gut. Basilio let out a choked gasp and folded.

LoriAnne snatched her phone from her pocket then yelped as Pirate Guy smacked it out of her grasp. It skittered down the alley and into the shadows. *"Help!"* she shrieked.

Smoker slapped a hand over her mouth and threw his arm around her waist, then hung on for dear life as she kicked and elbowed and bit. "Ow! Jesus, stop trying to scream—ow, fuck!"

"Oh for God's sake," Jacket Girl said with a disgusted roll of her eyes. "These asshole kids can't take a fucking joke. Just get 'em inside."

LoriAnne jabbed her drumstick hard at Smoker's thigh while she thrashed and twisted, but despite her best dirty-fighting efforts, the thugs succeeded in dragging her and her friends through the doorway.

The metal door clanged shut. Smoker released LoriAnne and shoved her away. Asti caught her as she staggered, then they backed against the wall with Basilio. They were in a workshop of some sort, with benches and tables and tools. A half-dozen empty beer cans littered the floor along with cigarette butts and a potato-chip bag.

"Get their phones," the girl ordered. "Don't want any of them calling nine one one."

Smoker scowled and shook his hand as Goatee relieved Basilio and Asti of their phones. "The little bitch bit me!"

"You attacked us," LoriAnne shouted, her fierce defiance somewhat spoiled by the awful quaver in her voice.

"Well, you attacked my little bro," Pirate Guy said with a sneer. "Fair's fair."

"We haven't attacked anyone," Asti retorted.

"Oh yeah?" Pirate Guy pulled out his phone and thumbed his pass code in. "Hang on," he muttered as it buzzed a rejection of the code. "I, uh, changed it the other day." It buzzed again, and he swore. "Fuck. What the hell is my birthday?"

Smoker gave him a perplexed frown. "You don't know your own birthday?"

"I know my birthday, dammit. I mean what number month is August?"

Goatee started counting on his fingers, muttering, "January, February, March—"

"Eight," LoriAnne said, then exchanged a *What the heck?* look with the others.

"Right. I knew that." He entered the correct code then spent several seconds swiping and scrolling before finally announcing, "See?" He thrust the phone screen at them in triumph.

LoriAnne, Basilio, and Asti peered at the image of the three of them after dinner, sitting at Basilio's table.

"What the hell?" Basilio said, echoed by Asti. LoriAnne stared, dumbfounded. Had Pirate Guy been at the hotel? And who was his little brother?

"Melvin!" she cried out. "Your little brother is Melvin."

"Uh-huh." Pirate Guy glared down his nose at them. "And you lot fucked with him."

"Oh my God, are you *kidding* me?" LoriAnne rolled her eyes.

"Melvin acted like a jerk, and I set him straight," Basilio cut in. "What's the big deal?"

Pirate Guy leaned in close to Basilio's face. "My bro makes one little joker joke, and you and your piece-of-shit friends gang up on him. Trip him. Curse him out. Then try to get him fired." He shoved Basilio's shoulder. "Not such hot shit now, are you?"

Basilio swallowed. "That's not how it went down. I told the manager I didn't want him to get in trouble."

"You calling my kid brother a liar, spic?"

LoriAnne mentally screamed for her skeeters to hurry. "We have a dozen witnesses who'll say Melvin's full of crap."

Pirate Guy grabbed the front of Basilio's shirt and cocked his fist back. The girl started laughing. "Melvin's the biggest whiner in the world," she said. "I bet he doesn't have a single person to back his side of it."

Smoker yanked Pirate Guy away from Basilio. "We were just messing with you fucktards," he growled. "But y'all gotta get freaked out about it and blow everything up into an international incident."

LoriAnne opened her mouth with a furious reply but closed it as Basilio grabbed her hand and gave it a hard squeeze. She glanced over, dismayed to see him white-faced with distress. Asti was quiet and barely fizzing at all, and his peachy scent had a sharp edge to it, like tar on hot asphalt.

Arguing was only making things worse. How was she supposed to reason with idiots? *This is my fault,* LoriAnne thought in misery. If she hadn't been cocky enough to suggest they look for TheFeels less than an hour before curfew, they'd still be safe at the hotel.

"This is my fault," Basilio said in a ragged whisper.

"No more talking," Pirate Guy shouted, then he flicked open a pocketknife. "Or I'll be snacking on some peaches."

Goatee stared at Pirate Guy with a look on his face as if he'd just tasted sour milk. "You gonna *eat* the joker?"

"What? No, you dickwad. It was a figure of speech!"

"I ain't never heard no figure of speech about having someone for a snack."

Smoker laughed. "Prolly means he wants to suck Peachy's dick."

"I do not!" Pirate Guy yelled. "And that's not the point anyway!" His face screwed up. "I been arrested twice already, and I'm not going in again just because my little brother is a goddamn wuss."

Goatee narrowed his eyes. "What are you saying, Marvin? You wanna get rid of 'em?"

Pirate Guy Marvin rounded on Goatee. "Why you gotta use my name, you moron?!"

The girl shook her head. "Jesus, you're *all* morons."

Goatee scowled. "Marvin's the one who's talking about killing these kids."

"I ain't talking about killing anyone, *Gerard*!"

"Fuck!" Goatee Gerard flicked frantic eyes from Asti to Basilio then to LoriAnne. "Th-that's not my name. Don't listen to him!"

"Is too!" Marvin shouted. "And she's Jess, and he's Eugene." He stabbed a finger at Smoker.

"Eugene?" Jess snorted. "You told me your name was Turk."

"Turk's my, uh, middle name," Smoker insisted. "Eugene is my granddad's name. No one calls me that."

She shrugged off the jacket and threw it at his feet. "There you go, *Eugene*."

They're all insane, LoriAnne thought. *And idiots. We're going to die.* Her skeeters whined on the other side of the metal door, but they couldn't find even the tiniest opening around the frame to get through.

"Okay, Marvin," Jacketless Jess said with a smirk. "You started this crap. Whatcha gonna do now?"

"Me? You're the one who said to bring them in here!"

"Yeah, to buy time so you numbnuts could get your heads out of your asses."

Gerard made a slashing motion with both hands. "All y'all shut the fuck up!" He froze, shocked when everyone quieted and looked at him. "We'll lock 'em up in here. Then we go find us some airtight alibis so as no one'll believe 'em if they go to the cops."

Jess put a hand to her head. "Oh, sure, that'll *totally* work. But, hey, I didn't hit anyone, so what do I care."

No hitting, but kidnapping for sure, LoriAnne thought. Being locked in was better than getting hurt or killed, but it would still be a disaster. She and the others would probably get kicked out of the competition for being out after curfew, and then the Plano jerks would no doubt win. Ugh.

"Asti, LoriAnne," Basilio suddenly gasped. "I'm really sorry."

Before LoriAnne could ask why, a *braaaaap* cut through the small room.

Jess laughed at Marvin then coughed and waved a hand in front of her face. "Dude, what the hell did you eat—" Her eyes went wide. "Oh shit."

Braaaaaaaaaaap.

"That's nasty, Jess!" Gerard backed away and clapped a hand over his nose, then visibly trembled as he cut loose a backblast of his own. "What the fuck!" he cried. Then Eugene clutched at his stomach and dropped to his knees, groaning as he ripped out a thunderous fart.

LoriAnne gagged as an I-ate-cabbage-steeped-in-toxic-waste smell rolled over her, thick and pungent enough to make her eyes water. The stench was worse than the time a skunk died in a porta-potty by her school. It would've been hysterical watching these jerks go all thunderpants if they weren't friggin' trapped in a small room with the fumes.

But maybe she could reach the door while they were distracted by their butt blasts? She started to rise, then froze as her lower gut gurgled. *Oh no.*

Asti let out a low moan, skin tone more sickly-salmon than pretty-peach. He shuddered, and then an odor like rotten fruit soaked in dog poop enveloped her. As if that was a signal to her own bowels, her booty belched out a methane bomb worthy of its own disarmament treaty.

I'm going to die of farts, LoriAnne thought in the one part of her mind that wasn't occupied with gagging or farting. Rectal honks echoed off the walls as the stench grew thicker. Everyone was doubled over, fighting in vain to control the flatulence.

Everyone except Basilio. He lunged up and grabbed his and Asti's phones from an unresisting Gerard, then seized LoriAnne around the waist, yanked the door open, and hauled her outside. She fell to her hands and knees, gasping in fresher air as Basilio ran back inside. A few seconds later, he emerged with a staggering Asti and slammed the door behind him.

"C'mon. We need to get out of here!" Basilio dragged LoriAnne to her feet then shifted to steady Asti as he swayed. "Hurry. Before they come after us." He threw his arms around their waists and urged them down the alley. She and Asti stumbled forward, continuing to rip out foghorn-psycho-geese blasts of noxious fumes.

They'd barely made it fifty feet when the metal door banged open behind them.

"Oh shit," Basilio moaned.

"Wait," LoriAnne gasped. "I got this." She pulled away from Basilio and turned, mentally calling to the skeeters. At her command, they eagerly swarmed the four hoodlums. But she needed thousands, not dozens, and it was darn near impossible to concentrate with all the fart fumes. She tried breathing through her jacket sleeve, but poly-cotton didn't do much to filter the toxic gases. Plus, her eyes were streaming so bad she could hardly make out the four shapes lurching toward them.

"Can't breathe," she choked out. "Can't concentrate!"

"LoriAnne!" Asti seized her arms. "My head! Put your face by my head!"

His fizz. Of course! LoriAnne shoved her face by his scalp then sucked in a deep breath of the sweetest, purest air a body could ever hope for, made all the more wonderful by not smelling at all like farts.

Her mind cleared in an instant. With laser-sharp focus, she reached out to the skeeters and duplicated each one hundreds of times over. Within seconds, the alley filled with thousands of skeeter-clones, each nearly twice as big as a normal mosquito. The size difference was new to her, but she told herself to wonder about that later, and sent the turbocharged skeeters to attack Jess and Gerard and Marvin and Eugene, biting and buzzing and crawling and flying into ears and noses and mouths.

Fart sounds mingled with shrieks and cries as the four slapped and flailed. They finally took off in a staggering run in the opposite direction, while clouds of skeeters trailed after them.

LoriAnne kept her gaze locked on to the skeeters until she lost sight of them around the corner and felt them dissipate. "Let's get out of here," she mumbled, not looking at the others as she retrieved her phone from beside a dumpster. Would Asti think she was horrible and selfish for keeping her talent a secret? And what would Basilio think about her being a wild card?

Wait a second. She rounded on Basilio, eyes narrowed. "Why aren't you farting?"

He hung his head, misery etched in every line of his face. "Because I'm immune to the effect."

"You make people fart!" Asti exclaimed, punctuating it with a *braaaaap.*

LoriAnne burst out laughing. "Basilio, you're an ace! That's amazing!"

But Basilio only grew more dejected. "No, it's awful. It's the dumbest ace power ever."

Asti hurried everyone around the corner then said, "Not dumb at all. It just saved our asses." He paused, farted. "Mostly." He turned to LoriAnne as she snickered. "And you're an ace, too?"

"Dunno if I'm an *ace*," she said. "Maybe deuce and a half?"

"Gimme a break. You just sent those four packing. That sounds like an ace to me." He tugged his hood up and looked up and down the street. "Those asstards know what hotel we're staying at. They're *probably* not stupid enough to come after us again, but just in case, we should take a less-than-obvious route back to the hotel."

"We can head north a few blocks then cut over," LoriAnne said, peering at her phone's GPS.

They walked up the street, eyes and ears open for signs of trouble. After a couple of minutes, Asti broke the silence. "Basilio, I can totally understand why you keep your talent a secret."

"Yeah, I really don't want to go through high school being known as Fart Boy," he said, voice bitter.

"Your secret is safe with us," LoriAnne assured him.

Asti gave an emphatic nod of agreement then furrowed his brow at her. "But, LoriAnne, why did you pretend you didn't know anything about having the virus?"

"Because I *don't* know anything," she insisted. "I live in a small town, and I've never really had a chance to talk to another wild card. I mean, is that even the right term? I'm *clueless*."

"You know enough to kick ass," Basilio said, but then his steps slowed. "Asti. LoriAnne. You've been so nice, and I don't deserve it." He gulped. "That thing I said about people in the elevator talking about TheFeels playing at the Alamo? I made it up."

LoriAnne stopped and blinked at him. "Why would you do that?"

"Because I like you, LoriAnne," he said with a quiet sigh. "You're cute and smart, and we both play drums." His face reddened. "But you're so into Asti. I figured if I could just get some time alone with you then maybe I could . . . have a chance." He hunched his shoulders. "It was so stupid. God. The dumbest thing ever. I never expected it to blow up the way it did. You both might've been really hurt or killed."

Basilio *liked* her? LoriAnne shook off her surprise and smiled reassuringly. "It's okay. Don't forget, I was the one who insisted we go out tonight. And I'm really sorry I was so oblivious." She gave Asti a grimace of apology. "I've kind of been a stalker girl, and might have developed a bit of a crush on you."

Asti shook his head. "No, I'm the oblivious one. All this time, I've been trying to get close to someone *I've* been really attracted to." He gestured to Basilio.

Basilio's eyes widened.

LoriAnne farted.

All three descended into a fit of giggles.

LoriAnne wiped tears of laughter away. "Dude, how long will this fart thing last?"

Basilio grinned. "Should only be a few more minutes." He glanced at his watch then sighed. "We totally missed the curfew."

"Then a bit longer won't make a difference." LoriAnne pulled the others into the entryway of a closed pawnshop and sat. "I'm not going back until I stop tooting."

The others plopped down on either side of her. Basilio leaned out to look at Asti. "Hey, man, if I was gay, I'd be all over you."

Asti laughed. "Thanks."

"Okay, Basilio," LoriAnne said, "what's your origin story?"

"Origin story, huh? On my thirteenth birthday, I fell into a giant bowl of *queso*."

"Seriously?"

"No!" He chuckled. "I was ten, an usher at my cousin's wedding, when a drunk groomsman farted right in front of me. I thought it was hysterical and started laughing, then, out of nowhere, barfed all over his shoes. Ended up spending the entire ceremony in the bathroom throwing up, but recovered enough to make it to the reception. The groomsman was even drunker and tried to give me shit about barfing on him." Basilio spread his hands. "He started farting. Then everyone around us. My cousin still cries whenever anyone brings up her first dance with her husband."

LoriAnne giggled . . . and farted. "And you learned how to control it?"

"Can you imagine if I hadn't?"

Asti shared his eczema story with Basilio then turned to LoriAnne. "What about you?"

"No idea," she said. "Mosquitoes have always been around me as far back as I can remember, though I've never once been bitten. I must've been around six or seven when groups of them started flying in shapes that I thought of. One time I was playing with them and made a cat shape. My mom swatted it with a broom then sprayed the whole porch down with bug spray." LoriAnne made a face. "I was real careful not to play with them around the house after that. Couple of years later, I realized I could make temporary clones. A whole cloud from one mosquito. I had a few thousand all whirling around me when my mom came around the house and saw me dancing with a bunch of bugs. She freaked out, yelled that she'd had enough of this weird shit, threw the basket of clean clothes in the mud, and left. Ran off that same night with the butcher from the Cajun meat store. Me and my dad haven't seen or heard from her since."

"Damn, LoriAnne," Basilio said. "That bites. Um, no pun intended."

"Sounds like she was looking for an excuse to leave," Asti said. "I mean, for the butcher to run off with her."

"Oh, she was a real ho," LoriAnne said, then grinned at their reactions. "What? She ditched me and my dad. I can talk trash about her. Besides, you can be sure every gossiping biddy around made sure I heard all about each and every man she fooled around with." She wrinkled her nose. "That's a big reason why I kept this whole mosquito whisperer thing to myself. It's a small town, and people love juicy gossip."

"And you'd get blamed every time someone got bit," Basilio said.

"Yeah, but I think maybe I'm ready to start letting more people know." LoriAnne smiled. "Who knows. Maybe *American Hero* will start up again, and I can audition."

"I'd vote for you!" both boys chorused.

"Awesome! All I have to do is get the show back on the air, get *onto* the show, then make it to the finale."

"Details," Asti said. "And I think the farts have stopped."

They climbed to their feet and continued walking. "Half an hour late," Basilio said, expression pained. "I'll take the heat for this since it's all my fault."

"Would you cut that out?" LoriAnne said with a glare. "It was my dumb idea to go out so close to curfew."

"And I should've stopped you both from going," Asti said.

"Oh, please," LoriAnne said. "Like you had any chance of getting through my stubborn head."

"True," Asti said. "You are a teensy bit determined."

"How about this," Basilio said. "No matter what happens, we stay friends."

"Are we going to make a super-sappy-friends-forever vow?" Lori-Anne asked, mouth twitching in amusement. "Because I can handle toxic farts, but that might be too much for me."

Basilio lifted his hands in surrender. "Fine, no sappy vows."

They approached an intersection and waited for the light to turn green. To their left, a petite woman with blond-streaked hair and sky-high heels stepped out of a nightclub. LoriAnne allowed herself a moment to admire the woman's amazing shimmery dress. It fit like a glove but came off as classy instead of slutty. The woman turned to smile at the man beside her, and LoriAnne got a good look at her face.

"Oh crap!" She yanked Asti and Basilio back around the corner. "That's Bambi Coldwater," she said under her breath. "If she sees us—sees Asti—we're toast." She herded them across the street to hunker in the shadowed entrance of a parking garage where they had a good vantage to watch dear Miss Bambi.

Asti grimaced. "If she catches us, she'll cause trouble for my whole band."

"We won't get caught," LoriAnne stated.

A second couple exited the club, and Bambi lingered to chat with them. The valet brought around a sleek silver Lexus, yet neither couple seemed in any hurry.

Finally, after nearly fifteen minutes, Bambi climbed into the Lexus and drove away.

LoriAnne called a nearby skeeter to her, just in case, then stood with a groan, legs stiff after crouching for so long. "All right, we're clear. Let's keep moving."

They retraced their steps to the intersection, crossed the street, and continued up another block before hanging a left. At the second corner, LoriAnne stumbled to a halt.

"Do you hear that?" she asked in a strangled voice. An intricate guitar riff floated to them through the quiet night air. "It's him!" A car passed by, drowning out the music.

"Him who?" Basilio asked, frowning. "Wait. Do you mean The-Feels?"

"Yes!" The music returned. She whirled, struggling to pinpoint the source.

"Are you sure?" Asti said.

"I'm positive. Believe me, I know his sound." She started up the street to her right, trusting that the boys would follow her. After half a block, the melody grew clearer, and she picked up the pace, pulse thumping in a staccato beat. The music plucked at her with nimble fingers, drawing her along. At the next intersection, she turned left and broke into a run.

She came to a stop in front of a seedy little dive bar with greasy windows and flickering neon. A handwritten flyer in the window announced *Live Music by TheFeels!*

Asti and Basilio caught up with her, puffing.

"See?" LoriAnne said, breathing hard herself. She pointed to the flyer. "I was right."

"But there's no way we can get in," Asti said with a wince. "None of us look anywhere near twenty-one. Sorry."

"Nah, it's all good." She smiled. "It's a beautiful night, and I can hear the music perfectly well out here." Not nearly as well as inside, but good enough. She looked up and down the street then crossed to where a low wall bounded a grassy area containing a couple of small trees. With a contented sigh, she settled on the grass. Asti and Basilio flopped down beside her. The shadows enveloped them, hiding the trio from view and giving them the freedom to relax. All that mattered now was the music.

TheFeels's style touched classical, rock, jazz, and folk, with a hint of Celtic thrown in. It was all, yet none of those. His unique signature. The music evoked sadness, joy, despair, hope, and a host of other emotions as it transported her on a silky roller-coaster ride of sound.

This was a life experience she could use to enrich the texture of her own music. In fact, now that she thought about it, this whole day had been packed chock-full of them.

Songs flowed seamlessly from one to the next, but at long last the final note died away.

"Wow," Basilio murmured. "Okay, that was worth chasing you through San Antonio and missing curfew."

"Right?" LoriAnne said with a grin. She pushed up and returned across the street to stand by the entrance to the bar. A dozen or so patrons trickled out, gave LoriAnne and her friends only the briefest of glances, then wandered off.

Several more minutes passed with no one else exiting. LoriAnne screwed up her nerve and pulled the door open. "Um. Excuse me?" she called into the dim interior. "I was wondering if we could meet the musician?"

A tattooed woman with a rag in her hand stepped into view. "Sorry, sweetheart, he already left. He keeps to himself."

"But I was waiting out front and didn't see him."

The lady hooked her thumb toward the back. "We got more than one door, hon."

"Oh." LoriAnne swallowed down the crushing disappointment and managed a wavering smile. "Thank you anyway."

She let the door close then took several deep breaths.

"You all right?" Asti asked, peering at her in concern.

"Yeah," she said, then smiled. "I really am. That was amazing. I got the chance to hear TheFeels live and, even better, I got to share it with y'all."

Across the street, a guitar sighed a mellow chord.

Heart pounding, LoriAnne spun, searching the shadows beneath the trees.

"There," Basilio whispered. He lifted his chin toward the very spot where they'd been sitting only minutes earlier. A hooded figure sat there now and cradled a guitar in white hands.

LoriAnne wanted to dash to him and go all fangirl, but she forced herself to walk in his direction like a not-crazy person and stop at the low wall. "I love your music," she blurted. "I've listened to all of your YouTube recordings about a million times each. I can't believe I'm here. I mean, you're here. With me." *Oh, that's nice. I sound like a blithering idiot.* "And . . . and you need to be careful because Bambi Coldwater might sic protesters on you because she hates jokers." LoriAnne gulped.

"I mean. If you *are* a joker. A joker-ace." She tried to get a glimpse of his face, curiosity burning. "Are you?"

The hooded man stroked his fingers over the strings, setting them humming. "I'm not a joker," he said, voice low and rich. "Or an ace."

"Then why don't you set people straight?" she asked, confused. "Tell them who you are."

"Wouldn't make a difference to those who want to hate, though, now would it? People believe what they want to believe. Truth doesn't enter into it half the time." He picked out a lilting riff. "Besides, *I* know who and what I am. A musician, doing my thing."

Asti shook his head in disbelief. "But you're incredible."

He let out a soft laugh. "I practice a lot. But it doesn't feel like practice, 'cause I'm doing what I love."

"You're an albino?" Basilio said.

One shoulder twitched up. "Something like that."

He's just a nat, LoriAnne thought in chagrin, then realized how stupid an attitude that was. No, he wasn't *just* anything. He was a brilliant musician. It made no difference *why* he was so brilliant.

Her fangirl respect for him skyrocketed. Nat or joker or ace, The-Feels didn't give a crap what other people thought of him. He knew exactly who and what he was, and everyone else could take it or leave it. Earlier today, Mr. Sloane had been forced to remind her that she was, indeed, a dedicated musician. If she could learn to believe in herself as a musician and a wild card and a *person* with even half the cool factor TheFeels had . . . Wow.

Pale fingers danced over the strings, plucking out a subtle refrain. "You three must be here for the band competition," he said, then he laughed softly. "I remember those days."

LoriAnne's jaw dropped. "*You* were in high school band?!"

"Couldn't do marching band, of course." He raised a white hand. "But I did a couple years of orchestra and jazz. Like I told ya, I'm no magic man. I'm just a guy with a bit of talent and a lot of love for music." His head tipped back enough for her to see his smile within the hood. "What's your name?"

She straightened as if coming to attention. "LoriAnne Broom, sir. I play the drums." She gestured to the others. "Basilio's a drummer, too. Asti plays guitar."

"It's real nice to meet you, LoriAnne, Asti, and Basilio. Most people know me as TheFeels. A few people call me Feeley Fitz." He leaned forward. "My real name is Greg Fitzmorris. But I like to keep things private. Low-key, y'know? So I'm trusting you'll keep it under your hats."

LoriAnne felt as if she'd been honored with the secret of the universe. She and the others solemnly promised to never reveal his name to another soul.

Greg "TheFeels" Fitzmorris tucked the guitar into its case and flipped the latches closed. "Well, I need to get going, and I have a feeling y'all are out a bit later than you should be." He chuckled as they groaned. "Just head to the corner and hang a right then keep going. Hotel'll be on your left."

Before LoriAnne could say another word, he stood and sauntered off into the shadows.

"So, yeah, it's almost midnight." Basilio laughed. "Go big or go home, right?"

LoriAnne sighed in mock despair. "Not sure how the rest of the week can measure up to tonight."

"It was worth every minute," Asti said fervently, then he blew out a breath. "Now to get back to our rooms without anyone catching us."

She glanced at her phone. "Mr. Sloane hasn't texted or tried to call. Believe me, if he'd done a bed check, my phone would be blowing up."

Asti and Basilio pulled out their phones and confirmed no messages for them either.

"At least we avoided Bambi," Basilio said.

"So far." LoriAnne wrinkled her nose. "We still have to get through the lobby and to our rooms. I'd be willing to bet there are some nat chaperones who'd come down hard on Asti just for being a joker." Probably not Mr. Sloane, but best not to take the chance. "What about Rubberband? I mean, Mr. Ruttiger? Do you think he'd help us out?"

Asti rubbed the back of his head. "It can't hurt to try. Any trouble I get in with him is sure to be a billion times less than with anyone else." He thumbed in a text. "Crap. I'm probably going to wake him up. Hopefully, he'll understand." He hit send. Less than ten seconds later his phone buzzed.

LoriAnne winced. "I guess he wasn't asleep."

Asti sighed as he skimmed the text. "Guess not. He says to meet him at the hotel parking garage entrance." He grimaced. "And to stay out of sight."

Fortunately, their route took them right to the parking garage. They slipped in and threaded their way between the cars as covertly as possible.

Rubberband was waiting for them in the shadow of a van, not far from the entrance. The dim light made it impossible to read his expression. Or maybe it was always tough to read.

"Asti. Miss Broom. Mr. Morales-Soto. I trust you are all well?" His eyes skimmed over them, lingering briefly on the thin scrape on Basilio's chin and Asti's scuffed sleeves.

All three hurried to assure him they were okay.

Rubberband nodded. "Asti, you can tell me all about it tomorrow." He glanced behind him. "For now, wait thirty seconds, then come in and go directly to the stairs and up to your respective rooms."

He slipped into the hotel. Asti stared glumly at his watch. "That'll be a fun conversation. But he's pretty cool. I'm just going to be honest and tell him we went looking for a musician and things went south."

"*Deep* South," LoriAnne said with a snort.

Asti smiled. "Okay, let's go."

As they entered, a screech of surprise came from the far end of the lobby, followed by a crash and shouts of dismay. Taking that as Rubberband's not-so-subtle diversion, they sprinted and reached the stairs without any chaperones spotting them.

But not completely unseen. A certain scrawny busboy stood in the entrance of the bar across the corridor. He stared at the trio in comical dismay as he clutched a bundle of dirty tablecloths to his chest like a shield.

"Heyyyy, Melvin!" LoriAnne stage-whispered with a fierce smile and wave. "It sure was great to meet Marvin."

His eyes went wide. "I . . . I didn't tell him to mess with you."

Basilio laughed under his breath. "You two stay right here." He shot a quick glance toward the lobby then darted over to Melvin.

"Hey, man," Basilio said. "I just wanted to apologize for yelling at you." He clapped a hand on Melvin's shoulder, paused a second, then dashed back to the others.

Melvin scowled and stalked back into the bar. Basilio whispered, "Three, two, one . . ."

Braaaaaaaaaaaaaaap.

"Jesus, Melvin! What the hell's wrong with you? Gah! Get out!"

Smothering laughter, they ran up the stairs.

When they reached the sixth floor, Basilio stopped. "This is me."

Asti nodded. "Same here."

"I'm on the seventh," LoriAnne said.

They cautiously peered out the stairwell door.

"Looks clear," she whispered. "Y'all be careful, okay? I guess I'll see you tomorrow."

Asti smiled and leaned in and kissed her on the cheek. "Definitely."

Basilio kissed the other cheek. "You're stuck with us now."

Blushing, LoriAnne closed the door to a mere crack and watched the two boys creep silently down the hall. She stayed until each one slipped into a room, then she continued to her floor.

Fortunately, her room wasn't far from the stairs. She eased in as quietly as possible and sloooowly closed the door, pleased when it latched with the tiniest of clicks. Using her phone for light, she crept to her suitcase to find her sleep clothes.

The sound of a keycard in the lock sent her heart spasming. *Bed check? Crap!* She dove for her bed and scrabbled to untuck the very well-tucked sheets, then blinked in shock as Cassie slipped in.

Cassie startled at the sight of LoriAnne but recovered enough to shut the door. "Why are you still up?" she demanded in a hoarse whisper. Her eyes widened as she took in LoriAnne's attire—which was certainly not pajamas. "And where have you been?"

LoriAnne folded her arms over her chest. "I might ask the same of you." Cassie had on a slinky purple dress, and a pair of stiletto heels dangled from one hand.

Cassie pursed her lips and gave LoriAnne a calculating look. "Why, I've been in here reading while my roommate . . ."

LoriAnne considered. "While your roommate listened to music, ever since dinner."

Cassie grinned in relief. "Dibs on the shower," she said, already heading for the bathroom.

LoriAnne smiled. "Have at it."

A familiar whispery whine brushed her senses. She moved to the window to see her Louisiana skeeter drift upward from the pool area and settle on the outside of the glass. Beyond it, the lights of San Antonio twinkled with promise as Greg Fitzmorris's music echoed in her memory.

LoriAnne let out a happy sigh. "This is going to be the best week ever."

♠ ♦ THURSDAY ♥ ♣

Bubbles and the
Band Trip

Part 8

GHOST SHOOK MICHELLE AWAKE at midnight.

"Holy shit! What are you doing here?" Michelle asked. She was bleary and a little disoriented. "And how did you get in?"

Ghost put her hands on her hips and looked at Michelle as if Michelle was incredibly stupid. But she also looked furious.

"Oh, right," Michelle said. "The walking-through-walls thing. Sorry, I'm not awake yet. Seriously, didn't Rusty talk to you about doing that here? And where is he?"

"He's asleep," Ghost said in a rush. "I just . . . I just couldn't sleep." She shivered. On top of the anger, Michelle saw a raw fear. "I hate those people! They want to kill us! They want to kill me and Adesina, and you!"

Michelle threw back the covers. "It's okay, Yerodin," she said, reaching out to her, but Ghost just floated away. There was nothing to be done when Ghost got into this frame of mind. Even living with Rusty couldn't completely repair the broken part of Ghost. "You want Wally or Sharon? Or you want to stay with me?"

"Sharon. If we get Wally, Mr. Ruttiger will wake up, too."

"Okay."

Michelle walked across the hall and knocked on Sharon's door. A few moments later, a bleary-eyed Sharon opened it.

<What's going on?> she signed. Ghost floated inside the room.

"She's having a rough night," Michelle replied softly. "You okay to spend some time with her?"

<Of course!>

"I'll see you tomorrow," Michelle replied. She turned and went back to her room.

And then she couldn't get back to sleep. She got up and threw on a pair of dove-colored baggy pants, sneakers, and a loose, leaf-green tunic top.

When she got to the lounge, there were no tables available. She went to the bar and ordered a vodka tonic. Light on the vodka. As she was waiting for her drink, she couldn't help but overhear a conversation from a table behind her.

"Yeah, I saw those freaks," came a slightly slurred woman's voice. "Walking down to the River Walk like they were normal tourists. Big as life. That one with the wings. And the one with the wheels. Creepy as hell, if you ask me."

The bartender put her drink down in front of her. "Here you go, Ms. Pond. Light on the vodka. On the house." She gave her a nice smile that surprised Michelle. "Don't mind the idiots."

"Too late," Michelle said, fishing a twenty out of her pocket. She tucked it under the drink on the bar. "Those are my kids out there."

"I understand."

Michelle slid off her stool.

I'm so going to ground Adesina. And Peter. Even if he wasn't her kid, she was going to ground him. *Now all I have to do is figure out where the hell they are.*

She stopped at the front desk. The clerk was a tall girl with a blond bob wearing a navy blazer and red kerchief around her neck. "Did you see a couple of joker kids leave here?" Michelle asked.

The clerk nodded. "They wanted to see about getting into Bohanan's next door. The jazz is great there, but there's no way they'd get seated given . . . well, you know. Also, it's expensive.

"They left about five minutes ago. Asked me where the Indigo Night jazz bar was. I gave them a map and showed them." She reached below the counter and pulled out a map of the River Walk. "You go to Navarro and turn south. When you get to the bridge, go over and down the steps. Head east and you'll find it."

"Did you mention that they were too young to be going to a club?"

"I did. But they told me that they were just going to hear music. I know that club, they weren't going to get in no matter what. I used to date the bouncer." The desk clerk gave Michelle a bright, disconcertingly gummy smile.

◆

The River Walk was swampy. Despite the cool temperature at street level, down along the walk there was a hint of heat. The man-made concrete river was arched by metal bridges, some leading to the streets above, some that just went from one side of the walk to the other. The water was a dirty jade color and looked as if it would be nasty to fall into. Tour boats made their way slowly through the murky water.

The River Walk was still busy, even at a quarter to one in the morning. There was a steady stream of tourists, but it was mostly small groups and a lot of couples.

After getting a heady, smoky whiff of barbecue from the County Line as she went down the stairs from Navarro to the River Walk, she saw the Hard Rock Cafe nestled back among the liriope, Texas lilies, and boxwoods overhung by live-oak branches. Round metal tables with white umbrellas and wood slatted chairs were set out on the patio. "I swear, there's a Hard Rock everywhere," Michelle muttered.

A couple jumped up from their seats and hustled over to her. Both men wore tailored khakis, short-sleeved madras print shirts, and Top-Siders with no socks. One had light brown hair with blond streaks and the other's hair was salt-and-pepper.

"Oh. My. God!" said the blond one. "It's you! I told you, Ben. It's really her!"

Ben smiled at her, then said, "I apologize for my boyfriend. He gets a little excited. You're Michelle Pond? You're much prettier in person. Could we get a photo with you?"

"Well, I'm trying to find my daughter and her friends," Michelle said, attempting to keep the annoyance out of her voice. "Did you see a girl with blue wings and a boy with wheels for legs come by here recently?"

The blond man chuckled and said, "How could we miss them? They went by a few minutes ago. There was a short, brunette girl with them. But no one bothered them, if you're worried."

"Thank you! I appreciate the help! I'm so sorry about the photo, but I really have to catch up."

Ben and his companion gave her the sad-face, then Ben said, "It's okay. I understand. We already got a pic of you as you were coming up."

"Thanks for understanding." She started walking again, passing Joe's Crab Shack, where the smell of frying *everything* hung heavy in the air.

♥

It didn't take her long to see the kids. Kimmie and Segway were holding hands, and Adesina was walking behind them. They were causing something of a sensation—as any jokers might—but no one was harassing them. However, Michelle was getting stopped by almost everyone. She hated disappointing people who wanted autographs or pictures, but sometimes she just wished she could be part of the crowd. It would make things easier.

The pathway curved and narrowed as it went under one of the bridges at Presa. Under the bridge, vendors' tables selling Dios de los Muertos and other kinds of tchotchkes narrowed the path, and people stopping to look-see or buy merchandise forced everyone to walk in single file. As Adesina, Kimmie, and Peter emerged from under the bridge, Michelle saw the Indigo Night bar on the other side of the river.

There were two popping noises. Then a pinging noise off the metal bridge.

Michelle knew what gunfire sounded like. Apparently, so did a lot of the sightseers. There were screams and some of the tourists hit the ground. Adesina unfurled her wings, then wrapped them around Kimmie, Peter, and herself. *"Get down!"* Adesina shouted.

Michelle knew Adesina's wings were tough enough to resist bullets, but that didn't address the problem of everyone else's well-being. And she was trying very hard not to freak out about the whole my-daughter-and-her-friends-almost-got-shot thing.

Michelle thought she knew which direction the bullets had come from. She began running toward the stairs leading to the top of the bridge at the corner of Crockett and Presa. She yelled at Adesina, Kimmie, and Peter, "You guys are in a world of hurt! And, oh my God, be careful!"

Michelle took the steps two at a time, then dashed across the bridge. She was at street level now, but there were only a couple of drunks staggering away from her. "Did you see anyone up here?" she asked them.

They turned and gave her tipsy smiles. "Nah," said one of them—a pretty girl with straw-colored hair in goth clothing. "Just us." Then she and her companion giggled. A car drove by with Tejano music blaring through the open windows.

Michelle swore under her breath. She looked around. But if this was where the shots had come from, the shooter was long gone. Frustrated, she turned and headed back over the bridge. It was a lousy night for the River Walk to be slow.

Adesina, Kimmie, and Peter had taken refuge under the bridge. Some of the patrons had joined the kids under there, but they looked like they were ready to bolt as soon as it was safe. Vendors were frantically packing up their wares or ducking under their tables. Michelle heard sirens in the distance.

Adesina, Kimmie, and Peter were huddled together, Adesina's wings no longer wrapped around them.

"What in all the hells are you doing out here?" she snapped. "You're *supposed* to be in bed. Instead I find you've snuck out. And now you get caught in the middle of a shooting. Which, I'd like to add, might have been aimed at you!"

The three kids didn't meet her eyes. It was for the best because Michelle was pretty sure they would be smoking ash heaps if they did. "I don't think anyone was shooting at us," Adesina said.

"Do you seriously want to get into a debate with me about this?" Michelle snarled. "That is such an epically bad idea."

Adesina pursed her lips, but stopped talking. She crossed her arms. Michelle wasn't sure if Adesina was pouting or ashamed.

"And dammit now we're going to have to talk to the police. *Again.*"

The seizure test of flashing red and white lights played across the sidewalk from street level. A couple of police officers came down the Presa Street bridge Michelle had gone up. They looked extremely pissed.

"We hear there were gunshots down here," said the first officer. A bit of middle-age pooch pushed against his belt. His uniform was neatly pressed, as if he'd just come on duty. He had dark eyes and his skin had a golden-brown sheen in yellow light. The other cop's raven hair was tied back into a neat bun. Her eyes were lighter, a color similar to Michelle's, but her skin was a little darker than her partner's.

Michelle wanted nothing more than to stay the hell out of this, but like everyone else, she'd have to make a statement.

"Yes, sir," she said. "Two shots. One hit here—" She pointed at a chunk of paint stripped away from the metal. "And the other went in the dirt, I think. I went the way I thought the shots had come from—where you came down, but no one was there except a couple of goth kids. Really drunk."

"Can I get your name?" the officer asked.

"Michelle Pond," she replied.

The cop had to look up at her. She had a good six inches in height on him. "Yeah, we heard you were in town. Officer Reyes got to spend some time with you today. Poor bastard. Susannah, you wanna start talking to those folks over there?"

"Hey," Michelle began.

The cop held up his hand. "Something always seems to happen when aces are around. Not saying it's your fault, just seems like bad luck follows you." He jerked a thumb at Adesina, Kimmie, and Peter. "Those belong to you?"

"Yes, they're in the band competition at the Tobin Center," she replied. "I'm chaperoning."

"I can see you're doing a bang-up job. Isn't it a little late for them to be out?"

Michelle had had quite enough. "I'm sorry, I don't see how us taking a turn around the River Walk is cause for attitude. What does this have to do with the shooting? What's your name?"

"I'm Officer Leos," the cop replied. "I doubt this had anything to do with your kids. Probably some drunken asshole.

"I hate it when this kind of stuff happens. No obvious perp. Random. It scares the tourists. Everything is going to be cordoned off until tomorrow. You going to be in town for a while?"

"Until Sunday."

"Give me your cell number in case I need to contact you." She gave him her number and he wrote it down. Then he reached into his shirt pocket and pulled out a business card. "If you think of anything helpful, call me."

Michelle took the card and slid it into the back pocket of her pants. "Thanks, Officer Leos, I will."

♣

Michelle pounded on the door to Rusty's room.

"Wally! Robin! Get up!"

Bleary-eyed Wally opened the door. "Oh gosh, Michelle," he said, his voice cracking and grating. "What's the problem?"

"My room. Now."

Sharon's door opened and she gave a low whistle and signed, <What is going on?>

"My room." Michelle's calm you-need-to-stop-talking-and-do-what-I-say-right-now voice had kicked in.

She held the door to her room open and everyone shuffled inside. "These three"—she pointed at Adesina, Peter, and Kimmie—"decided to sneak out and go to the River Walk tonight. And someone shot at them."

"Mom, that's not what happened," Adesina said. "C'mon, we were just having a Pekinese, sorry, a peek at the River Walk. And Officer Leos said those bullets weren't meant for us."

Michelle's eyes narrowed and she cocked her head to one side as she spoke. "Are you talking? Really, you're talking *right now*? And you can't see what a bad idea that is?"

<I told you Texas was dangerous,> Sharon signed. <But gunfire?>

"Who knows how long it'll be before the whole thing is up on You-Tube." Michelle glared at everyone in the room.

Kimmie looked like she had swallowed a bug.

"Mom," Adesina said, "no one bothered us. Like, Kimmie's a nat. Peter's hella cute, and I'm super-pretty. We're not like other jokers.

People aren't afraid of us. And who knows who they were shooting at? Maybe someone else, maybe they were just showing off. Mom, it's Texas!"

"All the more reason for us to shut this thing down," Michelle said. "We should withdraw from the competition and go back to New York. It's just too dangerous."

"Mom, no!"

"Ms. Pond, no!" Peter said. "How could they have known we were going out? If we leave it'll look like it's because of the smoke bomb. And then they win. I grew up in Jokertown. After what goes on there, none of this stuff could freak me out."

Ghost floated through the door to the bathroom. "Wally, I don't want to leave either," she said. "And yes, I was listening in. I came through the wall of the bathroom."

"Rusty, honestly, have you never had a conversation about this? I mean it's fine around friends, but here?"

Wally looked ashamed and Michelle felt terrible. She thought Wally was the best, and now she was being mean to him.

"You," she said, pointing at Adesina. "You're staying with me now."

"Mom!"

Michelle gave Adesina a look that could have melted glass. "You've blown your privileges. And you . . ." She turned to Peter. "I better not hear a peep from you for the rest of the competition. You . . ." She turned to Kimmie. "I'm going to get you to your room, and you better hope your mother isn't anywhere around.

"As for the adults here—we've really dropped the ball chaperone-wise. Myself included.

"Now everyone, out. Except for you." She pointed at her daughter.

"Kimmie," she said, "let's go. And Adesina, you better not move from that spot until I get back."

I may just bury her and dig her up when she's thirty.

♠   ♥   ♦   ♣

Dust and the Darkness

by Victor Milán

Part 1

"¡HIJO LA!" I SAID, stopping my fork with a load of hash browns just shy of my mouth. "He gave them his truck?"

"Yeah," Fabio said in his funny accent. "And his credit card."

"He told all this to you, a stranger? A cowboy from Brazil? Dang, maybe it's no big deal he gave away his truck and credit card to a pair of runaway kids."

"He seemed pretty, what do you say? Broke up about it. So, like, I don't think this happens all the time."

Fabio Fernandes was an old Professional Bull Riders junior circuit buddy of mine, from the days when we were both up-and-comers. He's still up-and-coming. I'm looking for alternative opportunities, ever since a bull named John Dortmunder rolled on me and dislocated my spine.

Which is how I wound up playing detective by sitting in a Truck-R-Nation coffee shop outside New Braunfels, trying to track down this famous seventeen-year-old high school music prodigy—the Mozart of Modesto, *USA Today* called her. *And* the drifter who'd bragged to everybody at the Gunter Hotel where he was tending bar how he was an ace, before smooth-talking her into running away from some big jazz band contest happening there. Where she was fixing to sign a deal with a big record label, no less.

It's my *abuela*'s fault—my grandmother's. Stuff like this usually is.

"But he told you all about it," I said.

Fabio shrugged. He was a long, narrow drink of water with a dark, kind of chubby face, curly black hair, and a pencil-thin mustache like some kind of old Latino heartthrob movie star. He was dressed like any other cowboy in the place, with pearly snap buttons on his shirt, battered and faded jeans, and cowboy boots.

"He was sitting in a booth. He was telling everybody who slowed down long enough how he'd offered these two broke kids a ride, only to have them jack his pickup and strand him right on the asphalt. Like a character in one of those old Russian novels, you know?"

"Yeah. I hate those. So where'd you see him last?"

The second I'd disconnected from my grandmother browbeating me into playing detective the night before, I mass-texted all my old contacts from PBR days. I figured, if the kids I was looking for had blown out of San Antonio for L.A. like her family thought they had, they were likely doing it on Interstate 10.

My pal Fabio was first to respond, with a tale of a strange encounter the day before at the Timberwood Park Truck-R-Nation, right there on 10 heading northwest out of San Antonio. Truck-R-Nation is as popular on the circuit as it is with truckers. It's clean, and the food is cheap, plentiful, and good enough, if not a touch better. I was trying to finish off a delayed and much-needed breakfast of pork chops, eggs, biscuits, and sausage gravy. I'd had to bolt the house all the way over near the New Mexico border with just a cup of predawn coffee burning a hole in my stomach to start my kid-genius hunt.

"I left him there, gazing out the big old front window like a lost soul. He called his daughter to come pick him up. He lives right nearby. Said she was gonna ream him a new one."

"Thanks, amigo. Uh, *muito obrigado.*" I stood up and scooped up the check. Grandma said the girl's family promised to pay expenses, which I certainly planned to hold them to. "How's the family?"

"Still back home in Paraná, where I like them. Yours?"

"Hanging in there on the ranch outside Lamesa. Where I wish I wasn't stuck living."

He stood up, too. He frowned and scratched his right eyebrow. "Be careful, man. I gotta wonder if you're maybe getting into something here that's gonna get over your head in a hurry."

"Me too, my friend. Me too."

♠

"So, yeah," the old dude said, "it was the damnedest thing I ever did see."

My informant was not what I expected. I'm not sure what I expected, but a little old guy with brick-colored hair that was going all grizzled, who looked like you put Lyle Lovett in one of those dehydrators and shriveled him up some, was not it. He insisted I call him Rooster, because of course.

"I mean, these were some good-lookin' kids. Boy coulda been a movie star, if he'd lose that East Texas bayou trash accent. And the girl put him in the shade: six feet tall in her sneakers, big brown eyes, brown hair in pigtails, knockers out to here."

It took me a minute to remember what *knockers* were in old-person talk, while he blew smoke out the open window of my twenty-year-old RAV4 five-door at the passing suburban scenery of Timberwood Park. Which looked like the suburban scenery everywhere else in southwest Texas, except newer and tackier. Rooster insisted I drive him to the Circle-K from his daughter's house, where the folks at the truck stop said I'd find him, and buy him a pack as the price of talking. Man, those things are *expensive*. I don't know if I can afford this detecting.

"Said they were headed to Hollywood to follow their dreams. I told 'em sorry, I was nigh home already, and I'd get in dutch with the daughter if I got home late. Next thing I know, the boy holds out his hand, and like this rainbow thing shines out of it right in my eyes. And the next thing after that, I'm standing in the parking lot, breathin' diesel fumes and wondering where my pick-'em-up went to."

"He shone a light in your eyes?"

"Colored light. Couldn't look away. Didn't want to. Like a rainbow, it was. Purty. Only gave him the one card. Noticed it was missing right away, once I came out of it. Bank card—don't have no ID photo. Yeah."

"They didn't force you or anything?"

"No. I recollect a little now—him asking real nice and proper if he could borrow a few things. And—it seemed reasonable. I really wanted to help, you know?"

Great, I thought. *He really is an ace.*

"So what's your interest in this gal and her friend with the rainbow hands?"

"I'm trying to talk her into going back to her parents." That seemed the simplest explanation. "Just doing a favor for some bingo-playing buddies of my granny's."

"Word to the wise: Don't look at that blond kid's hands, whatever you do."

Good advice, I thought. "Good advice," I said.

Rooster blew smoke out the window again. He was having me drive him around. His daughter didn't want him smoking in her house any more than I wanted him smoking in my dang car. He said she'd ask questions if she caught him hanging around outside talking to some stranger. I'd have called that smart of her, given his propensity for giving his bank card to random strangers, but the rainbow thing put a whole new spin on it. Then again, he'd offered a lift to a couple of hitchhikers at a truck stop, so maybe she was right after all.

"You know," he said to the hot breeze, "I reckon them kids are in a pack of trouble, since I reported the truck stolen to the Staties and all. And my daughter made me call the bank to put a stop on the card."

My heart sank. He put words to a tune I was already hearing in my mind.

He flicked his butt out the window and turned back to me with a grin spreading across his narrow withered-up face. "But, you know, if I got my truck back and didn't take no losses, maybe got a little something for my trouble, I might suddenly remember I did lend those kids that stuff voluntary like, after all."

◆

I put my smartphone on speaker and hit up my grandmother's number as I drove the State Highway 46 shortcut from New Braunfels to Boerne, which I-10 passed through. (Kids, don't dial and drive. I'm an ace detective. Don't do that either.)

She picked up right away. *"Abuelita?"*

"You want something." Luckily she always talks loud, since she's a bit hard of hearing and too stubborn to get a hearing aid, since I still had the passenger window open to clear the smoke remnants and the wind was rushing something powerful. "You always want something when you call me that. It's money, right?"

"Right."

"No."

"Not from you," I told her. "And not for me. It's business."

"Okay. Talk to me, Jesse. You have my interest."

I told her.

"You want to buy off a witness."

"Not a witness. The crime victim. He says we get his bank card charges covered, get him his truck back, give him a little extra for his trouble, he's not gonna press charges, okay?"

"You actually have his truck?"

"Well . . . not yet."

"I never knew whether you were my favorite *nieto* in spite of being such a devious little shit, or because of it. I'm beginning to see now. Okay, I'll talk to the girl's family in Cali. They're pretty eager to avoid a scandal; they should pony up pronto. And I'm pretty eager to see if you can actually pull this off."

Me too, I thought.

She disconnected. "I love you too, Grandma," I told my phone.

I was just tucking it back in my shirt pocket when it played the whistled bit from the theme for *The Good, the Bad and the Ugly.* I fished it right out again.

It was my cousin Florene, who works as a dispatcher for the Texas Highway Patrol in Kerr County, on I-10 northwest of Boerne. I'd also text-spammed pretty much my entire extended family. Which, if you're not familiar with Latinos, really leans hard on the *extended* part. Us Rodríguezes, and my mom's Márquez clan, have been living in this part of the world since San Antonio happened in the early 1700s. The ones who were Comanches at the time've been here even longer than that.

"Got good news and bad news for you, *primo,*" she said.

"Are you chewing gum? You're not supposed to do that on duty, are you?"

She popped it in my ear. "What're they gonna do, fire me? I'm

Simple Service. Also, last I heard, our *tía* Luisa is still director of the Texas Department of Public Safety, or did you forget?"

"Right." It wasn't as if Florene calling me was strictly legal. Or at all. I've always been a do-what's-right-rather-than-what's-legal kind of guy, and Florene . . . well, my older sisters used to joke her name should be spelled "fluorine," for the dangerously unstable element.

"Which do you want first?"

"Give me the good, so I can enjoy a brief moment basking in the sunshine of optimism."

"Such a poet." I could hear the sneer. "You oughta go into fertilizer sales with a line of bullshit like that. Okay. We got a report matching the description of your missing kids as of twenty minutes ago."

"Sweet! Where are they?"

"A pair matching their descriptions were reported at a convenience store in Kerrville."

The sun was still shining hot and bright through the open windows—okay, I don't just keep 'em down to let the smoke out, my AC is *todo fregado*—but I felt my heart sinking slowly in the west. "I think I can guess the bad news."

"Who's telling this? Yeah. The bank card they were trying to use had been reported stolen. So was the big-ass Ford pickup they drove up in."

"Is there video?"

"Reckon it's likely." *Pop.*

"You reckon? Didn't the Highway Patrol impound it?"

"You watch too much TV, dumbass. It's just probable credit card fraud. The cops don't actually give two pinches of sour owl shit about that. They won't even do a drive-by to look for the truck; clerk said the suspects took off in it."

"So it's not a worry?"

"Didn't say that, *primo*. The video's still evidence. They find the missing truck, or other crimes start getting reported, it'll get grabbed right off. You know how prosecutors love to pile criminal charges all on top of each other."

I didn't. But mostly what I was thinking was, *Dude's an ace-powered con man who ripped off some good-natured good ol' boy for wheels and whatever money he had in his bank account. What're the odds he's not doing more crimes?*

I sighed. "Nothing's ever easy. Except—still no names? No alert for a Runaway who look like that?"

"Not yet. So I guess you get two bits of good news for the price of one."

"Okay, thanks, Florene. Give my love to Oscar and Ruby." Oscar Ishikawa was her mortal saint of a husband. He worked for a landscaping business in Kerrville and was studying garden and landscape design at the vocational school there. Ruby was their year-old daughter. "I, uh. I owe you one."

"Hold that thought, buddy boy. Give my love to your *mamacita* and the finger to your snooty bitch sisters."

♥

I'm not Sherlock—which by the way is the name my older sisters are totally going to hang on me once they get wind of my current gig. (They really aren't that bitchy. They just don't like Florene. They are snooty, though. And, well, older sisters.)

But I didn't need to be Sherlock to notice that the big front windows of the little gas station store showed nothing but this strange, deep blackness that clearly wasn't Mylar taped over them inside. Nor did I need to be to realize some ace power was in play, or had been very recently. And that was before I spotted the weird tendril of sight-swallowing black that ran out the top of the window to envelop what I took was the security cam on the store roof in its own tiny cloud o' impenetrable darkness.

I turned right down the next side street. I also did not have to be a real detective, much less a wizard fictional one, to realize whoever was responsible for the blackout was up to something they probably wouldn't feel like leaving by the front door afterward.

The gas station was located in a settled, lower-middle-class-looking suburban part of Kerrville. The neighborhood was pretty nice, with lawns and established trees. Luckily most people seemed to be at work. Some kids were playing in a sprinkler a block and a half down the side street, but I didn't see any adults watching them. Which twitches some people out something powerful, a thing I do not understand.

I parked the RAV4 under a scrawny ash tree alongside the Stop 'n Save—can't speak to areas outside of Texas, Oklahoma, and New Mexico, but convenience stores here got abbreviation issues, it seems to me. I walked up to the back corner of the little cinder-block building as if I was the Kerrville Alley Inspector and peeked around as if I was a not very experienced spy. Which I was.

Sure enough, a person was emerging from the store's green-painted metal back door, looking even more guilty than I was sure I did. It was a young black woman, girl maybe, with a short Afro, dressed in a nice black T-shirt, jeans, and sneakers. She had a little black plastic box, like maybe a video recorder, tucked under one skinny arm.

She was looking the other way. I started walking toward her. I don't know if she heard my cowboy boots crunching alley gravel, but she swiveled her head right toward me. She was not hard on the eyes, if in an underfed way.

"Hold on, there, ms. We need to talk."

She opened her mouth and eyes wide, and black stuff poured out at me. Like squid ink but airborne. The world went black. Like, dead black. Like bottom of a coal mine at midnight black. (Coal mines are deep underground, right? I don't know anything about mining coal other than it's dirty and dangerous.)

Too black. I couldn't see the end of my nose.

The first thing I thought was, *Stop, drop, and roll!*

The second was, *That's for when you're on fire, which you clearly aren't, itonto!*

But by then I was already halfway to the ground and noticing, *Hey, I can see again! Which just goes to show, you might as well go ahead and give it a shot.*

I landed hard, which gave the mostly healed-up microfractures in my lumbar spine a twinge, but nothing I hadn't felt before. The woman was hightailing it the other way down the alley. So I resorted to the good old playground trick of scooping up a fistful of dust and tossing it in her face.

Now if you've been paying attention, you likely noticed that I was sitting on my butt watching her a good thirty feet from me and receding fast. Meaning that I was in precisely no position to go grabbing up dust with my hand and throwing it in her face.

But I don't have to use my hand. I'm an ace too. Dust's my power. Really, it's the sort of power that strikes most people as a deuce. But I figured out a few uses for it long before it ever dawned on me that other people couldn't just make little bits of fine powder dance around on command.

It was a good thing she wasn't any farther, or she'd have been out of reach. But I got her dead-on. She stumbled and fell headlong, coughing. The recorder squirted out from under her arm and went skittering along the gravel like a startled squirrel.

I picked myself up and ran after her. She had obviously used the same ace on me she'd used to black out the surveillance camera out front, and the store's inside. I didn't know if she was fixing to use it again—nor what to do about it if she did. So I did what my *abuela* always accuses me of doing, which is lead with my face and hope for the best.

Hey, sometimes it works. It did now. I hauled her up off the ground by one arm—she was heavier than she looked, suggesting some wiry muscles packed on that skinny frame—just as a siren began to sing its doo-wop song, not right nearby, but not too far and getting not-farther in a hurry.

"Whether he could see you or not, looks like the clerk in there had the presence of mind to hit the silent alarm. We gotta get out of here."

She glared at me. Which was not too effective, given that her right eyelid was blinking furiously all on its lonesome. The eye behind it was red. "'*We'?*" she demanded.

"I don't wanna answer their questions. I'd just as soon you not either." I let go her arm and retrieved the recorder. "Come with me. My car's right around the corner."

"Aren't we enemies?" She had an odd little accent. Thought it was French.

I waved the recorder at her. "Fact we're after the same thing sounds to me like we might be allies. Come on. Talk on the run."

"No, I can take care of mys—ow! Shit, shit, shit, shit. *Merde!*"

"Doesn't that just mean—"

"Shut up! This is your fault. I got a piece of dust under my eyelid and it feels like a knife on my eyeball. It won't let me concentrate. I can't call the Darkness."

You could hear the capital letter.

"Then come with me, all right?"

She didn't argue anymore but followed, blinking her right eye like she had a serious tic, with tears running down her cheek.

We jumped in the RAV4. You know those horror movies when the kids are fleeing the cabin with the chainsaw murderer hot on their trail, and they pile in a car, and the car doesn't start? Yeah, fortunately the RAV4 didn't see those movies. It started right up and purred right on down the street toward the kids hopping obliviously around in the Rain Bird spray.

My passenger was pulling her right eyelid down with a finger and sticking her head up in the rearview to see it. "Stop that," I said. "You're getting in the way."

"But I need to get this out of my eye."

"Been there. There's a mirror on your sunshade."

She glared at me again, but sat back in her seat and flipped the shade down.

"When you get a chance," I said, "you might put your seat belt on. The car yelling at me about it gets tiresome in a hurry."

She did, then went back to trying to extract the grit from her eye. Had to be feeling like a jagged boulder by now. "Can't you drive this piece of shit faster?"

"Not without looking suspiciously as if I'm fleeing the scene of untoward events at the convenience store. Which reminds me of Bill and Ted. Did you ever see—"

"No! What's wrong with you?"

"Well, to start with, I'm a permanently out of work bull rider who got roped into doing a job I got not the first inkling of how—"

"No! I mean, why are you here? And why are you helping me escape?"

"Wave to the kids, now, real nice." I turned left, after signaling, of course. Nothing to see here. Just a West Texas Latino kiboy with an angry young black woman whose kidnapper he was. *Or accomplice, depending.* "I was fixing to answer that first part. But like I say, we seem to be in the same business."

"How do you think that?" She took a finger away and blinked experimentally. "Fuck."

"See, I happen to know the clerk at that store back there just happened to call in an attempt to pass a debit card reported stolen not too long ago. I come here to talk to the person, and what do I find? A whole mess of unnatural darkness, and a person creeping out the back door with the very evidence of that attempt tucked under her arm." I gave her a little frown. "Unless that's the decoy. Sometimes these stores—"

"It's not the decoy, you—you hayseed. It's the real thing. I know what I'm doing."

"Yeah. Your subtle little ninja act back there proved that. The back-door creep that shouted to the world, 'I'm stealin' stuff here!' That weird darkness that adds, 'And I'm an ace while doin' it! Woo-hoo!'"

"You're an ace, too," she said accusingly.

"Guilty. Name's Jesse, by the way, since we're confessing our life stories here."

She sat back in her seat and looked sulky. "I'm Candace. People call me the Darkness."

"You must be a big hit at parties."

"What is that supposed to mea—"

"So what I am doing here is, the family of a girl called Mindy-Lou hired me to bring her back to a band competition in San Antonio, from which she was lured away by a sweet-talking lowlife goes by the name of Billy Rainbow. He's an ace."

I was trying to drive without running into anything, but also I was looking around. Playing a hunch. We'd turned back onto the bigger street the Stop 'n Save fronted on. A police cruiser with its light bar going passed us heading the other direction.

I glanced at the rearview. "That big old cloud of Darkness filling the Stop 'n Save is gonna clue them in there's a little more going on than a robbery."

"No. It melts away. Like fog. Police usually don't believe the people I use it on." She squinted at me. "My job is to bring the girl back as well."

"Her family didn't hire you, too? Honestly, I don't know anything about 'em, other than her aunt plays bingo with my *abuel*—my grandma."

"The record label hired me."

I slapped the top of the steering wheel. "Who-ee! Then we're not rivals after all!"

She looked at me narrowly. Her eye wasn't doing its semaphore-signaling thing anymore, suggesting she'd got the last fleck of dust out. "How do you arrive at that? Aren't we after the same thing?"

"Exactly! And when we find this girl, and deliver her back to the big-band thing—*quietly*—"

"Which is how my employers want it, too."

"Then we each get paid, and we go our merry ways. It's two for the price of one! Or one for the price of two? Or something!"

"Don't you ever shut up?"

"Sometimes. My mama always taught me it's rude to chew with my mouth open." I glanced past her, kicked the brakes, and yanked the wheel right into a sudden strip mall. The harness brought her up pretty hard as she rocked forward.

"See?" I said. "Seat belts."

"What are you doing?"

I turned right again, around a walk-in barbershop at the front of the lot. "Now, what is this I see to my right?"

"A bunch of cars? Mostly outsized American pickup trucks?"

"Yep. And you will notice among them a faded red 2010 Ford F-150, four-door, with a V8 engine, approximate size of the flight deck on the USS *Leo Barnett*. Whose license plate happens to match the one on the truck our boy Billy Rainbow allegedly used his ace to get a citizen to hand over to him in the San Antone suburbs. Billy ditched it once he realized it was reported stolen, just like I thought."

"How do you know these things?"

"That's what I do. I drink soda pop and I know things. Or at least it's what I do since my grandmother called me up on the phone last night and informed me I was going into the detective business if I knew what was good for me."

She twisted around in her shoulder harness to look. "So what are we going to do about it?"

"I am going to carefully note the location and inform a good old boy who calls himself Rooster—you met him, you'd know why—where to get his truck back. And add the towing fee to my bill to the family, since he's agreed not to press charges if I make him whole, as the saying goes. And you are being not subtle again. Will you sit down? You act like you're as new to this crime business as I am to detectiving."

"I am a very experienced criminal," she said stiffly. But she sat back again.

I put my blinker on and turned back onto the road.

"So why did you want the recorder?" she asked.

"I don't. I wanted to get the clerk to agree that, being as no crime had been committed—both the stolen-truck beef *and* credit card beef bein' withdrawn, and all—there was nothing for the video to be evidence *of*. And to give him a little gift from the Gutiérrez family, if that helped sweeten the deal."

"You mean bribe a witness. I thought you were supposed to be a good guy."

"I am," I said, "as I see it. I've just always been of the opinion that there's what's lawful, and there's what's right, and the twain don't always meet. I reckon if everybody comes out of this fandango as well off as they went in, or maybe *un poquito* better, then no harm, no foul."

She picked up the recorder and stared at it as if it had just fallen out of a flying saucer. "So what am I supposed to do with this?"

"I guess putting it back where you found it is out of the question? We gotta figure a way to ditch it without it getting tracked back to us—since it's evidence of the only actual crime that's been committed here, far as we know."

"Listening to you makes my head hurt."

"That's a surprisingly common reaction."

"I can get the recorder taken care of." She took out an iPhone and swiped it on with her thumb.

Connections started coming together in my mind so hard I was surprised she didn't hear the clicks. "Wait," I said. "You got a smartphone. I got a smartphone. All God's children got a smartphone."

She held the phone away from her face and looked at me in irritation.

I guess I don't really need to specify that, since that's pretty much the only way she had looked at me so far. I'll let you know when it changes, okay? "Who says that?"

"Groucho Marx. You got some gaps in your education, Little Ms. Frenchy. Or is it French Canadian?"

"I am West African."

"Okay. Now, if you'd just quit digressing, I was about to say that a modern teenager like Mindy-Lou Gutiérrez most assuredly has a smartphone."

She looked worried. Which is different from looking ticked at me, so I thought I'd mention it. "The police can track those by cell phone pings."

"Which makes it mighty handy for us nobody reported her as a runaway yet, much less a kidnap victim, giving the police no call to do that thing."

I turned off down another side street—less shady, with some none-too-hospitable-looking apartments on either side—and stopped.

"What're you doing now?"

"Not getting a traffic ticket," I said as I hit speed dial for the *abuela*.

"But you said you didn't care much about the laws."

"I do care much about being found with a self-professed hardened criminal and a boosted video recorder in my car. Now give me a minute. . . . *¿Abuelita?* Yeah, it's me. Yeah, I know you got caller ID. No, it's not money this time. . . ."

♣

Several minutes later I had my old-ass Galaxy III giving me directions to the nearest I-10 westbound on-ramp in the Google lady's voice.

"What are you doing now?" Candace asked.

An incoming SMS notification popped up. "Scoring!"

I pulled into a thrift store lot. Getting quite the tour of Kerrville's finer parking lots and side streets, today. I called the number.

"What now?"

"I'm calling Mindy-Lou. Family gave it to my grandma. She's blocked their numbers. But I'm hoping she'll take a call from me."

"From a complete stranger?"

"She ran off with a dude who calls himself Billy freaking Rainbow," I reminded her. Then I held a finger briefly in front of my lips. "Hello, Mindy-Lou? Please don't hang up! My name's Jesse Rodríguez, and I want to help you. . . ."

♠

"They're holed up in something called the Motel Hide-a-Way on the far outskirts of Fort Stockton," I said, putting my phone back on GPS directions and back in my shirt, and the truck back on the road. "Seems she saw through Billy's rainbow act and is pretty mad at him now."

"He's still with her?"

"Yeah. Apparently he pointed out to her they're both in this together."

She crossed herself as I slid into the traffic heading to El Paso.

"Hey!" I said. "You're Catholic too?"

"Of course. I am from *French* West Africa."

"I thought everybody there was Muslim or something?"

"Not my family," she said sniffily. "So, this girl just *told* you where they are?"

"Yep."

"Where is this Fort Stockton?"

"'Bout two hundred fifty miles west along Interstate 10."

"How much is that in kilometers?"

"A hair less than three and a half hours, if we stick to the speed limit. Which we will. Staties are pretty hard-nosed along this stretch. You don't, like, have a metric system for time, do you?"

"Three and a half—*nom d'un chien!*"

"What does that mean?"

"It's so far!"

"Well, those're the cards we got dealt, so they're the ones we play."

"Why Fort Stockton? Is it a major city?"

"It's not even as wide a spot in the road as scenic Kerrville."

"Then why are they there?"

"Billy's been up to his little rainbow games again. I get the impression

Mindy-Lou isn't feeling any too cut out for a life of crime—leastways, not with a screwup like him. But needs must when the Devil drives."

"Where did you get a phrase like that?"

"Read it in a book."

"American cowboys read?"

"This one does. My mom never had much truck with my reading anything but schoolbooks and the Bible. Said it was a waste of time. My mom loves me, but, truth to tell, she's wrong about a lot of things."

I took a breath. "All the latest contributor to the Billy-Mindy-Lou Follow Your Dreams to Hollywood Tour had in her billfold was enough money for two bus tickets to Fort Stockton. Luckily for everybody concerned that's so penny-ante the cops just laugh at you if you report it. So we're still clear."

"*Non.*"

"What's that mean?"

"They must eat. Is this girl not supposed to be a genius? Why did she run off with a con man?"

"Used his ace on her. Just blinked his pretty blue eyes at her. Genius means she's smart, not that she's got any common sense. I learned from playing *D&D* that Intelligence and Wisdom are so not the same thing."

"You are a nerd?"

"What? West Texas cowboys can't be nerds? I'm what you call a Millennial, lady. I'm a child of the age."

"I'm Millennial too," she said, "and I don't think either of us is what people think of when they hear that word. And you are full of surprises."

"Hey. I'm just some guy. Not that complicated."

"Then how did you get mixed up in this?"

"Girl lives in Modesto, but she got family here. Us Latinos got big families. Tend to be spread pretty far apart. Her auntie plays bingo with my *abuela*—my grandmother. She said the family was going nuts because their daughter lit out from the band contest last night. They were willing to pay to get her back—real quiet like."

"Why did you say yes?"

"Other than the fact nobody says no to my grandma?" My granny is a mean old Mexican lady—she was born in Zacatecas, though she speaks English like any other West Texas shitkicker—who cusses like a rap star, smokes big cigars, and is maybe the smartest person I know. "Well, I lost my sort-of-semi-promising career as a bull rider after a bull and I had a little disagreement about which way my spine should curve."

"You are crippled? You seemed to move pretty briskly in that alley back there."

"And I'm paying for it now. I get around fine. I just don't dare take another ride on fifteen hundred pounds of fired-up Brahma, 'less I'm eager to ride a Rascal Scooter forever after that. Lost some of my riding friends when I left the circuit. Said I didn't have the grit to be a pro bull rider if I wasn't willing to risk a little thing like becoming paraplegic for my career. They're right, I reckon. So I needed a job. I don't want to lie around leeching off *mi familia*. And, just between you and me and the fine vintage vinyl upholstery, ranching work is starting to bore the backside off me."

"You are not as dumb as you look."

"That's a less common reaction to me. So how about you? How did a nice girl from the Congo wind up in West Texas with a broke-down old rodeo cowboy?"

"You are not old," she said. "You are younger than I, probably. I am a refugee from the . . . troubles in West Africa."

"The People's Paradise thing?"

She shuddered. I mean, like, it was like a big old hand grabbed her shoulder and shook her whole bony frame.

"Okay, no point dredging up any more bad memories," I told her. "Sorry. So after you left, what?"

"A family in Montreal adopted me and brought me over. Through a UN program. Not what you might think—they were a lovely older couple. They treated me very well."

"So what happened?"

"Winter. I took as much of it as I could, broke across the border, and headed south to Miami. I was looking for warmth. I found that, anyway."

"And then?"

She shrugged. "I was here illegally. I had no real skills. I will not become a prostitute. So I make use of my 'wild talent' to get by."

"You do crimes for a record label?"

"Let's say I am a person whom one calls when one needs results."

Bubbles and the Band Trip

Part 9

GOD'S WEENIES HAD STRENGTHENED their ranks, Michelle saw with dismay as she stepped outside the hotel into the cool morning air. They looked to be perhaps seventy-five to a hundred strong now.

But across the street, there was now a group of twenty jokers carrying signs saying, *Jokers Aren't Monsters*, *Jokers Are People Too*, and *Protect Jokers from Hate*.

Jinkies, Michelle thought. *How could this situation possibly go wrong?*

The Mob was clustered together, running the gauntlet from the hotel to the auditorium. A couple of God's Weenies broke off from the main group—a woman with stringy blond hair (Michelle wondered how she could be in the group coiffed like that) and a teenage boy with a raging case of cystic acne started following the band, yelling at them. Two of the joker protesters broke off from *their* group and caught up with the two GWs and began shouting back.

"Go on," Michelle told the band. "I'll catch up later."

One of the jokers was tall and looked like an apple tree from *The Wizard of Oz*. And it looked as pissed off, too. It pulled an apple off its branch, then threw it hard at the back of the teenage boy, clipping his ear.

The other joker was short and squat and wore overalls. Warty tumors grew from his neck, arms, and face. Michelle assumed he had them all over, as his overalls looked lumpy. Snot-yellow, viscous fluid dripped from the tumors and he smelled like four-day-old chicken left in the sun. He ran toward the GWs. As he got close, he stopped, then shook like a dog. Ropy fluid flew through the air. It landed all over the two GWs, making them shriek.

Michelle ran over to the four of them. "Knock this shit off. *Right. Now!*" A bubble was already in her hand.

"Yeah!" the tumor joker said. "You leave those kids alone."

"*Spawn of Satan!*" yelled the stringy-haired woman. She looked down at her clothes and looked like she was about to puke. The pimply-faced boy had much the same expression on his face. They turned and ran back toward the group of God's Weenies, leaving Michelle alone with the jokers.

"Oh, shut up," Michelle said wearily as she backed away from the tumor joker. His smell could gag a maggot. "You're all idiots."

"But we're here to help you," the tree joker said. "I don't under-stand."

"Because the more people running around being upset and angry, the more stupid is in the mix and the more likely someone is to get hurt," Michelle said with no small amount of annoyance. *Why was everyone being such a pain in her ass?* She *knew* she was going to hate this whole chaperone thing, but she hadn't expected it to be this bad.

"She's an ace. She doesn't understand," said tumor joker.

"No, well, I *am* an ace, but this is a wild card thing. They're afraid of *all* of us. Especially aces. You think they can intimidate me? Of course not. They're scared I'll do something like this. . . ." Two bubbles few from her hand and hit both the jokers square in the chest. Well, one square in the trunk. The bubbles were heavy, but she didn't make them too hard. Just enough to get their attention.

"Ow!" they said in unison. "Why did you do that?"

"To stop you from being idiots! Someone is probably recording this and it's going to end up all over social media. And I don't care because have you seen the search hits on 'Bubbles, video'? Now you two—and all the rest of the jokers here—you're vulnerable."

"We can stick up for ourselves," said the tumor joker. "You can't stop us, and you have no idea what it's like to be a joker. We have to fight for everything. And they still hate us."

Michelle gave him a *Joker, please* look that was one degree worse than a side-eye. And she suddenly found herself giving no fucks at all about either God's Weenies or the jokers.

"Please don't pull that crap on me, it makes my ass tired. Now I'm going to hear my daughter—my joker daughter—play bass in her jazz band."

She pivoted and started back to catch up with the band.

◆

The Modesto Melody Makers had been scheduled to lead off the performances on Thursday, but there was a problem, as Michelle discovered when they arrived at Tobin. Mindy-Lou Gutiérrez was still missing.

"Her parents hired someone to look for her," the Modesto band leader said, "but we don't know how long it will take. We need a postponement. Maybe we could go last. . . ."

Dr. Smith frowned. "We're all very worried about Mindy-Lou, of course, but it would not be fair to the other bands to rearrange the entire schedule without notice. Modesto goes on in the next five minutes, or you will have to withdraw."

Michelle and the Mob watched as the Melody Makers huddled together. Some of the girls were crying softly—whether from concern or nerves was unclear. Jillian, the girl who had quarreled with Mindy-Lou at the mixer, stood rigid with her hand clenched around her alto sax, eyes blazing. "I *knew* she was going to screw this up for us," Jillian said furiously.

"What do you want to do?" Dr. Smith asked them.

"We'll go on," the Modesto director told them. "You're already warmed up, kids. We're a damn fine band, Mindy-Lou or not. Let's go out there and do ourselves proud."

Michelle watched as the Melody Makers filed past the Mob. Tears and noses were wiped on the backs of hands. Basilio looked like he was about to cry.

Their performance was a train wreck.

Even Michelle could tell that Modesto wasn't at the same level without their star player. Or maybe they were just so demoralized by her absence that it threw them off their game.

"Oh. My. God," Adesina whispered. "It's . . . it's . . ."

"Awful," Marissa finished.

"Bad," Antonia said with a hush.

"The worst," Peter continued.

"So not good," Sean added.

"Badosity," Yerodin said softly. "Hella bad. Badarific."

"Shush," Michelle told them all.

The performance seemed to go on forever. When it was over, the Modesto band stood to take their bows, to anemic applause from the audience. They filed backstage looking shell-shocked.

Michelle's heart went out to them. Several years' work for all the Modesto musicians to get into the competition had likely been laid to waste.

"I feel guilty going on after them," Adesina said. "It seems really . . . unfair."

The rest of the Mob nodded in agreement.

♠　♥　♦　♣

The Secret Life
of Rubberband

Part 7

THE AUDITORIUM FILLED FAST Thursday morning. Fortunately Jan, who didn't sleep, had saved Robin a seat. "Christ," he said, lowering himself by degrees. "I'm tired."

"Coffee?" Jan offered him her cup.

"Don't mind if I do." His fingers brushed her glove as he took the cup, and the mild jolt, at least, helped. So did the cup's contents, though not the way he intended. "What the hell is this stuff?"

"Coffee."

"Did you use all the sugar in the Starbucks, or just most of it?"

"Supposedly black coffee is part of a vast culinary conspiracy to hide the bitter taste of the brainwashing agents added to franchise coffee, pursuant to FDA Secret Regulation 7732-Apple. You can read all about it here." She passed him a pamphlet. He passed her back the coffee cup. "Sugar denatures the chemicals. Plus, it's delicious."

Onstage, the Jokertown Mob busied about their instruments. The Detonators waited in the wings. Robin glimpsed Vicky arguing with her band's bassist. "Your niece looks happy."

"Killer kid. She'll be okay." Jan removed the lid of her cup to get at the last of the vaguely coffee-soaked sugar mash at the bottom. "Care to bet on the outcome?"

"I'm flat broke. I'd have to borrow money from you to bet."

"I can handle that. Hundred bucks says my niece takes your kids for a ride."

Robin grinned. "You're on."

Adesina plugged in the bass. The amp crackled. At the drums, Antonia, ungloved, flourished drumsticks through the forest of her hands.

Robin and Jan shook hands.

And the bands played on.

Dust and the Darkness

Part 2

THE MOMENT WE GOT off the highway in Fort Stockton, she said, "Wait! Turn right here!" I did. It took us between a Motel 6 and some kind of redbrick office building thing. "Stop here!"

I did. "What's up? You sound like it's mighty urgent."

"It is. You seem like a sweet boy. So I am very sorry."

"For—"

She puked Darkness right in my face.

I tried to weave out of it, but my dang shoulder harness trapped me. It's amazing how hard it is to keep track of even simple, everyday things when ace-powered blackness suddenly blots out your vision. I'd just tripped the belt release when I heard my door open and felt hot air wash over my left side.

She yanked me out onto the hot asphalt on my back. "Ouch!"

"Sorry. You'll get your car back, too. Eventually."

My vision cleared in time to watch the back end of my RAV4 dwindle down the street and hang a sudden left. Without a signal.

"Shoot," I said, slowly picking myself up. My muscles hurt more than the vertebrae, at least. I rubbed my lower back. "I need to wash Baby something awful."

Yes, I named my *troca* after Dr. Tachyon's spaceship. Yes, I really am a cowboy nerd.

♥

All three of 'em were standing in the middle of a motel room that was precisely as crappy as you'd expect a motel called the Hide-a-Way in the nether reaches of Fort Stockton to be, talking loudly, when I walked in the open front door.

"Knock knock," I said. Then, to the striking girl who was towering over me from several feet away, not, "Really? Pigtails?"—though I surely was thinking it—but, "I'm Jesse. I'm the one who talked to you on the phone."

"How the *fuck* did you get here?" Candace said.

"Uber." *La Familia Gutiérrez* was running up quite the expense total. Well, I didn't ask them for the job.

"Who—" Billy started.

"He answered that, dumbass," Mindy-Lou snapped. *Ooh, trouble in Paradise.*

But nothing compared to what came in through the big black hole that suddenly appeared in the water-stained wallpaper.

I already said I was no Sherlock. Looks like I'm not an action hero either. These two dudes came strolling in, right through the wall, one a weedy little runt in overalls with a shock of dirty-looking hair, the other being what looked for all the world like a human crossed with a hound dog, with the lovely parts of neither. The weedy one had him on a leash. The doggy one looked us over with sad, bloodshot brown eyes sunk in saggy folds like a bloodhound's, and drooled down his slack lower lip.

And me? I stood there staring like somebody had sneaked in and superglued my boot soles to the scary brown-like carpet.

"We'll take it from here, Darkness," the guy on two legs said in a Louisiana drawl as the hole vanished behind them. "Looks like you lose."

The piteous joker guy, who seemed to be wearing ratty gym shorts, for which I was powerfully grateful, pulled rubbery lips back from a mouthful of yellow teeth whose disturbingly human appearance was only made worse by prominent fangs.

His baby blues practically bugging out of his head, Billy Rainbow started pointing at the dog-man and gibbering. *"What is that?"* seemed

to be the essence of what he was trying to get across. Candace just
stood there looking cool as always. "Buck and Blood. Eh, *bien*. So our
boss double-crossed me and farmed the contract out to you. What
makes you think he won't do the same to you?"

"'Cause we win," the one I took for Buck said, with the air of a
man who's discovered an irrefutable argument. "We bring him back
the goods."

"Are you talking about me?" Mindy-Lou demanded. "Because if you
are, that's, like, totes demeaning."

"You *cochons* haven't won, as you Americans say, dick," Candace
said. And suddenly, where the two interlopers stood, was one irregu-
lar blob of Darkness.

"Let's get out of here," she said. "They are dumb but danger—"

With a savage snarl the dog-man came flying out of the black
cloud and hit her with his palms. His weight knocked her right over.
I heard her head bounce off the edge of the writing desk with one leg
shimmed up by splints of wood. Then she landed on her back beneath
the high wall mount where a TV that was older than me was shack-
led as massively as if it would've brought more than five bucks at a
pawnshop.

The standing man was laughing nasty-like. "Ol' Blood, he don't
need to see you to strike. He can smell your brown sugar just fine!"

Candace had to be groggy from the head crack, but was gamely
fending those scary-toothed canine jaws from her face, while managing not to let the joker get a tooth lock on her arms. I reached out
with my mind for a handful of dust.

It's like groping with my own physical hand, best I can describe it.
Housekeeping here was the sort where they charge you extra if you
want the sheets changed before you take the room, and we were in way
southwest Texas, which meant dust should not be in short supply. But
for some reason it took me a spell to feel some. Then I ran my mind
over it—that sounds way creepier than it is, but let's keep moving—
and managed to scoop a pinch off the bedspread and stain-mottled
pillowcase.

This I tossed in Blood's nose, open mouth, and hound-dog eyes. My
power doesn't work just on literal dust; all it has to be is what you call
your fine particulate matter. I reckon this was mostly human dander

and dust mites, which sounds disgusting, but that might not matter much to some poor son of a one cursed by the wild card to be as much dumb animal as man. What did matter to him was that he started sneezing and choking violently, and left off trying to bite Candace to dab at his own eyes and whimper.

She got her feet up against his chest and heaved him right off her. She got up smart quick, then, but swayed.

"Dumb cunt don't know when you're beat," Buck said, and pulled out a gun. A snub-nosed .38 of some kind. Not my first choice, or second, and he held it down by his hip, which is second worse only to holding it sidewise for hitting what you think you're shooting at. That didn't make him any less deadly. Especially since he struck me as none too tightly wrapped.

So here we were: Candace too woozy to Dark him. Me needing a minute or so to recharge the mental batteries to go foraging for more dust. Billy apparently still losing whatever mind he had in buckets over the admittedly unsettling and unhappifying appearance of Blood.

And Mindy-Lou, all six feet of her in her little short Catholic schoolgirl–looking skirt and blouse, brown pigtails flying, said, "Fuck this," rared up, and fetched Buck a mighty clout over the ear with a wooden chair.

Somehow Buck managed not to trigger off a shot as he went down in a heap of busted-up chair parts, a lucky man it was too cheap-ass to cave in his skull. He also managed to keep a hold of his snubby. He was moaning and stirring his limbs vaguely, like a drunk penguin, even before he finished sitting down hard on his skinny butt.

"Good job," I said, grabbing Mindy-Lou by the wrist and towing her in the direction of the still-open door. Fortunately, the Valkyrie fury, if that's a thing Latinas can catch, had drained right out of her. She came along docile as a puppy.

"I don't understand," she said. "That was supposed to knock him out."

"That's just movies," I said, as we emerged from the hot and dim of the motel room to the hot and bright of late afternoon. "Reckon you gave him a concussion, though, that makes you feel better."

The RAV4 was unlocked and running, which of course meant the keys were in. Candace seemed to have wanted a quick getaway more than she worried about getting her car stolen. *My car. Which she had stolen.* Easy come, easy go, I guess.

I bundled Mindy-Lou any which way into the passenger seat, trying not to pay an unseemly amount of attention to bare brown legs that looked as long as all of me. I vaulted the hood, which made my durned back twing but looked *boss,* I'm just sure, and ducked behind the wheel. Which was blistering hot, of course. Apparently Candace's limited driving experience had not clued her in to things like sunshades.

"Ow, ow, ow," I whined as Candace yanked the right-side rear door open and literally dove across the seats. She got herself righted just as a second, longer person folded himself into the other side.

"Shut the door!" I yelled at Billy Rainbow as I screamed Baby in a backward arc, shifted, and sent her squealing and bouncing across the cracked and weed-sprung asphalt parking lot toward the street. "And what is he doing here?"

"The exit's that way," Mindy-Lou said, pointing off to my left and waving her hand in front of my face in the process.

"Irrelevant." We bounced over the curb, I screeched us more or less parallel with the road, and off we went.

"Why are you turning here?" Candace demanded as I hung the second left on two wheels, between a warehouse with a forklift parked outside and a strip club that looked as if it had been closed for years.

"Getting out of line of sight of those clowns who walked in on our cozy little soiree. I don't want 'em dropping through the roofs in our laps."

"Helps if he shoots at us, too," offered Billy, who had recovered his composure smart quick out of Blood's presence. Though Buck had about as much chance to hit us if he threw that snubby.

"So what was all that back there about?" I gobbled. "Who *were* those guys? Is everybody an ace these days?"

"Was that a *Dr. Strangelove* reference?" Billy asked.

"Yep."

"Well," Candace said, tentative for once, "perhaps I didn't tell you the whole story of who I'm working for."

"Which is to say?"

"The record label that's so hot to sign Mindy-Lou is owned by the Syndicate. So am I, you might say. And those two *connards* back there."

"*What?*" Mindy-Lou and I said at once. I was still driving around at random. If I got lost, Google Maps remembered where I-10 was. I had faith.

"Fuck," said Billy. He seemed pretty quick on the uptake for such a dedicated screwup. "We are so fucked."

"*I* am fucked," Candace said.

Beside me, Mindy-Lou burst into tears.

Little as I could blame the child, current events considered, it did nothing to help my considerably frazzled composure. "Listen," I said over her wailing. She had a good voice even doing that. "I think we all need to sit down together, calm right the heck down, and talk about all this in a rational matter."

"So says the big, strong cowboy," Candace sneered. Which was unfair, since I am by no means *big*. I like to think of myself as average height for an American. Plus I'm a wiry little *lagarto,* as my grandma likes to say. "Why didn't you shoot him? You're an American. This is *Texas*. Where is your gun?"

Why, it's right there in the glove compartment in front of our Ms. Gutiérrez, I thought. *Where you never bothered checking.* I had, though, right quick before walking into that motel room.

"We still need to deliver Mindy-Lou back to the contest without raising a public ruckus," I said. "If I shot him, no matter how justified, a mighty ruckus would ensue. So far the police still don't care enough to connect the dots on our little petty crime spree. Somebody dead on the floor around a bullet wound would change that pronto. So we need to think in terms of less drastic solutions. Or at least less noisy ones."

"Take her back?" Billy chirped up from the back seat. "So you're kidnapping her? *Cool!*"

That brought us a moment of blessed silence. Mindy-Lou gave off sniffling and sobbing to stare at Candace and me with big, brown, deer-in-headlight eyes.

"That . . . depends," I said. "Now everybody please pipe down while

I figure out a place we can light without attracting any more unwanted attention."

♣

"First things first," I said, as we all tucked into the bags of Mc-Donald's we had set before us on the weathered wood picnic table tucked away in a corner of Pat Taylor Athletic Field on the southwest side of Fort Stockton. Where fortunately no athletic events were taking place, nor seemed in the offing. "How did those slasher-movie nutjobs find you?"

Candace sat across from me, chowing down on a Filet-O-Fish. She looked thoughtful, chewed, and swallowed. Raised up proper, whatever else she was. "I told you the cops could track Mindy-Lou's phone by cell-tower hits, *non?*"

"*Sí.* And I told you they had no reason I could see to do so, since the crimes involved were minor."

"Just because they do not do so officially, does not mean they cannot do so as individuals, on the side."

"You're saying the Syndicate bought a cop?"

She laughed. "No need. I'm saying they have any number on the inside of any law enforcement agency you know about, and very, very many you do not. Or perhaps they rented somebody else's mole. They do that a lot too. Somebody made an official-sounding request for the data, and the cell company obediently handed it over without raising any fuss about due process. One thing I learned since joining your underworld is what a very great favor all your antiterrorism laws do for criminal organizations. Your law enforcement groups all share information so freely these days, there is hardly any infosec at all."

"They're not mine," I said. I wished I could've said I was surprised. "So now we get to our big question: Mindy-Lou, do you want to go back to San Antonio now?"

She nodded vigorously. Her mouth was occupied by being stuffed with a big old bite of Triple Cheeseburger. I already knew the kids hadn't gone hungry on their little jaunt. That was the source of one of the biggest problems I could see in our road that wasn't a pair of murderous sideshow freaks. "Yes, please," Mindy-Lou said, wiping her mouth with a napkin. "I wish I'd never laid eyes on this asshole."

Billy looked as hangdog as a body can who's stuffing his face with Chicken McNuggets and sucking on a strawberry milkshake like a five-year-old. "I'm sorry, hon."

"Don't 'hon' me, you—you *loser*. I trusted you. I believed in you. And then your car broke down before we even got out of San Antonio, and you've been getting me deeper and deeper into this—this *shit* since!"

He looked at us as if expecting sympathy. Yeah, lemme point that out in the dictionary for you, pal. "Man, I feel so bad about everything," he said. "I never thought it'd all go south like this."

Well, for that I *could* sympathize with him. Almost. The plain fact was, he and Little Miss Muffet here had made a truly wondrous mess of things in a really short period of time. It was an impressive achievement, looked at from the perspective of someone who wasn't me and staring down the three horns of a joker dilemma: Who was least terrible to wind up on the wrong side of, the cops, the Mob, or *mi abuela*?

Okay, maybe just a nat dilemma. Disappointing Grandma was not an option.

"I mean, I woke up this morning and suddenly it hit me: I probably shouldn't have boosted that poor peckerwood's truck and his bank card, even if it was only just the one. I mean, he probably misses 'em mighty bad 'long about now. That was just mean. And 'mean' just isn't me."

"You know," Candace said, swigging a bottled water, "I make a habit of trying extremely hard not to kill anybody. But I am much more tempted to make an exception for this one than even for Buck and Blood."

Leaving aside the odd little tint to her voice that suggested this no-murder policy was a relatively new development on her part, I was gut-inclined to believe Billy. He was coming across to me not so much malicious, or even stone cold like a real con man, as somebody who had never learned the habit of thinking things through.

Billy had lost what color he had in his face and, at least for the moment, his appetite. "I'm so sorry," he said. "I—I just want to make everything right. Like all of this never happened."

"Well, *one* of those things is actually going to happen," I said. "You are most certainly going to help us make things right, my friend. And you best pray it's possible."

"I'm an atheist," he said.

"Well, thank God you're not a Protestant, as my mom would say. But right now, Candace, I think we all need to hear a little more detail of what kind of people you've been bent on delivering Mindy-Lou to."

She sighed. "Bad ones."

"What's all this about Titan Records and the Syndicate, anyway?" Mindy-Lou asked.

"They are the same. They want you back very badly, child."

"But they were gonna make me a star!"

"Why'd you run off with Billy Sunshine, then?" Candace asked.

"Rainbow," Billy said.

"Shut up," we all three said.

"He was gonna make me a *Hollywood* star! The first marquee actress and movie scorer, like, ever!"

I had to admit she had the looks for it. And apparently the talent. The "Mozart of Modesto," remember?

The *abuela* and I had had another conversation about Mindy-Lou's family applying healing transfusions to my own fast-fading bank card. "You want *more* money, *pendejo?* They're already making unhappy noises about how much all this is going to cost them."

"They ain't seen nothin' yet. And tell them even that is going to mightily pale beside how much it would cost to defend their little songbird from all these criminal charges she's been ringing up. Anyway, they agreed to cover expenses."

"That they did," Granny said, and I could *hear* the twinkle in her eye. "And they better not try to weasel out!"

Guess who paid for dinner? Yeah, I was hungry, too.

"I am worried," Candace said. "Not just that they sent out Buck and Blood after they'd promised me the job. But what the job really is. They may not be intending to groom the girl as America's next pop star. Someone like her could fetch quite a price in certain corners of the world. Especially if she is a virgin."

"Hey, man," Billy said, "don't look at me. I didn't touch her."

"He most certainly did not!" Mindy-Lou said indignantly. "I told him I was saving myself for marriage, and he was a perfect gentleman. Well, that way, anyway."

"Then may God have mercy on your soul," Candace said.

I was looking at her pretty hard. "So that's what you were going to give her up to? To be sold for a sex slave?"

She dropped her eyes to her grease-stained yellow sandwich wrapper. "I hoped not. They can make a great deal of money if she hits big as a performer in the U.S., or even in Europe. The Syndicate owns a lot of the pop music business, you know."

"I didn't, no. Easy to believe, though."

"But not even they can control all the outcomes. It is always a gamble. If they are offered a big enough amount up front, that will tempt them strongly. In a way such people are not used to resisting."

"You reckon they got an offer?" I asked. Mindy-Lou and Billy, who also sat opposite each other at the table, were following our conversation like onlookers at a tennis match. You could almost hear their eyeballs clicking left and right. At least they weren't saying anything. Small favors, you know?

"First I must give you more background."

"Make it fast."

"Please. This is important. I never meant to work for the Syndicate. I was a freelancer, doing all kinds of jobs where my talents proved useful. Some of them were even legal. Most of them were gray. Then I found out I'd unwittingly contracted with a minor Mob boss, a Ukrainian. And once you sign on with them, they have a way of sinking their claws into you."

"Just like a movie!" Billy said, and I swear he perked right up.

He perked down at the look she gave him. "I spent the last couple of years . . . not wholly my own woman. Doing things even I find distasteful. At one point in my life, I was a monster. I never want to be one again. I would rather die—and I am a survivor, I assure you. But their tasks made it hard. I worked out an arrangement: one last score, and they'd let me walk. I trusted this was it: they believed enough in Ms. Gutiérrez's star potential to offer a premium contract to get her back. Enough to buy me out of what they thought of as my obligation to them.

"Or so I thought. Until the wall opened up and Buck and his brother walked through, back at the motel. That's Blood's power: he can make a tunnel from anywhere to anywhere. Otherwise, he is simple—impaired."

"I kinda gathered," I said, starting on my second Triple Cheeseburger with jalapeños. Which were not as good as real green chiles, but the alternative was "chili," and nobody wants that.

"The gun is new, though. In the past Buck has been content to let his brother do the violent work. You saw. They've mostly played taxi for heavier hitters. It looks as if Buck is aiming for promotion."

"So maybe they're auditioning—like, for your old job?"

"My place in the hierarchy, perhaps. Their involvement makes very clear to me that the Syndicate has no intention of letting me leave their employ. Alive, anyway."

"What does all this mean for me?" Mindy-Lou sounded as sick as anything else. And who could blame her.

Candace shook her head. "I—I will not take you back. Fuck them."

"But I want to go back!" Mindy-Lou said. "I miss my band. Well, except Jillian. She's why I left. She's a total bitch, and I'm sick of her pushing me around. But I've worked so hard for this. I want to be in the contest. Let Billy run off to L.A. This is what I'm supposed to do."

"My employers do not take happily to disappointment," Candace said.

I put down my sandwich—regretfully, because I still felt a powerful hunger upon me—laced my fingers together, and thumped my hands down on the table. "Okay," I said. "There's a way to work this out. There's always a way."

"Yeah, what?" Mindy-Lou said, a beat after Candace did.

"We'll get to that." *When I pull it out of my narrow fanny.* "See, you have a problem, Mindy-Lou. Which is the little crime spree you and Charlie Starkweather Junior here have gone on. Now, it's too small-time for cops to bother with. But it gets out you ran away from the big-band contest in San Antonio, with the national spotlight awaiting you and all, that'll change *muy pronto*. If they put all the petty scams together and douse the heap with possible publicity, prosecutors start pulling out their lighters."

Okay, it's possible I let my metaphor kinda run away with me, here.

"Best bet is to claim you were flat kidnapped. That Billy used his rainbow power to make you commit crimes. That makes you a victim instead of an accomplice."

"He didn't," she said. "The only time I saw his rainbows before was when, like, he shone them in other people's eyes at the contest. Sort of a party trick, like hypnosis. I didn't see any harm in it. But I wasn't kidnapped."

"Good for you," I said, and meant it.

"But you saw through his bullshit pretty quickly," Candace said.

"Hey!" Billy burst out. "I'm right here!"

Candace gave him a quelling look. He quelled. Then to Mindy-Lou, "Why did you keep going along with his rip-offs, then?"

"Well, we needed to eat. And a place to sleep. And he was like, 'Sorry, bae, but we're already in this together.'"

"Wait," I said. "He called you 'bae'? Literally that?"

"She's still beyond all else to me!" he said proudly.

"I never killed anybody at all," I said. "But that makes *me* want to reconsider."

"You're the one losing the plot, now, Dust," Candace said.

I blinked at her. It was a childhood nickname—never Dusty, which I hated. People started hanging "Dust" on me once they noticed I had something going for me normal people didn't. Years before I ever did. "Sorry. Been a long day for me too. Anyway. These things happened. Fortunately nobody's gotten hurt, nothing major's gotten broken. *Right?*"

"Right!" Billy almost yelled.

"Cross my heart and hope to die," Mindy-Lou said, and actually crossed her heart. I don't think I'd seen anybody do that since I was thirteen.

"Here's our situation. We got to track down the victims of your various misdeeds and get them all to agree to forget about pressing charges. And quit looking eager, Billy. We will do that without making use of those rainbows of yours."

Against honest folk, I thought. Because the seed of a plan had started sprouting in my mind. It was not a good plan. It was an insanely risky plan. But it was also way better than every other course I could see.

All of which wound up with us certainly boned and maybe dead, instead of just probably.

"Once we do that, and we are on a tight schedule here, we will deliver you safe and sound back to the contest."

"You just want to make sure you get paid," Billy sneered.

"Of course he does," Mindy-Lou said. "He's not an idiot, like you."

"Of course I do. But keep in mind that none of the things we are about to do will stand the light of day. They may be legal, I hope. Some of them. But—once people start looking for dirty bits here, they're gonna find 'em."

Mindy-Lou had been nodding along. Now her face turned green. "But won't that mean the record company—"

"Nobody is selling you into slavery. All right?"

"But how do we stop them?"

I ticked a finger at her. I hoped it made me look more grown-up than I was feeling, right then. "In due time," I said, because for a fact I hadn't got it thought all the way through. And also because if I told them what I was thinking of, they would have all gone bounding off across the plains like ol' jackrabbits. Including Candace.

"First we got to get you off the hook with the law. Then we work things out with the, uh, the record label. And, yes, for you, too, Candace."

"So you, the White Knight American Cowboy, aren't even considering calling the police?" Candace asked.

"No. You're not from around here, so maybe you don't know how things go. I was raised to walk the straight and narrow by a mama who believes things authority figures tell her. But I'm a working-class, rural *Latino*. Brown skinned in Texas, *¿sabes qué?* I did not grow up believing that *la policía* are my friends."

"You know, Mexico's right nearby, and bein' as I got my powers, and all, the border won't hold us up—" Billy started off, giving Mindy-Lou a soulful blue-eyed look. I could see how he was used to melting a girl's heart.

Too bad hers had annealed, at least where he was concerned. "No! And fuck you and the horse you rode in on, Billy McConaghy!"

That was the first I heard of his last name. He shrugged it off with a sad smile and began sauntering around the table toward Candace. "Y'all seem like well-intentioned people," he drawled, "even toward a sinner like me. I think you mean that, honest I do. But I think it's really best for me to—"

He rolled his right palm over. A rainbow spurted out of it, arcing directly into Candace's big black eyes. It even dazzled me, off to one side.

For a moment she just stood there. Then she whipped out a shin and caught him in the crotch so hard she lifted his boot heels plumb off the ground.

The rainbow went out.

"If you ever try that again," she said, "I swear I will cut your throat and bury you under a cactus."

Billy looked at me with a tentative grin. "Keep that shit away from me, *gabacho*," I told him, "or I'll dig up the cactus for her."

His shoulders sagged. He honestly looked about to cry. Which I took for sincere. "Make you a deal," I told him. "You help us, and don't try any more funny business, and at the end we will let you walk away with a bill of health as clean as Mindy-Lou's. On the other hand, if she or any of the rest of us sink, you will sink as well, and a good deal deeper and more painfully. *¿Me intiendes, ese?*"

"I don't really speak much Spanish," Mindy-Lou said, "but he means, do you understand?"

"I know what it means." Billy swallowed hard. "And yes, sir, I do. You may not trust me, and your reasons are sound, but I do trust you."

"Especially on that 'sinking painfully and deep' part," Candace said.

"Mindy-Lou?" I asked.

"Do I have a choice?" She brightened, slightly. "Whatever you've got is better than any kind of future I can see. Probably."

"Fair enough. Now, while we're still on the clock, here, we got a little prep work to do. You got a smartphone, right, Candace? And I bet it's a burner?"

She nodded at that first part, looking a little suspicious, which didn't seem any out of the ordinary for her. Her look curdled up plenty on that second, like I'd asked for her PIN to her bank account or something. "You have a plan?"

"It's coming." I stood up. "Well, now that we're all happy friends and all, we got us a job of work to do. Grab up your dinners, kids, and eat 'em on the run or chuck 'em in the trash. We got no time to sit around chewing!"

♠ ♥ ♦ ♣

Bubbles and the
Band Trip

Part 10

THE MOB HAD JUST finished "Turtle Bop" when the fire alarm went off.

"Please file out to the nearest exit," came the announcement. "Please file out to the nearest exit."

A groan ran through the audience and the bands waiting to play.

"Well, this sucks," Asti said. There was much agreement among the other Mob members.

Michelle walked onstage. She'd been hanging out in the wings with Robin, Wally, and Priscilla Beecher. They were watching the band play and keeping an eye on things.

"There's an exit back here," she said. "Let's head out that way."

The band stood and began to file out carrying their instruments.

"You need to leave those."

"We can't just leave them here on the floor!" Sean exclaimed.

"Our cases are right by the exit door," Asti said.

"This could be something serious, you betcha," Wally said.

"Rusty is right," Robin said. "This could be something real, let's get a move on."

"Can we just stick our instruments into the cases? Please?" asked Peter. "It won't take any time at all."

"Okay, be quick," Robin said.

The kids did as they were told, not even bothering to fasten the catches.

♠

The fire trucks pulled away. And much to everyone's relief, it was a false alarm. At the all clear, everyone trudged back inside. Michelle was glad to get back into the auditorium. They'd been waiting on the concrete walkway that wrapped around the building. Despite the beautiful day, it had gotten warm standing outside on it. It was cool and dark inside, and it took a moment for her eyes to adjust.

The Mob filed in through the backstage door, and the kids made a beeline to their instrument cases.

"You know, I'm beginning to think this trip is cursed," Michelle said to the other adults.

Even though her hair was securely braided, Michelle still ran a hand across the top of her head as if to smooth it down. She had bulked up some, weighing in at about a hundred and fifty pounds. She wore a loose-fitting black skirt and a snug-fitting gray jersey top that showed off her cleavage.

"I just hope—"

A gasp and a strangled scream from Adesina interrupted her. A surge of panic went through Michelle. Nothing much scared Michelle, but her daughter's cry terrified her.

Adesina was standing in front of her open case, but her bass wasn't inside. Michelle saw two diamondback rattlesnakes where the bass should be. They were coiled side by side, heads starting to raise, rattles shaking.

"Don't move," Michelle said. There was a crack in her voice. A sound she only vaguely remembered having just as her card turned. A sound fragile and full of fear.

Michelle lifted her left hand and two bullet-sized bubbles formed.

"*Mom! No!*"

"What!?"

"My bass case! Don't mess up my bass case!"

Two thoughts ran through Michelle's head: *Are you insane?* And: *Are you insane?*

She let the bubbles go. They began to expand in the air and in a moment, they encased the snakes in hard shells. The rattlers struck the inside of the bubbles, but their fangs slipped off harmlessly.

"Kewl," Adesina said.

The movement of their strikes sent the bubbles falling to the floor. The snakes began rolling around. Their rattles sounded like maracas.

"Eep," Antonia said as one of the rattlers rolled near her. She slid to one side to avoid it. "Seriously, I'm not going near that thing."

The other rattler rolled under the table where some of the instrument cases were. Asti got down on his hands and knees to grab it, but it slid off his fingers and began rolling toward Sean.

"Oh, hell no," Sean said, scooting away from the bubble. "I'm with Antonia." He nudged the bubble away with his foot. It slipped in Peter's direction and he wheeled back.

"I've got nothing against them, but I'm not for them either."

Ghost went noncorporeal and floated up a couple of feet. Rusty made a lunge for them and only succeeded in falling on his face as they spun out of his grip.

"Mom, do something!"

"Hey, you were the one who wanted her bass case kept non-gross."

"That's totes unfair."

"Fine," Michelle said. "*I'll* get the snakes."

◆

"I cannot believe something like this happened," Priscilla said. There was a frantic, birdlike quality to her hands as she spoke, and there was a rose bloom on her cheeks. Michelle found it incongruous with the normally composed Miss Beecher.

"Of course, y'all will want to withdraw the children from the competition," she said.

Michelle was pissed, but she was also scared and she didn't like feeling scared. She'd rarely felt this stomach-roiling panic. (*Don't kid yourself about that,* a little voice whispered.) Someone was willing to endanger the life of her daughter as well as the other band members.

She was certain now that the series of events that seemed to be pranks or accidents were something more sinister. She held the bubbles with the rattlers in her hands, uncertain what to do with them. Maybe she could put them in her room fridge until they went to sleep. The Big Sleep. But that seemed fucked up and cruel.

"I don't know what I want to do first," Michelle said, her voice tight with anger. "Obviously, they need some real security backstage. We need to find out if there were cameras back here." Just then, her phone started vibrating. She ignored it.

"Mom," Adesina said, "I need to see if someone from one of the other bands will lend me their bass."

"You're not going to play now!" Michelle said hotly.

"Yes, yes we are," Adesina replied. She looked at the rest of her band members. "Right?"

They all nodded in agreement.

"My trumpet is missing, too," Peter said. "We need to find replacements, quick."

"Someone could have been seriously hurt, or worse!"

"But they weren't," Adesina replied. "Ghost and I just got to the band this year, but everyone else has been practicing for this for three years. Someone is trying to scare us away! We leave, they win."

"Next time it'll be something worse."

Adesina didn't reply. She had a look of such mulish determination that it took Michelle aback.

"I'll be right back," Adesina said.

♥

The overhead floods made Adesina's wings gleam. Her coppery dreads shone.

"Uhm, I hate to be a bother," Adesina said in a cool voice as she faced the audience. "But my bass and Peter's trumpet were stolen during the false alarm. I know this might make us late to finish our performance, but there were diamondbacks in my bass case, and, well, I thought we might be given a few more minutes to get some replacements."

A shocked gasp went through the audience.

"Are y'all all right?" Dr. Smith asked. "Where are the snakes now? Good Lord! Do we need to clear the auditorium?"

"Oh, we're all fine," Adesina said. She even sounded cheerful. "Mom took care of the snakes. That's no big deal. We just need to have someone loan us instruments. I need a bass and Peter needs a trumpet."

"I got my axe right here," Buddy Robins said. He came down the aisle with his bass case and laid it across the arms of three empty seats in the front row. He opened the case, revealing a well-worn Fender five-string jazz bass. After taking it out, he attached the guitar strap, then walked up to the stage and held it up to Adesina. "Here you go, little lady."

An incredulous expression was stamped on Adesina's face as she took it from him. "Th-th-thank you, Mr. Robins," she said breathlessly. "I—I don't know what to say."

He smiled. "Just play the best you can. And I'm getting that back from you."

Adesina nodded.

Just then, a small voice piped up. It was Jan's niece, Vicky. "Peter can borrow my trumpet, but he better have his own mouthpiece."

Peter went out onstage and held up his mouthpiece. "Always carry one with me."

Now that Adesina and Peter had instruments, the band came onstage and settled into their chairs. Sharon stood in front of them, then brought them in on the downbeat.

♣

Robin, Michelle, Wally, and Priscilla stood backstage watching the kids play and keeping an eye on their instrument cases.

There was a metallic creaking noise. Michelle looked and saw that Wally's mouth was downturned and his face was scrunched up as if it were a ball of aluminum foil. "Oh, this is bad," he said. "Cripes, who would do something like this?"

"I have a theory," Robin said. Like Wally's, his mouth was pulled into a frown, but it kept going, stretching like Silly Putty. "Those Purity Baptist Church jerks are my number one suspects."

"But they've been outside this whole time," Wally said. "Someone would have seen them come into the building. It has to be someone else."

"Let's just stop speculating," Michelle said. "I know someone who'll help sort this mess out. In the meantime, we need to decide what we're going to do about keeping those kids safe until the end of the competition." To keep the snakes from rolling around backstage, she'd put them into Adesina's open bass case after the kids started to play.

She pulled her phone out of her back pocket and searched for a name, then she tapped on the number. A woman answered and said, "Ackroyd and Creighton Investigations. How may we help?"

♠ ♥ ♦ ♣

Dust and the Darkness

Part 3

I SHALL SPARE YOU most of the details of cleaning up Billy and Mindy-Lou's messes, of which they left a surprising number for a couple of kids who claimed they were trying to keep on the down-low. There was no squaring accounts with the woman who emptied her wallet to give them bus fare to Fort Stockton back in Kerrville, since they had no idea who she was, and the woman had raised no peep that either my or Candace's contacts could find out about with the law. Apparently the Mob were hedging their bets and hadn't cut off her access. Or maybe they aren't really a lot more efficient than any other big organization. Maybe the bus money really was a gift from a concerned citizen who took pity on a couple of destitute and really pretty kids.

The pizza joint from whose all-you-can-eat buffet the pair had walked out without paying last night was a potentially nasty sticking point. Like borrowing Rooster's high-dollar pickup, dine-and-dash is a felony in the state of Texas. Luckily the Mordecai's Hammer Pizza franchise they had ripped off lacked internal surveillance cameras, because the chain's owner, retired ace Mordecai Jones, had something of a paranoid streak and didn't believe in spying on his employees and customers. (He'd dropped the "Harlem" part of his ace name right before he founded the chain a few years back, pointing out that black aces always got hung with some kind of moniker that called attention to their race.) Even better, the owner-manager was another distant cousin of mine, so the criminal report the restaurant put out on the pair—no names attached—got withdrawn as mistaken.

None of which is to say it was *cheap*. Business is business, and I most particularly was not going to stiff my *primo*, distant or not, after he'd agreed to cut us a truly immense quantity of slack. Nor did I dread the inevitable "perpetually growing expense account" conversation with my granny. For once in my life I was enjoying talking to the fearsome old *bruja* on the phone, since she'd decided the Gutiérrez family's understandable concern about the money hemorrhage this whole thing had turned into constituted an attempt to stiff *us*. Admittedly, since Mr. G was a financial adviser and Mom was a big-time dentist in Modesto, they probably weren't hurting for funds.

We found ourselves in a pawnshop on the north side of town, near the Flying J airport, trying to untangle the transaction by which Billy and Mindy-Lou—meaning, as usual, Billy and his rainbows—had gained the funds needed to front the bucks for a second night at the Hide-a-Way. On the one hand, Billy omitted to actually say he owned the amp he'd hocked. On the other, the members of the Bon Iver cover band he'd rainbowed as they were breaking down from a barroom gig at weird o'clock in the morning were drunk, usually drunk, and in the habit of losing important bits of gear like their instruments, and apparently their van, when in that condition.

They'd filed no police reports before we tracked them down, which ate precious hours and more than a few dollars more of Daddy and Mommy's patience. Also in our favor, Pocket Aces Pawn had failed to perform its due diligence to ensure the amp was really Billy's before agreeing to lend him money for it. There was a chance the band may have stolen it themselves first, but that wasn't our problem.

Candace was doing most of the talking at this point. I did her share of fidgeting alongside my own. It was more than five hours' drive back to the Tobin Center the quickest way, and as I mentioned before, the county Mounties and Staties along the way were ever eager to enhance their revenue. If we didn't wrap this up quickly, it didn't matter how things shook out here; we'd never make it in time.

I just reckoned potential legal questions about the situation accounted for the amount of sweating the goateed young Asian dude with the unfortunate man-bun—if I do not repeat myself—was doing despite the surprisingly adequate AC blowing through the shop. Until a short black revolver barrel got stuck up against the side of Mindy-Lou's neck from behind, and a voice that had grown unpleasantly familiar on really short acquaintance snarled, "Keep facing away from us, bitch. And don't try none of that Darkness shit. Ain't need to see to blow this little girl's pretty head off."

"You don't dare," Candace said. For my part I stuck my thumb in my pants pocket and did a thing with it pretty quick. "LaCanfora will skin you alive if you hurt her." But she didn't turn around, or use her Darkness power.

"Keep telling yourself that. Maybe them big bosses decided they'd rather have you back for a little talk than Little Miss High-Ass, here. And you, shitkicker—stop playin' pocket pool and put your hands up behind your head."

"All right, all right," I said, obeying. I turned to face him and his unlovely brother. Behind them Blood's magic tunnel was just closing up in the front door and parts of the barred plate glass windows to either side.

"Where the heck did y'all come from this time?" I asked. If they'd done the cell-tower trick on Mindy-Lou's iPhone again, I hoped they'd enjoyed walking into the insides of the particularly rank-smelling *carnicería* dumpster we'd chanced to drive past yesterday evening. Blood, maybe.

"The back room," the clerk said miserably. "Sorry, man. I had no choice. They got my grandfather tied up back there. Dude said he'd let the dog-joker eat his face if I didn't play along."

From outside an electrical-sounding voice snarled, "This is the Fort Stockton Police Department. We have the building surrounded. Come out with your hands up."

Well, that was fast, I thought. Did you know you could text 911? Turns out you totally can. Before we stopped by each and every station on our way, I paused to prep an SMS on Candace's burner phone. When Buck and Blood finally caught up with us, as Candace and I reckoned they would, all I had to do was a couple quick blind thumb swipes to text, *Armed robbery in progress this address.*

Quick response. Apparently the Pocket Aces Pawn made regular donations to the FSPD widows and orphans fund.

Buck's eyes went wide. As if on cue a whole slew of police cruisers hit up their light bars. Best light show ever. *"Blood!"* he shouted. "Get us the fuck out of here!"

His canine-looking brother obediently opened a tunnel in the wall to my right, right through a rack of electric guitars. And Buck began blinking and gagging as I blanketed his and Mindy-Lou's upper torsos with the biggest handful of dust I could handle, gleaned from shelves and shelves of random old junk. *"What the fuck?"* he choked out, and yanked the trigger.

Now, as Candace kindly observed, I am a Texan and a proud American, and a lifelong rancher, so I know a thing or two about firearms. Buck's little five-shot Taurus snubby was a double action with no spur to the hammer. Meaning to shoot, he had to cock the piece by hauling back pretty hard on the trigger, which pulled back the hammer and rotated the cylinder to bring a new cartridge into place beneath the firing pin.

It's kind of a clockwork mechanism, and turns out it jams up mighty tight when you suddenly stuff a bunch of pawnshop dust into the works. The hammer got stuck partway back, the piece locked up, and Mindy-Lou showed a surprising plucky streak by knocking the gun away, then wheeling around and knocking Buck on his skinny backside with a very creditable left hook.

Candace grabbed her arm. "Go!" I yelled, digging in my other pocket.

"Blood," Buck coughed out, "sic 'em, boy!"

"No," I said, bringing out the tennis ball I'd scavenged from outside a local court that afternoon. *"Fetch."*

And I bounced it off the linoleum tiles in front of him.

He smiled in a way that made my heart go out, half kid, half puppy, and entirely disturbing as it was. His head bobbed up and down to follow the bouncing ball. But he was a good boy, according to his not-so-bright lights. And human enough to remember to keep open the tunnel his brother told him to make.

I turned and dove through, with Candace, Mindy-Lou, and Billy right behind me. I managed to tuck my shoulder and roll right up onto my feet on the Persian-looking rug on the polished hardwood floor upon which I suddenly found myself. I have a little experience in falling off things, as you might gather. Though I did my back no favors.

I found myself looking back into the Pocket Aces through a fancy liquor cabinet in an oak-paneled wall. I heard Buck squawk something, and saw Blood, tennis ball in mouth, get a stricken look in his all-human eyes. Then blackness blotted the scene.

The tunnel vanished, making the rest of the cabinet appear. Some mighty fancy crystal work there. "Whatta we got here?" a voice sneered from behind us. "Candace? And our little girl lost?"

Right behind us stood a couple of Hollywood Central Casting Heavies in Suits, down to the bulges beneath their armpits. One, the size of the shaven Kodiak he so resembled, glowered at us from beneath thick black eyebrows. The other, a shorter but no less wide Latino with a round shaven head, was grinning at us like we were a winning lottery ticket. He had a gold tooth, *La Guadalupana* protect us.

"You know," he told Candace, "we're kinda gonna miss you."

Candace smiled. Though she had a nice face—not on a level with Mindy-Lou's, but presentable—it was not a nice smile. "Ah. *C'est si bon.*" And Darkness poured from her mouth, her ears, her nose, filling the room like black fog.

But I could see.

Before we walked into the Pocket Aces, Candace had told me to shut my eyes, then kissed both the lids, lightly. "For luck?" I asked.

"You'll see."

"Huh? I don't—"

"No. You'll *see.*"

I did. It was as if the fancy lighting got a bit dimmer, was all.

"Why the knife?" I asked Candace in alarm. "I thought you didn't kill anybody anymore?"

"I make exceptions." Suddenly she was on Bear Dude's back with her legs clamped around his massive rib cage and the edge scoring his neck. "If you don't surrender now, for instance, Bogdanovich."

Bogdanovich raised his paws. "Wait," the *vato* said. "You can't—"

And then I nailed him in the nuts with the pointy toe of my boot from behind, and clocked him hard on the back of the head with a fancy green bottle off the cabinet.

You may not knock 'em out that way. But you can make 'em feel too sick to do much for a minute or two.

Enough. I went to work.

♠

The man beneath the wall full of photos of celebrities—mostly pop stars, unsurprisingly, and politicians—looked up from a desk you could have put wheels on and lived in down by the river. "Hog-tied with their own belts and neckties," I said. "I grew up a working cowboy before I joined the PBR circuit."

"What? The fuck are *you?*"

"Billy," I said.

Billy opened up his hands.

"Ooh," Mindy-Lou said, impressed despite herself. "*Double* rainbow."

I held up my phone. "Mr.—LaCanfora, is it?"

He nodded vaguely. "Sure. Yeah."

Candace had told me the Mob's shot caller at Titan Records—he played the role of chief financial officer—was one Giulio "Julie the Weasel" LaCanfora. You could see why, with his pointy, chinless face and black button eyes. I have to say, a ferret face looks powerfully cute on an actual ferret—my oldest sister kept 'em as pets—but on a human being, not so much.

"We're your new best friends." As long as you keep gazing at the pretty colored lights. "You want to help us, don't you?"

"Sure." He looked eager as a high school kid about to make his first visit to a strip club. I glanced at Billy. When it was hitting on all cylinders, as apparently it was, that ace of his was pretty scary.

"Then listen real carefully to what we say, and repeat it, word for word, into my phone, here. You got that?"

He nodded. "Repeat what you say. Listen hard. Sure."

"Candace," I said, "take it away."

◆

Fifteen minutes later LaCanfora was glaring bloody blazing death at us across the deck of the USS *His Desk*. Not pictured: Billy's rainbows.

He had already discovered that the emergency backup-goon call button under his desk didn't work so good when it was all choked up with dust. His cleaning service did a pretty good job; hadn't been easy to find enough. Then again, mostly what else I had to do was click the voice recorder app on my Galaxy III on and off as Candace prompted him, line by line. Line by astonishingly, *fatally* incriminating line. I was kind of in awe of her, and not even for her totally overpowered ace, this time.

I clicked off the replay.

His face had gone a purplish color, underneath a real torrent of sweat. That was not a good look for the ferret features, either.

"What . . . the fuck . . . is that?" he managed to choke out after a couple tries.

"You recounting enough crimes in enough detail for the Feds to lock away half the district bosses across the American South," Candace said, with obvious relish. More than a little Louisiana Red, too. "Including your boss, Shevardnadze."

His round eyes got so much rounder you could see white all around the irises.

"More to the point," I said, "the contents of this brief but enlightening recording, should it come to the attention of said bosses, you would most assuredly find yourself hanging from a hook alongside the Houston Ship Channel minus some of your favorite body parts. Though maybe not so short as you'd prefer."

He kept his mouth opening and closing as he processed that. That pointed-face thing also makes you look like a carp, when you do that. TIFO.

"You are now going to record a contract, releasing both Mindy-Lou here and Candace from all ties and obligations. And promising not to try to take out your understandable frustrations on either me or, uh, Billy, here. In fact, in case any of us stub our toe real hard in the next few years, it'd be a good idea to have your affairs in order."

He glared from one of us to the other. "You're joking, right?"

I looked at Candace. "Can I?" She nodded.

"Okay. I know what you're thinking, Mr. LaCanfora. And it won't work. Here's something I forgot to tell you. Everything you said earlier was recorded using a nifty little app called FiVo-Film. It's designed to record encounters with the police, in case they get a bit overzealous in the pursuit of their duties. As they sometimes tend to with those of us of a darker-skinned persuasion. Now, what this does is regularly dump the feed, in this case audio, to a Dropbox in the possession of the app company. You can't get to it. We can't get to it. But if something should happen to us, it will be released to the public, including WikiLeaks. So if your goons intercept us on the way out, you'll have only bought yourself a ticket to getting hung out to dry in a most literal way."

"My partner likes to talk," said Candace. "He means, you fuck with us, your friends will peel you like an orange."

"You wouldn't," LaCanfora said. "This is a good little girl here. All-American, even if she is a Mexican. Brought up all prim and proper and middle-class. She's not gonna go along with that. Are you, sweetheart?"

"It would almost be worth letting your pigs take us out," Mindy-Lou hissed at him, "just knowing what would happen to *you*, you motherfucker. You were gonna sell me to some sheikh as a sex toy!"

"Actually, our best offer came from Punjab—"

"You're not helping yourself." I shook my head. "Kids these days. No respect. Right? So, time is running out for us, which means it is also running out for you."

"Do you wish to wiggle on the hook anymore, Mr. the Weasel?" Candace asked.

He could only shake his head. The look in his eyes reminded me of the sadness I'd seen in Blood's eyes, when his nasty brother hadn't got him worked into feral fury. Except it stirred less sympathy. None, point of fact.

"Great! Win-win for everybody." I held up the phone. "And go."

Is Nobody Going to San Antone?

by Walton Simons

JERRY HEARD A *POP* and experienced the expected moment of vertigo as he was sent hundreds of miles from the comfortable confines of his office at Ackroyd and Creighton. He heard voices behind him. Well, voices and noises.

He turned and saw a blond woman straddling a man on a king-size bed. She was wearing a cowboy hat, gun belt, spurs, and nothing else. The man was totally naked.

"Oh shit," he said out loud without meaning to.

The woman swiveled her head in his direction and screamed. "It's the ghost!"

The man snatched the gun out of her holster and pointed it at Jerry.

"No, wait. Please, I'm not a ghost." Jerry held up his suitcase. "Ghosts don't have luggage. I'm not even sure how I got in here." Over the years, Jerry had faced a loaded gun plenty of times and had gotten very good at reading the intent of the person holding the weapon. He figured this guy was going to pull the trigger and dived headlong for the door.

The reports from the gun banged in his ears and plaster rained down from the wall. He wrenched the door open and ran toward a stairwell. Once inside, he ditched his coat and luggage. If he ran down the stairs he might take a bullet if the man pursued him and he was unlucky; better to defuse the situation.

He changed his face to Jack Elam's. Elam was one of his favorite grizzled character actors and he rarely had the opportunity to use his features in New York. Physical and vocal impersonation was Jerry's stock-in-trade, courtesy of the wild card. It was one of the things that made him an ace detective.

He stepped back into the carpeted hallway just as the naked gunman bolted out of the doorway, weapon at the ready.

"Son," Jerry said, stroking his chin, "would you mind not pointing that in my direction."

The man lowered the gun. "Did you see anyone else here a second ago?"

Jerry shook his head. "I didn't mean the gun." He pointed at the man's crotch. "Waving that thing around is probably a felony in these parts." Jerry looked closer. "Then again, maybe just a misdemeanor."

"So no one else?" The man's voice trailed off. "Maybe it *was* the ghost."

The blond woman peeked out, clutching a bedsheet, and took the man by his shoulder. "You need to get back in here, hon. This ain't a bull-riding contest, so an eight-second ride won't earn you no prize."

The man shook his head, but reluctantly went back inside.

Welcome to Texas, Jerry thought.

♥

A few minutes earlier Jerry had opened the door to the offices of Ackroyd and Creighton and stepped inside like he was sliding into an old, comfortable shoe. The office space was located in a stately Manhattan brownstone, appropriate for the most respected detective agency in the city.

Jay and Ezili were waiting in the interior office. She'd taken the investigator spot vacated by Peter Pann when he'd opened his own agency out in L.A. "Good morning, Jerry." She gave him a wink. "I mean, Mr. Creighton."

Calling him by his made-up last name was a bit of a running joke. Everybody in the office—Ezili, Topper, Sascha, and Jay—knew his real name was Jerry Strauss. He'd invented the Creighton moniker partly out of paranoia at being outed as an ace, but more to honor Lon Chaney Jr. Jerry, like Chaney Jr.'s once famous father, was the man of a thousand faces.

His Creighton face was similar to that of Richard Denning, a 1950s Hollywood leading man who never hit star status. Jerry spared a moment to glance at Ezili. She looked great, of course. Then again, she'd looked great for the two decades or so he'd known her. She didn't look the same, though. Nobody around the office did. Everyone's hair was a little grayer, their faces a little more lined; everyone, that is, except him. Unless he was on the job, Jerry always kept his looks at early thirties. He felt kind of bad about the unfairness of it, but no one else seemed to mind. They were his surrogate family.

He entered the main office, plopped into his chair, and nodded at Jay. "Morning, partner."

Jay looked up and his mouth twisted ever so slightly. "What?" Jerry asked.

"I've got some good news and some bad news."

"Why do I have a feeling the bad news is pointed in my direction? Let's have it."

Jay raised a hand. "First the good news. We're set to finish up the Nesbitt case tonight. I expect our client to be completely satisfied with the result."

"Right. I knew that already."

"Yep, you did. Here's the rub, you won't be there tonight."

Jerry cocked his head. "Where exactly am I going to be?" He drummed his fingers nervously on the mahogany desktop.

"San Antonio, Texas." Jay smiled. "I hear it's beautiful this time of year."

"Texas! What the fuck is going on in Texas that I need to miss out on wrapping up a case we've worked weeks on?" Jerry bolted out of the chair and put his hands on his head.

"Calm down." Jay almost sounded conciliatory, which wasn't his style. "This is a major new client, and we didn't get to be one of the most respected detective agencies in New York by turning down heavy hitters."

"How heavy?"

"Michelle Pond, the Amazing Bubbles."

"Wow." Jerry sat back down. Like everyone else on planet Earth, he'd heard of the Amazing Bubbles. He put his skepticism on momentary hiatus.

"Your travel gear is in the briefcase by your desk."

"What are the specifics of the case?" He picked up the briefcase.

"There have been threats against a group of young joker musicians she's chaperoning," Jay replied. "Your cover is that young journalist we've used before."

"So, kids or something. What kind of threats?"

"Ms. Pond will give you all the particulars." Jay shaped his hand like a gun and pointed his index finger at Jerry. "You'll be arriving at the Gunter Hotel. Nice place. I spent a couple of nights there once looking into a supposed haunting. You want to show up in the lobby, or the haunted room?"

"Oh, the haunted room, of course." Jerry took a deep breath and began slowly exhaling.

"As you wish, partner."

♣

The hotel desk clerk dutifully told him there were no rooms, but after Jerry flashed his fake government ID he'd landed a suite. What the hell, it was on the agency's dime and this wasn't where he wanted to be anyway.

He called Michelle Pond. She answered on the sixth ring. "Yes."

"Ms. Pond, this is Mr. Creighton of Ackroyd and Creighton. I understand you have some issues with a band you're chaperoning. I'd like to meet with you as soon as possible."

There was a moment of silence. "You're here in San Antonio already?"

"We pride ourselves on our response time." Jerry was trying to sound more professional than indifferent. "How soon would you be able to meet with me?"

Another longer pause. Jerry heard a lot of chatter in the background. "I'm finishing up with the police right now. Give me fifteen minutes."

"Police?"

"Yes," she said. "It's about the rattlesnakes."

"Ah." Jerry realized this might be a bit more complicated than some rowdy teenagers. "See you in a quarter hour."

♠

Her model-perfect features didn't mask the worry on Michelle Pond's face. That she was so obviously concerned was hard for him to figure. This was one of the most powerful aces on the planet. She could turn him into a grease spot on the wall in the blink of an eye. Either teenagers were far scarier than he imagined, or there was something else going on.

Jerry tapped notes into his phone. "We've escalated from smoke bombs and falling lights to rattlesnakes." The snakes were potentially a good lead; not just anyone could handle them safely. If nothing else, it could eliminate some suspects.

She nodded, taking a sip of bottled water.

"I assume the auditorium has security cameras. Have the authorities gotten anything useful from them?"

"No," Michelle said, "I think they spray painted them or something."

"Were any of the locks forced?"

"I don't think so." She stared at Jerry and sighed. "What exactly is it you're going to do? We're only here for a few more days and things are getting serious. Do you have a plan for dealing with this?"

Jerry stopped tapping and looked up. "I understand your concern. The truth is, I just got here. The more information I have to work with, the more likely I can produce positive results for you. Are there any individuals or groups that have been overt in their hostility to your band?"

"The Purity Baptist Church. They're complete assholes. And there's always going to be tension among competing bands. The Plano Originals, for sure." She pressed her lips together. "Probably won't stop some of them from trying to have sex with people in other bands, though."

"A major problem for a chaperone, I expect. Still it could be worthwhile to talk to your band members. Someone might have heard something useful. You never know." He put away his phone. "We have one other operative here, a reporter for the *Jokertown Cry*, or that's her cover. I'll send her over to talk with them. Her name is Tess Harding."

"What will you be doing in the meantime?"

"Staying busy, trust me," he said, smiling. "I'll be in touch."

◆

Clothes were the bane of his existence. He could change his face and form all the livelong day, but clothes would always give him away if they weren't right. Jerry handed the stack of garments and his company credit card to the woman behind the counter. If she thought it was odd that a man was buying women's clothes, her smile didn't give even a hint of it. She was disarmingly friendly. In fact, outside of the gun-toting lunatic who'd tried to shoot him, all the people Jerry had encountered were among the nicest he'd ever met. How was it that a state filled with people like this invariably elected bigots and morons? There was no point in trying to square that circle. He didn't have the time.

"Thanks so much for shopping with us today." She returned his credit card and neatly placed the clothes into a bag. "Y'all please come visit us again, soon."

Jerry wandered over to the ladies' dressing rooms and snuck in when no one was looking. He put on the new clothes and altered his body to fit them perfectly, checking the mirror to make sure everything was working properly. The crotch bulge wouldn't do, so he shrank his junk down to minimal size. He could get rid of it altogether, and had done so when it was necessary, but he liked to keep a little. A therapist, if he had one, might be able to tell him why, which was one of many reasons he didn't have a therapist. He tucked his Creighton clothes into the bag, hit the makeup counter, and decided to walk back to the hotel.

Jay was right about the weather. It was glorious. The temperature was ideal and the gentle breeze was indecently pleasant. The San Antonio River Walk was busy, but not overly crowded. Most of the people looked to be tourists like him. They didn't move with the speed or assurance that a local would.

He worked to put himself into a Tess mind-set—young, energetic, and inquisitive. Realistically, he was only one of those things, but pretending otherwise was the job. Becoming Tess physically was easy. Jerry couldn't disobey the laws governing conservation of mass, so Tess was tall and well-muscled. Big breasts were hard on his back so he kept them small. Tess did have substantial hips, though. Tess was a joker too, but Jerry hadn't added those features yet since jokers sometimes drew unwanted attention and aggravation.

Jerry felt a hand on his shoulder and turned, wondering who could possibly want anything from a stranger. There were two young men staring at him. One had a drunken smile on his face; the other had a more drunken one. Aggravation had showed up in spite of Jerry's best efforts.

"Piss off, boys. I don't have the time." Jerry's Tess voice was concise, brusque, and very New York.

The boys looked at each other. The larger one leaned in. "Looking at your ass we thought you had it going on, but there's not much up here." He grabbed a breast and squeezed.

Jerry owned guns, but he didn't like carrying them. So over the past couple of decades he'd taken self-defense courses in various disciplines and was highly skilled at hand-to-hand fighting. He grabbed the big boy's pinky and twisted it hard. There was a satisfying snap.

The injured punk fell to his knees. "You broke my fucking finger!"

Smart guy number two moved in, fists raised. "I've got this, bro."

Jerry stomped on the kid's instep, elbowed him in the solar plexus, and hip-checked him over the metal railing into the dirty, shallow water. A boat cruised by, loaded with passengers. Many of them pulled out their cell phones and pointed them in Jerry's direction.

"Cunt!" the broken-fingered boy screamed.

Jerry walked away quickly. The last thing he wanted was an encounter with the local police. So much for everyone in Texas being friendly. Young punks were pretty much the same everywhere. Although those two wouldn't have lasted out a day in New York City.

♥

Ezili had taught him how to put on makeup, but Jerry had never really mastered it. His hands were steady and he understood the basic concept of what to do, but the aesthetic of the process eluded him. Luckily, he didn't have to do anything with her hair. Tess had a multicolored mohawk of feathers, as well as a mane of smaller, softer feathers around her neck. The only other aspect of her jokerdom was her finger- and toenails, which looked more like talons. He gave his Tess look one final check in the mirror and then grabbed his tablet. He'd Googled "teen slang" and was scanning the page. The number of terms was daunting, to say the least.

"This is hopeless," he said. He'd just have to fake his way through it. The story of his life.

He was nervous about being in a room full of teenagers and couldn't really place why. It wasn't just the way they talked. That couldn't be it. There was something else. Jerry was in his mid-seventies, although he never looked it unless it was for a job. He'd spent two decades as a giant ape, which had messed with his mind to the extent that a lot of his pre-simian memories were becoming fuzzy or nonexistent. Teenagers were like aliens to Jerry. Maybe worse. He would probably have been happier if Jay had popped him to Takis.

He arrived at one of the band's rooms. It must be the right place, because there was the sound of a saxophone being played behind one of the doors. At least, Jerry thought it was a saxophone. He smoothed his clothes, took a deep breath, and knocked. The playing stopped and a few moments later a teenager with sax in hand opened the door. At first he looked totally normal, but then Jerry noticed an expanding blob of sky blue on his neck. It disappeared and moments later a crimson one showed up on his right arm.

"May I come in?" Jerry leaned into the open doorway and smiled. During the course of his decades as a detective, he'd flashed a ridiculous number of introductory smiles at people and had gotten really good at it.

The joker boy opened the door and backed away. Jerry stepped in and looked for a place to sit. The room was littered with instrument cases, laptops, tablets, and random piles of clothes. The boy was alone, which surprised Jerry. He figured teenagers ran in packs. Still, the kid might speak more freely without his bandmates around.

"My name is Tess Harding." Jerry extended a clawed hand and the boy shook it cautiously. "I'm a reporter with the *Jokertown Cry*. I'm working on an article about the band competition, featuring the Mob, of course. Would you be willing to talk to me?"

"Me? Sure, I guess." He scratched his head and took a seat on the couch, holding his sax carefully in his lap. More circles of color bloomed on his skin. "I never met a joker reporter before."

"I never met a joker saxophone player, so we're even." Jerry sat down. "What's your name?"

"Sean Malone."

"Nice to meet you, Sean." Jerry noticed Sean trying to not look at him. Tess wasn't a stunning beauty—women who were exceedingly pretty attracted too much attention as a rule—but she was still plenty cute. Jerry's vanity demanded that much. He guessed Sean hadn't been around too many women. Jerry flipped open his tablet for note-taking. "You want to tell me about yourself, Sean?"

Sean took a moment. "Well, I'm from Pennsylvania. After I changed, my parents wanted me to continue playing sax, so they sent me to high school in New York. To be with other people like me. That part's worked out great. Our squad is hella tight. I miss my folks, though."

Jerry nodded. "I understand you've had some problems since arriving here."

"It's been totally effing nuts. The smoke bomb was no big deal, but this morning we had rattlesnakes in a couple of the instrument cases."

"That's serious. Who do you think would want to do that?" Jerry leaned in a bit.

"Nobody knows. I wouldn't be surprised if it was that bunch outside the hotel. You should have seen how they acted when we got off the bus. If Bubbles—Ms. Pond—hadn't been there, I don't know what would have happened." He clutched his sax a little tighter. "All we want to do is play our best. We're not hurting anyone."

"What about the other bands? How do they feel about you competing?"

Sean twisted his mouth thoughtfully. "They're mostly okay, I guess. The Plano Originals aren't crazy about us. Some of them, anyway."

Jerry tapped the info into his tablet, his clawed fingers clicking on its surface. "Sean, do you have any other notions, no matter how wild you may think they are, about what—"

The door opened and a crowd of kids pushed into the room. It was like an inversion of the stateroom scene in *A Night at the Opera* but with joker kids.

Sean popped up off the couch to greet them. "Did you have any luck?"

"Oh yeah," said a girl with wings and antennae. "We'll be back in business soon."

Jerry stood. "Hi. My name is Tess Harding. I'm a reporter with the *Jokertown Cry*. I'm here to do a story on your band. Do any of you have a few minutes to talk to me?"

A young joker rolled up to him, literally: his legs were fused together with a wheel at the bottom. "Do you blog?"

"Not really. Some of my stories have been picked up by mainstream media, though." It was half a lie. There actually were stories under the Tess Harding byline that had appeared in the *Jokertown Cry* and elsewhere, validating her faux existence. Ezili wrote them, though. She had quite a talent in that area.

Sean picked up his sax and raised it to his mouth. He glanced around at the others and started to play. The sound filled the room, reverberating off the walls.

"Please, if you could just spare me . . ." A couple of the others joined in. The insect-girl fingered an imaginary bass, bobbing her head and mouthing the notes in *bum-ba-bum* rhythm with the rest. The wheeled boy started gliding, dipping, and, well, dancing. He moved like Cab Calloway on a unicycle.

Jerry was overwhelmed, not just by the noise but by the kids' unbridled enthusiasm. His head swam and he started to feel a bit faint.

"Excuse me," he said, and bolted for the bathroom.

Once inside he checked his face, which had slipped ever so slightly back to his actual countenance. Jerry sat on the toilet and did some deep breathing. He'd studied yoga for a bit; it helped him focus and he was able to quickly get back into character. He stepped back into the room and headed for the door.

"I'll try to come back later, if anyone would like to talk to me." No one noticed.

Outside, Jerry encountered a large, slow-moving metallic person. He immediately recognized Rustbelt towering over him.

"Who the heck are you?"

"I'm Tess Harding with the *Jokertown Cry*. I was trying to get an interview with the kids, but it didn't really work out."

Rusty slowly shook his head. "Cripes, once they get going it's hard to stop them. I gotta break it up, though, or the hotel folks will complain. You might have some better luck later on." He paused for a second. "I never do, though." He ducked his head and entered the room.

Jerry walked quickly away and heard the music slowly fade as he moved down the hallway. That had been a bust, for the most part. Still, Sean had given him a little bit of info to go on. Might as well check it out.

♣

Jerry sat on the edge of his bed, trying to make the pieces of the case fit together in a way that made sense. The problem was he didn't have enough pieces to work with. He needed to find some, and soon.

He had the TV on in the background, tuned to the local cable news channel. There was a blue bar at the bottom of the screen showing upcoming stories. The next up was titled *Snakes Alive*. Jerry turned up the volume.

The picture cut away to a young woman reporter. "As if the situation with the jazz band competition wasn't already tense enough, reports this morning indicate that instruments were stolen from the Jokertown Mob band, and in their place were left a pair of baby rattlesnakes. We are informed that the Amazing Bubbles herself disposed of the dangerous reptiles. In her own inimitable fashion, I would imagine."

Jerry clicked the TV off and used his tablet to find the contact number for the San Antonio Zoo. Moments later he had a telephone receptionist on the line.

Jerry mimicked the reporter's voice. "This is Ms. Garcia. I'm researching a story for our station on what happened this morning with the snakes at the band competition. Do you have a herpetologist on staff?"

"Yes. I'll connect you."

After a long wait, a woman answered. "This is Dr. Shelton. I've been told you're a reporter. How may I help you?"

"Thank you for your time, Dr. Shelton," Jerry said. "Regarding the incident with the snakes earlier, is there a special permit required to handle rattlesnakes? If so, who would issue such a permit?"

Dr. Shelton cleared her throat. "My understanding is that those snakes were diamondbacks. There's no permitting process for the handling or housing of indigenous snakes, regardless of how danger-ous they might be. Only if it were a non-indigenous species would a permit be required. Texas Parks and Wildlife would handle that."

Another swing-and-a-miss. Jerry sighed. "I see. Thank you for the clarification." He was about to hang up when Dr. Shelton spoke again.

"Most of the people who handle rattlesnakes and such are . . . well, they do it for religious reasons. They don't really show the animals the proper respect and many of them wind up getting injured. Sometimes the Lord works in mysterious ways, but other times he just smacks you upside the head."

"Indeed. Thanks so much for your time, Dr. Shelton. You have a nice day." Luckily, Jerry knew exactly where to find a group of people who were both religiously inclined and hostile to the Mob.

♠

He was hungry as hell, but Jerry was determined to make some head-way before letting himself eat. The gnawing in his gut was motiva-tion after the debacle with the kids. As Tess, he'd established a bit of a relationship with Sean, but there was no guarantee that would pay off in a meaningful way.

After changing back into his Creighton clothes and body, Jerry headed downstairs. He moved quickly through the lobby and stepped outside. The weather was still pleasant, if a little more sunny. He scanned the crowd, spotted a face he liked on a man walking by, and bent down to pick up nothing in particular. When Jerry stood, he was wearing his new face. With all the cameras around, there was no point in running the risk of being identified as Creighton. It had been eas-ier when he started out in this business. Now almost everything wound up on video. He worked his way through the bystanders toward the stage, where a woman representing the Purity Baptist Church was speaking.

"We have been brought here by the will of our Savior." Her voice was brittle and her face was stern, like Agnes Moorehead's less fun sister. Her most distinguishing feature, other than her bigotry, was a shock of pink hair on her head. "I know that none of you have hatred in your heart for these creatures. I pity them, but they have been marked by God as abominations. It is he who has cast them out for their sins, and we cannot question his judgment. We must not allow them to bring their twisted bodies and tainted blood to our city unchallenged. It is God's will that we drive them out, and we will do so." She raised a black book adorned with a single silver cross above her head.

Jerry tuned her out. When he was growing up, which was admittedly a long time ago, Christians hadn't been like this. Not the ones he'd known, anyway. They were decent people who'd help you out if you needed it, because that was what you were supposed to do. He hoped that this was just the lunatic fringe. Every group had one these days.

He gave the small group of people behind the speaker a long once-over. There were a couple of men who looked like they might be body-guards or some other kind of hired muscle. The larger of the two was dressed in a dark navy suit and had a bored look on his face. Jerry didn't give him a second glance. The other was staring at the speaker with a look of rapt intensity. Jerry figured him to be a true believer and therefore more potentially useful. It would be nice if something would go his way on this case.

The larger man leaned in next to Jerry's mark and said something. His companion made an unhappy face and walked away slowly. Jerry figured maybe the big guy wanted a burger or some tacos. He tried to stop thinking about food and kept the man in his sight line as he walked away from the crowd and into the hotel lobby. Jerry tailed him, a half dozen or so paces behind. The man walked over to the elevator and pushed the up button.

Jerry held back. He didn't want to be in an elevator alone with his quarry; then again, maybe he could make it work to his advantage. That's why he got paid the big bucks. Two young girls, both focused on their cell phones, entered the elevator. Jerry moved in behind them, figuring the man would pay attention to the girls and not him. One of the girls pushed the button for the second floor. The third-floor button was also illuminated—no doubt the man's destination.

He let the man take a few steps down the hallway before ducking out as the elevator doors closed. Jerry had an idea how to deal with him that was either brilliant or idiotic. It wouldn't take long to find out which. The man stopped in front of a door and slid his keycard into the lock. Jerry changed his face as the man was stepping inside the room.

"What hast thou done in my name?" Jerry walked in behind the man and closed the door. He was wearing the Jesus Christ face he'd grown up seeing—long brown hair, beard, soft caring eyes, and perfect skin.

The man turned and opened his mouth in complete disbelief. "I . . ." He shook his head. "Why are you wearing a suit?"

Jerry raised his palms. "If I didst appear in my celestial raiment, your eyes would surely see nothing else for all eternity."

The man reached toward Jerry, then pulled his hand back, falling to his knees and pressing his fists into his eye sockets. He began to sob. "Please don't punish me, O Lord. I'm your servant."

"I know your every sin from the moment you came onto this earth until this very instant, but there is one misdeed you must confess to me now, or be forever damned." Jerry set his right hand gently on top of the man's head. This was going better than he'd hoped.

"Ask me," he said, whimpering. "I will confess."

"The joker children art my children, just as others are, and thou hast raised a hand against them." Jerry was having a hard time trying to talk like Jesus. His voice was fine but he wasn't at all confident of his word choices. Luckily, it didn't seem to matter to the man on the floor.

"All I did was locate keys. I didn't know what was going to happen after."

Keys. So that was why it didn't look like a break-in. Jerry would have to take the man at his word, since he was supposedly all-seeing and all-knowing. "Good, my son. Thou were wise to unburden yourself of this. Rise now."

The man stood, but avoided meeting Jerry's gaze. "Thank you, Lord Jesus."

"Your Savior has a task for you to perform as penance for your sin."

"Anything."

Jerry wanted him out of the way for the next few days at least, so getting the man out of town was his best bet. "You know Carlsbad Caverns, my son?"

"Yes, but I've never been there."

"You wilst go there now, my child. There is a sacred object contained within its vastness. Only you will be able to see it, guided by my divine sight." New Mexico seemed far enough to Jerry, and the caverns were huge.

"What will I be looking for?"

"Thou wilst know it the moment your eyes do behold it. You must then take it to Lourdes, France. It will complete a miracle long prophesied."

"France? But my passport is expired."

"The Lord will make provision for your journey, if you but trust in him. You must leave immediately, and tell no one, lest your tongue cleave to your palate." Jerry was probably enjoying this more than he should. Around the office he had a hard time getting his way.

The man looked around the room, then took a few slow steps toward the door. "This sounds kind of fishy. Can you do a miracle, or something, just so I know I'm doing the right thing?"

Jerry changed his face again. He'd dressed as Satan for Halloween one year. That was one childhood memory that had never dimmed. "Behold the visage of him who thou wilst serve for all eternity if you should fail in your appointed task."

The man took one look at Jerry's devil face and fell to the floor again. "No, not that, never that."

Jerry slapped on his Jesus face again and lifted the man up. He was heavier than he looked. "Thou wilst not fail, my child, not if your heart is true. Come, embrace your Savior before you depart." Jerry hugged the man and reached into his pants pocket with a pair of elongated fingers, pulling out a cell phone. Jerry tucked it out of sight and guided the man to the door. "Go now, and do the service your Lord commands." The words sounded more like something Don Corleone would say than Jesus, but the man left the room without speaking another word.

Now that he was alone, he actually got to be a detective. Jerry had searched a lot of rooms in his time. There was an art to learning where to look and what to look for. First things first, though; he pulled out the phone to see if it was locked. Jerry tapped its face and was rewarded by rows of apps.

"No security," he said, smiling. "Praise the Lord."

That was a break, but he'd check out the phone later. There was a Bible open on the bed. Jerry sat down and picked it up, scanning the open pages for anything that looked noteworthy. Three-quarters of the way down the page he saw a piece of scripture that was more than a little interesting. He accessed the camera function on his phone and took a picture of the pertinent language. The rest of the page and the one opposite had nothing of apparent relevance.

Jerry went through the dresser drawers and found nothing out of the ordinary. The bathroom was equally dull, a toothbrush, shaving gear, and a really strong cologne. He moved on to the closet and checked the clothing to see if there was anything of note in the pockets. Other than a pair of Spurs tickets and some change in a pair of gray suit pants, it was a washout. Jerry decided to take the suit with him. It might come in handy later.

A generic confession about keys and a Bible quote didn't exactly crack the case, but it was a step. Jerry decided at the very least he'd earned lunch.

◆

The hotel restaurant was noisy and crowded, but Jerry managed to snag a table in the corner. There were several high school–aged kids inside. He figured they were members of the competing bands, or friends and family. He'd texted Michelle Pond, asking her to join him. Might as well update her on what information he'd turned up, and talking to her could shake something useful loose. Not that he figured she was holding out on him, but she had a lot on her plate right now and riding herd on teenagers couldn't leave much mental energy for anything else.

Jerry had ordered the brisket sandwich; might as well get a taste of Texas BBQ while he was down here. He was sipping at a cup of coffee, waiting for his employer to show up. In the meantime, he decided to investigate the cell phone he'd stolen. The recent e-mails appeared to be almost entirely church business related; there was nothing of interest that stood out in the subject lines.

"Hello, Mr. Creighton." Michelle didn't look happy. She was likely to stay unhappy until Jerry found out what she wanted found out.

"Have a seat." He indicated the chair opposite him. "The company is buying if you're hungry."

"Thank you," Michelle said, taking a seat. "I understand your reporter was something of a bust."

Jerry was hoping to lead with the good news, but she'd jumped straight to the bad. Might as well deal with it. "True, I didn't have much luck there."

Michelle looked up over her menu and gave him an appraising stare.

Shit, he thought, *pronoun trouble.* Time to move on quickly.

"I did get some potentially useful information from your friends with the Purity Baptist Church." Jerry paused as the waiter came over with pad in hand.

"What can I get for you today, Ms. Pond?" He was young, freckled, and visibly excited.

"I'll have the Cobb salad and a water with no ice." Michelle handed him the menu with a practiced smile.

"If it's not an imposition, would you mind giving me an autograph?" the starstruck waiter asked. "If you don't want to, that's fine. I'm sure people ask all the time and it gets to be a pain."

Michelle raised her hand to keep him from nervously rattling on. "If you get us our food in a hurry, I'll sign something for you on the way out. I promise."

"Celebrity can be useful at times," Jerry said. The gods of genetics had been kind to her. Not only did she have striking good looks, but her wild card ability was one of the most powerful on the planet.

"It's not all it's cracked up to be. I wouldn't mind trying anonymity now and then."

Jerry nodded. She had a point. Other than his stint as a movie star back in the twenties courtesy of Croyd Crenson, his entire life was built on anonymity and the secrecy it provided. He was only recognizable if he chose to be, and could shed any physical persona in an instant. Still, it might be nice to be able to blow people to giblets with bubbles.

"You said you had something about the Purity Baptist Church."

"I had a chat with one of the church members. Although he didn't admit direct responsibility for anything, I got the impression at least some of them were involved in the actions against your band. And then there's this." He pulled out his phone and brought up the photo he'd taken of the Bible. "There was a Bible open on his bed and on that page was an interesting entry. I took a picture of it." He handed his phone to Michelle. "It's Matthew 23:33."

She read the passage aloud. "You serpents. You brood of vipers, how will you escape the sentence of hell?"

"It might be a coincidence, but I very much doubt it."

The waiter trotted over with their food. Jerry gave him a thumbs-up and took a bite out of his sandwich, which was tangy, warm, and delicious. He'd give the kid a generous tip.

"So, your money is on the church being behind all this." Michelle went to work on her salad, but maintained eye contact with Jerry.

"Well, signs point to them being responsible for the snakes. That doesn't mean there aren't other players. Your band has generated a lot of hostility. I understand a Bambi Coldwater filed a lawsuit."

Michelle nodded. "Yes. The suit isn't going anywhere but it's still a dick move. Her daughter Kimmie is the flautist for the Plano Originals, one of the other bands here."

"Okay, that makes sense." Jerry took another bite and gave it a few extra chews while he was thinking. "So the Plano bunch doesn't like the Mob either."

"Apparently some do and some don't. One of the kids told me that Jax, their drummer, really has a hate-on for us." Michelle turned her head at the sound of piano music.

Jerry looked over Michelle's shoulder to see who was playing. It was a young couple who looked like they were making music together in more ways than one. He'd heard the tune before, but couldn't place it. In any case, they were very good. "I assume they're with the bands."

Michelle took a bite of salad and then raised a finger. "She's Marissa Simpson from our band and he's Cesar Chao of the Seattle Wailers, who had the dubious pleasure of a date with Jade Blossom."

"Jade Blossom from *American Hero?*"

Michelle gave a distinctly unsmiley smile. "That's the one. Thankfully, she's out of our hair for good."

Jerry imagined there was an interesting story behind Michelle's reaction, but he doubted he'd ever find out what it was. "Is there anyone else—" He stopped at the sound of an angry, high-pitched voice. A middle-aged woman was standing by the piano, looking down at Marissa and Cesar. Her face was red and her eyes bulged uncomfortably in their sockets.

"How dare you, you inhuman . . . whatever you are. Stay away from my son." She grabbed Cesar's shoulder. The kids looked angry and embarrassed. Marissa was more of the former, Cesar the latter.

"Mom, leave us alone," Cesar said. "Just let us play. We were really getting into it."

"You'll do as I tell you, when I tell you. I'm your mother." She put her hand under his armpit and lifted him from the piano bench.

A tall man, probably the restaurant manager, rushed with quick steps to intervene. He whispered something to Cesar's mother and gestured to the exit.

"You stay away from my son." She wagged a finger at Marissa. "You're not nearly good enough for him and you never will be."

She stormed out with Cesar in tow. Marissa paused a second or two, straightened her shoulders, and began playing "Clair de Lune." After a few bars of Debussy, spirited conversation and the clatter of silverware brought the restaurant back to normalcy.

"Cesar's mom is also no fan of jokers, I'm guessing."

Michelle rolled her eyes. "That's Lara Chao, another charter member of the bigot brigade."

Jerry sighed and entered more names on the list he was making of potential bad actors. He felt like this was a detective movie and he'd missed the entire first act.

Michelle finished up her salad and took a sip of water. "You've got this, right?"

"Yes, I do," he said.

Michelle stood, located their waiter, and quickly gave him the autograph she'd promised. Jerry chewed slowly on the remainder of his sandwich. No point in dwelling on the fact that he was somewhere he didn't want to be, doing something he had no interest in doing. This was the job. He wasn't sure what his next step was, but he had a hunch this would be his last downtime for the day. If this were a *Thin Man* movie, he'd have to do without a Nora. Unless he wanted to be her.

♥

Jerry had mentioned the possibility of multiple perps to Michelle to cover his ass if that turned out to be the case. He didn't really buy it himself, but given the high population of joker haters in the vicinity he wondered if it might not be true after all. A city the size of San Antonio had to have a decent-sized joker community, and in Jerry's experience nothing incited joker hate more than having to be around them.

He took the elevator to the seventh floor, where his room was. Maybe a shower would clear his head or provide a moment of inspiration. There was still the stolen phone to look through.

"Hey, Jax, wait up." It was a young male voice.

Jerry turned to look. The name Jax had come up during his lunch with Michelle, and not in a positive way. The person Jerry assumed was Jax, a tall blond kid, didn't bother to look back at the person who'd called out to him. There was another, smaller boy standing shoulder to shoulder with Jax.

"Keep up or get left behind," said Jax. "We're hitting the River Walk before I have practice."

They clustered together at the elevator, laughing loud enough for Jerry to hear. He had no idea what they were laughing at, but that was probably just as well. So much for a shower. He entered the stairwell and scampered quickly downward to the ground floor. He gave his face a Dwight Frye look. Frye had always been one of his favorites.

Jax and his wingmen were shoulder cutting their way through the crowded lobby to the street. Jerry fell in behind them, a few paces back. He passed an older man headed the other direction. To Jerry, he looked like a storybook Texan; his face was weathered, drawn, and tanned, with bold features. It was a great face. Jerry bent down to pick up an imaginary coin and made it his own. No one was likely to have noticed. Still, he hated that he couldn't be sure if there were cameras nearby. They were omnipresent in big cities now. Jerry knew where most of them were in Manhattan because it was in his best interest to know. What the hell, if a camera busted him changing faces it wouldn't matter. This wasn't his turf anyway. He just hated being sloppy in his work.

Changing faces had dropped him several more paces behind his quarry, so he lengthened his stride a bit to catch up. When he was close enough to hear, one of them laughed in a nasty, high school jerk way.

"That wheeled guy," Jax said, "we could just superglue his wheel to that—whatever the fuck you call his lower body. He'd never roll anywhere again."

"Or we could glue training wheels to him. People would laugh wherever he went."

"What about that bug-girl?" The kid speaking was the smallest of the three. "My uncle's an exterminator. I could get some industrial-strength insect killer and we could take her out completely."

Jerry had heard this kind of patter before. People in groups often talked tougher than they actually were. That didn't mean they wouldn't do anything harmful. The same dynamic that pushed them to sound badass to each other could also encourage them to push the envelope on bad behavior.

A phone vibrated in his pocket. It was the one he'd lifted from the Purity Baptist Church goon. He swiped it open and saw a text message.

Where the hell are you? The texter was identified only with a phone number.

Jerry thought about it for a moment, then tapped in, *Church.*

About thirty seconds passed before he received a reply. *Get yourself organized and get over to the Alamo for the meet-up.*

The kids had gotten well ahead of him and Jerry quickened his pace to get back within earshot. He had two choices—follow Jax and company to see if they were up to no good, or head to the Alamo and potentially get busted pretending to be someone he knew very little about. If he chose option two it was high-risk with potential high-reward, but there really wasn't time to go back to the hotel and put on the suit he'd lifted from Aaron. At least he assumed that was his name since the phone was named "Aaron's cell phone."

Jerry decided to ditch the kids and head to the Alamo. What was the worst that could happen?

The Alamo was nearby, but Jerry pulled out his phone and tapped in the location of the famous landmark just to be sure he didn't take a wrong turn. Time was clearly important. He put on his Aaron face and legged it at a good pace to the Alamo.

He was more than a little disappointed when he saw the main structure; it was far smaller than he'd imagined. The grounds surrounding the actual church building were fairly sizable, and that posed a problem as to where Jerry should situate himself. He wanted a good vantage point to keep an eye on things. There was likely a specific place he was supposed to be for the meeting, so he'd be looking for a person or persons who were trying to find Aaron.

There was a shaded gate to the left of the church. Jerry put his back to the wall and settled in for what he hoped was a short wait.

The plaza was crowded, lots of tourists out enjoying the beautiful weather. There were families of all sizes, looking and pointing, and several groups of kids and young adults just hanging out. On a day like this, why not visit the site of one of the most famous massacres in American history?

Jerry didn't see anyone who looked like they were trying to find Aaron, but he stayed where he was. He didn't want to stick his neck out by walking into the bright sunshine of the plaza. Better to watch and wait. He played out scenes from the John Wayne version of *The Alamo* and *Pee-wee's Big Adventure* in his head to pass the time. "There are thousands and thousands of uses for corn. All of which I'm going to tell you about right now."

A girl, maybe six years old, broke away from her parents and ran over to Jerry. "Do you know where Davy Crockett is, mister?" she asked, hopefully.

Jerry shook his head. "I plumb reckon Mr. Crockett has left the building, little one."

The girl's parents hurried over and led her away. "We're sorry," said the mom.

"No need." Jerry looked back out over the plaza. Four people walking together caught his attention: three men and one woman, and they didn't move like tourists. Jerry figured they were all in their late twenties, definitely out of college, and dressed well enough to have a fair amount of disposable income. The man in the lead, half a head shorter than any of the others, spoke to his companions and they wandered over to a shaded area under the trees. The leader walked forward slowly, glancing from side to side. Jerry backed farther into the shadows by the gate and studied the man's face and gait. The more time Jerry had to watch him, the better his chances of impersonating him if it came to that. Jerry decided to roll the dice and go meet him, but before he took a step forward there was a commotion at the far end of the plaza.

A sizable knot of people were entering the area. Even though they were still a fair distance away, Jerry could tell it was a group of jokers. He heard raised voices, some yelling at the joker group, others asking that the jokers be left alone. Jerry didn't see the short young man or his companions anymore, and walked toward the disturbance. When he got within twenty feet or so, Jerry saw that several of the jokers were wearing *I ♥ The Mob* T-shirts. Maybe they were local jokers, or had traveled to San Antonio to support the band. At this point it didn't matter. The anti-joker voices were getting louder and the jokers were closing ranks and huddling together. Most of them were young and looked scared. A bottle whizzed past Jerry's ear and into the jokers. He looked for police, but didn't see any nearby.

This wasn't what Jerry had signed up for, but he couldn't sit on his thumbs and let a riot happen. Particularly since the end result would likely be jokers in the hospital or the morgue. He needed to draw attention away from the group of jokers and do it in a hurry. Impersonating an ace was a bad idea; appearing to be an ace without having ace powers was a losing hand. He needed a startling look that would scare the hatemongers just enough to let the jokers get away.

Also, he didn't want to mess up his clothes. Running naked, or nearly so, through an unfamiliar city would end badly for him.

He decided to go with a flying monster, something humanoid. The harpies from *Jason and the Argonauts* had always been a favorite of his. Buzzing the crowd would be sure to draw plenty of attention. Somebody, maybe several somebodies, would have a gun. He'd risk that, though.

His first order of business was to ditch his clothes. He transformed his hands into claws and pulled himself up the side of the famous mission building to the rooftop. Jerry removed his garments and tossed them in a pile, then completed the transformation. He rarely did anything that allowed him to fly, and the large bat wings felt somewhat cumbersome. He flapped them and was quickly airborne, but he felt smallish for the job at hand.

Jerry soared over to a nearby power line and perched on the pole. People were pointing and taking video. He could add mass to his body by channeling electricity, but it required concentration or he'd take the current the same as anyone else. He used a taloned finger to slice into the wire. The surge tingled and he began to grow. At about three times his normal mass, he stopped and took to the air again. He wobbled a bit as he banked sharply toward the jokers under siege in the courtyard.

To make sure they saw him coming, Jerry let out an extended shriek while circling the crowd. Most of the people around the jokers scattered, but a few diehards remained. Jerry saw one of them reach toward his waist.

He dropped out of the sky like a stone, beating his wings to slow his descent only when he was a few feet over the man. Jerry grabbed him under either armpit with his scaly feet and lifted the screaming man into the air. He veered over to a tree and deposited him, not too gently, in its branches.

He checked the plaza. Everyone, including the joker group, had run for cover. Jerry shot into the sky a couple of hundred feet and released the energy he'd absorbed with a sizzling pop, returning to his normal size. He flew back down to the Alamo and scooped up his clothing, then landed on the roof of a nearby building. After returning to his previous form, except for his hands, Jerry dressed as quickly as he could manage and lowered himself down an exterior wall. Once his feet touched the ground he returned his hands to normal.

Flying was great fun; he should do it more often. He walked around to the front of the building, which turned out to be the Alamo Gift Shop.

Word of the incident must have reached the shop. People were exiting and buzzing about the attack of a "joker monster." Jerry walked inside to a display of coonskin caps and picked one up. He passed it in front of his face and changed again, back to someone younger. He walked over to the understandably distracted clerk at the register. Due to the commotion he'd caused there was no one in line to check out.

"I'll take this, please." He paid in cash and stepped out into the beautiful Texas late afternoon. The sunset promised to be spectacular.

As he strolled through the Alamo, glancing at the exhibits, Jerry indulged himself by putting on Fess Parker's face. When he returned to the plaza, it was swarming with police. Several officers were moving toward the joker group, which had returned and was milling about at the edge of the plaza. The posture of the officers indicated that they were there to protect them. Curious onlookers clustered in small groups, discussing what exactly had happened.

"It was a goddamned flying devil, I saw it with my own eyes," said a heavyset older man to anyone who was listening. Not many were.

Whether or not they got their tour, the jokers were safe. He'd done that right, at least. Jerry walked away whistling, then started singing, "Born on a mountaintop in Tennessee . . ."

♣

Jerry's shower was refreshing, but hadn't yielded the hoped-for inspiration. He was trying to talk himself out of the idea that the trip to the Alamo had been a fiasco. Jokers had been bailed out of a bad situation . . . and how could any scenario where he turned into a harpy be a fiasco?

His cell phone whistled an incoming text message. It was from Michelle Pond. *Need to see you asap.*

I'm in my room. Give me five minutes, he texted back.

Jerry hurriedly donned his clothes and made sure his Creighton face was on right. This could be good or bad. If she wanted a substantial update on the investigation, he didn't have much to offer. On the other hand, maybe she had come across some useful information and wanted to pass it on. That could be a major plus.

He heard a knock on the door. Jerry opened up and let Michelle in. She was carrying a box. "What's that?"

"A present, sort of." She gave him a knowing look. "Did you hear about the incident at the Alamo earlier?"

Jerry parked himself on the edge of the bed facing her and tried not to react. "Yes, something. I didn't pay too much attention. It didn't sound good, though."

"No, it wasn't. A group of jokers were threatened by some of the locals. The odd part was the large flying creature that showed up and took the heat off the jokers."

"That was a lucky break." Jerry didn't know what she was playing at, but it made him uncomfortable.

"Yes, but I don't believe it was mere luck." She set the box on his dresser and stood, then opened the top drawer. "I do believe in an ace power that allows a person to impersonate someone else." Michelle took out Jerry's makeup supplies and set them on top of the desk. "I'm not sure these go with your coloring."

Jerry's skin went cold. How the hell had she busted him? "I'm not sure how that got in there," he lied, unconvincingly.

She went to the closet and pulled out the dress. "This is actually pretty cute."

Now he was starting to get pissed. He took a deep breath and pushed those feelings way deep down. Being angry with someone as powerful as the Amazing Bubbles was largely pointless. "What do you want?"

She put the dress back. "Sorry, I'm being a bit of a bitch. It's been a long day. The Committee has files on—hell, I have no idea what all the Committee has files on, but definitely aces. The information on Ackroyd and Creighton, which is quite extensive, strongly suggested one of your agents was an impersonator. After your pronoun slipup earlier, and the scene at the Alamo, I put two and two together."

"And some people still insist women can't do math." Jerry felt trapped. He hated this assignment.

Michelle sat down. "Look, I don't know if you're Mr. Creighton or someone else, and I don't care. I'm not interested in making your secret known to anyone else. But you're working for me, and I need you to do something specific for me tonight."

Jerry exhaled. "I'm doing the best I can. I've only been here a few hours."

"You're misunderstanding." She waved her hand. "I have to be gone tonight. Maybe until morning, although I'm hoping it won't take that long. I want you to take care of my daughter, Adesina. Make sure she stays inside and out of trouble."

Jerry mulled it over. "I can look like you, and mimic your speech patterns pretty well, but don't you think she'll see through this? I mean, you're her mother."

"Sit on the couch and watch TV or read a book. If she comes out of the bedroom tell her to go back in and go to sleep. Don't get into an argument with her. She's a teenager and she'll wear you down." She opened the box she'd brought. It contained a top and pants. They were very nice. "Put these on and I'll do a little makeup on you."

Jerry picked up the box and trudged into the bathroom. He put the outfit on and checked himself front and back to make sure it was fitting properly.

Michelle smiled when he came out. "I'm not sure why I'm enjoying this so much," she said. "I guess I've had precious little else to enjoy the past few days."

"Boo-hoo," Jerry said, picking up a chair and sitting dutifully in front of her.

"Luckily for you, I don't wear much makeup, so this won't take long."

"So what time do I show up at your room to report for duty?"

Michelle looked at her watch. "I'll come back here at a quarter to eight and you can start your shift then."

"Right. Do you drink?"

"Not tonight I don't."

He sighed. "Well, that's just perfect."

After Michelle left, Jerry realized how attractive she was. Beautiful, intelligent, and dangerous were the trifecta for him. There was no way he was going there, though. Not with her, or anyone else. Not ever again.

Veronica had been one of his first great loves. In addition to being beautiful, intelligent, and dangerous she was a geisha for Fortunato back in the day, and Jerry paid for her services. Hardly the basis for a healthy or lasting relationship. Things cratered before too long, but over the long haul they'd formed something of a friendship. He was one of the first people she'd told about the cancer. Jerry had done as much as she would allow him to do. He brought in specialists from Europe, paid for in-home care when her wife, Carla, was at work, and visited often but not too often. Expense wasn't an issue. He'd had plenty of money even before his years in the past, and a hell of a lot more when he got back.

None of it had helped; Veronica was gone a few months later. Her death had damaged something in Jerry, maybe broken it. He'd expected to grieve, but this was more than that. Whatever it was he never wanted to feel it again.

Irina, his costar and lover at Fortune Films, was gone as well. They'd made several pictures, plenty of money, and what he thought was beautiful music together. Still, when he'd opted to come back to the present to resume his life, she'd stayed behind to continue her film career. He couldn't blame her. Money and fame, after all. But Irina had died less than a decade later, of a severe infection. Life was more precarious in those days, before antibiotics. He missed her sometimes, but not like he missed Veronica.

Women still mattered to him up to a point. Jerry had created a Tinder account and managed the occasional brief fling. It helped. Not much, but anything was better than nothing.

He pushed the unwanted thoughts away. He needed to be sharp if he was going to manage a teenage girl. It was time for adventures in babysitting.

♠

Adesina was in her bedroom, doing whatever semi-grounded teenage girls do. Not that Jerry had any idea what exactly that was.

He took advantage of the alone time by going through Aaron's cell phone. He checked the contacts section, but there was nothing there of any apparent interest. The recent e-mails hadn't revealed much either: lots of discussions about biblical verses and the end of days. Jerry had expected a fair amount of joker hate, but there was almost none to be found.

Stymied, Jerry paged through the photographs. There were pictures of San Antonio, groups of people who looked like family or church friends, nothing out of the ordinary. He flipped to the next picture and stopped cold. It was the same group of four young people he'd seen at the Alamo earlier. The photo's caption read *Keyz & Company*. It hadn't occurred to Jerry that Keyz was a person when Aaron mentioned it earlier. He quickly paged through the rest of the pictures, but found nothing.

He heard a noise behind him and tucked the phone away.

"Mom, can I go visit Ghost for a bit?" Adesina asked.

Jerry tried to get into the parental mind-set. "No."

"It will only be for a few minutes. We have stuff to talk about for tomorrow." Her voice was both plaintive and practiced.

"You can talk about it tomorrow." He heard a deep sigh and Adesina's footsteps retreated into the bedroom.

"Round one to the old man," Jerry said softly. He turned on the TV and tuned it to TCM.

Less than an hour later Adesina walked up behind the couch, but said nothing.

"What's up?" Jerry asked.

"What are you watching?"

"An old movie."

"Why would anyone watch an old movie?"

He was about forty minutes into *Mighty Joe Young*. Jerry could give her an hour-long lecture about stop-motion animation, but doubted that was something Michelle would do. "We had old movie night once a week when I was on *American Hero*," he lied. "Sit down for a minute and watch this with me."

Adesina plopped onto the couch with a practiced sigh.

Max O'Hara was introducing Jill and Joe Young at the Golden Safari.

"You ever heard the song 'Beautiful Dreamer'?" Jerry nodded toward the TV.

"No."

"Then this will be something new for you."

Jill Young played the piano as the platform slowly ascended, surrounded by nothing but darkness. As the song reached a crescendo, lights flooded the area below the platform, illuminating the giant gorilla.

"That looks so fakey, Mom."

"It won an Oscar for special effects." Jerry wondered if she even knew what an Oscar was.

"I did what you asked, can I go see Ghost now?"

"No."

"You're so lame, Mom." Adesina stalked back to the bedroom.

Jerry was thinking this parenting thing wasn't as hard as people said. He didn't want to think about his co-workers wrapping up the Nesbitt case tonight, or that he was flailing about on an important investigation. Better to concentrate on Terry Moore.

Jerry heard a knock at the door. "I'll get it. You stay put."

He opened up and saw the kilted, wheeled boy whose name he couldn't remember. "Yes?"

"Can I come in and talk to Adesina?"

Jerry shook his head. "Probably not a good idea. You can see her tomorrow."

The boy gave Jerry a sad look. "Is it okay if I try something? I'm just curious about the physics." He made a fist and cocked it.

"Don't." Jerry saw what was coming, braced his feet, and grabbed solidly on to the door frame. He took the punch in the midsection, but managed to not move.

"I didn't see you add any fat."

Jerry forced a smile. "It wasn't much of a punch." In fact it had been a pretty good one. He hurt like hell. "Now go to bed." Jerry closed the door. He doubled over, and after staggering to the bathroom, spent a minute or two on the toilet seat massaging his abdomen. Then he splashed some cold water on his face. Checking the mirror, he was pleased that his Michelle face hadn't slipped. Jerry took a few deep breaths, exited the bathroom, and stuck his head into the bedroom to check on Adesina.

"Oh, fuck," he said, but there was no one else in the room to hear it.

◆

It was late, but the streets were teeming with people—some drunk, some on the way to getting drunk, but all generally happy. Jerry borrowed the face of a harmless-looking guy outside the hotel and was pushing his tired legs as fast as he could to where he hoped Adesina would be.

In the end, it was Sean who'd given up the information. Jerry had gone to visit the kid as Tess. The kid had liked Tess, been attracted to her, whatever. Jerry hadn't tried any faux female wiles on Sean, though. In fact, he'd mostly told the truth, that Tess was working for a private agency hired to protect the members of the Mob. And that Adesina could be in big trouble wandering around outside. After a few minutes, Sean cracked. Jerry promised he wouldn't tell Adesina who had informed about where she was. Jerry was going to keep that promise; he liked Sean.

Jerry checked the GPS on his phone. He was getting close to the club and there was a faint, but soulful, melody rising and falling. As the music got louder Jerry got more nervous, afraid of what he might find. After the scene at the Alamo this afternoon, he couldn't rule out anything.

He spotted her outside the door to the club. Adesina was swaying side to side and bobbing her head up and down in time to the music. There was a small group of people standing near her, but they didn't seem to be paying her much attention.

Jerry was relieved to see her alive and safe. Hopefully she'd come back to the hotel without a fuss. He walked slowly over to her.

"Excuse me, Adesina. Can I have a word with you?"

She stopped moving and gave him a long, slow look. "Who *are* you?"

Before Jerry could answer, a large man grabbed him by the shoulders and swiveled Jerry around. He was well over six feet tall and built like an ex–football player; there were probably plenty of those in Texas. He wore a white tank top and had tattoos covering both arms.

"Is he bothering you?" he asked Adesina.

She smiled. "This is my friend Max. He works here. He said I couldn't go in, but I can stay outside and listen to the music. It's Buddy Robins."

"If you give her one iota of trouble," Max said, bringing his face close to Jerry's, "I'll toss you in the river and call the cops."

Jerry raised his hands. "I'm not looking for trouble." He was impressed by Max's use of the word "iota"—maybe he'd underestimated the big guy.

"What do you want?" Adesina asked.

"I'm a private investigator. I'm working for your mom. She wants to know who's behind these incidents. You know, the stink bomb, the snakes."

Adesina nodded. "So?"

"Well, she also wants me to keep an eye on you. She's your mom. She worries."

"I can take care of myself. Besides, Max will help me if anyone gets any ideas. He's awesome." Her antennae twitched. "And why should I trust you? How do I know you're who you say you are?"

Jerry had anticipated this might be an issue. She was a smart kid, and not totally naive. "Can you kind of wrap those wings around me enough that people can't see my face?"

She curled her wings around them. They felt strong and durable. Adesina might actually be able to take care of herself, but that wasn't the issue. He put on his Tess face. "Remember me from this morning?" Once she got a long look Jerry morphed his features back. "You can open back up."

Adesina unfolded her wings. "Okay. I believe you, mostly. You can stay if you want."

"There's not more than a dozen people in the world who know I can do that," Jerry said. "So I've put my cards on the table and now I need your help."

"I'm not a detective."

"No. I'm not asking you to help me with that. But as long as I'm here with you I can't be doing the rest of my job. I could miss out on a clue that would help me solve this." Jerry looked her in the eyes. "Please go home and let me do my job."

Adesina sighed. "All I want is to listen to the music."

Jerry looked over at the door to the club. A group of people pushed their way outside, laughing. It was Keyz and friends, and one other person. Jerry recognized the man's face from earlier today, but couldn't place it. He'd seen so many faces today. Keyz and his buddies weren't talking to the guy, but Jerry's intuition said they were together.

"Can you fly?" he asked Adesina.

"Of course."

"Then please fly back to the hotel right now. It's important." Jerry tried hard not to sound like a grown-up making demands of a teen-ager.

"You saw something, didn't you?"

He had a feeling not much got past her. "Please, Adesina."

She made an unhappy face and walked to the door. "Bye, Max. Thanks."

"You're welcome," Max said. He and Jerry watched Adesina flap away into the night. "She's a good kid."

"Yes, she is." Jerry saw Keyz and buddies disappearing down the River Walk. The fifth man was no longer with them. "Later, Max."

He closed the distance easily enough. Keyz and his friends weren't in a hurry. Jerry was within fifteen feet of them when they exited the River Walk, heading in the general direction of the hotel. Jerry wondered what his best plan of action was. If they had something going on tonight that was designed to hurt the kids, he'd have to find a way to stop them. Four to one wasn't a scenario that worked in his favor. Direct conflict would be his last option.

They crossed in the middle of a block and headed into a parking lot. The back of the lot was dark; whether the lack of illumination was an accident or by design didn't really matter. After a couple of minutes, he put on his Aaron face and started walking toward the parking lot.

"Fortune favors the bold," he said, trying to convince himself this wasn't a stupid idea.

They were moving back toward the street when Jerry got within speaking distance. "Hold on, Keyz. I've got some new information for you."

Keyz didn't look impressed to see Aaron. None of them did. He hooked his thumbs under his belt. "Well, if it isn't our friend who missed the meet-up earlier. We've got nothing to say to you."

"I wasn't going to stick around after what happened. You saw it. The police were everywhere after that." He stepped in closer. "Whatever you've got on for tonight can wait. Like I said, I've got new information."

"We just got our assignment from someone more connected than you. So, out of the way, Bible beater, or you'll be the one who takes the beating." Keyz pushed past him.

So much for fortune's favor. Whatever they were planning, he couldn't allow it to happen. This would burn his Aaron persona, but he'd live with that. "You're not going anywhere," Jerry said, changing as he spoke. He wanted a startling appearance mixed with the ability to do some damage if necessary. He made his skin green and his head block-shaped, and produced sharp thornlike protrusions on the backs of his knuckles. Jerry doubted any of them had seen *The Thing from Another World* but they certainly wouldn't have any weapon to electrocute him.

Keyz turned and pulled a gun from the back of his pants. Jerry high-kicked him hard enough to knock him into a nearby Audi. He hit the car with a thud and dropped his weapon.

Jerry turned to face the others. One of the young men had high-tailed it, which helped Jerry's odds a bit. The young woman and her friend both had knives, and took up positions on either side of him. Jerry lunged to the right and took a backhanded swing at the woman, who seemed more confident with a blade than her companion, but caught only air. She jumped in and sliced into Jerry's forearm. He bellowed.

The man tried to attack from behind, but Jerry spun quickly and grabbed his knife-hand. He wrenched the man's arm as hard as possible and threw him into the woman. The collision sent them sprawling and knocked both their knives free. Jerry advanced, making sure the thorns on the backs of his hands were visible, even in the dim light. He raised his right arm menacingly. The pair looked at each other and bolted.

Jerry turned to check on Keyz, who hadn't recovered his gun but was pointing a Taser at Jerry's chest. Jerry swung his arm, hoping to deflect the twin wires. The connects hit him first and delivered a massive jolt. Jerry's follow-through cut the wires, but he was still down. He struggled to get his feet under him, but his body wouldn't respond.

Keyz stood over him. He had his gun now, and it was pointed at Jerry. "Say hello to Jesus for me, ass-clown."

He was going to die as a space carrot if he didn't do something. Jerry tried to grab Keyz's leg, but his arm only flopped around. Keyz laughed.

There was a rush of air and a dark shape impacted Keyz, sending him flying a dozen or so feet away. It was Adesina.

"This one time, I'm glad you didn't do as you were told," Jerry told her.

"Lucky for you I followed you. You're not very good at your job, are you?"

"Not right now I'm not, but tomorrow is another day." She didn't appear to get the reference. Jerry lurched to his feet and walked over to Keyz, who was trying to locate his pistol. Jerry kicked it away under a car.

"We're not done, monster-man." Keyz's false bravado didn't faze Jerry. He'd heard it plenty of times.

Jerry brought his leg back and kicked Keyz in the face. "Keep watching the skies."

"You didn't need to do that," Adesina said, disapprovingly.

"Well, he was going to kill me. I take that sort of thing personally." He was going to pat her shoulder, but the wings were in the way. "Thanks. I owe you one."

"You sure do."

"Now fly back to the hotel. We've had enough excitement for one night." Jerry watched her wordlessly take off. Her wings propelling her into the night sky were a thing of beauty.

The cut on his arm wasn't too bad, but it hurt like hell. He'd never been good with open wounds. Given his power, Jerry should be able to make them close right up, but it didn't work that way. It was most likely the blood. He didn't care for blood at all. That probably accounted for his dislike of guns. Blowing holes in people was a bloody mess.

A police vehicle, rotating red and blue lights flashing, advanced slowly up the street. Jerry ducked between the parked cars and was gone.

Jerry bought some first aid back at the hotel while wearing a totally random face, and bandaged himself up back in his room. He changed into his Michelle body and clothes and headed back to her room. He'd have to make some kind of an outraged mom scene with Adesina, but he didn't want to go too hard on her. After all, she'd just saved his life.

She was watching TV when he came in, and didn't even meet his eye. "Everything's cool, Mom," she said. "Don't go crazy on me."

Jerry walked over in measured steps. "Where were you? How could you do something so reckless? Did you know I had people out looking for you?" Jerry kept his Michelle voice short of yelling, but loud enough to make sure she got the point.

Jerry stepped in front of the TV and glared down at Adesina. "You know what's been going on these past few days. It's dangerous out there." He waved his arms emphatically.

Adesina looked at his bandaged forearm and narrowed her eyes. The dime dropped for her in a hurry. "It's you. You're pretending to be my mom."

Busted again. Jerry didn't have the energy to try to think his way out of this. He sat down beside her on the couch. "Yeah, you're right. Your mom had something important to take care of tonight and she wanted me to keep an eye on you."

"That's totes lame."

"No, it isn't. I may be lame, but your mom wanting to keep you safe means she's a good mom." Jerry relaxed and let his body collapse into the couch. "I'll make you a deal, Adesina. Let's forget you got out tonight. We'll keep it a secret between us. That keeps both of us out of trouble."

She gave him an uncertain look. "You want us to lie to my mom?"

"A judicious lie can be a positive thing, and this would qualify," he said. "Let's face it, she's likely to chain you to the bed tomorrow night if she finds out what happened. I'm not sure what she'd say to me, but I'd just as soon not find out. Deal?"

"Deal."

"Great. Now why don't you go to bed, so that when your mom shows up she'll assume everything tonight went fine."

Adesina nodded and headed toward the bedroom.

"When your mom comes back, if she checks on you pretend you were asleep. You know, rub your eyes, yawn, that kind of thing." Jerry was trying to avoid anything that might make Michelle suspicious.

Adesina rolled her eyes. "Like I didn't already know that." She paused in the bedroom doorway. "Are you actually a man or a woman?"

"A man. I was born a man anyway, and that's what I am in my spare time."

"I figured. What's your name?"

He could have lied. There was no way she'd ever know. Then again, she'd saved his life tonight. "Jerry," he said.

She made a face. "That's such an old-sounding name. Perfect for you, though." She entered the bedroom and turned off the light.

♥

He got Michelle's text a few hours later. She was waiting for him outside his room. He changed his face and headed to the elevator. Upstairs Michelle was leaning against the wall; she looked even more tired than Jerry felt.

"Come on in. I'll get your clothes for you."

Michelle followed him inside. "Did she give you any trouble?"

Jerry smiled and nodded. "A little. No more than I could handle, though. She's a good kid."

"Yes, she is. But sometimes it takes everything I have to keep her in line." She sighed. "You have no idea."

Jerry pulled a fluffy robe from the closet and walked into the bathroom. "I'll change and you can have the clothes back."

"You took off your makeup."

Jerry shrugged. "Yeah, after she went to bed I didn't see the point."

Michelle nodded.

After a few moments in the bathroom, Jerry handed Michelle her clothing and walked her to the door. "I'll be back on the case tomorrow. Let me know if anything happens."

"Good night, Mr. Creighton, or whoever you are."

"Night."

Jerry couldn't sleep. For one thing, his arm hurt. For another, he hadn't had a very good day. He picked up his tablet and ran a YouTube search on the Jokertown Mob. There were several entries, so he picked the one with the most likes. Halfway through the video, Jerry was smiling. It wasn't really his kind of music, but these kids were great and they were loving what they were doing.

Jerry remembered something, a feeling from a long, long time ago. Before he'd been a detective, even before he'd been a giant ape, Jerry had worked the club circuit as the Projectionist. He'd used his ace to impersonate movie stars onstage. His act wasn't great; in fact, it usually wasn't good at all. But the times it did click were magic. Getting up in front of an audience, connecting, doing your stuff, and making it really work—that was something he'd forgotten until now.

It was how the Mob felt when they got onstage and performed. That was one of the best feelings in the world.

Jerry smiled as the memory faded. The kids deserved that moment, and there was no way anyone was going to take it away from them if he could help it.

He needed sleep, but first thing tomorrow morning he'd be on the job. It was time to get his game faces on.

♠ ♥ ♦ ♣

Dust and the Darkness

Part 4

I'D PHONED AHEAD, AND Mindy-Lou's bandmates had been waiting for her in the lobby for hours. As soon as we entered the Gunter they spotted her, squealed, and came rushing over to hug her and kiss her and generally squee that she was back. Beside me, Candace had a look on her face that I took for fifty-fifty contempt and envy.

One girl hung back, though. Blond, tall, though not nearly so tall as Mindy-Lou. Cover-girl pretty—but not quite as pretty as Mindy-Lou.

"And you must be Jillian," I said, as she marched up with rage kindling in her sky-blue eyes. "I know we're gonna be great friends."

She paid me no mind. "Mindy-Lou, you selfish *bitch!*" she screamed in Mindy-Lou's face. "We played for shit and we *lost* and all because of you!"

Beside me, I heard Candace utter a growl that wouldn't have sounded out of place coming out of Blood's throat. I touched her arm gently with two fingertips. More would have been impolite without invitation. Also I didn't want her gutting me with her hideout knife.

Mindy-Lou blinked, scowled, and decked Jillian with an overhand right.

Neither her bandmates nor the other bystanders hustled forward to help the stricken girl. She gave Mindy-Lou a look like a cat I'd once seen who'd found himself confronting an escaped coatimundi—long story; no animals harmed, etc.—and burst into tears. "This could be bad," Candace muttered to me across a sudden silence.

"Not our problem," I said.

♣

"So what now?" Candace asked.

I shrugged. "Billy's in the breeze. Our girl's back. We got paid."

"Well, you got paid."

"Yeah. But Mindy-Lou's parents don't know about you." Neither did my *abuela*. And boy, did I plan on keeping it that way. Though I had to suspect she'd find in Candace the Darkness a kindred spirit.

"Anyway, I meant what now for *us*."

"Umm—"

"Not like that!"

"Nothing could be further from my mind." It was true. Almost. I mean, she was pretty good-looking. But so is a sidewinder, from a certain point of view. Like a herpetologist's. Or a boy sidewinder's.

Candace leaned back on her elbows and looked up at me. "For such a nice, naive country boy, you are a sneaky little shit."

"Thank you kindly for the vote of confidence, Ms. Darkness. But I don't need compliments. I'm only in it for the money."

"*Merde.*"

"*¿Mande?*"

"Underneath the rough shitkicker exterior you are mush. A true Quixote."

"If you say so. Although some of these windmills turned out to be actual giants."

"Indeed. And we bested them, did we not?"

I had to allow that was true.

"We seem to work well together."

"But you're a hardened criminal. And I'm a piss-poor junior-grade detective, now retired."

"As it happens, I find myself at loose ends for employment. And so do you."

"There's always chunking bales of hay into the back of my uncle's Ram."

"You are not meant for such a life. You need adventure. Why else would you take up riding wild bulls?"

"I—" They're not wild. Fact is, in their way they're as much professionals as we are. But I didn't have the energy to explain."—Guess so."

Because . . . well, good question, ¿que no?

"You're not meant to be a ranch hand. You said it bores you. I think you're an ace detective."

"When I'm not getting my car stolen by shady women? And almost getting us killed?"

"Let us not speak of the car again. We each—underestimated the other. Besides, all ended well. Mindy-Lou's family will even pay for your Uber ride."

"Durn tootin'."

"What I meant was, you're an ace, who is also a detective. And do rather well at it, like it or not. We are both aces. So was Billy. Do the police always give proper attention to wild card–related crimes or disappearances in this country?"

"Some try. And there's the Feds. SCARE."

"So. We could . . . take the cases they will not."

"Nah," I said.

She laughed. "You won't dismiss it so easily once you think about it a while."

"Bet I won't even think of it again."

But I already was.

♠ ♥ ♦ ♣

FRIDAY

Bubbles and the
Band Trip

Part 11

"MY BASS IS STILL missing, and so is Peter's trumpet," Adesina said. She was pulling on her shoes. Her side of the hotel room was a disaster. *She's only been here since Thursday. How is this even possible?* Michelle thought.

"I know, but I bet Mr. Robins will let you borrow his instrument again. And Jan's niece will let Peter borrow her trumpet again. She seemed to think he was nice."

"*Mom,*" Adesina said with an exaggerated patience. "Peter is hella cute, super-nice, and really popular. Of course she liked him. So, did you really like the movie we watched last night? I was kinda surprised."

"Movie?" Michelle replied. She moved the bass case into the closet so she would stop tripping over it.

"You know, that old black-and-white one. The one with the giant gorilla. And the one you watched later, you know, the one with the lady with the cool hair who was a witch."

Michelle looked at Adesina blankly. Then she realized that Creighton must have been watching something on TCM. It was the only station she knew that ran old black-and-white movies.

Well, shit, she thought. *He might have mentioned that he was watching stuff with Adesina.*

"Yes," Michelle replied, lying smoothly. "It was a lot of fun. Didn't think I'd like anything like that, but you know, hair."

"Right." Adesina smiled at her. Then she hummed a little bit of a song: "Da da da de da. Da da da de—"

"You ready to go?" Michelle asked. She didn't like Adesina's smile. It was too sunny. And what was the deal with the song? It didn't sound like the kind of thing Adesina would go for.

Both Michelle's and Adesina's text message tones went off at the same time. They pulled their phones from their pockets and simultaneously looked at their messages.

"OMG!" they said together.

"We made it to the finals!" Adesina said with wonder.

♠

The Plano Originals, the Lubbock High School Jazz Band, and the Mob stood backstage waiting to perform.

<I can't believe we made it to the final round!> Sharon signed. <We did have a great day. But in all fairness, Modesto really dropped the ball.>

"I know," Michelle said. "I don't know much about jazz, but I do know they really seemed to struggle."

The high-drama return of Mindy-Lou Gutiérrez created quite the shitstorm backstage. Michelle was just happy Mindy-Lou was back safe and sound—and that she hadn't been the chaperone to lose a player. And apparently Mindy-Lou was now in the possession of a wicked overhand right.

But none of those other chaperones had to deal with rattlesnakes, so she figured she was ahead in the whole who's-having-the-MOST-fun-chaperoning game.

♦

"You ready?" Michelle asked. Adesina nodded and smoothed her skirt. It was below the knee, black, tight. Her shirt was a white halter top that left her wings unencumbered. Her vestigial legs peeped out from slits in the front of the blouse. A black-and-white ensemble. It was the normal uniform for performance.

"Go out there and show those Plano jerks how we do it in Joker-town. Kick their . . . bottoms."

"Except Kimmie," Ghost piped in. "She's really nice."

"Okay, kick everyone except Kimmie," Michelle said.

"Well, since she's an ace, we have to like her," Sean said. "I think that's why she was hanging out with us so much."

Michelle was baffled. "What do you mean, she's an ace?"

"I think she's a deuce," Antonia said with a laugh. "I mean, not having to breathe so your flute solos can go on forever? That's pretty deucey."

"What if she can hold her breath forever underwater, huh? That would be a great ace power," Sean replied indignantly. "Who knows what her power can do?"

"We should totes check it out after everything's done," Adesina said earnestly. Her vestigial arms curled in and out. "She's been hella nice to us when she didn't have to. I mean, no one in her band knows. Her mother, obvs, doesn't know. Just being around them would be scary."

"Yeah," Peter allowed. "I don't know how I never twigged to it."

The rest of the band looked at him with a collective *Dude, please* expression.

Slowly, he looked around the circle. Then he flushed red up to his hairline. "Oh, never mind," he said. Michelle would have laughed, but she was afraid it would make Peter feel bad. And she really liked him.

And she was a little embarrassed that she'd never noticed Kimmie's power, but then she didn't know much of anything about jazz.

♥

Now that it was down to three bands, each performed a song in one of the styles they'd chosen for the competition.

The Plano band did a hot and spicy rendition of "Bonga" by Duke Ellington. Both the Mob and Lubbock had chosen bebop as their special style. The Mob played "Ain't Got No Jokertown Baby" by Mysterious Shades fast and light. And Lubbock did "Scrapple from the Apple" by Charlie Parker, which was pretty much a no-brainer.

♣

Creighton looking like Creighton tapped Michelle on the shoulder while the Mob was playing.

She spun around, startled, a bubble forming in her hand. "Jesus!" she hissed. "You scared the hell out of me. You do know I could have . . ." She held the bubble out. He went pale.

"Is that your immediate reaction to everything?" he asked with a quiver in his voice. "Because that's a little peculiar."

Michelle tilted her head to one side and stared at him. He grew fidgety, then finally said, "Okay, I have some new information for you."

"Well, not now," Michelle whispered. The bubble popped silently in her hand. "My kids are playing."

"Yeah, I see," he replied. He gave a little smile, then turned his attention to the stage. There was a wistful expression on his face. "They sure are good, aren't they?"

Michelle nodded. "Yes, they are."

♠

The final three bands stood onstage, fidgeting nervously.

"How long do you think it's going to be before they announce the winners?" Robin whispered.

Michelle saw that Yerodin was rocking back and forth heel to toe. Toe to heel. The other kids looked equally nervous. Michelle looked over at Wally and he was biting his lip. It sounded like a pepper grinder.

"Dr. Smith is coming out," Wally whispered. "We'll know soon enough, you betcha."

A wave of whispers ran through the audience. Tension fairly hummed in the air.

Michelle saw Adesina and Peter holding hands and Adesina holding hands with Ghost. Most of the Mob had grabbed the hand of the person next to them. Tentacles wrapped around fuzzy peach fingers. Marissa's blocky hand was enclosed by Sean's shifting-colored hand. Robin took Michelle's hand and her fingers sank into his rubbery grip.

Dr. Smith cleared her throat and then leaned into the mic. "I just want to say that all the bands in the competition have been exceedingly good this year. You're all most exceptional." She looked around the room and beamed. You'd never know that there had been one dis-ruption after another during the proceedings. Or that there was a world of controversy swirling outside the doors to the auditorium.

She looked down at her card, then said, "In third place, the Lub-bock High School Jazz Band." The Mob looked at one another then dropped hands and started clapping. Michelle knew what they were thinking. They had a chance to win.

The Lubbock band stepped forward and took their trophy. A skinny, dark-haired boy stepped up to the mic. "Bacho," Michelle heard An-tonia whisper. "He's been hanging out with Jax and Darryl. Which is weird because he seems so nice."

"We're proud to have been part of the competition and we don't feel as if we've lost. We feel like we won because we got here at all. Thanks so much for this and for the awesome week."

There was warm applause as he stepped back in line with his band. The Mob joined hands again. Dr. Smith didn't look at her card. She just stepped to the mic and said, "In second place, the Xavier Des-mond High School Jazz Band." The Originals looked at one another and did silent cheers and clapped each other on the back. Some of them did fist bumps.

The Mob accepted their second-place trophy. They didn't seem very sad. They actually looked happy.

Peter rolled up to the mic. "I know that it's been an, er, interesting time. But we've met a lot of cool people who didn't treat us like freaks and we really appreciate it." He smiled at the audience. "I know some of you still don't like us, but we hope you respect us as musicians. Thank you again."

The Originals stepped up, accepting the first-place trophy as if it were their due. "It's awesome to be here and finally win! It was a tough year," Jax said. "We just want to thank everyone."

The audience started applauding, then, after a few seconds, stood. The top three bands began intermingling, congratulating one another on placing. Except Plano, who didn't shake hands—or tentacles—with anyone from the Mob.

After a few minutes, the applause died down and the audience took their seats again.

"Thank y'all again for a wonderful competition. The rest of the afternoon and evening are free! Remember, we have the showcase tomorrow! I expect everyone to be here ready to play at noon."

◆

Creighton had asked Michelle to come to his suite now that the competition was over. His suite was cold. Hanging-meat cold. Michelle was glad she'd put on some fat by jumping out of her window—it helped some. There didn't seem to be a time of year when Texas buildings weren't cooled to hypothermia. Even now when the weather was delightful during the day and pleasantly cool at night as it was right now.

Michelle was staring out the window looking out at the downtown San Antonio lights because Creighton had asked her to turn her back as he was changing into someone else. She obliged because . . . ew. Behind her, there was an electric pop as if a circuit breaker had blown.

When he said it was okay to turn around, she saw he'd changed himself to look like Bambi Coldwater. He wore towering heels and a crimson "ladies who lunch" dress. There was a black Louis Vuitton Pont-Neuf Mini in his hand. His hair was a little bigger than Bambi's usually was, but it looked magnificent.

"You look incredibly well-turned-out," Michelle said. She was impressed with the outfit.

"I went to Neiman's and told them what I needed," Creighton said. "Can you help me with this?" He held out a makeup bag. Michelle took it and looked inside.

"Yeah, this is suboptimal, but I think I can make it work. But these are not Bambi's colors."

♥

Creighton looked at himself in the mirror. "You did a great job," he said.

"Ya think?" Michelle said with a laugh. "It's almost like I've worked in the field of making things beautiful before."

"I thought you had people who did your makeup."

"Well, they're not around 24/7. Sometimes you have to do the heavy lifting yourself." Michelle gave him a once-over. "So, when do you want me to come up tomorrow?"

"You need to be here at eight thirty tomorrow morning." Jerry preened a little in the mirror. "I think I'm going to enjoy this." He grabbed his purse and waltzed out the door.

Drop City

by David Anthony Durham

BACHO STOOD IN THE bustling hotel lobby. Waiting. He hated waiting. It always made him feel awkward when he had to do it in public. He checked his phone. It was fifteen minutes past the agreed-upon meeting time and a full twenty-five minutes since he'd been waiting. It was stupid, but not only did he hate being late, he tended to end up being *early* because of it. He'd agreed to meet Jax and Darryl in the lobby and to walk with them over to the Hard Rock Cafe to meet a bunch of the other band members. He should've known they were going to be late. He'd only known them for a few days, but he'd noticed Jax seemed to get some perverse pleasure out of pushing people's buttons.

Dude, Bacho thought, *you really should try being cooler.* He focused again on the blank screen of his phone, for connection, for validation. Any new e-mails or texts? Nope. He texted Jax. *Where you at? I'm waiting.*

That done, he looked around the lobby again. He leaned an elbow on the glass shelves that wrapped around one of the tall light pillars, trying to looking nonchalant. This place was way too fancy for him. He worried it showed. He and his mom were more Econo Lodge types, and that only on rare road trips to his grandmother in Colorado. Even after a few days here, he still felt out of place, an impostor somebody was going to discover and chuck out any minute now. It only made the waiting worse.

He wore jeans and his *Walking Dead* T-shirt, the one with joker-zombie Carl staring out from beneath his sheriff's hat, snarling. He thought it was cool, and he was glad to be able to wear something other than his band clothes. He wished again that Jax and Darryl would show up. Maybe that was part of the reason he'd started hanging out with them. *They* certainly felt at home here. They acted like they owned the place, actually.

In all the motion of people coming and going, it was the girl's stillness that made her stand out. She lounged on one of the plush chairs not far from the main entrance. She sat with her legs crossed, leaning back into the cushions, looking bored. She held a phone propped up on one hand, absently rotating it around with her fingers. Bored, yeah, but also about as at ease and self-assured as possible, which Bacho found a little strange. She wasn't your average Texas fancy hotel–looking girl. Her short skirt was black. Her boots were bright orange. She wore two loose tank tops, white over black. And her hair was long enough on the crown of her head that it hung down her shoulder and onto her chest. That was just the top; the sides and back were shaved to the skin. She didn't look like she belonged here either, but she didn't seem to know that. Or maybe it was more that she just didn't seem to care.

"Hey Lurker, someone should call the cops on you." Jax, suddenly there right beside him. He grabbed hold of Bacho's ear and twisted it until he pulled away. When Bacho slapped, ineffectively, at his hand, Jax put on an offended pout, a look of insult and unfairness. It was one of his signature features. With his blue eyes, pert little nose, and that flare of blond hair that would've made Kevin Bacon green with envy . . . well, he could get away with it. To Bacho, it seemed like Jax could get away with most anything. Even if he didn't exactly like him, there was something about his confidence and privilege that drew you in.

Darryl was all smiles. He was a slim Asian kid. He'd admitted once that people always assumed he was Chinese because his name was Chang, but actually his family was Korean. And he said it like that: *his family* was Korean, as if they were and he wasn't and it was all quite a burden on him. His name wasn't technically Darryl, either. It was really Joon-ho, which he only admitted after pointing out that Bacho had a messed-up name also. Personally, Bacho thought he shouldn't fight it. His features were Asian, his slim physique was, and, not to stereotype, but his technical skill with the violin suggested hours of practice before the unflinching supervision of a Tiger Mom. When he spoke, though, in a pretend cop walkie-talkie voice, he could've been straight off the Ferguson force. "Suspicious guy of questionable ethnicity spotted lurking in the lobby."

Darryl, guaranteed to back up anything Jax said. They were kinda jerks, but at least they both knew the roles they were supposed to play. Bacho wished he did.

"So, you ready or what?" Jax asked. He started to move away. "Let's go."

"Yeah, I'm ready," Bacho began. "I've been—"

"Hey." Jax paused. "What do we have here?" He meant the girl by the main entrance. Jax looked immediately predatory. His posture loosened. His jaw shifted. He looked on the verge of licking his chops. "She looks a bit skanky."

"Dude," Bacho said, "that's not cool."

Jax rapped him on the chest with a thrum of his knuckles. "I mean it in a good way. Like, she probably does the weird stuff. She's probably got identity issues. Insecurities."

"I've seen her before," Darryl said. "She's pretty noticeable, huh? Don't know who she is, though."

"How about we find out?" Jax started toward her, weaving through the crowd.

Following him, Bacho had a harder time navigating. "Excuse me," he said to a middle-aged woman who looked mildly alarmed at almost bumping into him. "Sorry."

Jax sauntered up to the girl like a baseball pitcher to the mound, looking a little bored, a little cocky, and completely sure that all eyes were on him. The girl, however, didn't seem to notice him until he said, "Hey, what's up?"

She looked up. She wasn't exactly pretty. Her face was a little too gaunt, her nose a little too prominent, and her lips turned down at the edges. Her eyes were amazing, though. Gray, languid, lined underneath in black. She reminded Bacho of a girl version of a young John Lennon. That struck him as kinda strange, but there it was. With a bit of punk thrown in also. He couldn't figure out how old she was. Seventeen? Eighteen? Something about her disinterested air made her seem like she might be older than she looked. She made him nervous, in a bumblebees are suddenly buzzing around in his stomach sort of way.

Her eyes scanned the boys—first Jax, then the other two, and then back to Jax. She said, "Nothing whatsoever is up."

"I know, right?" Jax said. "Is this city lame or what? Where you from?"

The girl fluttered her eyes and said, "San Antonio."

An awkward silence, and then Jax shrugged it off. He was good at shrugging things off. "So what's your name?"

She exhaled an amused breath. "Are you really going to keep talking to me?"

"Sure," Jax said. "You in one of these bands?"

The girl's look of derision was withering. "Do I look like someone who would be in high school jazz band?"

No, Bacho admitted to himself, but he couldn't have said what type of music she might've liked.

Jax tsked. "I know. It's lame, right? Bunch of dorks."

She raised an eyebrow. "You didn't act like you thought it was lame earlier, when your team won the competition."

"You saw that?"

She pointed two fingers toward her eyes. "See these things? They're called eyes. Seeing is what they're for."

Bacho was starting to like her.

Undeterred, Jax went on, "So, if you were watching you saw how the Plano Originals crushed all competition. Right, Bacho? Lubbock was like . . . what, third place? Bronze metal territory. And Darryl . . . what band were you even in?" He put on—and then dropped—a perplexed expression. "But, anyway, I don't like to brag."

"I'm sure," the girl said, "but if you ask me the whole competition was sketchy. Stolen instruments. Stink bombs. Rattlesnakes. Those collapsing lights . . . I mean, seriously, somebody could've gotten hurt."

Jax shrugged. "A few squished jokers. Wouldn't have been that big a loss."

The girl exhaled and checked her phone, managing to make the gesture into a dismissal.

Jax didn't take the hint. He just changed gears. "So what are you doing later? If you're a local, maybe you could show us the real San Antonio or something."

"Just go to the River Walk like all the other tourists."

Which, Bacho thought, *is exactly where we were supposed to be right now.*

"Why don't you show us around? Something grungy that tourists don't see?"

"I don't think you guys are into the same sort of scene as I am."

Jax wheedled his way closer. "How do you know if you don't try us?"

"I know. Trust me." She turned away slightly and began typing on her phone. Another dismissal. This was getting ridiculous.

"Hey, Jax," Bacho began, but paused when a group of joker kids poured out of the elevator area and started across the lobby. More than a few heads turned to watch them. Several people stepped out of their way. If the jokers noticed, they didn't show it. The group laughed and chattered. One of them, the boy with the weird sienna skin, cut circles through the crowd, talking as he skated effortlessly on his wheeled feet. How does someone get a mutation like that? It was weird, but also pretty cool. And the kid had personality, that's for sure. Confidence, but the kind that welcomed you on your own terms. Pretty different from Jax, who, on cue, spoke up.

"Fucking jokers," he said. His voice changed completely. He dropped the smarmy hitting-on-a-girl vibe and went full disgust.

The girl looked up from her phone, watched the passing group for a moment, and then asked, "What about fucking jokers?"

"Hey, I'm not prejudiced or anything." He pointed at the jokers as they exited the hotel. "But they're sick. You know what I'm saying?"

She stared at him, finally giving him her full attention. "Yeah, I know what you're saying."

Jax grinned. "They're sick and dangerous and they can spread it. I know they say they can't, but people keep becoming jokers. So . . . it's spreading somehow. And that stuff in Afghanistan? Damn. They should be kept separate from us. You know what I'm saying?"

"I think you mean Kazakhstan," she said. "Are you for . . . like . . . a quarantine?"

"Permanently," Jax said. "Don't hate me for telling it like it is!"

The girl smirked. "No, I wouldn't hate you for that. We haven't met properly. I'm Dina. No need to introduce yourselves. You're in the program."

Considering her crack about not looking like someone who would be in a band, she certainly seemed to have followed the competition. Bacho wanted to ask her about that, but he'd yet to open his mouth in any significant way.

Jax got smarmy again. "You sure you don't want to hang out tonight?"

Dina pressed the question between her lips for a moment, and then let them curve into a mischievous smile. "I might. No tourist stuff, though. If we hang it's gonna be with locals, local style. Underground, you know? You ever heard of Drop City?"

The boys drew blanks.

"It's a dance club."

"Oh, yeah, that one," Jax said. "I heard it was cool."

Dina smiled, let her head float a little loosely on her neck, flirty like. Bacho couldn't figure her out. He had the feeling she totally saw through Jax's shit—which made him like her—but she also seemed kind of into him. Maybe guys like Jax just had it that way. Even when they were jerks girls fell for them.

"You're in luck, then. DJ Tod's performing tonight."

"What kind of music does he play?"

"Psychedelic deep house. And I mean *seriously* psychedelic."

Darryl frowned and looked about as clueless as Bacho felt. Jax seemed unfazed. "Right," he said. "Cool. Love that stuff."

"Okay, then," Dina said. "It's a date. I'll get my cousin to come, too. Meet outside at twelve. I figure you kiddies need to sneak out, so let's meet around on that side." She pointed. "It's more out of sight. Just go like halfway down the block."

"Twelve?" Bacho asked. "But what about the—"

"Done," Jax said. "A date, just like you said."

Dina answered by clicking her tongue off the roof of her mouth. With that, she got up and started to walk away.

"Where you going?" Jax asked. "I thought you were waiting for somebody."

Dina swirled and walked backward. She scrunched her nose, which

Bacho found to be terribly cute. "Nah, changed my mind. I gotta go. See you at twelve, if you don't wimp out." And then she was weaving into the crowd, heading for the elevator bays.

"Oh, you'll see us, all right," Jax whispered, too softly for her to hear. He looked between Bacho and Darryl, grinning like a wolf. "She's totally into me."

Afraid he was right, Bacho returned to the topic that had been cut off. "Yeah, but what about curfew?"

"Who cares? This whole thing is almost over. Let's have some fun. We sneak out; that's all. Don't be such a trump."

"Yeah, grow some balls, Bachacho," Darryl said, though he glanced at Jax for approval.

Jax ignored him. Staring vaguely toward the elevator, he said, "*And she has a cousin*. This is gonna be epic."

"Totally," Darryl said.

♣

When Mrs. Robertson stopped by the room for the curfew check-in she found Bacho snugly under his covers, eyes slitted in imitation of sleep. Dion sat up in bed reading a book, and Troy and Sam were on their sleeping bags on the floor, taking turns playing an app on a tablet. The teacher wore her sleepy-time cap and bathrobe, and looked like she was well on the way toward catching her zzz's. "It's been quite a day," she whispered. "You should all follow Bacho's example and get a good night's sleep. I know I will. You boys promise you'll go lights out by twelve thirty?"

Troy and Sam assured her they would, and she yawned as she wished them all good night.

As soon as the door shut behind her, Bacho yanked back his covers and sat up, fully clothed. He grabbed his sneakers and began to lace them up.

"What exactly do you think you're doing?" Dion asked.

"I'm going somewhere," Bacho said, trying to make it sound completely mundane. "Don't worry about it."

"Going somewhere?" Troy paused the game on the tablet and looked up. "You can't *go* anywhere. It's after curfew. You'll just get in trouble."

"Or get us in trouble," Sam added.

Bacho was all too worried that they were right, but instead of answering he just tugged his laces tight and stood up.

"What if Mrs. Robertson comes back?" Dion asked. "We're not lying for you, you know."

"I know," Bacho said, grabbing his light jacket and slamming his arms into it. "I didn't ask you to lie or anything. Anyway, she's not coming back. You know how fast she crashes." They didn't dispute that. They'd all seen the way she fell into a deep sleep as soon as the bus was moving on band trips. She rarely woke up again until the bus engine turned off and students were clamoring down the aisle with their instruments. "If anybody asks just say you don't know where I went."

"Yeah, but where *are* you going?"

"Better you don't know. Plausible deniability and all that."

"Plausible what?"

Bacho didn't answer. He went to the door, turned the doorknob, and listened through the narrow crack. He heard a couple talking, down the hall to the left. He waited as their voices faded and then a door clicked audibly shut. He let the silence sit for a moment and then opened the door more. He peeked up and down the empty, silent hallway.

"You're probably going to regret this," Dion said.

"Yeah, I know," Bacho whispered. He slipped out the door and pulled it, softly, shut behind him.

He slid down the hallway sideways, arms stretched out in front and behind him, as if he was afraid of running into something. He feared the ping of an arriving elevator, and his adrenaline ramped up each time he passed a door. When he finally reached the stairwell door, he exhaled a breath he hadn't known he'd been holding. He stood, taking in the humming silence of the concrete chamber, and then he tore down the flights of stairs, taking them three and four steps at a time all the way down to the ground floor.

In stealth mode again, Bacho cautiously opened the door from the stairwell into the lobby. Low music greeted him, voices, the sound of someone's wheeled luggage being pulled across the polished stones. Crap, why was he doing this? He was sure he'd step out and promptly

collide with one of the chaperones. He had decided he would pretend
to have a headache and say he'd come down to see if he could find
some aspirin, but he had zero confidence he'd actually get through the
lie convincingly.

He might've hesitated indefinitely, except that a door opened somewhere above him in the stairwell. That pushed him out into the lobby.
He walked quickly, hugging the wall, head down, and was out the lobby
doors faster than he thought possible. Nobody collided with him. Nobody called his name. The night air greeted him with a delicate cool-
ness. He didn't pause to take it in, though. He shifted down the
sidewalk, along the old awning, across the street to the tree-lined area
he thought Dina had specified. Once there, tucked in near a clump of
bushes that hid him from the front of the hotel, he scanned both sides
of the street while trying to look nonchalant. A few people strolled
by, chatting. He turned from the street as several cars passed. It was
a normal enough night and fairly quiet. He checked his phone: 11:45.
Of course, he was early. He couldn't help it. It was a pathological dis-
ability with him.

"Hey," a female voice said. Bacho started, turned quickly around.
It was Dina, surprisingly close behind him. He hadn't heard her ap-
proach at all. She looked awesome, dressed in a short black skirt with
colorful leggings. Her gray short-sleeved shirt had a symbol at its center that Bacho couldn't make out. And he didn't want to look like he
was staring at her breasts. "Where are your pals?"

"Dunno," Bacho said, feeling immediately tongue-tied. "We
weren't, um . . . in the same room. Like, we're . . . in different rooms."

"Good to know you're not attached at the hip."

"Nah. Really, I don't even know them that well. We're all from different bands and all."

Dina considered that. Made a sound low in her throat, a humpf.
Then she said, "We'll give them a few minutes. It's not twelve yet."

She looked down the street, head loose on her neck like she'd grown
instantly bored. Bacho thought about texting Jax and telling him to
hurry up, but that had never helped before. He needed to say something. They couldn't stand there in silence. Reaching for anything, he
asked, "So, what about your cousin?"

Dina maintained her head tilt, but her eyes swiveled back to him.

She watched him a moment, during which he kicked himself for being nosy. "She's probably not your type."

"Oh, no, I didn't mean . . . I was just . . ."

"Calm down. I'm just kidding. She's probably *not* your type, but . . . just relax. Anyway, she's coming."

Back to the awkward silence. Bacho rallied again. He tried, "So what's this place like? The club, I mean."

Dina shrugged. "It's a club." It seemed like that might be all the answer she was going to offer, but then she said, "Don't worry, it's a cool crowd. It doesn't really attract many jokers, if that's what you're worried about. A few, but mostly it's a nat scene, the kind of thing you guys are into."

"Right," Bacho said. He thought of the kid with wheels instead of feet, the way he seemed so at ease with himself, friendly and funny. It didn't really seem right to let her think he was as anti-joker as Jax and Darryl. Normally, he wouldn't have said anything, but with the two of them just standing there his mind jagged on it and wouldn't let go. "You know, it's not like I have anything against jokers."

"Sounded like you did."

"Not really. I mean, why should I? I haven't even really known any."

"How can you not know any jokers?"

"I mean, like, personally. So, if I just decide I don't like all of them that's kinda . . ." He stopped, not so much because he didn't have the word for what it was kinda like, but because of the way Dina had turned her full interest on him.

"It's kinda like what?" she asked.

Shit. Why was he talking? For all he knew he was on the verge of insulting her. He tried to think of a way to change the subject, but when she went, "Hmmm?" he said, "Well . . . I mean, kinda like . . . prejudiced."

She stared at him for a long moment, and then shifted her jaw back and forth. "A deep thinker, are you?" Bacho started to respond, but she said, "You should lose the cap. You've almost got style without it. With it, not so much. What are you anyway?"

"What am I?"

"Like ethnically."

"Oh." For a moment, he considered lying, just shrugging and saying,

You know. White. Mom's from Colorado. That was the safest thing to say. The neutral thing. But for some reason he kept just wanting to say the truth to her. "I'm a mutt. Half white, half Native. Navajo."

"Right. That's the part I was wondering about. So I guess you know a thing or two about prejudice?"

"Well, not really. I know my dad dealt with a lot of shit, but he died when I was like two. Never really knew him."

Dina touched his arm. It was just a quick, light touch of condolence, but it sent a surge of electric energy through him. "Sorry. But you *did* know him. Other than your mom he's the first person you knew. Right?"

She had a point. He'd never quite thought of it that way. "But I don't *remember* knowing him."

"Yeah, but that's not the same as never knowing him. You probably know him more than you think. He's alive in you, you know? All of our ancestors are. Pretty cool to think about that, huh?"

Though he wanted to—though he felt himself falling into the idea as much as he was falling into her eyes and smile—Bacho didn't get a chance to contemplate it.

They both turned at a sound. Bacho's pulse raced, first out of fear of being discovered. And then out of disappointment. For once, Bacho wished Jax and Darryl just wouldn't show. But there they were, jogging toward them, looking elated. "Dude," Jax said, "we came so close to getting busted. Bambi was like roaming the halls."

"She's insane," Darryl added. "You should've seen her."

Jax silenced him with a wave of his hand. "We dodged her, though. And guess what? I grabbed some liquid gold to loosen us up." He turned Darryl halfway around, indicating his backpack.

"What are you talking about?" Bacho asked.

"Booze, man. They were breaking down one of the events in the conference rooms. A guy parked a bar cart in the hallway and I was like, *What do we have here?* I grabbed a bottle."

"A bottle of what?" Bacho asked.

Jax shrugged. "Sherry."

"Sherry?"

"Hey, I only had a second. Don't complain."

Dina did not look amused. "You don't really need to drink, you know? The Drop is cool enough by itself. You don't need to get sloshed, especially not on sherry. That's like . . . muck."

"Muck?" Darryl asked.

Jax ignored him. "I'll be the judge of that. Where's your cousin, anyway?"

Looking past him, Dina smiled. "She's here. Hey cuz."

♠

The boys all turned as another figure stepped into the shadows and moved down the alley toward them. When she stepped into the light from the streetlamp, Bacho recognized her. Antonia, the joker drummer girl. What was she doing here?

"You've got to be kidding me!" Jax said. "This is a joke, right?"

"What's Fish-fingers doing here?" Darryl added.

Turning back to Dina, Jax said, "No, seriously, what's this joker doing here? She's your—"

"Cousin." Dina slipped through the boys, embraced Antonia. With her arm around her shoulder, turned back to the boys. Now that Bacho saw them side by side, he noticed a vague family resemblance, in the shape of the jaw and mouth mostly. There was also a marked contrast in their expressions. Dina looked beside herself with amusement; Antonia looked ready to punch someone, with her tentacles squeezed into two bulbous fists. What would it feel like to get punched by one of those? Bacho wondered, but he didn't want to find out.

"She's my cousin," Dina repeated, "and she's coming out with us, like I said."

Jax seemed to have a hard time finding a response. Lamely, he fell back on his favorite indignation. "But she's a joker! I hate jokers."

Smirking, Antonia flipped one of her tentacled hands over, curled most of the writhing appendages into a knotted ball, with just one long squirming digit standing upright. A recognizable gesture if ever there was one. "What you hate is that I drummed you into the ground today. If the voting had been fair—"

"That's bull. You shouldn't even have been in the competition! None of you jokers—"

"Would you stop saying *jokers*!" Antonia snapped.

"Jokers, jokers, jokers!" was Jax's response.

That led to a rapid-fire verbal exchange of insults, which, in Bacho's estimation, Antonia was winning on points. Dina watched them, that mischievous grin on her face again. Eventually, Antonia turned to her and said, "This wasn't a good idea. I can't hang out with these assholes."

Dina was as calm as ever. "Sure you can. They're not necessarily all assholes." She glanced at Bacho when she said that. "Listen, we don't have to be best buds. Let's just go to the Drop, like we planned. It's not going to kill you guys to be seen with . . . with my awesome cuz. You already snuck out. The hard part is done. Might as well make the most of it. And you," she added, squeezing Antonia's shoulder, "can settle it on the dance floor. How about that?"

Antonia kept her face hard, but Dina's smile eventually wore her down. "Fine," she said. "On the dance floor."

Jax scowled. "I'm not dancing with her!"

"I'm not dancing with *you!*" Antonia fired back, her face a mask of disdain. "God, I'd rather hurl."

On that note, the group moved off. They weren't exactly the cohesive unit Bacho would've hoped for, but he was glad Jax and Darryl didn't bail. He certainly didn't want to, and he wasn't sure how he'd have handled that. Stay with the girls, as he wanted to? Or hang with the boys, as they'd pressure him to? He didn't, really, have anything against Antonia. She was a damn good drummer, and if she was related to Dina . . . well, that went in her favor.

Her hands kept drawing his eyes, though he tried not to show it. They were always in writhing motion, like creatures separate from her, each tentacle moving like it had a mind of its own. Bacho thought they changed color, too. At least, he'd thought they were dark red when she was arguing with Jax. But as she strolled along with Dina chatting to her, they faded to a light hue, pinkish, with occasional dark or light flashes, like different shades of ink tossed into water. Weird. But also kinda cool. He wanted to look at them more closely, to ask her about them, to touch them. Not in a weird sexual way. Just . . . he was curious. He kept that to himself, though.

Jax and Darryl stopped a couple times to take swigs from the sherry bottle. Bacho declined, saying he would, later, but not really wanting to. He wasn't a drinker in any event, but moreover he didn't want Dina to think he was *muck*. Whatever that meant, it didn't sound good. He wondered how strong sherry was. Could the two of them get smashed off one bottle? He hoped not. Who knew what they'd get up to drunk.

They'd just started through a small, quiet park when Darryl stopped in his tracks. "What the . . ."

Something flew through the air, over the trees, and toward them. It was a tumbling stretchy form, like a giant loogie hocked into the night sky. The kids all froze and watched it hurtle toward them, so fast they didn't have time to react. Just when it was occurring to Bacho that they should dive for cover, the thing changed shape. It suddenly billowed, expanded, became a parachute as it caught the air, checked its speed, and drifted gently to the ground. As it touched down it changed form again. It congealed into a glob that morphed into human form, a tall, lanky man, who squirmed into trousers and a V-neck sweater even as his body took shape. And then it was done. He stood there, stooped over slightly, with a crooked smile on his wide mouth. Bacho recognized him as one of the chaperones from the competition.

Antonia said, "Mr. Ruttiger?"

"Antonia," he responded, half-sternly and half-gently. He nodded at Dina and said, "Dina."

Fortunately, the bottle of sherry was zipped away in the pack on Darryl's back. But if he demanded to check it . . . Jax clearly had the same thought. He inched away from Darryl, looking, for once, small and meek. Silent.

"How did you do that?" Antonia asked. "I'd no idea you could—"

"That's a topic for another time. What, young lady, are you doing out in the middle of the night? It's well past curfew, as I'm sure you know." He looked the group over, his face growing grave as his eyes bored into the boys one after another. "I'm not sure I approve of the company you're keeping."

"Tell me about it," Antonia said.

"Are these boys bothering you?"

"It's okay, Mr. Ruttiger," Dina said. "They're with us. No abuse . . . or, nothing we can't handle, at least."

The teacher sighed. "You shouldn't be out here. Come with me. I'm afraid I'll have to report this to your respective teachers."

"Crap," Jax said.

"Oh, man," Darryl added.

"Wait," Dina said, for once not looking completely calm and collected. "We can explain."

"I'm sure you can, but that won't—"

"Please, Mr. Ruttiger, just listen. Um . . . Could we just talk over here for a second?"

The teacher began to protest, but Antonia tugged on his arm. Dina motioned for the boys to stay put, and the two girls led the teacher a little ways down the street. As soon as they were far enough away, they launched into a fervent, whispered conversation with him. Both girls gesticulated as they talked, Antonia's tentacles all taking part.

At first Mr. Ruttiger just crossed his arms, shook his head, and kept trying to cut in. But the more they talked, the more he leaned toward them, listening. Several times Dina pointed back at the boys, making Mr. Ruttiger turn and look at them.

"Should we bolt when he's not looking?" Darryl asked under his breath.

"Don't be stupid," Jax said. "He knows who we are. That'll just get us in more trouble. Shit. Whose stupid idea was this?"

"Ah," Bacho began, "if you recall it was—"

Jax smacked him in the chest with the back of his hand. "Shhh. What do you think they're saying?"

"I don't know," Bacho said, "but it better be good or we're all toast."

Darryl began to squirm out of the backpack. "Here, take this."

"No way!" Jax backed away from him.

"It was your idea!"

"I'm not touching that. Keep it on your back and don't act like—"

Bacho said, "They're coming."

Both boys snapped to attention. Darryl grudgingly pulled the backpack into place again. Jax sidestepped away, putting Bacho nearer to him. *Jerk,* Bacho thought.

Dina, Antonia, and Mr. Ruttiger strolled back, the teacher walking in that strange, not-quite-right gait of his. "You'd better not make me regret this," he said, once they reached the boys and he'd looked them over, gravely.

"We won't," Dina and Antonia said in unison.

"It's your safety that matters most."

"We know," Dina said. "This is all absolutely safe. And it's not far away and—"

"Okay, okay. You explained it all well enough." He waved them away. "Go on before I change my mind." To the boys, he added, "I just hope you learn from this." With that, he started back toward the hotel. A few strides and his body began to stretch and morph. He stayed in human shape, but became a melted, Gumby-like version of himself.

"That dude is weird," Darryl said.

"No," Dina corrected, "that dude is cool enough not to bust us."

"He's letting us go?" Jax asked. "Holy fuck. I thought we were grilled cheese. What did you all say to him?"

Dina flashed her mischievous smile again. "Oh, don't worry about it. Point is, we're free to go. So . . . let's go."

She and Antonia began walking across the park.

Jax held Darryl back. "Hang on a minute." He looked around, suddenly cagey. The streets weren't empty, but nobody was particularly near them, and the trees at the edge of the park provided some cover. "Gimme the bottle," he said. He spun Darryl around and tugged at the pack's zipper.

"Oh, *now* you want it!"

"Shut up, douche!" Jax got the sherry bottle out. Holding it close to his chest, he scanned the park again. He uncorked the sherry and took a chug. He pulled away suddenly, spilling a little and looking like he was about to hurl. Then he shook that off. Smiling, he said, "Damn!" He handed the bottle to Darryl, who took a somewhat less robust swig.

Dina and Antonia walked back to them. Dina looked from one to the other for a moment, and then stretched out her hand.

"I thought you said we didn't need it."

She shrugged, and gestured impatiently with her fingers.

Jax smiled. "Now we're talking." He took the bottle from Darryl and offered it to her. "You can make it a double if you want."

Dina held the bottle by the neck. She sidestepped slightly, taking her off the grass and onto the paved path that bisected the park. Smiling at Jax, she held the bottle out. She said, "Oops." And dropped it.

The bottle hit the cement with a muted crack. The glass shattered into large, jagged chunks and the sherry gushed across the cement.

Jax and Darryl both surged toward it as it dropped, and then jumped back as it broke, and then crouched forward again, hands out as if to undo what had just happened. Or, failing that, as if they could scoop up the sherry before it drained away. Neither worked, so they fell back on swearing and moaning.

"What'd you do that for?" Jax yelled. His body jerked in a dance of frustration, his cool completely gone.

Dina checked that none of the liquor had splashed on her sneakers. She calmly said, "Sorry, I'm a clumsy girl."

"Bullshit, you did that on purpose!"

"Did I?" She put on an expression of mock confusion, and then made it evaporate. "I promised Mr. Ruttiger there'd be no drinking. It was one of the conditions of him letting us slide. So, you're welcome." She pulled out her phone and checked the time. "Let's go. DJ Tod will be on soon. We have to get there before he starts."

She hooked Antonia's arm in hers and the two of them walked away. Watching them, Bacho imagined being on Dina's other side, feeling the soft flesh of her inner elbow brushing against his. Like that was ever going to happen. . . .

"This is so lame," Darryl said.

"*She's* so lame," Jax corrected.

"Maybe we could get someone to buy us some beer or something. You think anybody would?"

"Not unless they're creeps," Bacho said. He crouched and began gingerly collecting the shards of glass. "Buying underage kids liquor? Creepy."

"Screw this whole thing," Jax said. "Let's go back to the hotel."

"Yeah, she's just messing with us."

Bacho stood, holding the smaller pieces of glass within the larger ones. He looked at both boys frankly, knowing they were waiting—expecting, requiring, demanding—that he agree. Normally, he would have gone along with them, but he found he didn't feel like doing that. "You can go back if you want, but I'm going with them."

"You'd bail on us?"

"Well, in a way you're bailing on *us*, actually."

Jax scowled. "Now you and them are *us*? Coming out wasn't even your idea, remember?"

Of course he did. But that was then. "I just want to go," he said. "If Dina goes there it must be cool."

"'If Dina goes there it must be cool,'" Darryl whined. "Crush much?"

Bacho's face flushed warm and embarrassed. "No, I'm just . . . you know . . . saying. It's gonna be cool, I think. So, I'm going."

He turned and, carrying the shards of glass held away from his body, followed the girls. He deposited the broken bottle in a trash bin at the edge of the park. Dina watched him from the other side of the street. He'd just crossed over when he heard Jax's and Darryl's feet slapping on the pavement. Bacho sighed, but Dina looked pleased. Before the two boys reached them, she said, "Thanks for that. Picking up the glass, I mean. That was cool of you." And then, to Bacho's amazement, she slipped her arm through his and tugged him into motion. "You're gonna love this," she said.

He already did.

◆

The club didn't look like much from the outside. With its squat, windowless gray façade, Bacho might've taken it for a warehouse and walked right past it. A single sign hung on the bland wall: DROP CITY in muted brown letters. They weren't exactly screaming their presence to the world. Still, a line of people stretched from the door halfway down the block, a diverse crowd: white and black, Latino and Asian, mostly nats, but with a few obvious jokers here and there. They dressed in all manner of clothing, with no rhyme or reason or particular style to it. Bacho was relieved about that. He was no clubber, and he'd worried about looking out of fashion. Clearly there wasn't any particular way these clubgoers dressed. Everyone seemed happy, which was another relief. Excited, chatting, smiling, laughing, embracing friends as they arrived.

As they passed into the dim interior, the music that had been a dull thrumming beat from outside became louder, more physical, pulsing and vibrating in the air. Bacho had the feeling he was leaving the normality of the outside world behind and stepping into unknown territory. As they stood waiting to pay the entry charges, Bacho read another, smaller sign: *By entering you give your consent to full Drop City*

Experience. Bacho thought, *Okay. Bring it on.* He couldn't have said where that newfound confidence came from, but, despite all the ways he feared he'd make a fool of himself, there was an energy building in him, humming at his center and radiating up into his head and out through his arms. It made him feel tingly, loose. Maybe it was the music, and maybe they were all feeling it. Dina was swaying slightly, her head bobbing to the electronic beat. Antonia was stiffer, but her tentacles . . . well, they couldn't be stiff. They moved in rhythmic pulses, those colors shifting.

They each paid the cover charge and an added "clothes deposit." Bacho, not wanting to sound stupid, didn't ask what a clothes deposit was. Jax didn't have the same reserve.

The cashier, a skinny girl with a red heart tattooed on her cheek, said, "It goes into a fund. We buy clothes and bank them. If you need any clothes replaced you can take your pick. If you don't . . . maybe next time."

"Why would we need new clothes?" Darryl asked.

"You know. If things get ripped, shredded. The usual sort of stuff. Who's next?"

With that, the line pressed forward and they didn't get to ask anything further. Bacho thought, *Rips and shredding are the usual sort of stuff?* But, again, he held his tongue. She was probably joking with them. Nobody in the crowd seemed the least bit menacing.

A second girl met them at yet another door. She handed Bacho an iPad, seemingly assuming he knew what to do with it. He didn't. "What's this?" he asked.

"Terms and conditions. Type your name and sign."

"He's read them before," Dina said. She flicked the screen until the text scrolled up and only the signature square was on display. As efficiently as if she worked here, she typed in his name and said to Bacho, "Sign. Use your finger."

He did, though he was thinking more about Dina's arm brushing against his—and the fact that she'd known his last name—than about what he was signing.

"What's it say?" Darryl asked, when the tablet came to him.

Dina pushed him playfully on the shoulder. "It says, 'I hereby confirm that I'm not a complete Monti.' Okay?"

"But he *is* a complete Monti," Jax said. He punched Darryl's other shoulder with enough force that it looked like it hurt.

As they stepped through a haze of pink smoke the music went silent, just for a second, and then it came back, one throbbing electronic beat, slowly mingling with what sounded like quivering tambourines. It almost seemed like the music was acknowledging their entry, coaxing them in, letting them take in the scene. The dance hall opened up before them like a large subterranean cavern. Bacho couldn't believe the dimensions of the place. So much bigger than it looked like from the outside, with a maze of dance floors on different levels, some elevated, some sunk into a lower level. The DJ booth at the center stood like a squat tower from a medieval castle. Strobe lights blinked and twirled from the ceiling. The place was packed. Some people danced, but in a subdued, swaying way. Most seemed to be waiting, just hanging out.

A tall guy with a tray of plastic water bottles hanging from his neck stopped in front of the group. He handed them each a bottle, saying, "Hydrate. Hydrate. Hydrate."

Jax sucked on the little straw protruding from the top of his, and then scowled. "It's water."

"Best stuff in the world," the guy said.

"How about something stronger?"

Smiling, the guy said, "You must be a first timer. Don't worry, there's no need for inebriation here, my friend. DJ Tod will take care of all your needs."

When he moved on, Bacho pointed to the DJ booth and asked, "Is that DJ Tod?"

Dina laughed. "Nah, that's just some warm-up. He'll be on soon, though. He's in the building. I can feel him. Can't you?" She didn't wait for answer. "Come on. Let's get a space on the dance floor."

She grabbed Antonia's tentacled hand and began weaving through the crowd.

Bacho started to follow, but Jax said, "Hey, forget them. We should do our own thing. There are plenty of other girls here. Like her." He thrust his chin toward a pretty blond girl not far from them. "Bet I could nail her."

"But Dina brought us here in the first place," Bacho said. "We can't just—"

"She brought us to a place that serves water!" Jax said. "I can't believe she had to go and drop the sherry. And bringing her joker cousin . . . It's like she's enjoying messing with us."

"Yeah," Darryl said.

"Let's dump them," Jax said. "It'll serve them right. Bet we hook up in no time. They certainly won't. Not with tentacle-girl there. Think about it. Dina's *related* to her. I wouldn't even touch that now that I know. I vomit a little just thinking about it. But anyway, we're here. Let's at least get some action. Come on."

Jax began walking in the blond girl's direction, Darryl just behind him. This time, it was Bacho's turn not to move. Noticing, Jax swung around, smirking. "What?"

Bacho stood there for a moment. He knew what. The thought had come to him fully formed, a sentence that summed it up. He heard the words, and realized he was even up for saying them. So he did. "You guys are jerks." He turned and walked away. Jax called after him, but Bacho's eyes found Dina and the sight of her pulled him through the crowd.

When he reached her and Antonia, Dina smiled. "Hey." She let the word and the smile sit for a moment. Then asked, "Where are your pals?"

"You know, I don't really care," Bacho responded.

"They didn't leave, did they?"

"No, they're here." He dipped his head to the side and admitted, embarrassed for and by them, "They're trying to score."

"I wish them good luck with that." She stared at him for a moment. "You're really not much like them, are you?"

Bacho shrugged. "I guess not."

"Good to know." Again, her eyes studied him, her mind clearly thinking through something. "There's something that maybe I should—"

A voice replaced the music, cutting her off. The DJ. He thanked the crowd for letting him spin for them, but admitted he knew they weren't here for him. "So, without further delay, let's get to why you're really here. With pleasure, I hand you over to the one and only, *DJ Tod*. Feel the love, people. Feel the love!"

Judging by the rapturous response from the clubbers, they did.

"It's time," Dina said, leaning in close and shouting. "Bacho, are you okay with surprises?"

"Sure."

She exchanged a glance with Antonia and said, dryly, "Good to know."

♥

Dina clapped her hands excitedly. "Look, there he is!"

For a moment Bacho couldn't make out anyone specifically in the throng and with the flashing strobes and the careening beams of light. Standing on his tiptoes, he noticed people in the crowd reaching to touch someone moving through them. He couldn't see him clearly, but the adoration of the masses around him seemed fervently religious, as if he was Jesus about to hand out loaves or something. He climbed into the DJ booth and, above the crowd now, Bacho could see him. He was a tall guy, wearing what seemed to be a white lab coat and black gloves. That was strange enough, but to top it off he wore a metal mask that covered his face. He held up one arm, leaned close to his mic, and waited for the commotion to die down. When it did, he re-leased the intro, a slow eerie tune played on some sort of wavering flute. It started low and he spoke over it. He said, calmly, "Welcome to the Drop City Experience. Love is a transformative force in the world. Tonight, I hope you all feel the love and are reborn through it." He paused a moment, and then added, "Oh, and I also hope you dance."

DJ Tod caught the word "dance" and looped it instantly into the sound system. The word became a rapid-fire repetition, starting low and rising, rising, rising in pitch until it boomed into a long, trem-bling command. An explosion of rapid techno beats cut in and, just like that, the crowd went wild. The club became a churning mass of writhing, jumping, undulating bodies. Bacho couldn't have stopped himself from dancing if he'd wanted to. But he didn't want to. It was as if the music suddenly controlled his body and standing still would've been impossible. He bounced on his toes, thrashed with his arms, twisted his torso. He just moved. The more he did so, the more exhilarated he felt.

Dina was dancing like crazy, all of her running and bouncing, her head bobbing side to side, hair snapping. She pumped her water bottle in the air. She was gorgeous. She was all in. She was the music, and, watching, so was Bacho. When she met his eyes, smiling, he leaned in and shouted, *"This is awesome!"*

"Just wait," she said.

"For what?" he asked.

The music cut suddenly, dropping into an entirely different tune, with different strings of music and pulses, all of them instantly addictive. Instead of answering, Dina fell back into full-on dancing. Bacho did too. In no time at all he was sweat-covered, breathing hard. But it didn't matter; he didn't want to stop. For a while there was only music, dance, measured by the additions of new riffs, hooks that came and went. Samples from song after song, vocal hooks that layered over each other.

"It's starting!" Dina exclaimed. She shouted the same to Antonia, and then turned to Bacho. Unexpectedly, she grabbed him and kissed him. Pulling away, she pointed at the DJ booth. "Just watch."

DJ Tod worked within a strange light show. A ring of shimmering yellow brilliance surrounded him. *Neat trick,* Bacho thought. Inside it, he was a whirlwind of intense motion. His body swayed as he worked. His hands flew about, shoulders bouncing. He was a mad scientist of crazy beats. That's not all he was, though. Still dancing, Bacho watched the glowing ring coalesce around DJ Tod's head and start to climb. *How are they doing that?* It became a peak of light that slowly rose above his head. Watching it, Bacho realized that it vibrated with the same rising intensity of the pulse in the music. It was climbing, energy building, getting faster, containing a staccato tension that was too much. The cone of light was as high as the ceiling. Bacho felt like he was going to erupt.

Then, when it couldn't possibly go any higher, all the tension in the music exploded, an auditory bomb as the beat dropped. The cone of light fell. It collapsed onto DJ Tod's head and shot out in a radiating ring from there. It surged through the crowd like a blast shock wave. It hit Bacho with a physical euphoria that took his breath away. It was so intense he closed his eyes, head thrown back, his whole body in an ecstatic spasm. He flushed as warm and rich as molten gold. He'd never, ever, felt anything nearly as good. It was emotional also, like being possessed by a physical embodiment of rapturous love. He stood, trembling, gasping, stunned. The beat emerged again as throbbing bass, fast and furious. That brought him back. It was impossible not to want to dance to it.

Bacho opened his eyes, and he froze, gaping. He beheld a scene that seemed ripped from some medieval vision of Hell. All around him, a heaving mass of demons writhed. Right in front of him, a girl with scaled crimson skin and tiny black horns pumped her arms in the air. A man brushed him on the left, a monstrosity with a smiling face of massive teeth and a pointed jaw. The entire crowd had been transformed. Each of them different, but all their own version of a demon from the depths of a deranged nightmare, all of them dancing like this was biggest party Hell had ever thrown.

Bacho turned toward his left, where Dina and Antonia had been. They weren't there. Only some demon girls were. They thrashed like all the others. One of them noticed him looking at her. Her skin was a glistening orange. Her overlarge eyes tilted up at the outside edges, between them a twisted, elongated hook of a nose. Her mouth, when she opened it, was crowded with pointed brown teeth. She was horrific. Only . . .

She leapt on him, arms around his neck. She shouted in his ear, *"Isn't it beautiful?"* Her voice was Dina's voice. When she pulled back, face near his, he saw her . . . Dina. Behind the demon features it was her.

"Dina?"

She squeezed him again. "I knew you'd make a great joker." She reached around and grabbed something. Bacho felt her hand on him, but he didn't know what part of him it was until she said, "Nice tail."

As soon as she said it, he felt it. He swung his tail around and stared at the fleshy point of it. "Wait . . . What am I? What do I look like?"

She shook her head, her eyes soft and sympathetic on him. "It doesn't matter. Now feel the love, and dance!"

As if responding to her, the beat shifted into a higher gear. She spun away and resumed her dance. Antonia was just as wild. She was a gaunt, elongated version of herself, with spots on her flaky-looking skin. Instead of tentacles, her hands matched her body, long, bony fingers that she pulsed in the air to the beat. *So weird,* Bacho thought. She was a monster, and yet all he had to do was look at her to recognize her. And, stranger still, though he *knew* they were all monstrosities, he didn't feel any revulsion. He'd been shocked, but not revolted. He looked at his hands. Rough-skinned, pocked, with jagged black curls for fingernails. He loved them. They were his. *Weird.* Part of him knew that he should have a million questions, that he should rush out of here and get help, that his whole existence might just've changed forever, that this might be the single greatest horror of life. All that he knew, but the part of him that knew it seemed a small, distant, boring voice. He decided not to listen. Instead he said, "Fuck it," and did as he'd been instructed. He danced like he'd never danced before.

The music was building again, a low pounding of drums with a pulse darting through it like swirling electronic flies. It rose and rose again. Soon, the halo of light formed around DJ Tod's head and then climbed into that cone shape. This time, when the beat dropped, Bacho was ready for it. It hit him again with that same euphoric impact, but he kept his eyes open and watched the moment of transformation. The bodies around him morphed in a strange, staccato motion, lit by the strobes and in time with the release of tension in the music. Bacho watched his hands go scaly and green. His arms thinned and he felt plates forming across his back and chest. His feet burst through his sneakers, leaving them tattered as his size thirteen lizard feet stomped them into the dance floor. His thighs, bulky with muscles, strained against his jeans. He glimpsed reptilian forms all around him, each of them different, but all of them sharing in the change. They were all beautiful to him. Every single bizarre, scaly inch of them seemed exactly right.

Dina flicked a thin ribbon of tongue from her mouth and tickled the end of his snout with it. *Is she into me?* he wondered. *I think she's into me.*

And then another song. Another drop. Another change. It happened again and again. Each time was just as euphoric, no matter that each time they morphed into different joker forms. Every one was as bizarre and horrible and gorgeous and perfect as the one before. They sprouted tiny wings from their shoulders. They emerged covered in thick hair from head to toe. One time they all had loose flesh that hung from their bones like melting rubber. It was, perhaps, the most hideous change, but in the moment the sensation of flesh flapping as they danced was wonderful. Another time they all ended up with thin, frail bodies and enormous, bony, Afro-shaped bulges around their heads. They tottered more than danced, barely able to support the weight, hysterical until the next drop changed them all again. And again.

Once the change didn't distort their basic forms at all, but instead turned the sweat that drenched all of them into a sweet, sticky syrup. Dina said, "Hey honeyface," and swiped a fingertip of the gook from Bacho's chin and popped it in her mouth. "Yum."

Had anything ever been sexier?

She's definitely maybe into me, Bacho thought. Hoped. Prayed.

And danced.

What must have been a couple hours in, he caught sight of Jax and Darryl. "Look," he said, pointing at them for Dina and Antonia. Somehow, the two had gotten themselves up onto one of the raised platforms. They had all just emerged from the drop with bodies that seemed virtually boneless, held upright by sinewy, serpentine muscle. Darryl started popping and locking, and Jax followed suit. In no time the entire place was waving undulating arms about with more fluidity than any nat break-dancer could ever dream of. Clearly, Jax and Darryl were feeling the love.

A little later, in a canine, werewolf-like body, Bacho felt a strange sensation. It came from inside him, the feeling that he had an infinite cavern that stretched beneath him, inside of him, yes, but also unfathomably deep. And from those depths, something climbed. He felt claws moving up the walls of his insides. It felt quite different from the magic DJ Tod was working, but still, he welcomed it. The crawling thing climbed the vertebrae of his spine, using his ribs like ladders. It squeezed through his throat and out his mouth. He raised his snout to the ceiling and released it. A howl of joy. Others joined him, their cries mixing with the music. Bacho had never heard anything more wonderful. He didn't want any of it to ever stop.

♣

Bacho, Dina, and Antonia stumbled out into the cool of the night, propelled by the flood of jokers leaving the club. It was strange leaving the temple of sound and sensation and motion behind. Bacho would've stayed on forever, but all things had to come to an end at some point, as DJ Tod himself said as he signed off.

The world expanded around them, the air cool and fresh. Bacho sucked it in, his body hungry for it as if he needed to make up for the hours of constant motion. "Oh my God I'm exhausted," he said. "My legs feel like rubber."

"Well, you *are* a bit flabby," Antonia said.

They all laughed. Yeah, they were flabby all right. The last drop—before the music faded, DJ Tod said his goodbyes and waded through the adoring crowd—had left them all short and pudgy, with skin that had the texture of lumpy cottage cheese. They had wide, swinish snouts instead of noses. Bacho's shirt clung tightly to his chunky torso. His legs, stubby as they were, wouldn't have fit into his trousers. No matter, he'd replaced them with a pair of shorts from the clothes bank. He would have had to anyway, as his tail from the first change had made an embarrassingly noticeable rip in the seat of his pants.

"DJ Tod . . . that guy is epic," Bacho said.

"You bet he is." Dina slipped her hand into his. Before he could get too excited about that, she grabbed Antonia's as well. "Come on. We should head back."

As they moved away from the club, Bacho felt some of the euphoria slip away from him. With each breath of the fresh air his head cleared a bit. The pulsing ecstasy of the club faded. With it, a realization dawned on him. He looked down at his lumpy body, at the stubby fingers of his free hand. "But wait . . . I'm a . . ."

Jax finished the thought for him. "Joker!"

He and Darryl shoved through the jokers on the sidewalk, eyes on Dina. They both looked comically furious. Jax carried most of his body weight in the jiggling fat of his thighs and ass. He waddled more than ran, and clearly couldn't move as quickly as he wanted to. For some reason, he had a checkered necktie wrapped around his forehead like a bandanna. Darryl walked on thinner legs than normal, the length of them on display beneath a rather short miniskirt. Above that, his bulky upper body strained to bust out of a short halter top.

Bacho stepped in front of Dina, arm raised to fend them off. Jax pressed his chest against it, fuming. "Move it, Bacho! This is between me and her." To Dina: "This is your fault. You turned me into a fucking joker!"

Dina looked them over. "I had no idea you guys were so fashionable. That tie is a nice touch, but, a skirt?"

Looking sheepish, Darryl said, "I had to change into something and it seemed like a good idea at the time."

Jax, unable to contain his anger, thrashed his arms like a child going full-on temper tantrum. "Look at me! Look at me! *Look at me!*"

"We are," Antonia said.

"I'm hideous!" He abruptly stopped his thrashing. His snout twitched and face paled, as if the reality of what he just said drained the life out of him. He mumbled, "I'm a . . . a . . ."

"Yeah, we know," Dina said. "You're a joker. *Surprise!* And don't worry about thanking me. The looks on your faces are all the thanks I need."

Jax looked baffled, at a loss for words. For once, there was no cockiness in his voice. "What type of monster are you?"

Dina held up her fleshy arms, jiggled them. "I doubt there's a name for it. Other than joker. It's quite a catchall term, really."

"We are so screwed!" Jax yelled. "My dad will sue you. He'll sue the DJ, the club. He'll sue—"

"If your parents don't disown you first. That happens, you know. Not everyone—including parents—wants a joker as a child."

Something about thinking of his mother blew away the last remnants of the club's magic. *Oh my God,* Bacho thought. How would he tell her? How could he explain it? How would she respond? He wanted her here, right now, and yet the thought of her seeing him terrified him. They'd really all been turned into jokers. In the club it had been all awesome, but now they were outside in the real world. All around him, newly minted jokers walked down the street, trickling out into the city's streets. None of them seemed troubled by it, but a feeling of dread began to squeeze him.

"Dina?" he asked, his voice a whisper that she didn't hear the first time. He tried again. "Dina?" She cut off whatever she was saying to Jax and looked at him. "Are we really . . . changed . . . into this?"

For a second it looked like she was going to say something sarcastic. Whatever it was, she let it go. She inhaled a long audible breath through her snout, paced away a little. Somehow, despite being a short, pudgy, cottage cheese version of herself, her clothes still fit. "Okay, I guess it's about time for me to explain. That's fair. So . . . obviously DJ Tod isn't just any DJ. He's an ace. His ability is what you experienced. He turns people into jokers."

As if this were news, Jax said, "Oh, *fuck! Fuck!* I knew it."

"Would you stop with the hissy fit and listen? It's not like you think. You're not permanently a joker. The last change lasts for about a day. It's a little bit different for everyone, but at some point tomorrow you'll all just realize you're back to normal. You probably won't notice when it happens, but I promise it will happen. I've done it plenty of times. All the regulars in the club have." She paused, but the boys stared at her, waiting for more. "You guys were being such jerks, over the whole competition, really. All your anti-joker crap. I just . . . thought you should see the world from the other side."

"You had no right," Jax said. "People will see us and think we're jokers!"

Dina dipped her head to one side and observed, "Right now you *are* jokers."

"I am not! I'm exactly the same person I was before I went into the stupid club. Nothing's changed except"—again, he jerked and twisted in exasperation—"the way I look."

"Exactly," Dina said. "You're the same person you were before. Nothing's changed except the way you look. Exactly what I was hoping you'd learn." She reached out and pinched him on the cheek.

Jax squirmed away, ranting again, vomiting vitriol.

Dina ignored him. She turned to Bacho. Her voice softened. "I'm sorry I didn't tell you. It's just . . . I didn't know what you were like until things were already happening. I hope you don't hate me."

"You hope he doesn't hate you?!" Jax cried. "After what you did? Of course we—"

"Didn't you feel something in there?" Dina asked Bacho. She spoke close to him, gesturing with her hands, her snout twitching with the passion she clearly felt. "Each time the beat dropped. Each time we changed. The beauty of it. The connection. Didn't you feel that?"

Bacho thought for a moment, and then answered, honestly, "It was like love."

Jax, annoyed, snapped, "Oh, shut up!"

"Yes! Exactly. We all loved each other in there. Even you two." Dina crossed her pudgy arms. "Tell me you didn't feel it."

"Whatever I felt wasn't real," Jax said. "It was all part of a scam! That's what it is. No, it's a crime! I'm pressing charges." Suddenly inspired, Jax struggled to get his phone out of his pocket. It was made harder because of both his pudgy fingers and the tightness of his pants over his thickened thighs. He twisted and hopped on one foot and finally got the phone free. His efforts to dial with his chubby fingers were soon too much for him. He had a fit, looking like he was on the verge of smashing the phone on the pavement.

"Hey, look," Darryl said, pointing.

They all followed his finger. DJ Tod and a small entourage walked down the sidewalk on the other side of the street.

"Hey, you," Jax called, "DJ guy, you've got to do something!" He ran out into the street, causing a Toyota truck to slam on the brakes to avoid hitting him. The driver shouted out the open window, leaned on his horn. Jax ignored them. While the truck was still stopped, the rest of the group crossed. Bacho waved at the driver apologetically.

When they reached the other side, Jax was already pleading with DJ Tod to turn them back to normal. With the DJ wearing a mask, Bacho could only see his eyes, but something about the way he held himself suggested that he was staring blankly at the teenager.

"Change us back! I want to be normal again."

"Oh, I see," DJ Tod said, "you got a bit more than you expected, huh?"

"I could call the cops. Look what you did!"

DJ Tod shrugged. The tilt of his head somehow conveyed his boredom with the conversation. "Law enforcement has weighed in on this already. There's no crime. You'll all be back to normal tomorrow. No damage done. There have been cases already and they've gone nowhere. Anyway, if you were in the club, it means you signed the terms and conditions."

"But I didn't read it!"

"Your signature says that you did. There are no grounds for a claim of harm. And, even if there was, it won't change you back to your old self any sooner. Wait it out, kid. Try seeing the world with different eyes for a little while. It'll do you good."

"You could do it if you want to," Darryl said, though it was more of a whine than a real assertion.

"No can do." The DJ shook his head. He began to back away, his companions protectively close. Speaking loudly so others in the pass-ing crowd could hear him, he said, "I show people the joker light. Not the other way around. Man, just find peace with yourself, and with all jokers."

"I'm not a joker!"

Bacho could hear the smile in the man's voice. "You keep telling yourself that. But, truth is, we're all jokers, kid."

Jax went into convulsions again, barely managing to stay on his feet. He didn't seem used to the change in his center of gravity yet.

Bacho couldn't help it. He laughed. Dina and Antonia did as well. A good, long, bellyaching laugh.

♠

Walking back to the hotel, Bacho, Dina, and Antonia played through the best moments of the night again. They talked about the weirdest changes, argued about which were the most enjoyable joker bodies to dance as. They'd seen so much, almost too much to believe. Speaking about it, they fed off one another, remembering more and more things as they walked, slow and casual, caught up in their conversation. The streets were quiet, dawn not far away, the air lovely cool. Bacho felt comfortable with these two in a way he never had with Jax and Darryl. Yeah, he was crushing on Dina, but . . . in a cool way, not terribly awk-ward. And Antonia had let down her brittle exterior armor. She was relaxed in a way Bacho had never seen her. It was nice. Her tentacled hands? Well, they weren't tentacled just now, but the very thought that he'd once found them weird seemed foreign to him now.

The streets were quiet enough that they paused in the middle of an intersection, enjoying the way the empty streets made them the center of an asphalt X. Dina said, "What about when we got all rubbery?" She made a rather pathetic attempt at a wave. Bacho caught it as it left her thick fingertips and let the wave flow from his wrist through his elbow and shoulder, and then down his chest all the way to his feet and back up again. It was a funky little dance, made all the more amusing by his joker body. All three laughed.

Antonia held up a hand to calm them. "Okay, that's funny and all, but it's not always like this. You know that, right? I mean it's not always joy and laughter. For a lot of people the change is pain, suffering. Body and mind. Don't forget that and think that being a . . . joker . . . is all a joke."

Dina took her hand. "Of course we won't." Bacho mumbled his agreement as well. They carried on walking, quieter now, but still talking.

They reached the park they'd cut across earlier. They were about to cut through it when Antonia said, "Hey, do you see that?"

Down a little ways, a group of nat guys had a couple of jokers surrounded. It was Jax and Darryl. The four guys hemmed them in like pack hunters around prey. It didn't take more than a glance to know they'd had a long night of drinking, or to assess that they were trouble. As if to confirm it, one of the guys shoved Jax, who stumbled, tripped, and landed hard on his substantial bottom. The nats hooted with laughter.

"What do we do?" Antonia asked.

"Go get help," Bacho said. "Wake someone up and come back."

"Are you kidding me?" Dina asked. "By the time we'd explained everything it would be too late." She paused a moment, watching the nats get bolder. One of them offered Darryl a drink, but when he reached to accept it the guy yanked it back, punching him with his other fist instead. Jax tried to run, but one of the nats clotheslined him and tossed him back into the circle.

"We can't leave them," Dina said. "This is my fault." She started running toward them.

"Shit," Bacho said. His short legs had to work to keep up with Dina. He tried to think. He wasn't a fighter. Never had been. He avoided conflict whenever he could. And that was before, in his own body. As a four-foot-tall, stubby, fleshy joker? He'd be toast. They all would be. But none of that stopped him from pulling up beside Dina, and then passing her as they neared the group. Still not having the slightest plan, he ran between two of the guys, right into the circle that had Darryl and Jax trapped. He stood with them, trying to look larger than he was.

"Whoa! What the hell do we have here?" the guy with the bottle asked. "*More* of them? Holy shit. Look at them! Oh God, there are girls, too."

Dina and Antonia joined them. Both girls crossed their arms defiantly, the sight of which made the nats howl. "We don't want any trouble," Bacho said. "We're just walking back to our hotel. These are our friends."

One of the nats dangled the half-empty bottle of bourbon from his fingers. He took a swig of it. He was a white guy, wearing khaki shorts and a polo shirt. He had the build of an athlete, the swagger of privilege, and the hungry eyes of a guy who'd just found a bit of amusement after a night that might have been lacking it. "Why do people who are about to get their asses kicked always say that?"

"Try being more original," another one, a light-skinned black guy sporting a lacrosse jersey, said. The other two, also athletic-looking white guys, added their two cents.

"I told you they'd be out again," the leader said. "Every Saturday. Sun comes up. Fucking jokers come out. Where do you all come from? Do you hide somewhere during the day? I bet you do. Like vampires."

"B-b-but I told you," Jax stammered, "I'm not a joker." He gestured at his decidedly joker body. "This is just . . . a . . . thing. I'll be normal tomorrow. Like you. I play baseball."

"Normal like me?" The guy took a swig and then passed the bottle to one of his friends. "Yeah, right."

"You don't understand. Oh, God . . ." Jax scrunched his eyes closed. His snout trembled with fear. "There's a club where—"

"Shut up," Dina said. She cast her voice low, but it was rock hard. To the nats, she said, "We're going. Okay? We're just going."

She began to slip between them, but they closed the gap. "You're not going anywhere until we say you are. Your kind nearly destroyed the fucking world. Nice try, shitheads. Now it's payback time." He glanced at his friends. "Let's take this into the park."

"We're not going into the park," Dina said.

The leader looked at her, strangely contemplative all of a sudden. Then he said, "Deal with the rest of them. This one's mine."

The others sprang into action. They surged forward, shoving the jokers from the sidewalk into the trees at the edge of the park. The leader grabbed Dina by the wrist, yanked her to him, and then lifted her, screaming and kicking, off the ground. He began to carry her away, into the shadows and toward a thick clump of bushes.

Anguished, Bacho fought to break free and get to her. But the guys were too fast, too brutal and strong. They kept knocking them back. One punched Darryl in the gut. Another lifted Jax with one arm and body slammed him. The two others converged on Bacho. He saw them coming, but his eyes looked past them. They locked with Dina's for a brief moment, before she and the leader disappeared into the bushes.

"*Noooo!!!*" Bacho yelled.

The two guys were upon him, but suddenly he wasn't scared of them. Fury filled him. As it did, something strange happened. His vision doubled. He saw the men with his normal eyes, almost frozen in time, reaching for him, one with his fists cocked and starting toward him. But also a second pair of eyes rose to a higher vantage, as if another version of him was growing out of his back. He tried for a moment to find Dina. With astounding clarity and detail, he saw the trembling in the bushes that indicated where they were.

That made his rage complete. His *Noooo* became a roar. He looked down at the two men, so close to his joker body, so large and fierce next to it. He shot out a hand—not his normal hand, not his pudgy joker hand, but a large, long-fingered claw of a hand—and grabbed the fist of the man punching him. He crushed it in his grip until he felt small bones begin to break, and then flung the man away. He back-handed the other man, impacting with his head so hard the man's feet came out from underneath him and he dropped to the ground.

Bacho ran toward the bushes that hid Dina and her attacker, but his legs were too short. He couldn't run with the speed he wanted. His eyes could, though. His view through his second pair of eyes shot forward at incredible speed, tracking the faint signs of motion. Doubled vision. And with it two different views. From the vantage of his running joker body, Bacho saw a large, dark shadow leap over him and bound, wolflike, into the bushes. His second set of eyes, he realized, saw from within that canine body. They took the wolf crashing through the bushes, arriving as the attacker pulled back his hand to smack Dina, who was still struggling to pull away from him. The wolf bit down on the man's arm and yanked it savagely. He felt the man's shoulder dislocate, the arm go limp. He heard the man scream, his voice high-pitched and frantic. Bacho shoved him away. It was Dina that mattered.

She stood leaning back into the bushes as if she'd been thrown there, arms stretched out to hold her up. She stared, mystified, into the wolf's eyes. The joker Bacho ran all the more frantically, worried that she would be afraid, desperate that she not be. He scrabbled through the bushes, saw the hulking, shadowy form of the wolf, highlighted at times by shimmering waves of silver light. It was a tangible form, and yet Bacho walked right through it. His joker vision went dark for a second, and then he pushed through and there was Dina. His two pairs of eyes saw her from slightly different angles, but they saw the same scene again.

When Bacho reached out, gently offering his hands, Dina's eyes left the wolf, saw him. After a long moment, she reached out to him as well.

◆

When Bacho emerged from the bushes with Dina, the spectral wolf hulked behind and above him. It moved as he moved, paused when he paused. It stretched to nine feet or so, a bulky form that had substance and yet was ethereal as well. Wide shoulders, long arms, furred in glistening black. Above the shape was that wolf head, long-muzzled, with black canine eyes that glimmered as they moved.

Seeing him, their attackers fled. Two of the men took off running. The third urged the man with the crushed hand to walk faster. Their leader clutched his dislocated arm to his chest, flinching as the slightest movement sent jolts of pain through him. They all kept looking back, clearly fearful of Bacho following them. He didn't. He just stood, his little fists clenched, panting as he watched them go. The wolf shared the posture, watching as well. The rage in Bacho burned hot, but instead of feeding it by chasing them down and tearing them apart—as he knew he could do—he embraced the fury and let it fill him. But just because he could have torn them apart didn't mean he wanted to, or should. He'd done enough. He let the anger burn itself out, saddening slightly as he felt it fade away.

Around him, the others stared. First at the retreating attackers, and then at Bacho himself. The vision through his second pair of eyes faded, blinked a few times, and then cut out completely. He was one being again.

"What was that?" Antonia asked. "You all saw that, right? The . . . the . . ."

"It was like a werewolf," Darryl said.

"How come only Bacho has it?" Antonia asked.

"I don't know." Dina looked perplexed. "I've never seen something like that happen from a DJ Tod drop."

"This joker stuff is insane," Jax said. "I just want to be normal again."

"What?" Dina asked. "Like those guys?"

Jax put his fingers to his temples, and then he shook his head. "No, not like them. Screw them. Thank you all for . . . you know, not just leaving us."

"We're not jerks," Antonia said. She smiled. "We have to watch out for fellow jokers."

Jax wasn't quite ready to get on board with that. "Can we just go now? Let's go back and get in trouble and normal stuff like that."

The five youths made for a sad procession as they hobbled back to the hotel. Jokers, battered and beaten, fatigued from the long night, traumatized both by what had happened and by what had nearly happened. Back at the hotel, Jax and Darryl were the first to go inside. Bacho waited near the entrance as Dina had a private conversation with Antonia, who then went inside also, waving good night to Bacho. Dina walked back to him. She didn't say anything immediately. They shared the night for a bit, both of them watching the salmon-pink hues creeping into the eastern sky.

"That was some night," Bacho said. He began walking, the two of them strolling absently in front of the hotel.

"More than I bargained for," Dina said. "Sorry if you're mad at me. It was a stupid idea, taking you all to Drop City. But . . ." She exhaled. Pursed her lips. "Antonia's my cousin, Bacho. I love her. Always have. Loved her before her card turned. When we were little, at family gatherings, she and I were inseparable. We'd clasp hands and be glued to each other. Then she changed. At first I didn't know what to feel. All I saw was the deformity and I hated it. It felt like God or someone had taken my cousin away and made her a freak. For a while I didn't even want to see her. I was a jerk. Stupid. She didn't get mad at me, though." She laughed. "She's too cool for that. Instead she sent me a Snapchat. Just one where she held out her hands in front of her and talked to me, asked me to see her, to remember her, to understand that she was still the same Antonia. She said, 'I'm here for you. Are you there for me?' And then the Snapchat ended and that was that. I replayed it once, and that was it. There I was staring at the empty screen, and I realized I still loved her. Of course I did. I'm not saying it's like that for all jokers. I know it's not. But still, I see them differently now. That's the point. This stuff tonight, that wasn't just me being a jerk. I was hoping you guys would see things differently too. I didn't plan for the assholes."

"That's part of it, though," Bacho said. "Right? Dealing with the assholes."

They'd come to stand in front of one of the hotel's large glass windows. They stood there, looking at their joker shapes in the reflection. It seemed so strange, but not because it was strange, but because it *should* be strange and yet wasn't. He could look at himself and see something completely hideous. A joker. And yet at the same time it was the same as looking in the mirror always had been. What looked back was . . . him. And Dina. She didn't look anything like the girl he'd met yesterday in the lobby. He recognized that her snout was a thing that only a mother pig was likely to love. But he did love it. It wasn't even that he saw her beneath it. It's just that he saw her. She—no matter what she looked like—was still her.

"None of it was stupid. Dina, I think what you did was pretty awesome. I don't regret it, but . . . I'm sorry about the stuff that happened. And the stuff that might've—"

Dina stopped him. "What happened happened, and it sucked. But we're all okay. I'm okay. Thanks to you."

Bacho flushed, looked away. "Thanks to that wolf thing, you mean."

Dina touched his face, brought his eyes back to hers. "Whatever that was, it was a part of you."

Bacho hesitated a moment, almost giving in to his old, tongue-tied reticence. But that was force of habit, not because he really felt it. Actually, the words came more readily than they ever would have before. He just said what he thought and knew to be true and wanted her to know. "I think that you're pretty awesome." He took Dina's pudgy, soft hand in his. He squeezed it, and he watched her in the reflection.

She squeezed back. "You're cute, you know? I thought so before. I think so now. Chances are, I'll think so tomorrow, too." She turned toward him, leaned in, and kissed him.

Behind them in the reflection from the window the spectral wolf materialized. His canine eyes watched them a moment, tenderly. Sadly. Proudly. But not for too long. The wolf turned his head away, giving the two their privacy. He was there a little longer, nostrils flaring as he smelled the sunrise in the air. Then he faded to invisibility and was gone.

For the time being.

♠ ♥ ♦ ♣

SATURDAY

Bubbles and the
Band Trip

Part 12

MICHELLE KNOCKED ON THE door to Creighton's suite at eight thirty Saturday morning. When he opened it, he was wearing a sharp navy pin-striped suit. But she couldn't place the face he was wearing. It was a handsome face with dark eyes and dark hair that was Brylcreemed back from his forehead. Under a grown-up version of Segway's mustache, his lips curled into a bemused expression.

"I feel like I should know who you are," she said. Her suspicion was this was another dead movie star from one of Creighton's black-and-white films.

"You really need a movie education, Ms. Pond." He tucked one hand into his pocket and pulled out a cigarette and lighter. With a practiced touch he popped the cigarette into his mouth and then lit it. "This"—he gestured to himself—"is William Powell as he appeared in the Thin Man movies. I've decided I should go all Nick Charles on these clowns."

"I don't understand," she said.

"Oh, you will."

♥

"Ms. Pond, I confess, I'm perplexed," Priscilla said when Michelle opened the door to Creighton's suite. Priscilla had knocked promptly at nine. "Dr. Smith texted me and told me to meet her here this morning. So why are *you* here, Ms. Pond? And who is that?" She pointed at Creighton.

"That's Mr. Charles," Michelle answered. "I hired him to investigate the incidents that happened to the Mob during the competition. Since the police didn't think there was a problem, I took matters into my own hands."

"Beg your pardon," Priscilla said. "Then why am I here?"

"Everything in good time." Creighton gestured to the sofa. "Why don't you have a seat?"

Priscilla eyed him warily. "Is Dr. Smith on her way? This is very strange. Ms. Pond, your students are due at the auditorium at eleven." She made no move to sit down.

"It shouldn't take that long," Creighton said. "Please make yourself comfortable."

A few minutes later, there was another knock. Michelle opened the door. Bambi and Kimmie Coldwater stood without. Bambi glowered at Michelle. "Where's Dr. Smith?" she asked imperiously, then grabbed Kimmie's arm. "We're not staying in this room with you."

"Mom, stop." Kimmie yanked her arm free. "I'm sure Ms. Pond is here for the same reason we are. Dr. Smith asked her to come." She smiled at Michelle, and Michelle wondered why Kimmie had been called in. Surely she wasn't a suspect. "C'mon, Mom, let's just go inside."

No sooner had Michelle closed the door behind them than there was yet another knock. "Splendid!" Creighton said. "Things are going well!"

Michelle gave him a dubious look. "What exactly is going on, Mr. Charles?"

"Have you ever seen the stateroom scene from *A Night at the Opera?*"

Both Bambi and Priscilla nodded their heads. Creighton looked pleased. Michelle was confused. "No, I haven't," she said. "But I'm not a big opera fan."

An expression of sheer exasperation flew across Creighton's face. He took a puff of his cigarette. "Well, it's not going to be that bad."

"Mr. Charles," Bambi said with a delicate cough. "Can you please extinguish that cigarette. The Gunter does not permit smoking. It's vile."

Creighton smiled. "I would be happy to, my dear lady."

♣

"Welcome!" Creighton said cheerfully. "You're right on time!"

Michelle stared in disbelief as Creighton stepped aside and revealed Earl Walker and Betty Virginia.

"Who are you?" Betty Virginia asked Creighton. "*Bambi!* Why did you tell us to meet you here?"

"I didn't tell you to do any such thing, Betty Virginia," Bambi sputtered. "I'm as confused as you are."

"I think we should leave." Earl's right hand went to his holstered gun. "She's here." He pointed at Michelle with his left. "And we don't know what she might do to us."

"Earl's right," Betty Virginia said grimly. "You're a menace, Michelle Pond. God will punish you someday." She put her hands on her hips. "But I confess, now I'm curious. And Bambi, you most certainly *did* tell us to come."

"I did not," Bambi said hotly.

"Well, since I'm one of the 'chosen people,' I'm not really worried about the whole God thing," Michelle said cheerfully. "Though being a lesbian could counter the whole chosen people thing, depending on one's interpretation of the Bible. By the way, do you eat bacon or ham? Because if you do, you're violating God's law." This was turning out to be more fun than Michelle had expected. "I'm pretty sure you're also wearing clothing that has different fibers in it," she continued. "Unless that's a polyester jumpsuit, Betty Virginia. In which case, I'd argue you've already sinned against God."

Creighton interrupted. "We're not here for theological discussions, ladies."

There was a tentative knock on the door. Michelle opened it to find three jokers standing in the hallway. One had lumpy skin that looked like curdled cream. He was at least a foot and a half shorter than Michelle and had a long tail. His legs were encased in shorts and he had probably the worse case of cellulite she'd ever seen.

The joker on the left side also had skin that looked like lumpy milk, but instead of being short, he had massive thighs. The joker on the right wore a miniskirt and a halter top. His legs were long and skinny. His skin was the same color and consistency as the other two. And they all had snouts.

"And who might you be?" She didn't remember these jokers from the joker protesters outside. And she couldn't imagine why Creighton might invite them to the proceedings.

"Dr. Smith got in touch with us," one of them said. His voice sounded familiar to her. "I'm Bacho and that's Darryl, we're from the Detonators. And there's Jax from the Originals."

Michelle was stunned. What had happened to these boys to trigger all their cards at the same time and in similar ways?

By this time, Creighton had come up behind her. "Well," he said. He sounded pleased. "This should make things even more interesting. Come in, boys."

He opened the door wide and they shuffled in single file. But when they saw the rest of the people in the room, they stopped. "Wh-what's going on?" Darryl asked. "And where's Dr. Smith?"

"This is all of us." Creighton leaned over and whispered in Michelle's ear, "Make sure no one leaves."

"I'm already in trouble with the locals for doing that," she hissed. "It's called unlawful imprisonment, and after I did it to God's Weenies on Tuesday morning, doing it now to Bambi, Earl, and Betty Arizona Bialowsky might get me into trouble."

"Virginia. Her name's Betty Virginia."

"Whatever."

Creighton grinned. "Just watch." He turned back to the rest of the room. "Dr. Smith asked me to take over this meeting," he lied smoothly. "Here's what we know. One of our young friends here is responsible for the stink bomb that was set off on Wednesday."

"I didn't do that!" Bacho said with real bewilderment in his voice. "I'd never do anything like that. It's so . . . so . . . *jerky.* . . ."

"How do you know one of us did it?" Jax asked.

Creighton smiled. It was full of glee and confidence. Michelle suspected he had nothing concrete. "Because you boys were followed, and overheard talking about what sort of things you might do to the Mob."

"That doesn't mean anything," cried Jax. "It was just bullshitting. Everyone does it."

Creighton smiled enigmatically, then walked across the room and started making a drink. "Anyone else for a martini?"

"It's ten in the morning!" Betty Virginia said. "And Earl and I don't drink. It's a sin."

"I'm pretty sure it's not a sin," Michelle said. "Don't you guys do the whole 'This wine is my body' thing?"

"We use Welch's," Earl said.

"Ew," Michelle replied. "Sounds like no fun at all."

"Back to the matter at hand." Creighton poured vermouth over ice cubes and swirled it around. Then he added gin. The juniper fragrance of the gin floated in the air. "Now, we've accounted for all the other suspects except for the three of you."

"I'm telling you, we didn't do it," Bacho said. This time there was a real thread of anger in his voice. Michelle thought she saw something blooming around him. Then it disappeared as he said more calmly, "I was in the bathroom. When I was on my way back to the auditorium, I ran into everyone leaving. You can ask Mr. Gunderson!"

Michelle pulled out her phone and texted Wally. A minute later, he texted back: *Yup. I saw him. Nice kid.*

She looked up at Creighton and nodded.

"Well, that just leaves the two of you," he said, pointing to Jax and Darryl. "Odd that all three of your cards turned at the same time."

"We're not jokers!" Jax said, clenching his fists at the sides of his massive thighs. "This is temporary."

"That would be new," Creighton said. "There's only one person I know whose wild card changes."

"He's right." Darryl's voice quavered and he sounded like he was going to cry. "At least that's what we were told. This isn't permanent. We're not going to be jokers forever."

"And who told you that?" Creighton took a sip of his martini and seemed pleased with it. Then he tucked his left hand into his suit pocket and patted a bulge there.

The boys glanced at each other, then pursed their lips and said nothing. "Would it be the worst thing in the world to be a joker?" Kimmie asked. "I mean, if you could still play music. Wouldn't that be okay?"

"To look like this?" Jax gestured at his misshapen body. "I'm disgusting."

Kimmie got a mulish expression on her face. "And what if you had a wild card like Ms. Pond? What if you had an ace? Would it be okay then?"

"That's different," came the reply.

"It's most certainly not," Betty Virginia said. There was a righteous tone in her voice. "All people with the wild card virus are marked with the sign of Satan. They can appear as demons—like these boys." She waved her hand dismissively. "Or, they can have wings like angels, or they can even be like Ms. Pond here, using her powers in the service of the United Nations, that great destroyer of American sovereignty."

Creighton seemed to be enjoying her tirade.

"Okay, Devil's work, blah, blah, but Kimmie makes a good point. What difference would it make?" Michelle asked.

"Kimmie doesn't know what she's saying," Bambi replied. "I don't know what's gotten into her."

"God, Mom!" Kimmie said, throwing up her hands. "I'm an ace! Or maybe a deuce. I'm not sure."

The blood drained from Bambi's face. Then it flushed. Her eyes narrowed. "Kimberly Coldwater, I don't know why you just said that, but you take it back this instant."

"Mom, I can't," Kimmie said. Tears were welling up in her eyes. "You know how I play all those amazing flute solos that go on and on? Well, I don't have to breathe when I'm playing. I just pretend like I'm doing circular breathing, but really, it's my ability. I guess you could say I've been cheating."

"You're going to get us disqualified!" Jax wailed.

"I think this is more like being a musical prodigy. Some people just can do things other people can't," Michelle said. She couldn't have been enjoying this more. "Her ability doesn't make her a great flutist. She did that on her own."

"Mom, please." Kimmie wiped her nose on her sleeve. She was crying in earnest now.

Bambi staggered, then sat down on one of the armchairs abruptly. Her shoulders sagged, and her hands flopped into her lap. "How could you do this to me?"

With that, Kimmie jumped up then went and knelt down by her mother. "Those people"—she pointed at Betty Virginia and Earl—"they hate me! They want to hurt me!"

Bambi looked up at Kimmie, then at Betty Virginia. Her eyes narrowed and she stood up with just a little wobble on her high heels. "No one messes with my daughter," she said. There was iron in her voice. "She may be a freak of nature, but she's *my* freak of nature."

"Bambi, don't be ridiculous," Betty Virginia said. "She might as well be a joker. And she *cheated*. You brought a case to court about this very thing."

"That Pond woman is right," Bambi replied. "What Kimmie can do may give her an advantage, but not everyone has the same abilities. And you have no idea how hard she practices."

Betty Virginia threw her hands up. "You *hypocrite*."

"I'm sorry I ever worked with you," Bambi said. "You have terrible taste in clothes and, yes, you went too far harassing those children."

"Harassing those children? I did no such thing," Betty Virginia replied. "There are limits to what I'm willing to do, Bambi. It's clear *you* were involved. You were in the auditorium for performances. *I* never set foot in there. Also, you wear too much makeup. You look like a tart."

Michelle noticed that Earl was slowly backing toward the door as the exchange went on.

"Whoa there, pardner," she said, putting on a Texas accent. "Where yew going?"

"I don't have to stay here." Earl put his hand on the grip of his holstered gun. "None of this has anything to do with me."

"You know, Earl, I had the most interesting chat with a friend of yours," Creighton said. "Name of Keyz. And you seem awfully fond of that gun." He took a sip of his martini, then refilled it from the cocktail shaker. Michelle wondered how the hell he had an entire martini-making setup in his room. Much less one out this early in the morning.

"Two of the Mob and Kimmie were shot at after midnight on Thursday. The police managed to locate the bullets that were fired and are running ballistics on them even now. I'm guessing you don't have an alibi. . . ."

Earl was sweating. His white western shirt had perspiration stains under his arms, and his forehead looked oily. "I do have an alibi, don't I, Priscilla?"

A chorus of *"What?"* sounded and everyone turned toward the liaison for the Mob.

"You idiot," Priscilla said. Her eyes narrowed. There was a feral look to her. "I *told* you to keep your mouth shut."

"But they have mah bullets!"

"My God," she continued. "They didn't know those were your bullets. *Until just now.* They had nothing but supposition until you opened your mouth."

Creighton grinned. He looked like he'd gotten exactly what he wanted for Christmas. "You've done yourself no favors either, Miss Beecher."

"I'm leaving," Priscilla said.

"I'm going with you," Earl said. He dropped his hand from the butt of his gun and reached out to Priscilla. She swatted it away. Michelle almost felt sorry for him when she saw the hangdog expression on his face, but then she remembered the gunshots and hoped he would go to prison for a long time.

"She *told* me to do it," Earl said, pointing at Priscilla. The sad expression faded from his face, replaced with hurt and indignation. "She said to scare them, but not to hit them. It was tricky to do without being seen."

"Shut up," Priscilla hissed. "Shut up, you, you *liar.*"

"*She* loosened the lights," he said, pointing at Priscilla. "You know she's been doing this competition for years, and she knows everything about the auditorium. If it hadn't been for that stink bomb, who knows what would have happened."

"I set the stink bomb," Darryl blurted. "I thought it would be funny. I knew we didn't have a chance after I went on YouTube and heard all the other bands play. We're good, but we're not in the same league as the Originals or the Mob. I thought if we couldn't win, then we could at least have some fun. I'm so sorry."

"Oh, I didn't expect that," Creighton said with genuine surprise. "Then who did the fire alarm and the snakes?"

Earl pointed at Priscilla. "She told me to."

"I'm leaving," Priscilla said. "All you have is the word of this lunatic."

"Goodness," Michelle said with complete insincerity. She turned and placed her hand over the lock and let a tiny bubble go, crushing the lock into place. "Something has happened to the lock on this door."

"You did that! You did that just now!" Priscilla exclaimed. "We all saw you!"

Michelle looked at her indignantly. "I most certainly did not," she said haughtily. "I use my abilities only for good."

"Did anyone see anything?" Creighton asked. No one answered. "I'm sorry, Miss Beecher, you seem to be mistaken."

"None of this will hold up in court," she said. Her voice was cold, all hints of the pleasant and helpful Miss Beecher gone. "You're keeping me here against my will. I'm certain the police will like to hear about that, Ms. Pond."

"Oh, we already have," Officer Reyes said as he sauntered in from the bedroom. "You were right, Mr. Charles. This was well worth my time. And it may just get me off bike duty."

"Officer! Surely you can see what's happening here. The broken lock. The harassment. The false imprisonment. I demand that you arrest this Pond person. And them too." Priscilla pointed at Creighton and then at Earl. Creighton drained his martini, then ate the olive.

"I'm prepared to overlook the stink bomb incident," said Officer Reyes to Darryl. "It appears you've been through an interesting time given your current appearance. And since setting it did avoid a terrible accident with those lights, I'm going to let it skate. As for you, Miss Beecher, I'd say you and Earl have a lot to answer for."

Priscilla glowered. "I'm not saying anything else."

"I'll tell you what happened," Earl said in his West Texas drawl. "Long as I don't take the rap for what she had me do."

"Go on," Creighton said. He went and started making another martini. "I'm sure we're all fascinated."

"She wanted them instruments stolen and them snakes put in the cases. Said that Bubbles' kid's bass and that Segway kid's instruments should go. The Segway kid 'cause she thought he was disgusting," he said. His eyes were turned down and there was almost a pout on his face. "You know you wanted that done, Priscilla. And to think I loved you like Johnny loved June."

Priscilla rolled her eyes.

"My friend, Keyz," Earl continued. "He's got a friend who's good with the snakes. Did some snake handling back in the day. Hooked us up with them rattlesnakes. But we had to do it on the sly seeing as how you can't just grab one of those anytime. Did you know there's a black market for rattlers?

"Anyhow, Keyz got us in. I grabbed the bass and the trumpet, Keyz's friend dropped them snakes, and we skedaddled while the excitement with the fire alarm was going on." A pleased smile crossed his face as if he'd just eaten a MoonPie.

"And you contacted your friends at Miss Beecher's request?" Officer Reyes asked.

"Oh hell, yeah. She had a burr up her butt about them jokers. Said she'd have the Plano band again this year if it weren't for them freaks. And you gotta admit, they can be pretty revoltin'. But we didn't expect them to be so stubborn. Well, she just got angrier every time somethin' didn't work." Michelle glanced over at Priscilla, who looked mad enough to spit nails.

"And you know, I felt pretty bad about them snakes," he continued, warming to his topic. "But the heart wants what the heart wants. Yew know? But I'm beginning to think she was just using me. And that hurts."

"What happened to the instruments?" Creighton asked. He sounded remarkably untipsy.

"Oh, they're in the back of my Escalade. I was planning on hocking them over in Austin. They got a lot of bands there."

There was a long silence. Then Bacho piped up, "Can you get the instruments back? I know we'd hate to lose ours. It's weird just playing any old instrument. Your instrument is a part of you."

"Don't see why not," Earl said. "I got the keys right here. I mean, if it'd help. I can pop right down and bring them back."

"I doubt Officer Reyes would allow you out of his sight now." Creighton poured himself yet another martini.

"Oh hell, I don't have no need to run," Earl said amiably. "Now Priscilla, I'd keep an eye on her."

"Those instruments are evidence now," Officer Reyes said. "I can't let anyone have them."

"Why are you holding me when it's obvious Earl did all the crimes?" Priscilla asked. "I did *nothing*."

"Well, Earl isn't very bright, Miss Beecher," Officer Reyes said. "That much is obvious. But you, now, it's clear you did all sorts of things to encourage a simple guy like him to do awful stuff for you."

"But, but, but," she sputtered.

"Don't get me wrong, Earl's going to do some time," Officer Reyes said. He and Creighton gave each other delighted smiles.

"Hey!" Earl said. "I thought I wasn't gonna get in any trouble seein' as how I gave you the skinny on her."

"Now, no one promised you anything, Earl," Creighton said. He'd started stirring up a new batch of drinks. He was in the process of making short work of his current martini. "I merely said to go on."

"I hope you know y'all aren't very nice."

"What are you going to do now?" Michelle asked. She bubbled the broken lock again, smashing it to bits. It left a neat hole and that pleased her. It took more concentration to be tidy about things like that.

"I'm going to arrest Miss Beecher and that helpful guy, Earl," Officer Reyes said. "Give a call to a couple of detectives I know who won't hog all the glory. Have them come pick them up." He gestured to the three boys on the couch. "You three jokers get on out of here."

"Are you sure there's no chance to get the bass and trumpet?" Michelle asked. "My daughter and her friend will be heartbroken if they don't get them back."

"I'm afraid not, Mrs. Bubbles," he replied with real sadness in his voice. "We'll likely need them for the case. And who knows how long that'll be."

Michelle didn't know how to break it to her daughter and Peter that their instruments would be in police custody for an indeterminate amount of time. She didn't know about Peter, but Adesina practically doted on her bass. Replacing it wouldn't be easy and wouldn't happen fast.

♠

"Gross, Mom," Adesina said as Wally knocked Michelle down the hallway. "Why don't you just jump out the window like you usually do?"

Michelle had insisted on Wally walloping her so she would have fat to bubble with, just in case. A little fat went a long way in civilian situations.

Michelle shrugged. "I wanted to go downstairs with all of you. You know, like a normal mom."

Wally, Ghost, and Adesina exchanged looks.

"Fine," Michelle said. She was a little embarrassed. "I want to *pretend* we're normal, 'kay? Let me have my little fantasy."

A few minutes later, they were crammed into one of the small Gunter elevators. A Muzak version of Nine Inch Nails' "Closer" was playing. Wally took up a healthy chunk of real estate, as did Michelle in her somewhat zaftig state.

Adesina's wings kept trying to open, hitting Ghost in the face.

"Stop it!" Ghost said, slapping them away, then going noncorporeal. "You and those wings."

The elevator stopped at the lobby and when the doors opened, Ghost floated out, leaving Wally to grab her sax cases. Adesina was still struggling with her wings, but eventually got out. Michelle followed them.

The lobby was as jammed with people as it had been on Tuesday before everything went to pieces.

Kids holding instrument cases were talking animatedly, but there were concerned expressions on the chaperones' faces. And a couple of them looked at Michelle with narrowed eyes and ugly frowns.

Sharon pushed her way through the crowd until she stood before Michelle. "What's going on?" Michelle asked. Sharon's hair and clothes were messy, as if she'd thrown them on and was too rushed to bother with her hair.

"I thought everyone was supposed to go to the Tobin Center for the concert."

<That was the plan,> Sharon signed. <But things have gotten out of hand. Look.> Sharon grabbed Michelle by the wrist and pulled her to the wall-sized window that fronted East Houston Street. Michelle couldn't get a good look at what was happening because there was a wall of people blocking her view.

"Shit," said Michelle with frustration. "We'll just have to go out the other entrance."

<Good luck with that,> Sharon signed. <It's just as crazy back there.>

Michelle looked at the opposite set of doors. The automatic doors were open, unable to shut because of the crush of people. Two police officers stood just outside the doors making sure no one else came in or went out. An overwhelmed security guard was trying to look cool and in charge and was failing miserably at both.

"I'm going out there," Michelle said. The rest of the Mob, who had gathered together by now, raised a babble of protest, as did Wally and Robin. Even Sharon was signing frantically that Michelle should stay out of it.

"Look, I appreciate your concern, but, hello, impervious to harm. Well, pretty much. You can break mah heart." The last she said with a heavy southern accent.

No one laughed. "Seriously?! That was funny." She mock pouted. "Look, just stay here. I'll see what's up and try and figure out a way to get us to the Tobin Center."

Outside, by standing on her tiptoes, Michelle saw God's Weenies, a host of jokers, police, and a camera crew from KSAT.

The intersection of North St. Mary's and East Houston was blocked off by police cars and barriers. Several dozen God's Weenies held the west. A slightly smaller group of jokers and a few nats the east. Looky-loos had filled in the north and south sides.

Michelle shoved her way through the looky-loos. It helped that she had some fat on and she used her girth to push people out of the way. She popped out of the crowd, where she ran smack dab into the police barricade. Eight officers were spread out—two on each side of the intersection.

"Officer Reyes," she said, taking a step back so she wasn't pressed up against the orange barricade webbing. She was genuinely happy to see him. "I'm surprised to see you here after this morning's events."

Reyes shrugged and gave her a wan smile as he walked over. "Well, it seems the wheels of justice grind slow and so do the detectives I turned everything over to. And then there's this big protest mess going on and I got roped in because, well, I was downtown already."

"You know how to have fun," she replied. "Me, I'm just trying to keep things cool."

"*You're* ready for a fight," he said dryly.

He had her there. Ever since she'd gotten off the bus on Tuesday and run into God's Weenies, she'd wanted to—in all honesty—kind of blow them the hell up. She felt proud that she'd only bubbled them in ways that were non-blow-uppy. But it had done little to assuage her anger. They were fucking with the Mob and that wasn't going to stand.

"Are you suggesting I might do something violent?"

She was drowned out by the jokers and God's Weenies trading catcalls. Most of the crowd had their phones out and were recording. Michelle wondered if all of them were on Livestream.

"You're kidding, right?" Reyes said as he gave the crowd a quick look. "You do have a reputation for making stuff go boom."

"I only make stuff go boom when it's absolutely necessary," she replied huffily. "I want you to notice how little boom there's been this week."

A puff of wind blew her platinum hair into her face. She usually wore it in a single, long braid, but today she'd decided to leave it unbound. She also wore her sensible bubbling clothes. Stretchy everything and comfy Vibram Furoshiki shoes. They were ugly as hell, but forgiving when she changed sizes.

"Hey, Mom."

Michelle looked up, and hovering over her was Adesina. Her wings were fully unfurled and they flapped slowly, keeping her aloft a few feet above Michelle's head.

"Are you *kidding* me?" Michelle said hotly. *I want my little girl back! I want the little girl who wouldn't do dumb shit like this.* "Adesina, what are you doing out here? You should be inside with everyone else."

"But I can't see from there. This has a much better view."

A barrage of catcalls was suddenly aimed their way, led by Betty Virginia.

"There's one of those joker freaks!" "Hey, butterfly girl, look over here!" "Bubbles! Bubbles! Can you give me an autograph?" "You're a heifer, Bubbles. No wonder you can only screw other women."

"Adesina! Seriously!" Michelle exclaimed. Then she glared at the hecklers. *If you're going to try and insult me, at least make it something new. And lay off my daughter.* "You come down this instant."

"Mom!"

A cry went up from God's Weenies' side of the street and they strained against the stretchy orange barricade webbing.

One of the officers held up a bullhorn and said, "Step away from the barricade!"

God's Weenies started chanting: "God hates jokers! God hates jokers! Keep us pure!"

The joker protesters began a chant of their own: "God loves everyone! Down with hate! Down with hate!"

The barricade webbing on all four corners was stretching now. Michelle was shoved against it. The cop with the bullhorn said, "Settle down! Y'all just settle down. Right. Now."

"Adesina, dammit, go back inside!" Michelle tried jumping up to grab her ankle, but Adesina just fluttered up a little higher. "The police have this handled. Stop making me repeat myself."

"Mom, we can get to the Tobin Center if we can just get those people to move." She pointed at the looky-loos to the north.

The barrels keeping the barricade webbing in place on the joker side of the street gave a loud *thunk* as they tipped over. For a moment, the jokers looked surprised, as if they weren't expecting to be sprung. Then a couple of jokers—one whose misshapen crimson body was covered in black eyes; the other who had a praying mantis body topped by a tiny woman's head—glanced at each other and, with a yell, dashed across the intersection toward God's Weenies. Another joker—whose head looked like a 1950s Jell-O mold with his features and brain floating inside—followed them.

God's Weenies shrieked. In fear or anger, Michelle couldn't tell.

Dammit, Michelle thought. *I'm going to have to do something. And I'm going to catch hell for it no matter how things turn out. So, fun.*

A giant bubble flew across the street and stopped abruptly in front of the jokers. The Jell-O joker stopped, his eyes widened, and then his gelatinous face collapsed onto his navy-blue suit, sliding down his chest and belly as if his head were melting. His brain ended up on his shoulders, and his eyes, ears, and mouth were now residing on his torso. Apparently, this was some kind of survival reflex.

Ew, Michelle thought.

She let the bubble break into twenty smaller bubbles. The wall of them shimmered iridescent in the sunlight. Then she turned them rubbery and dropped them. They began to bounce around and off Jell-O joker and the rest of the joker protesters.

"Ah, c'mon," said the Oz tree joker as he swatted a bubble away. It came back to pester him like a mosquito. "That's just not fair!"

Michelle ignored him.

Now she had to turn her attention to God's Weenies, who were planted on the opposite side of the street. And after sorting *them* out, she was going to deal with the media. And then there were the idiots on the sidelines who thought they should be involved in this situation by watching the scene unfold, all the while filming everything on their phones. This was *not* how she'd planned her afternoon.

"It's incredible how many morons can be in one place at the same time," she said. There was a lifetime of annoyance in her voice. Five baseball-sized bubbles rose from her hands.

"You guys *do* remember me, right? Or did you become really confused over the last four days and decide I wasn't the Amazing Bubbles anymore? Seriously, I'm kinda hurt, here. As my daughter would say, 'I'm totes sad-like.'" Now the bubbles were careening around the intersection. It was the best human pinball machine ever.

"There's a frosty margarita and some spicy Tex-Mex in my future," she continued. Now people on each side of the intersection were smacking bubbles away. "Also, you're keeping all the kids inside the Gunter from their final performance and I'll be damned if you're going to stop me from hearing my daughter's recital. You're all that's between me and a fine time. And *that* makes me *very* uncheerful."

To her surprise and exasperation, God's Weenies ignored her and were still pushing against their barricade. Then, suddenly, it came down with a loud *bang!*

Great, she thought. *My daughter is refusing to stop flying around. There's a ridiculous protest conflict going on. I'm trying not to end this little get-together in a bubbly explosion because, apparently, that's not a happening thing right now. Of course, because that's the way things are going today, the sun will go supernova. How on earth did a simple band trip turn into* this?

"Mom!"

Michelle looked up. Her daughter had a stricken look on her face. "Mom! Seriously, you're embarrassing me here."

Michelle's bubbles quivered for a moment, as if they were about to pop. "Are you kidding me?! *I'm* embarrassing *you?* Are you paying attention to what's happening here?"

Adesina rolled her eyes. "God, Mom, of course, but you don't have to make such a big deal about it. You know things kind of . . . escalate when you're around."

Out of the corner of her eye, Michelle could see the jokers and God's Weenies were in a standoff, but most of the intersection was clear now. More bubbles flew off her hands to join the ones she'd already made. Both groups turned and glared at her. She wished she had more fat.

"You're being adorable," Michelle said to both groups. A headache was starting behind her right eye. She hadn't had headaches until Adesina turned into a teenager. "But I'm bored with this nonsense now. I've decided we're playing a variation of Mother May I? And I haven't said you may." Her bubbles stopped bouncing around and formed a large circle in the middle of the intersection, forcing God's Weenies and the jokers to back away from each other. "Now everybody freeze," Michelle said.

Both groups froze.

Michelle smiled. This was the most fun she'd had in the last few days. "Now in this variation, I tell you what you're supposed to do and you ask me if you can do it. And then you better do it. Take a step back," she said. The Jell-O-faced joker and the many-eyed joker stepped back. Everyone else said, "Mother May I?"

"You may," she replied. "You two. You go sit on the curb."

"I don't have to do anything you say," Jell-O head said sullenly. His lips were near his belly button. Slowly, his head was starting to form again, his features sliding up his chest.

Michelle planted her hands on her hips. "You seem confused again. My game, my rules. Now the two of you, scoot."

They glared at her—it was disconcerting having all those black eyes staring furiously at her—but then they went to the curb and sat down while the joker protesters and God's Weenies stepped back.

"Mom!"

"What?!"

"You can't play Mother May I? in the middle of a standoff," Adesina said. "Mom, you *can't!*"

"Hmmmm," Michelle replied, trying to keep the glee out of her voice. "I might be mistaken, but I'm pretty sure I can. Check this: Take a jump to the left!"

A chorus of "Mother May I?" rang out. Michelle nodded and both groups did so.

"Now take a step to the right!"

"Mom!"

Michelle giggled. She couldn't help it.

"Mother May I?" came the reply.

"Put your hands on your hips and bring your knees in tight!"

"Mom!"

"Mother May I?" both groups said. One of the twins from God's Weenies forgot to say, "Mother May I?"

Michelle shook a finger at him. Her bubbles swung back and forth in time as she wanted them to. "You're out, Tweedledee. Go sit down."

"You disgusting freak lover! You can't make me."

Michelle gave him a long-suffering look. "Oh, kitten," she said. "Yes. Yes, I can." One of her bubbles zoomed and stopped, then hung in front of his face. "You have a really simple choice here. Mind Mother, or, well, you get the idea."

"Whore."

Michelle was having a good time. Beautiful weather, she was getting to bubble—which was always a plus—and she'd managed not to kill anyone. Win-win.

Tweedledee turned and walked to God's Weenies' side of the street, then sat down on the curb. Michelle could hear him muttering about her various Christian shortcomings.

Good thing I'm Jewish, she thought.

"Now where was I?"

"Mrs. Bubbles," Officer Reyes said, "this is beneath you. And don't for the love of God have them do the pelvic thrust. That's something I don't need in my brain."

Michelle sighed. "Fine," she said sullenly. "Okay, just stay where you are for now."

Her fat was waning, which was to be expected given how little she started out with. Meanwhile, the press and most of the looky-loos continued recording everything. *Well,* she thought. *I'm nothing if not good at putting on a show.*

"Hey, Officer Reyes, could you stop calling me Mrs. Bubbles? Ms. Bubbles if you must. Or just Bubbles now that we know each other. I'd even be good with Michelle."

He smiled. The impish expression surprised her. There were many things Michelle could see Officer Reyes doing, but grinning mischievously wasn't one of them.

"Oh, I know you don't like being called Mrs. Bubbles," he replied. His smile grew bigger. "It just bugged you so much when I used the Mrs."

"Aren't you cute?"

"Michelle!" She turned and saw Creighton pushing his way through the crowd. Or more like staggering his way. Apparently, he was still feeling the effects of the number of martinis he'd consumed that morning. "Hey, Michelle," he said. It came out as *Heh, Meeshill.* "You need to get these morons out of the way so the kids can get to the concert." He pointed at the looky-loos and then swayed a little. But he managed to look pretty dapper all things considered. Probably because he was still in his Nick Charles form.

"Thanks, Nick," she replied. "I'm pretty sure I know that already. Hence the bubble action."

He blinked his eyes and gave the scene before him a quick once-over. "It does appear as if you have the situation under control." *It dosh appear ash if ew have the sishuashun under control.*

"Mr. Charles, maybe you should go to your room and get some sleep," Adesina called down, with concern in her voice. She dropped a little lower. "You look pretty drunk."

Creighton gave her an indignant stare. "This isn't drunk, my dear. This is merely a normal day in the life of Nick and Nora Charles."

"Mom says you had like four or five of those martinis."

"I'm not sure what you're getting at, my dear, but my only concern is for you."

"Thanks, Mr. Charles, but—"

A shot rang out and Adesina shrieked.

Grabbing the outside of her right thigh, she gave another yelp of pain, then fell from the sky, landing hard on the pavement. Michelle wanted to scream herself when she saw her daughter put her hand on her thigh. When Adesina looked at the blood on her hand she gave a hysterical laugh.

"Oh, God!" Michelle ran to her daughter. "Adesina, honey, are you all right?"

"Jinkies, Mom, I just got shot." She swayed as she got to her feet, favoring the right leg. Her face turned ashy. "I've been totes better. Being shot, I confess, not my favorite thing."

"You're awfully quippy for being shot," Michelle said as she grabbed her daughter by the waist. She was shaking all over as if she were in the grip of a high fever, which was how she felt. Adesina trembled, too. "Someone get a doctor. Or an ambulance. Jesus, don't just stand there, you morons—do something!"

Adesina took her hand away from the wound. Michelle saw a pencil-thick wound seared across the outside of her thigh. It was bleeding a little, but nothing as serious as Michelle thought it would be. It was the most minor in nature she'd seen. A couple of inches to the side and . . . well, Michelle didn't want to think about it.

"Mom, it doesn't really hurt so much as it burns. Like when I put my hand on the stove that time."

"It's a graze, thank God," Michelle said with relief. "And it'll hurt until it heals—and maybe some after. But luckily it just got the fleshy part of your thigh." She was trying to keep Adesina calm, but she was babbling like a maniac.

Her daughter, who had stopped shaking by now, was remarkably cool. "It helps that my skin is so tough now." Adesina looked down at herself. "And these are my favorite pair of pants!"

"You should lie down," Michelle said. The immediate fear was wearing off, and it was being replaced by rage. Some asshole had shot her daughter.

"Sonofabitch!" Creighton yelled. "Whoever did this is going to pay!" He swayed a little, reeling, then staggered into the crowd of looky-loos. Nonplussed by his actions, Michelle looked away from Adesina for a moment.

She turned back to her daughter and started stroking Adesina's copper-colored hair. "Honey, an ambulance is going to be here soon. Try not to bleed too much in the meantime. And lie down."

"First," Adesina said as she tentatively put weight on her right leg, "it's just a flesh wound. It's not even a flesh wound, it's a graze. You said so yourself. I'm not dead yet. Secondly, I'm not missing the performance. Third, you really want me to lie down in this street? It's filthy. I'm okay."

"You are not okay!" Michelle replied vehemently. "There's only one person in this family who is impervious to harm, and that's me, young lady. You are going to the hospital."

"Mom!"

Just then, there was a scuffle in the group of looky-loos and a ginger-haired woman dressed in tight jeans and an elaborately embroidered Roper western wear shirt was dragged into the open part of the intersection.

"I didn't mean to do anything!" she cried as she struggled against the people holding her. "I was getting some lip balm out of my purse and it just went off! I have a conceal-carry license! I know my rights. You can't—"

There was a loud *pop!* and the lights for the block flickered out.

"No one better move," Michelle said as she spun on her heel, a bubble forming in her hand. "What the hell is wrong with you, lady? There are kids here. Do you know how to use that weapon? Did you even bother to put the safety on?" She'd tried not to be all let's-just-bubble-the-fuck-out-of-this-crazy-bitch, but she was pretty sure she could get away with it.

"I'm just taking care of myself! A woman can't be too careful these days. And besides, it's my Second Amendment right. We can't all be like you."

There was a hush as Michelle's other bubbles abruptly stopped moving. Officer Reyes stepped in close and said quietly, "I know you're angry and upset, but let us do our job. You don't need to go all Bubbles on her."

Michelle's green eyes narrowed and she said, "I'm pretty sure this is *exactly* the time for me to go 'all Bubbles.'"

"Hey," Reyes said loudly, putting his hands on his hips as he turned and addressed the crowd. "Now that we know who shot this young lady, y'all can disperse quietly. Go on home now."

One of the police officers came over and took the red-haired woman by the arm. One of the looky-loos held her purse out for him. He took her to one of the cruisers and put her in the back seat. Then he put the bag in the front seat and locked the car. He sighed and went back to his original position.

"I wouldn't say I'm a lady," Adesina interjected. "That implies a certain type of behavior that conforms to societal expectations." She gave Officer Reyes a bright smile.

"I'm pretty sure that's not the most important conversation we could be having right now," Michelle said. Adesina changed the conversation so fast sometimes it was like having a conversation with Chico Marx. "Also, where did you read about that?"

"*Jezebel*," Adesina replied with a shrug. She put more of her weight on her right foot. She didn't wince this time. "I think the bleeding has stopped." She wiped her hand off on her black pants and then put it over her wound again, giving a sharp hiss as she did so. She lifted her palm up to show no blood on it. "See, no big dealio. Also, leathery skin. Very helpful in these gunshot situations."

Sirens wailed and horns honked like geese on steroids as the ambulance and fire truck arrived, further blocking looky-loos on the north side of the intersection. The crowd barely moved as the EMTs and firefighters jumped from their vehicles and tried to get through to Michelle and Adesina.

"Move aside, people! Let them through!" Officer Reyes shouted. "What's your problem? I said move!"

Tweedledee replied, "*She*," he said, pointing at Michelle, "didn't say we could."

"Seriously?!" Michelle exclaimed. "Really? Are you all that stupid? *Move!*"

The jokers and God's Weenies glared at each other, then turned and hustled back to their respective sides. The crowd of looky-loos began to part to let the EMS responders through.

And that's when the giant ape showed up.

◆

"*Jesus Christ!*" a joker yelled. The arms of his cloth-thin body were wrapped, like a cloak, around the back of a fellow joker. The other joker—his head looked like a bishop from a Staunton chess set, but with eyes and a mouth—gave a squeal, turned, and began pushing his way through the gaggle of other jokers. For a moment, the rest of the crowd, the EMTs, and the police stopped what they were doing and stared at the massive ape.

The ape staggered toward the crowd from the west side of East Houston Street. He shoved the police cruisers blocking the intersection aside. Then climbed on top of one and roared.

A scream went up from the crowd. Instead of running, the looky-loos continued to film. But the jokers and God's Weenies began running east down East Houston. The giant ape climbed into the intersection. He stopped and put his hands down on the ground in order to give it a good pounding. Then he got up and lurched forward a few more steps. The ape's coffee-colored eyes rolled and his mouth was pulled into a twist of sadness and then rage as he bared his teeth and let out another bellow.

The ape bounded forward and swiped one of the reporters aside. Her skirt flew over her head as she tumbled ass over teakettle toward the looky-loos on the north side of the intersection. When she came to a stop, she popped up and ran to her cameraman. "Did you get that on tape?" she asked. "Should I do it again for the B roll?"

Michelle stared at the ape. The giant ape. The giant drunken ape.

Oh shit, she thought. *Creighton. Why did you have to go and do this? This cannot end well.*

A bubble formed in Michelle's hand. The pandemonium was going to get people hurt. She grabbed Adesina's arm and dragged her back toward the Gunter.

"Mom! Don't hurt him," Adesina hissed in Michelle's ear. A couple of people shoved them from behind, sending them stumbling forward. "I'll explain later . . . just stop him from hurting anyone . . . and stop anyone from hurting him! He's not . . . well, I can't say who it is, but you wouldn't want to hurt him. I mean, you'd feel really, really bad."

"I know who it is, and that person is an idiot and drunk to boot. And you'll be explaining later how *you* know who it is."

The gorilla stopped and pounded the ground some more. Then he lunged toward the looky-loos near where Adesina and Michelle were standing. The looky-loos scrambled back, climbing over the cop cars, but they bottlenecked as they tried to squeeze past the fire truck and ambulance. Some took shelter under the marquee of the Majestic Theatre.

Adesina let her wings unfurl. It forced the people pushing next to them to get out of the way. "This is totes messed up," Adesina said, wings twitching. "We can help him faster this way." She grabbed Michelle by the waist and began to rise into the air before her mother could react.

It wasn't the first time Adesina had carried Michelle. She gave a grunt, her entire body shook, and then they were aloft. "Mom, do something quick," Adesina said. She sounded out of breath. "Someone might shoot him."

The ape stood on his back legs and swung his arms around. An angry cry escaped him. *Shit,* Michelle thought. *How the hell do you stop a giant ape?*

From her vantage point, she saw the jokers and God's Weenies were still running down East Houston Street. At least half of them had their cameras out and were slowing because the ape wasn't following them at the moment.

"All I wanted was for you to have a good competition, go play this concert, us to have a meal of Tex-Mex and drinks, and then go home!" Michelle exclaimed.

"Mom, seriously, can you melt down some other time?"

"No, this is *exactly* when I should be melting down. And why can't I just blow the ape up? Boom! Problem solved. Except for the blood and guts everywhere. That won't play well with the locals. But, it's you-know-who, so that makes it right out of the question. Dammit." Michelle glared at the ape. Creighton was still staggering and having trouble hitting people. Mostly, he swung his arms around, lost his balance, and sat down abruptly. Then he would howl with frustration.

Michelle opened her hands and between them a bubble began to form. It grew and grew, and then she let it fly toward the gorilla— expanding as it went. By the time it reached him, Michelle was thin and the ape was encased in an enormous bubble.

"Pretty kewl, Mom," Adesina said admiringly. Even Michelle was pleased with herself.

"Why would he turn into an ape?" Michelle asked. She understood

Creighton changing form for his detective work, and maybe even for other reasons, but becoming a giant ape? "He could have turned into anything!"

"Uhm, I think it was this movie we were watching last night," Adesina said. There was a guilty tone in her voice. "It was *Mighty Joe Young*. It's this black-and-white movie about a big ape. Pretty much that ape." She nodded toward Creighton as she began to drift down.

"You hate black-and-white movies," Michelle said. Michelle wasn't too crazy about them either, except for *Casablanca*. Or the Marx Brothers because . . . funny. Or anything with Katharine Hepburn. Michelle liked the cut of her jib.

The ape looked at the bubble and gave an angry roar. He beat his fists on the ground, then roared again, the whites of his eyes showing. He threw a punch at the inside of the bubble, but his hand bounced back. This time, he cried dolefully.

"Did he hurt himself?" asked Adesina.

"Nah, I made it all rubbery like the ones I made for you when you were little. You know, when you were a child, just last year. When you weren't all . . . like this."

The ape took an experimental step forward, and the bubble rolled as he did so. He gave another sad wail.

"I feel really sorry for Mr. Creighton," Adesina said.

"Don't let anyone hear you saying his name," Michelle said sotto voce. "Maybe we should call him something else."

"How about Mighty Joe Young?" Adesina suggested.

"That's a mouthful, maybe just 'Joe'?"

"Believe me, that'll get hella boring in a hurry," Adesina replied, as she lowered Michelle to the ground. "But Joe is okay. What are we going to do about him?"

The bubble wobbled as Joe staggered forward then flopped on his face. A mournful groan followed.

"We should get a hamster, Mom," Adesina said, veering off into a non sequitur as she let go of her mother's waist. "You could make it the happiest hamster ever. Think of all the bubbles you could do for it. I wonder if Joe will remember his awesome time in the bubble. Look, he's so cute." Joe was on his back with all four feet in the air like an infant. It wasn't the most elegant of positions for a giant ape to find himself in.

Joe rolled onto his belly and then climbed to his feet. He ran forward a little and the bubble tumbled with him. He rolled toward the looky-loos on the south side of East Houston and North St. Mary's. Now that Joe was in a bubble, they didn't run off like the group on the north side had. Instead, some of them climbed onto the police cruisers to get a better angle.

"You aren't helping things," Officer Reyes said to Michelle. "How am I supposed to call this in? 'Giant ape in bubble heading for the Alamo'?" He pointed at Joe, who was now on all fours weaving his way east.

"He's heading for the Alamo?" said Michelle with dismay. "Why did it have to be the Alamo? Of course, it's the Alamo. Because that's just perfect. And why don't you have someone else call it in? There's a nice-looking officer over there, why not ask him? Or any of these other police officers. Oh, never mind, they just started chasing Joe. Though he is moving pretty slow."

The police had surrounded Joe, but seemed baffled as to what to do next. "Can't have pretty boy call it in. He's a moron," Reyes replied with resignation. "But he's the brother of the chief's sister-in-law. And he's a pain in the ass."

"But cute," Adesina interjected. Her wings fluttered. "I mean, not hella cute. But cute in that older-brother-of-your-best-friend-who-you've-had-a-secret-crush-on-since-you-were-eight way, but you now realize is a complete doofus."

Michelle and Officer Reyes turned and stared at Adesina. She shrugged. "I'm just sayin'. . . ."

Joe had slowly rolled halfway to Navarro with the cops providing escort.

"Well, what are *you* going to do with the giant ape in a bubble?" he asked Michelle. Then he looked up at Adesina, who had floated up into the air again. "Aren't you supposed to be having a visit with these nice EMS girls?"

"I'm okay," Adesina replied. She did a loop in the air.

Reyes put his hands on his hips and frowned at Adesina. "I think you should see the EMS girls anyway. After all, they've come all this way."

"Nope. Nope. Nope. Not gonna do it." Adesina fluttered her wings and rose a few more feet into the air. "That's soooooooo not going to be a thing. Mom, tell him. There are bigger things that you need to be dealing with right now, Officer Reyes. Mom, you gotta go stop Joe."

"The ape has a name?" Reyes asked. "Exactly what do you know about this monkey, Bubbles?"

"I suppose I should go after him," Michelle said with a sigh. And she deliberately didn't answer Reyes. What he didn't know and all that. Just then, the rest of the Mob, LoriAnne Broom, Vicky, and Kimmie Coldwater came out of the hotel. Michelle noticed that some of the looky-loos on the south side of the street had started following Joe.

"Are you okay?" Kimmie asked Adesina. "We saw the whole thing from the lobby. Mr. Ruttiger wouldn't let us come out." She cast a baleful eye at Robin, but then Segway gave her arm a pat and she relaxed.

"It burns pretty bad," Adesina replied, floating back to the street. "I'm good, but it ruined my best pants! Totes suckage."

Yerodin ghosted to Adesina, then turned corporeal and gave her a fierce hug. Michelle heard Ghost whisper, "I can kill her for you. The red-haired lady with the gun. It would be easy. She's in that car."

Adesina hugged her back and said, "No killing. Wally talked to you about the killing."

Ghost released Adesina and gave an annoyed shrug, but then she grabbed Adesina's hand. Joe was almost to Navarro and wasn't staggering as much. Occasionally, he'd turn and roar at the police or the looky-loos.

"I guess I should go deal with the gorilla." Michelle began to jog down East Houston after Joe. How was she going to get Joe to change back into Creighton? She doubted he could be reasoned with in his current condition. There was also the issue of the fat. As in not having as much as she wanted given the situation. She'd only had Wally knock her around some. And that only got her so much because he got all weirded out about it. He always said something about hitting girls. Even though he knew she could hit back.

As Michelle caught up to the looky-loos, Joe put on a sudden burst of speed. A cry went up from everyone and they started running faster, too. Michelle was glad of her commitment to being in shape. It helped her no matter what size she was and she was getting pretty skinny now.

"Don't be idiots," she yelled as she ran by the looky-loos. "Go the other way. Don't go toward the giant ape. That's, like, Survival 101. Run away from the danger. Sheesh."

The looky-loos stopped and stared at her as she sped by.

"Oh, never thought of that," said one of the looky-loos sarcastically. He was a tall, beefy guy with a military-style haircut and a ruddy complexion. "You know," he said as he lifted his phone up and began running after her while recording, "I've always wanted to meet you."

"You're an idiot!" Michelle snapped. She could hear the padding of feet on pavement behind her. *Goddamn civilians.*

"Now that's no way to talk to a fan," he replied.

"Trying to catch a giant ape here," she said.

"Oh, don't mind me." He was having trouble catching his breath.

"You know, you are not helping," Michelle said as she released a bubble. It was baseball-sized, rubbery, and heavy. It caught him in the chest. His phone flew out of his hand and landed on the pavement with a satisfying crunch. A BB-sized bubble shattered it. He landed with an "oof" and reflexively grabbed the bubble. "Hey!" he complained. "That's a new phone! You're paying for it!"

"Okeydokey," she replied, running backward. Then she pivoted and began running toward the Alamo again. Joe was outrunning the police now, and Michelle was gaining on them. Glancing over her shoulder, she saw that more of the looky-loos had broken off from the group and were heading back toward the Gunter. The rest were tenaciously following her. And still filming. *I bet there's a Chinese Hell for those people. Maybe the Hell of Upside-Down Sinners,* she thought. *The Chinese have a lot of Hells.*

As she passed Presa Street, a group of tourists on Segways rolled off the sidewalk. A little sign hung off each one: *National Segway Tours.*

"Don't mind us!" one of them said as she ran by. He sounded giddy. "But this is the most exciting thing we've had happen here in a long time." The Segway tourists gave excited squeals, then leaned forward on their machines.

"You have got to be kidding me," Michelle said, dumbfounded. "Did you not see the drunken giant ape in a bubble?"

The Segways were speed-controlled and she easily pulled away from them. Joe was a block ahead, almost to Losoya. He'd gotten the knack of running in the bubble and was gallumping along, though unsteadily. Some of God's Weenies and the jokers were slow moving and Joe caught up with them.

The acrid sour odor of fear floated to Michelle as Joe overtook one of the joker protesters whose body looked like a century plant, arms and legs pointy and jagged. As he ran on the tips of his leaves, she could see the blossom stock rising from the top of his head. Buds began opening, but he didn't stop running even as they bloomed and began to fall off, leaving a trail of petals behind him like a flower girl.

He bumped off Joe's bubble, flew a little forward to the left, and smacked into a crying teenage girl from God's Weenies, who was sent tumbling. "Fucking jokers!" she yelled.

"*Language!*" Michelle yelled back at her.

The girl sat up and flipped Michelle the bird as she ran by. It was a very un-Christian thing to do.

Joe had a real head of steam going as he passed Losoya. By now, Michelle had caught up with the police, who looked pissed. She realized she couldn't get to Joe before *he* got to the Alamo. And it being Saturday, the Alamo would be overrun with tourists.

"Joe!" Michelle yelled loud as she could. "Joe, stop!"

And much to her surprise, he did.

He looked around, cocking his head to one side like a dog.

"Joe!" Michelle was a half a block away from him now. "Joe!" she yelled again. "Joe!" She stopped running. The police stopped with her.

"What should we do?" one of the officers asked. "What's that bubble made of? If we shoot at him will it burst? Will our bullets bound off and ricochet? What's the story?"

"How about we don't go shooting stuff just yet," she replied. "He's in a bubble. He can't do much right now."

There was a giggle behind her and then she found herself surrounded by a phalanx of the Segways.

Joe turned and looked at Michelle with a blank expression. It was clear he didn't recognize her. He started toward her. The Segway tourists rocked back on their vehicles, then there was a chorus of "eep"s, and they spun around and trundled slowly past her. And then, zooming toward her, past the Segway tourists and crowd of looky-loos, was Peter. He glanced with scorn at the tourists on the Segways and said, "Amateurs."

Michelle fired a bubble off at Joe. It rocked his bubble backward and sat him on his ass.

"Peter! Dammit! What are you doing here?" Michelle asked. *Again* with the heading into danger. "You do know that if you get hurt, maimed, or killed in any way, your parents are going to be really upset with me. And why do you have your trumpet?"

Peter put the trumpet to his lips and piped a few notes. It caught Joe's attention. "Just because," he said with a smile. "Adesina sent me. She has a plan."

"Is it a cunning plan?" she had to ask. "Fine. I guess I can't make you leave." Peter shook his head. "But try to stay out of range of the big gorilla. You know, the one over there."

Joe began lurching toward the Alamo once more.

Crap, crap, crap, she thought as she sprinted off again.

She hadn't had enough of a chance to really bulk up. She was model-thin now and her clothes hung on her as if she were doing a runway show.

Fortunately, most of the protesters parted like the Red Sea, pouring the jokers north and God's Weenies south down Alamo Street. Joe hit the intersection of Alamo Plaza and East Houston Street and caused the passing cars and buses to screech to a halt. The crunching sound of bumpers being hit made Michelle cringe. *Oh, the insurance bills,* she thought.

Joe continued into the grounds of the Alamo, running headlong into the Cenotaph. He bumped off the bottom part inscribed with:

IN MEMORY OF THE HEROES WHO SACRIFICED THEIR LIVES
AT THE ALAMO, MARCH 6, 1836, IN THE DEFENSE OF TEXAS.
"THEY CHOSE NEVER TO SURRENDER NOR RETREAT; THESE
BRAVE HEARTS, WITH FLAG STILL PROUDLY WAVING,
PERISHED IN THE FLAMES OF IMMORTALITY THAT
THEIR HIGH SACRIFICE MIGHT LEAD TO
THE FOUNDING OF THIS TEXAS."

Joe was not impressed with the sacrifice of the valiant Alamo heroes. The Cenotaph and its inscription slowed him down not at all. He barreled through the crowd that was milling around the plaza. Tourists shrieked and ran. Some bounced off Joe's bubble. A couple wearing flip-flops, cargo shorts, and Knicks T-shirts—Michelle assumed they were tourists, no one in their right mind wore a Knicks T-shirt to the Alamo—caught his eye and he rolled after them. They were remarkably nimble given their girth and they beelined it to safety.

"Joe!" she yelled to no effect. I knew this wasn't going to end well, she thought. Joe was in spitting distance of the Alamo. "You suck, Joe!"

Apparently, Joe was indifferent to his suckage.

She ran down the broad limestone path, using the last of her fat to fire bubbles to nudge people away from Joe. This bubbling was all well and good for the tourists, but it didn't address the Joe and the Alamo situation. Michelle heard sirens behind her. A police car jumped the curb and came toward her, driving into Alamo Plaza straddling the pavement and broad walkway. And then it slammed into her.

Delicious fat swelled her up. She popped into the air then landed hard on the hood. It wasn't graceful, but it felt marvelous. Behind the wheel of the patrol car was the police chief's young relative. Officer Reyes was in the front passenger seat. In the back of the car, Asti, LoriAnne, and Sean were crammed together. They leapt out of the cruiser and ran to the back of the car as the trunk popped open, grabbing instrument cases and pulling out their instruments.

She looked up and saw Adesina flying toward her, carrying Antonia, the band's drummer. And a block away, the rest of the Mob were running full-out. Ghost rode on Wally's back. He carried her alto sax in one hand and her tenor sax in the other. Following them was a passel of the band kids and their chaperones from the competition.

"What all the hells is this!" Michelle exclaimed. She glanced back at Joe and saw that he was bouncing off the ancient oak trees in the plaza. The trees trembled and she cursed under her breath. The live oaks were huge and she suspected the Daughters of the Republic of Texas would be less than thrilled if Joe uprooted them.

He lurched suddenly to the east and rolled into the courtyard in front of the Alamo, heading toward the famous façade. There he stopped and stood on his back legs and gave a roar.

Adesina landed in front of Michelle, dropping Antonia gently to the ground. LoriAnne whipped out her drumsticks. Antonia ran to LoriAnne, pulling out her own drumsticks as well. Michelle heard Officer Reyes telling the young police officer driving the cruiser to stay put.

"How many times do I have to say, 'Run away from danger'?!" Michelle said with dismay to the array of musicians, chaperones, and looky-loos. The looky-loos who were *still* filming everything. "Ever since he showed up"—she gestured at Joe—"people have been running toward and not away from him." As more chaperones and kids from the competition swelled into the plaza, she saw many of the kids carried instruments, too. Basilio ran up holding his drumsticks aloft as if he were Enjolras singing, "One Day More" in *Les Misérables*. He made a beeline to LoriAnne and Antonia. The three of them grabbed trash cans and flipped them over, but not before they pulled out the can liners and neatly tied them up.

What the hell? Michelle thought. *Well, at least they're civic-minded.*

Kimmie arrived with Bacho, who managed to get the crowd to part and let him through with his upright bass. He was panting and sweating, but in his normal form and he had an enormous grin on his face. Adesina rose in the air again. Her cobalt wings glistened with an iridescent sheen in the sunlight and her titian hair was lit like a halo.

"Okay guys, this is it," she said loudly. "Ready?" She held her hands parallel to the ground, then lifted them both up, and brought them down in front of her.

The kids with instruments started playing. Those in the crowd—including the chaperones, parents, and even a couple of looky-loos who were getting into the spirit of things—began singing while looking at their phones.

Beautiful dreamer, wake unto me,
Starlight and dewdrops are waiting for thee;
Sounds of the rude world, heard in the day,
Lull'd by the moonlight have all passed away!

Michelle recognized the song. It was the one Adesina had hummed yesterday. The lyrics were old-fashioned, and had a lovely lilting quality. The crowd of singers continued with the second verse, slowly walking toward the middle of the Plaza.

Okaaaaaaaaaay, Michelle thought. *This isn't going to help stop him at all.* She was about to try bursting Joe's bubble, and then hit him with something concussive enough to knock him out, but she didn't have the chance. Joe stopped. He gave a happy grunt, sat down, and looked over his shoulder.

Beautiful dreamer, queen of my song,
List while I woo thee with soft melody;
Gone are the cares of life's busy throngs,
Beautiful dreamer, awake unto me!
Beautiful dreamer, awake unto me!

Joe began to shake and an electric pool formed underneath him. The bubble burst. And then he rapidly started to shrink. His fur began to slide into his skin, revealing pale flesh.

In an instant, Adesina flew to him and encircled them both with her wings. When they opened again, there was an eight-limbed joker there. It had four hands and four feet. It cartwheeled off fantastically fast, zipping across Alamo Street in the direction of the River Walk. Adesina rose up into the air, then flew to the other players.

"Okay, guys," she yelled. "Let's make it swing!"

The band kids began to riff on "Beautiful Dreamer." LoriAnne, Antonia, and Basilio started using the garbage cans as drums. Suddenly, the sedate song had a fast, syncopated beat. Bacho started playing his bass; it was a little hard to hear him over the drums, but he did manage to get the bottom going. Just as Michelle thought he'd be drowned out altogether, Greg, the bass player from the Funkalicious Four, showed up with his upright bass. Together they thickened the sound up.

Kimmie did a quick, fluttery flute solo. Ghost ended up taking a wicked alto sax solo, trading back and forth with Sean and the sax player from the Plano Originals, who was the only Original aside from Kimmie who'd shown up to play.

And as Peter took his trumpet solo, Adesina nodded at Sharon, who took over and directed the musicians to start slowing the tempo of the song. It developed a cool, bluesy quality.

As the kids played, slowly the tourists came back to hear them. People smiled and bobbed their heads in time with the music. When "Beautiful Dreamer" was finally done, Mindy-Lou taking an impressive scat solo at the end, there was a clamor for more from the audience.

Sharon signed "Yardbird Suite," and the Mob started playing. It was a hot and fast bebop standard. After a couple of bars, the rest of the band kids joined in.

"You do know this is going to be a huge problem," Officer Reyes said to Michelle as they listened to the kids play. But he had a smile on his face.

"Yeah," she replied. "But there wasn't really any damage done. And see, the Alamo is fine. And no dead tourists—or anyone—so that's a plus."

"Texans are pretty emotional about the Alamo," Reyes said. "It's a good thing it's intact."

"I wouldn't have let anything happen to it," she replied. At least she was pretty sure she wouldn't have.

"You going to come with me to make a statement? Or are you going to be a pain in my ass?"

Michelle pretended to think it over. "Hmmmm, you're making it hard to decide there, Officer Krupke. Being a pain in your ass these last few days has really been a high point of this trip. But you did help out with the whole who-wanted-to-kill-my-kids thing, so I'll do my best to comply."

"You're not going to be very popular with the locals."

Michelle tucked her hair behind her ears, then jammed her hands in her pockets. "Wow, something I'm so not used to," she said sarcastically.

They reached the cop car. The bent-in fender and human-size dent in the hood was worse than she remembered. "I'm guessing I'll be paying for that," Michelle said. "And for that other guy's phone. And for some other stuff I've forgotten. And for those fines the city will be ladling on me."

"What about your daughter? Sure looked like she aided and abetted the ape dude."

"The ape dude? Is that really what you're going to go with? The ape dude?"

Officer Reyes blushed. "I'll come up with something better."

"I hope so. He has a name. Joe." Michelle sighed. "There are probably fifty people here who've recorded all this on their phones. It's all over the Internet already. There'll be a huge shitstorm for a few days until the next click-baity thing comes along. Adesina did what teenagers do: impulsive, stupid shit. And she was the one who stopped him."

"And let him get away!"

"You're really into the details, aren't you? Look, I'll come and see your superiors." She let a quince-sized bubble float above her hand, then another. Eventually she had five and she began to let them spin in a circle hovering above her palm. "I'll talk about how you and the Little Private over there helped me stop the giant ape—with help from all those band kids, of course. There won't be a dry eye in the house by the time I'm done."

"You think you can do that?" He gave her the side-eye.

"Cake."

He smiled. "I think this might be the beginning of a beautiful friendship."

"Ha! More like a one-night stand gone horribly awry. The full *Fatal Attraction*," she replied.

"That doesn't sound pleasant."

"I know. Right?!"

♠ ♥ ♦ ♣

SUNDAY

Bubbles and the
Band Trip

Part 13

THE WEATHER HAD HELD and it was a beautiful cool morning when Michelle and the Mob stepped outside the Gunter to board their bus home. Both God's Weenies and the joker protesters were gone. The media had vanished as well. No doubt there was some other Drama of the Moment that they needed to feed on.

Her phone gave a chirp and she checked her text messages. There was a short one from Creighton: *Thanks for the help. Sorry about Joe. Maybe we can make an adjustment on your bill.*

"Wait! Wait up!" Kimmie called. She dashed across the sidewalk to Adesina and Peter. "I'm going to miss you guys so much!" Then she threw her arms around Adesina. They hugged and then Kimmie turned her attention to Peter. Michelle expected a big emotional scene, but this was just a friendly goodbye, nothing Michelle would have expected after the past week.

Adesina got on the bus, and a few moments later rushed out. "OMG! Mom! You totes won't believe this! It's the best thing *ever*!" She grabbed Michelle by the hand and dragged her onto the bus. There, on one of the front seats, was Adesina's bass. On the seat next to it was Peter's trumpet.

There was a note written on an evidence tag attached to the bass. It said:

You'd never believe it, but sometimes evidence goes missing in certain police cases. It would be awkward should this ever be mentioned again. Try to stay out of San Antonio, Mrs. Bubbles.

"Mom," Adesina said, looking as if she was about to cry. "You told me I wasn't going to get it back."

"I guess you just got lucky," Michelle said. "Go get your case. And tell Peter to grab his, too." Adesina leapt off the bus with a whoop.

Michelle picked up Adesina's bass. It was heavy. Its purple sparkle finish was beautiful, though nothing Michelle would ever have chosen. But it was Adesina's style, at least for now.

A few moments later, Adesina and Peter climbed back aboard. Adesina turned to Michelle and pulled her into a fierce hug. "Thank you so much for being the most awesome mother ever! You were *amaze balls!*" Adesina giggled. "I love you."

"I love you, too." Michelle kissed Adesina's forehead. "But you're still grounded for forever when we get home."

Adesina pouted. Michelle wanted to laugh. "Okay, maybe just for a month." She returned Adesina's hug, then released her. A bubble began to form in her right hand, then one in her left. Michelle made them rubbery tough, but light enough to float. Then she batted both to the back of the bus. "Go on, get those instruments packed up."

While Adesina and Peter were putting their instruments away, Michelle got off the bus. Outside, she saw that the cinnamon-haired drummer, LoriAnne from the Funkalicious Four, was giving Asti a big hug and sniffing him at the same time. Cesar Chao seemed to have recovered from his date with Jade Blossom and was awkwardly asking Marissa to keep in touch. All around her, the members of the Mob were saying goodbye to the friends they'd made during the course of the competition.

For a moment, she relaxed. She'd made it to the end of the competition and was still standing. Maybe she had a handle on this teenager thing after all. A surge of pride and happiness soared through her. Her kids were going to be all right. Michelle smiled and decided she wouldn't rush them, and then turned around and got back on the bus. In the last row, she saw Adesina and Peter. They began to kiss, and as they did, Adesina's wings enveloped them.

Oh no, Michelle thought. *No, no, nope. I am not ready for this. Nope. Nope. Nope.*

But to her horror, she was going to have to face it. There was no going back.

Adesina really was a teenager now.